THE DEMON'S CURSE

PART ONE:

THE END OF MAGIC

ALLAN C. HOWARTH

 **New Generation Publishing**

TO
NATASHA MAIRE
AND
JAMES EARL TOMAS

THE BEST CHILDREN
ANY FATHER
EVER HAD

REMEMBER:

"LIFE IS WHAT HAPPENS TO YOU
WHILE YOU'RE BUSY MAKING OTHER PLANS."
(JOHN LENNON)

4

Prologue

The man stood on the edge of the precipice, staring out, into the void.

His face was unshaven. His advancing years betrayed by the deep lines etched into the skin of his forehead as he frowned. His cheeks were flushed, pink, in the afterglow of his recent exertion. His eyes were clear, a mix of blue and green, but watery, as the mixture of biting, cold air and unbridled emotion, forced tears, which he stubbornly wiped away.

The man's most outstanding features were large pointed ears, which, in his younger days had stuck out from the sides of his head, like the handle sticks out of a mug. In his youth they had been a source of much embarrassment, the butt of cruel ridicule, but that was long ago and only a distant, fading memory now. Years of being pressed down by the man's thick, curly hair had flattened his ears to his head, leaving them strange only in their size and how pointed they looked.

The man took a deep breath of the clear, fresh mountain air, then exhaled with all his might. He grimaced as he watched the small clouds that he produced float swiftly away into the darkness that obscured the valley, far, far below.

The sun had still not appeared; but the sky was just beginning to lighten over the hills to the east, in anticipation of the coming dawn.

The silhouetted outlines of mountains and hills began to emerge from the cover of darkness. Shades of dormant grey awoke and transformed into vivid greens. Pastel limes and glittering emeralds became the predominant colours of the landscape.

Features, previously indistinguishable in the dark began to appear; stone walls, ruined cottages, sheep, a few skeletal trees in the valley. A winding river flowing into a huge lake, which stretched out as far as the eye could see.

The lake began to reflect the vicarious reds, oranges, blues, whites and greys in the sky, a riot of colour, which belied the water's habitual silver-grey appearance.

On the opposite banks of the lake, a patchwork of small fields and hedges began to materialise through low-lying mist.

The white vapour rapidly retreated from the valley floor, but clung tenaciously to the flat-topped hills, rolling and churning in the chill breeze, like wild, unkempt wool on a giant sheep's back.

The man watched the rolling mist and thought of the similar churning in his stomach.

He took a chunk of dry, brown, soda bread from his jacket pocket, examined it for a moment, watched a few crumbs fall to his feet, and then, with a sigh, stuffed it roughly back into his coat pocket.

The man felt sick with hunger, but though his belly was empty he couldn't face the thought of food, perhaps the sickness was not in his gut, but in his mind. He sighed deeply and closed his eyes.

How had it all come to this?

The panorama before him never failed to impress him, but this was the first time he had seen the valley as the sun rose. It was spectacular. It reminded him of a time he and his wife had stood on the edge of the Grand Canyon as the dawn broke. A few Americans had whooped, cheered and applauded as the sun rose and the layers of Canyon rock had dramatically changed colour with a vibrancy that had been totally unimaginable.

Here, the light show was less spectacular, but no less impressive.

There was no wild cheering, or applause here though; the silence was all pervading.

As if to counter the silence, an epic piece of music flooded into the man's mind: a theme from one of the favourite movies of his distant youth.

In the movie scene, the hero was pictured standing just like him, with one foot perched on a rock, staring out at the landscape. Yet here, only one sun was rising above damp, green Irish hills, not two suns, setting beyond an arid desert plain, a long, long time ago, in a galaxy, far, far away.

The man in the movie had been young and blond and at the very beginning of his great adventure.

Here, the man on the mountain was old and greying and very possibly coming towards the end of his own adventure.

The man's feet and legs ached. He had walked only a mile or so to this spot, from the cottage way below, but that had been in pitch darkness, over treacherous rock strewn, boggy ground and then straight up an almost sheer mountain-side.

Even in daylight, climbing to the summit of Binnaw was serious hard work, but in the darkness it had been a foolhardy enterprise, bordering on madness, even with the large, silver maglite torch.

Madness or not, the man had a plane to catch later that day and time was running short.

Directly ahead of him, to the East, the light was getting ever brighter over Benlevy. The first rays of the sun burst gloriously above the mountains opposite and he felt a fleeting moment of joy and pleasure. Then he remembered why he was standing there and reality hit him like a heavy fist smacking into his unready stomach. He was going to war and despite the apparent confidence that he was desperately trying to display; he was, in reality, terrified.

It wasn't just the fear that he might die.

Death, as terrifying as it was, was easy.

The man's fear came from not knowing whether his actions would prove to be good, or whether he was in fact, going to do something evil. Of course, he had thought he was going to do the right thing, but a dream he had had recently had made him think again. One thing was for sure. If he was wrong, if he was evil, then billions of innocent people would die. Even if he was good, but failed in his mission, the same billions would die.

At that moment, as if in recognition of his misery, the nascent splendour of the sunrise was mercilessly strangled by the inevitable gathering of swift, dirty grey clouds.

The Lake took on a darker, almost threateningly sombre hue, reflecting the changing sky; reflecting the deep, impenetrable darkness of the man's mood.

Grey rolling mist crept slowly towards him, along the ridge of the mountain upon which he was perched, and he smiled, grimly.

The man turned and walked along the edge of the precipice towards a nearby cairn.

His ancestors had maintained a tradition of putting a stone on to the cairn for every new child that was born into the family. Over the centuries, the cairn had grown into quite a large pile of rocks and was visible for many miles.

The man had put his own stone on the pile many years ago. He had been raised far away in exile from his family and had known that no one would have celebrated his birth in the traditional manner. Since then he had put two more stones on top of the pile, one for each of his own children.

A solitary sheep bleated nervously before it swiftly scurried away, seemingly quite unaware and unperturbed by the apparent precariousness of its lofty position.

Somewhere in the distance, far, far, below, a dog barked.

The man closed his eyes and took a deep breath.

Then he gulped and prepared to face his greatest shame:

"Father!" He almost whispered the word.

The distant dog barked again.

"Father?" He repeated almost pleadingly this time, but louder.

A nearby lamb bleated for its mother, the tone almost mocking the man in its imploring indigence.

"Father!" This time he almost shouted.

In the valley below the dog barked yet again, as if in answer to the man's call.

A solitary thrush twittered noisily as it hurtled past the cairn, hunting for breakfast.

"Father, please, I need to speak to you. It is time!" The man shouted.

The sheep, now half-way down the mountainside, bleated noisily. The nearby lamb responded joyously and skipped off down the steep slope.

The only other sound the man could hear was his own loud breathing, echoing in his ears.

"Aillen Mac Fionnbharr. I summon thee!"

The man's voice now began to take on a desperate edge.

His voice broke as he shouted the last words.

"I am so sorry." He moaned.

He closed his eyes and sighed forlornly, all he could hear was the sickening sound of silence.

A cloud of mist swirled down from the mighty Maumtrasna mountain, which towered over its smaller sibling Binnaw.

The man felt a small surge of hope, but the mist drifted past him and rolled over the edge of the plateau on which he stood.

"Please, Father, I beg you." He whispered.

A last wisp of green tinged mist swirled up from somewhere near the cairn and enveloped the man.

Slowly, a grim-faced, spectral shape began to emerge.

The man shifted awkwardly, although he was apparently undaunted by the frightening apparition that appraised him disparagingly.

In a strong, deep voice that belied the insubstantial nature of its source, the translucent figure began to speak:

"You dare to summon me, Mac Aillen, Michael Sean O'Brien."

The man nodded.

"Yes, Father!"

"You, the son who betrayed me; who betrayed all of us by abandoning your birthright? You, who used the greatest gifts that your ancient and noble heritage granted you, to merely drink and indulge your flesh in the base carnal pleasures, instead of carrying out the appointed task that was your doom, your destiny?"

The man bowed his head and nodded like a guilty schoolboy.

"Yes, Father!"

The spectre stepped out of the mist and took on a more solid shape.

"So, my son, is it another grandchild I have, that brings you creeping back to this place?

I have watched you put rocks on the cairn for your two children. Yet you did not call on me then."

His voice betrayed the merest hint of mellowing.

The man bit his lip and glowered at the ghost.

"No, Father." He muttered.

"A shame." The spectre sighed despondently.

"Maybe one of my line, may yet be born with the courage to do that which must be done. Even though by then it will all be far too late."

His voice had regained its harshness and apparent contempt.

The man smiled:

"You give up on me too easily, my Father!"

He turned his back on the ghost and took a stone off the cairn and dropped it onto the boggy turf at his feet.

"The task is mine. " He stated.

"It has always been mine. It is just that the time has never been right. I wasn't ready. You once said to me that I had succeeded in passing two of my three great tests when I survived the assassination attempt in Finaan and then dealt with that lunatic in Dublin. You also said, on this very mountain, that you hoped it would be many summers until I faced my greatest challenge."

The spectre's visage softened in the shadow of the mist as the man continued:

"Well it has been many summers and I have passed many more tests, as well as failing a few on the way here, father. You should have seen me in action against two gangs of warriors just a few days ago."

The man continued to remove stone after stone off the pile until deep within the core of the cairn he found an old, faded, plastic Tesco shopping bag.

"But I can tell you one thing. The time is definitely right now!"

He picked up the plastic bag, shook off the dirt and woodlice, then put it down carefully on the ground and began, wordlessly, to replace the rocks, just as he had found them.

"The enemy has declared his hand at last and has placed his pieces on the board. The game is on and I am ready to play!"

The spectre's mouth opened, as if it was going to say something, but then thought better of it. The slightest curl of a smile appeared on its grey lips.

The mist swirled around the man and the ghost, the only sound, the clunk of rocks being placed on top of one another as the man worked to repair the cairn.

Finally, the man turned back towards the phantom that faded in and out of view as the mist brushed past.

The apparition wore his black hair long and loose, his stately robes touched the ground and around his head shone a circlet of gold. He looked like an ancient Prince, drawn from the pages of legend, which, as the last Prince of the immortal "Tuatha de Danaan," he was. His clean-shaven face had now lost its previous severity and had adopted a bemused, quizzical frown.

"So why now, my son? Why now, after all these long wasted years? Years in which the enemy has grown ever stronger and can now dictate the game, as you call it."

The man smiled sadly.

"As John Wayne once said: A man's gotta do what a man's gotta do."

The spectre slowly nodded his head:

"But would it not have been wiser to do this thing, before your belly got fat, your limbs grew slow, your eyes faded and the hair of your head started to turn grey?"

The man grinned sheepishly:

"It might have been, but I can't change the past. Like I said, things have changed. I have changed. Like all youths I was arrogant, I would have been over confident. I could never have killed the child anyway. The time is now right. Anyway as I said, the enemy has declared himself and his people have declared war on me. They started it, not me."

The man picked up the dirty plastic bag at his feet and opened it. He took a round stone ball, slightly larger than a tennis ball out of the bag. He examined it, then placed it in his jacket pocket. He then picked out a rusted pointed piece of metal, which, at his touch immediately and magically changed into a shining bronze spearhead. The man didn't seem in the slightest bit surprised. He put the spearhead in the inside pocket of his jacket.

"Sometimes circumstances dictate our actions, Father. Sometimes, you just know when the time is right. The time is right when someone tries to kill those that you love, those that you love more than yourself, more than you love life itself."

He looked at the shadowy figure of his father and smiled grimly.

"Anyway, I might be a bit plumper than I was, but life is a bit like tennis isn't it? I know the game much better now. I don't need to run quite as much. I can pick my shots. Let the other fellow do the running. I've never felt better."

The shade of Aillen Mac Fionnbharr, nodded and his lips creased into a smile:

"Then go, go do what you must, my son. Remember, I am always with you.

Go! At long last fulfil your destiny. Be what you were born to be, the "Slanaitheoir mor." You have my blessing."

Wayne Higginbotham nodded curtly, then turned to clamber back down the mountainside.

He had to get to Shannon airport and he didn't want to be late.

The mist evaporated, the clouds parted and the early morning sun kissed his face.

It was a beautiful new day.

Wayne Higginbotham wondered how many more of them he would see.

One

The corridor was long, its décor, stark and white. A series of evenly spaced, closed doors lined the walls on both sides. A straight row of fluorescent tubes on the ceiling, flickered and buzzed as the woman ran down the corridor, her eyes wild, darting left and right. Her breath came in short, sharp gasps, her blonde hair swung from side to side as she twisted her head nervously, glancing back down the corridor. Whatever it was she was fleeing from was obviously close.

The woman stopped running; she wiped the perspiration off her forehead then grabbed at a door handle, twisting it uselessly. She glanced down the corridor again before knocking frantically on another door, then another. She almost bounced from wall to wall, door to door banging on them, twisting the handles, all the time glancing back down the corridor.

All to no avail, every single door was locked.

Sobbing heavily, she came to a plain white wall at the very end of the corridor. She turned and pressed her back against it. Her mouth fell open as she gasped for breath. Her eyes closed.

Silently, gracefully, the black figure moved down the corridor towards the woman. It looked like a man in black robes, but it didn't walk like a man. It seemed to hover, gliding about six inches above the white tiled floor.

Its face was like that of a man, but was as white and featureless as the paint on the corridor walls.

Expressionless.

Its hair was black and long, tied back in a ponytail.

The woman opened her eyes and sobbed uncontrollably as the figure stopped before her. She shrunk back as though trying to disappear through the solid wall, then she sank down and curled up in the foetal position on the ground, her arms covering her head.

"Nooooo!" The woman wailed. "Please, I don't want to die."

The creature before her smiled: "We all die, my dear. Each and every one of us. The rich and the poor. The black and the white. The male and the female. The peasant and the King. It is the only thing that all of us have in common. It is simply a matter of when and how."

Its voice was deep, heavily accented, Eastern European.

"Come my child, stand before me. Your fate was written long before this day."

The figure held out an arm.

The woman stopped sobbing and looked up, helplessly, her eyes imploring the creature to let her live, her lips whispering pleading words.

The creatures' hand beckoned her to rise.

She slowly climbed to her feet.

The creature moved closer to her.

The woman closed her eyes and turned her face away from the horrific apparition before her.

The creature towered over her, it was over six feet tall anyway and the fact that it hovered above the ground made it seem even more monstrous.

Her fingernails dug into the white wall behind her.

The creature's mouth opened in a leering grin, exposing long white fangs where its incisors should have been. It reached out towards her and the index finger of its left hand traced a line from her mouth, over her chin, then down her slender white throat.

She turned her head, exposing the side of her neck. Her chin quivered.

"Please, at least make it quick." She gasped, as though accepting her fate.

The creature licked its lips as its mouth closed in on her neck and then its teeth bit into the tender white flesh.

Her eyes shot wide open, her mouth opened wide as she jolted, then shuddered and moaned.

Her eyes closed again as she slowly wilted. Her breath escaped in one long sigh then she slumped lifelessly into the arms of the creature.

"And cut!" A loud disembodied voice shouted.

"Awesome guys! That's a rap for today, great job people, great job."

Terri Thorne blew out a sigh:

"Jeez, if we'd had to shoot that scene one more time I think I'd have shot myself."

She laughed.

Brent Walker, "the vampire" laughed too as he began to disengage the harness that had allowed him to float above the ground.

"You died beautifully, Terri baby! I'm gonna miss biting that pretty neck!"

Terri rolled her eyes:

"You're an old flirt, Walker. I'm sure not going to miss those teeth." She laughed.

All around them the "corridor" was a hive of activity and noise as the film crew covered up the cameras and rolled back equipment.

Ron Seymour the director slapped Brent's back.

"Hey man, great job, you even had me peeing in my pants."

The tall actor laughed and the pair wandered off, discussing the next day's scenes while Terri slipped out of the hanger like studio into the blazing sunshine and made her way back to the trailer she shared with two other bit part actresses.

Terri Thorne, or Theresa O'Brien as she had been christened, (the Thorne was an abbreviation of her mothers maiden name, Thornton) stared at herself in the unforgiving light of the make-up mirror. The lines by her eyes were definitely turning into crow's feet; soon no amount of powder was going to disguise that. Her lips were definitely thinning too.

Oh well, even so, she didn't look half bad for a thirty four year old mother of two. She stopped in mid thought, thirty four year old mother of four, she corrected herself.

There was no doubt in her mind that the roles were drying up. She'd never had a really big part. Her biggest role had been in the disaster movie "Tornado," some six years ago. She'd had ten scenes in that, even if eight of them had involved her doing little more than running around screaming, as the malevolent wind had ripped off her clothing, item by item. She had shot the last two scenes, including her gory death, impaled by a flying "No Entry" road sign that the tornado had torn up, wearing nothing more than bra and pants.

She vigorously rubbed the make up off her nose with the small cotton wool pad.

The original script had demanded that she would be seen topless in her latest death scene, at the hands of Brent's vampire. Terri, however, even at the risk of losing the part, had refused. She certainly wasn't going down to the level of the booming San Fernando Valley porn industry, even if the roles were drying up.

Terri had been surprised that Dean, her agent and manager, as well as her husband had even considered allowing her to do the scene anyway. He had always been very jealous about anyone seeing "his prize possession" as he often referred to her.

She put the pad down and stared deeply into the eyes of her reflection. Who was she trying to kid? Dean hadn't been faithful to her for years; she knew that. She even suspected that she knew who his latest mistress was. Some blonde, bimbo tramp in her early twenties, who he'd recently started to represent. That affair had started when she had been pregnant with Marina, her second child to Dean in quick succession, she was sure of that.

He had been staying away an awful lot, recently, citing his various business interests.

Business, yeah right!

He also seemed to be spending more and more time with his family in Boston. He'd said a number of times that he was going to get out of the movie business soon and start working for the family law firm.

He had dropped out of law school just before graduating, much to the chagrin of his father. Dean reckoned he would soon be able to complete his studies if he went back to school. His cousin Aurelio had left the firm to take up politics, so there was a space available for him.

Terri stood up from the dressing table and slipped on her T-shirt and jeans just as Ebony Mars, another bit part actress opened the trailer door, letting in a blast of LA late summer heat.

"Hey Terri." She drawled in between chewing a huge piece of gum. "You leaving?"

Terri nodded:

"Yeah, my nanny, Conchita is looking after the kids and I guess she'll be climbing the walls by now. You know how hard it is to find a good nanny in the Valley."

Ebony looked at her blankly.

"I ain't got kids, sugar." She stated with a look that almost shouted: "Are you stupid?"

"Whaddya doing over the weekend?" She managed to articulate over her constant bovine mastication.

Terri thought for a second and then brightened:

"We're gonna take the little ones to the beach, you know, a picnic and stuff. Then I've got a big party to arrange for next weekend. It's my daughter's first birthday. Dean's going to be in Vegas, on business with his cousin all week, so he's going to be bringing him and his cousin's stepson, who is just sooo cute. Then, oh yeah, my, er, one of my relatives from England is flying in to stay with us for the later part of that week. So he'll be at the party and yeah, it should be fun."

"Awesome." Ebony stated unconvincingly as she sat at the dressing table.

"What about you?" Terri asked.

Ebony ignored the question as she screwed up her face at the sight of her reflection.

"Do I look old to you?"

Terri laughed:

"Ebony honey, you can not be more than twenty five."

Ebony peered closely at her face in the mirror.

"Yeah but we're sort of finished in this game by the time we hit thirty, aren't we?"

Ebony had a slighter bigger bit part than Terri in the movie, a part that involved quite a lot of nudity.

Terri smiled sadly:

"Yeah, sadly honey, I guess we are. Have a real nice weekend."

She stepped out of the air-conditioned trailer into the searing Southern California heat.

Two Roman soldiers marched past her on their way to nearby sound stage.

"Bitch!" she spat as she walked towards the parking lot.

Then she smiled as she thought about her babies at home, little Marco, now nearly two and Marina who was already one. They were her little treasures and whatever Dean did, she'd always be grateful that he'd given her two of the most beautiful children in the world.

Terri climbed into her car and slammed the door shut.

"Well I guess I'm going to be spending a bit more time with them now." She said out loud. Terri had no more scenes to shoot on "Valley of the Vampires" and much more worryingly; no more movies lined up in the foreseeable future.

It looked like Terri Thorne was going to be "resting" a while. Maybe Ebony was right. Maybe she was all washed up at thirty-four.

I mean, having an eighteen-year-old son coming to visit didn't make her exactly feel young. Oh well, at least she'd got one of her long lost twins back, sweet young Michael.

Terri Thorne wiped a tear from her eye and put her sunglasses on as she drove the Porsche towards the studio gates.

It had been seven years since she had been reunited with Michael, or Wayne as his adoptive parents had called him, but there had been no word from her daughter Charlotte. Not a peep!

"One day I'll have all my babies with me. All four! One day, God willing." She whispered as the Porsche shot out onto Barham Boulevard and began the long crawl home.

Two

Wayne Higginbotham was a very happy young man indeed. The prospect of escaping from the perpetual boredom of the long summer holidays and the seemingly endless grey skies that brooded over the small market town of Shepton, Yorkshire, for the sunshine of Southern California, was just about as good as it gets.

Even if it was going to be just for a week!

That he would then be going on to the University of Manchester, after achieving four good 'A' levels, made it even better.

Wayne stood at his bedroom window in the fading light and stared out at the fantastic view of the town that had been his home for as long as he could remember. Three dales stretched away to the north, east and west, below the huge moors, fells and crags, lined with dry stone-walls and dotted with clumps of trees.

The Yorkshire Dales had to be one of the most beautiful places on Earth, but Wayne couldn't wait to escape. Like most boys of his age, he wanted excitement and adventure, not views and spectacular landscapes.

The first lights were twinkling on in the town, as people turned on car headlights and the streetlights began to illuminate automatically, reflecting brightly in the rain-washed streets.

The view from 49 Greenwood Avenue sure beat the view of the Auction Mart and station buildings from his old room, in 18 Cavendish Street, the small, stone, terraced house, where Wayne had spent most of his first sixteen years.

Wayne and his adoptive mother, Doris, had moved to the new house on Greenwood Avenue after his adoptive father, Frank had died and the house on Cavendish Street had suffered extensive fire damage. Wayne and Doris had had to stay with Doris' sister Margaret for a while and Wayne had conspired with Margaret to insist that Doris make a new start. The old house, even when fully repaired, would be too full of painful memories. Frank and Doris had lived in that house long before they'd adopted Wayne. They'd had some good times there and more than a few bad, but they'd lived through them together. Now Doris was going to have to face a new life, alone; even if she hadn't quite realised it yet.

It had been Wayne who had discovered the ex-council house, halfway up Shepton moor. He had fallen in love with its magnificent panoramic views over the town and the countryside beyond. Plus, being a modern house, the bathroom in number 49 Greenwood Avenue was upstairs, unlike Cavendish Street, where the bathroom had been down in the basement. The basement bathroom where the insane Belgian Priest, Pierre De Feren, had tried to burn him to death.

Wayne grimaced as the memory of those awful moments flooded back into his mind.

Fr De Feren had been an assassin of "The Sacred Order of St. Gregory."

In fact he had been the second assassin of the "Order" that Wayne had encountered in his short life.

"The Sacred Order of St. Gregory" had been a secret organisation based in the Vatican City in Rome, dedicated since the Sixth Century A.D. to the elimination of all "unnatural creatures." What they meant by unnatural creatures was anything that was "not created in God's image," in other words, anything that seemed out of the ordinary to them. This included the usual denizens of the forces of evil; such supernatural and overtly demonic creatures as vampires and werewolves, but more surprisingly other groups who did not see themselves as a division of the army of darkness, including all representatives of the "little people" as they were called in Ireland.

And Wayne Higginbotham just happened to be the son of one of those "little people."

Wayne had been eleven when he had found out that he was "different" from the other kids at Gas Street Primary School. A difference that wasn't just limited to his large, pointed ears.

It had just been another normal early summer day and Wayne had been walking home from school when a local bully had decided to attack him. Wayne could not remember exactly what had happened, but he had found out later that, despite being already badly injured, he had used magical powers to defend himself. Magical powers that he had no idea he had. Magical powers that had seen the bully, Baz Thompson, blasted up into the air and rendered an unconscious heap several yards away, by Wayne doing no more than simply raising his hand and concentrating. Indeed, Wayne had heard that Baz was still mentally disabled as a result of that fateful incident.

He felt slightly guilty about that.

And as if that hadn't been life changing enough, in the same week, Wayne had subsequently discovered that he wasn't the natural born son of Frank and Doris Higginbotham at all, something he had taken for granted all his short life, but that he had been adopted and that his real name was Michael Sean O'Brien.

Wayne had been so traumatised by this discovery that he had run away from home in an attempt to find out who he really was.

In a journey that took him all the way from Yorkshire to London, then on to the West Coast of Ireland, Wayne had not only traced his real parents, but had found out that he just happened to be the son of the last survivor of the immortal and magical race of the "Tuatha de Danaan."

At least that had explained the magic.

Wayne smiled as he remembered how Mickey Finn, an elderly, rotund and apparently simple Irish farmer, living in splendid isolation among the mountains of County Mayo, had changed his shape, right in front of him, to become the imposing stately and regal Prince Aillen Mac Fionnbharr.

Tragically, Wayne's reunion with his father was very short lived, for, on the very night that they had met, "The Sacred Order of St. Gregory" had assassinated Aillen.

Wayne could still see his natural, or supernatural father if he was to be pedantic about it and a deranged Priest, trading thunderbolt-like blasts of energy, in his minds eye.

He could still hear his own anguished cry and see the flash of the assassin's blade, as a young Irish Priest called James Malone had tried to help Aillen, yet in so doing, had fatally distracted him.

Wayne wiped away a tear as he remembered the last Prince of the "Tuatha de Danaan" slumping to his knees with Fr Pizarro's dagger stuck in his chest.

Wayne himself had only survived because of the intervention of Wayne's brave, adoptive father, Frank Higginbotham.

Drops of rain began to hammer against the window.

Wayne sighed sadly as he remembered how Frank had vaulted over a wall, seemingly as if from nowhere and punched the assassin squarely on the jaw, sending him reeling.

The assassin had been the "Sacred Order of St. Gregory's" best agent, Fr Francisco Pizarro, a deranged psychopath who, like Aillen Mac Fionnbharr, had been born an immortal. An immortal, who had built a career out of killing his own kind for four centuries. A career that came to a sudden and abrupt end when Frank Higginbotham had given him a sledgehammer of a right hook that would have floored Mohammed Ali and had then had the presence of mind to hurl Pizarro's own fallen blade, right into the middle of his chest.

With a little bit of help from the power emanating from Wayne's raised hand, the evil Priest had staggered back into Aillen's burning cottage, just as it had finally collapsed, killing him instantly.

"Good riddance!" Wayne muttered to himself.

"So much for HIS immortality!"

Wayne, having been born of a mortal womb, had been denied the immortality of his Tuatha ancestors.

Oh well, who wanted to live forever anyway, especially now that all the other immortals were dead and gone? Such a "gift" would soon become the "curse" of perpetual loneliness.

And Wayne was already all too aware of the precarious, fickle nature of mortality.

His adoptive Dad, Frank, the only father he had known until the age of eleven, his saviour on that dreadful night, was dead now.

He had been killed two years earlier, when Wayne was just sixteen.

Wayne wasn't sure if the "Order" had had anything to do with it, but Frank had died in a road accident, just before Pierre De Feren had tried to burn him alive in that basement bathroom on Cavendish St. That time, Wayne had been saved by his friend, the now ex-Priest, James Malone.

Wayne smiled. Good old James. He would be seeing James as soon as he arrived in California, where Malone now lived.

A brief moment of excitement and anticipation crossed Wayne's mind, but the flood of bad memories were still coursing through his head like the raindrops cascading down the window panes.

Wayne wondered whether he really had heard the last of the "Sacred Order of St. Gregory."

The rain really was hammering on Wayne's bedroom window now.

It had been two years since the "Order" had last invaded Wayne's life.

Aillen Mac Fionnbharr had told Wayne that he would have to pass three tests and that so far he had succeeded in passing just two. The third and most dangerous right of passage still lay ahead. The ironic thing was, even Aillen hadn't been able to tell his son the true nature of the tests and the third test was still very much a mystery. Was there another Pizarro? Another De Feren out there?

Wayne shrugged. He wasn't a boy any more, nor was he an impetuous youth.

"Let'em come. Bring on the last test," he whispered with just a hint of a snarl as he turned and checked his bag.

He had tried to refrain from using magic, ever since the "Battle of Dublin" as he had called his defeat of Pierre de Feren. It had been his careless use of magic that had alerted the "Order" to his existence.

20

A drunken and ridiculously futile attempt to use his shape shifting abilities to capture the girl of his dreams had somehow been detected by the "Order."

The ghost of Aillen, who frequently appeared to Wayne, had told him that the all the pieces of the "Stone of Falias" glowed, whenever the Tuatha used magic, as the stone amplified their powers.

That must have been how they'd found out about him.

That must have been how they'd managed to trace him to his remote hideaway in insignificant little Shepton.

Wayne wondered how much of the stone was still out there, in addition to his own fragments?

Aoibheall the Banshee, who had tried to rob Wayne of his shards of the stone, had possessed a ring with a small piece of it set in the centre.

Bishop Donleavy had given him several more pieces, just before he passed away and had told him that a Priest in the Vatican City in Rome possessed yet even more shards.

Wayne strolled over to a chest of drawers and took out a cashbox. He instinctively looked around. His bedroom door was closed and no one could see through his bedroom window as the house was so high up the moor above Shepton.

Wayne lifted a model of the Starship Enterprise off the top of the chest of drawers and ripped a strip of sellotape from the base. A key dropped into his hand. Wayne put the key into the keyhole of the cashbox, opened it and poured the contents onto his bed.

Several rolled up socks bounced on his duvet.

Wayne took a deep breath.

Why was he doing this now? He wondered. He was flying off to California the next day and would soon be leaving Shepton, if not forever, then certainly for the bulk of the foreseeable future. Maybe that was what was causing his reminiscences and his subsequent desire to check his most precious possessions.

He slowly unrolled each sock. A grey pebble sized piece of stone, fell from each one onto his bed. Eventually ten pieces of the fabled Stone of virtue, the stone of the great Tuatha city of Falias, the Lia Fail, lay on Wayne Higginbotham's duvet.

Wayne shook his head. These unassuming bits of stone had seen things that he couldn't even imagine and had existed in places he could only dream about.

Ten magical pieces of a stone from an ancient, magical civilisation, plus the tiny shard embedded in the ring he wore on his wedding finger, a ring that had once belonged to Aoibheall, the Banshee.

Wayne shook his head. It was all so surreal. Like the sort of thing you'd read in a fantasy novel. Wayne heard Doris knock on his door.

He shuddered. He had been so lost in his thoughts that he hadn't heard her bumbling across the landing.

Doris opened the door before Wayne had even had a chance to say come in.

"Are you ready for tomorrow?" She asked after a quick, suspicious glance around Wayne's room.

"Yes." Wayne sighed with a nod towards his bag on the floor.

Doris pursed her lips.

"I don't know why you have to go galavanting off to America again, when you're going to be starting at that University in a couple of weeks. What am I going to do on me own?"

Wayne shrugged:

"I need a bit of sunshine." He suggested, hopefully.

"Aye, couldn't we all." Doris exclaimed as she glowered at him scornfully.

"We could have had a nice week in Blackpool, instead of you going off all that way on your own. I don't know why anybody would want to go to America, what with all them murders you see on the telly. It does me good, the sea air in Blackpool does. Aye, it would have been nice to have had a break, before you go off to Manchester. Never mind though, don't bother about me, nobody else does."

She shuffled out of the bedroom miserably and slammed the door shut.

Wayne heard her mutter: "Trevor would have taken me to Blackpool," as she wandered off along the landing.

"Sorry Eeyore." Wayne sighed, as he turned, reached down the side of his bed and picked up the stones.

Wayne replaced the stones in the old cashbox, which he wrapped in a pair of underpants and hid in the bottom of his underwear drawer.

Wayne stood and stared at his reflection in the mirror. The gawky teenager was turning into a man. His hair was getting longer by the day and only the very tips of his pointed ears could now be seen through his natural corkscrew curls. Some girl had told him in the pub that he looked like one of the guys in the TV show "The Professionals." Wayne had enjoyed that moment.

Wayne grinned at his reflection. The reflection grinned back as it morphed into the face of the actor Martin Shaw.

"Let's go see some of those California girls." He whispered as his face changed back into his own.

Life was definitely good for young Wayne Higginbotham.

Three

James Malone kissed the green card, which he clutched tightly in his fist. Now he could do whatever he wanted. He was officially no longer an illegal alien. He laughed when he remembered young Wayne looking horrified when he had described himself in those terms before his marriage to the beautiful Carrie Hordern.

"What, you mean you're not really human?" Wayne had gasped, his eyes as round as saucers.

"But I thought…"

James had interrupted him, putting his hands on his hips and laughing out loud:

"Hark the bloody kettle calling the pot black. I'm a damn site more human than you are for a start, Michael Sean O' Leprechaun. At least I'm not related to Mr. Spock!"

He had pulled his ears into points.

"Ha, bloody ha!" Wayne had responded with a snort and then a fit of giggles.

That had been last winter, just after Christmas, when Wayne had last visited California and had moaned about the rudeness of the immigration officer at the airport. James had described to him the infernal grilling that he had been given at U.S, immigration when he had tried to get back into Los Angeles after the "Battle of Dublin."

James had almost been refused entry and had been accused of being an "illegal alien," but he had used the gift of the Blarney, told a couple of whopping lies and had charmed his way back into the States. One of his lies, that his girlfriend was pregnant had, in fact, turned out to be true.

Now, here he was, James Malone with a beautiful American wife, a beautiful baby daughter and that precious green card permit. The world was his oyster.

It was quite a change in circumstance, for a man who had been a naïve young Irish Priest in the far west of Ireland just over seven years earlier.

It had been a long hard slog.

James had fled to America in the aftermath of the "Finaan Tragedy," as the Irish press had described it at the time. The more salacious gossip rags had termed it the "Finaan Scandal." In whichever way it was described, two Catholic Priests had died and one had disappeared and was widely presumed to have committed suicide. Rumours abounded about homosexual trysts, devil worship, or terrorist involvement. There had even been tales of a dark and handsome Spanish priest having been in the Priests house in the days leading up to the tragedy, but he had disappeared off the face of the earth. Even the most positive press reports had blamed the events on excessive drink. None of them knew the truth.

None of them knew that a fourth Priest really had been there and that he had burned to death in the ruins of a blazing farm cottage. None of them also knew that magic had been involved and that the last of Ireland's true "little people" had also perished that night.

James put the green card carefully into his wallet and picked up the steaming mug of sweetly aromatic coffee from the table in his yard overlooking the San Fernando Valley.

It was still early in the morning, yet the sun was already blazing in the clear blue sky.

An enormous buzzard wheeled in lazy circles over James' head, looking for a tasty breakfast snack amongst the Canyon rocks. While down in the valley, far below, amidst the busy rush hour throng, the smog was already beginning to shroud the taller buildings.

It had all been so different, seven years earlier, on that dark night near the village of Tourmakeady.

James could still see Father Francisco Pizarro hurling bolts of pure energy from the raised palms of his hands, across the flame illuminated cottage garden.

He could still smell the burning thatch and the noise of furniture exploding inside the inferno that had been Mickey Finn's home.

He could still see Mickey Finn, or Aillen Mac Fionnbharr, as he had discovered him to be, trading energy blasts with the assassin from the "Sacred Order of St. Gregory", while James got Wayne's Aunt and young cousin to safety.

He could still see young Wayne Higginbotham advancing towards the menacing Priest and the kneeling, mortally wounded figure of Aillen, whilst he, James Malone, superhero (failed), writhed in agony after Pizarro had blasted him. He had tossed him through the air as easily as an October gale tosses a fallen leaf.

He smiled wryly as he recalled little Wayne's defiance and the way the boy had used his own energy bolts to blast the evil clergyman to the ground, but how it had looked really grim when Wayne had exhausted his magical energy, until the boy's adoptive father had appeared over a wall, as if from nowhere, to deliver a tremendous right hook onto Pizarro's chin and had rescued his son.

That had been something to see.

In the midst of all that energy blasting and magical duelling, it had been a man using nothing more than guts and the raw power of his fists that had prevailed.

Yes, he'd come a long way from the events of that night.

He took a sip of coffee and remembered his friend, Father Dermot Callaghan. Fr Dermot had been found hanging in a village church. The authorities and press described it as a suicide, but James knew that Pizarro had murdered him. He had murdered him in cold blood because he had refused to help the "Order" and because he knew too much. He had been a brave man, much braver than the young James Malone, who had eventually helped Pizarro, much against his better judgment.

James took a deep breath and sighed as he remembered his futile, pathetic attempt to thwart Pizarro's plan by grabbing the steering wheel of the old Morris off Fr Burke and crashing into the wall.

"Not exactly James Bond, were we, James?" Malone whispered.

Old Fr William Burke had been Pizarro's chief accomplice. Neither Dermot, nor James had liked Burke and Dermot had shared the Priest house with him for many years. He had had a condescending, patrician air about him. Indeed it was said he had once been a Monsignor and was well on his way towards becoming a Bishop, when some serious scandal overtook him and he had ended up in exile in that rural Connaught village backwater.

Fr Burke had died crashing that old Morris, when he had been attempting to flee the scene of Mickey Finn's assassination.

"James!" The sound of Carrie's voice brought James back into the modern world with a jolt. The smell of Bougainvillea overtook the memory of the smell of burning and the heat of the burning cottage became the heat of the burning Southern California sun.

Carrie Malone, nee Hordern emerged from her house in Box Canyon carrying a beautiful baby girl in her arms.

James appraised his young wife and blessed his good fortune.

He had met Carrie over two years earlier when she had given the good looking Irish hobo a ride when he had been walking down the Highway in Santa Barbara. She had brought him home and he had never really left, except for that last trip home when he and Wayne had finally defeated the "Order" in Dublin.

"Yes babe?" He answered. Carrie tenderly touched their daughter's nose:

"Would Daddy get baby Aoibhell some clean diapers on the way home from his interview, yes?"

James grinned and put down his mug.

"Daddy would love to." He said in a baby-talk voice, as he stood and gave his wife and child a hug.

"Daddy's going right now, yes he is."

He smiled at his long blonde haired wife and stared at the beautiful clear blue eyes that never ceased to amaze him.

"How come I got so lucky?" He whispered.

Carrie cocked her head to one side and grinned:

"You've got the luck of the Irish to start with and then you just happen to go hang out with the last of the leprechauns. It's not like sooooo surprising, is it?"

Her face creased into a huge grin as she stared back into his brown eyes and ruffled his mop of brown curls with her right hand:

"But how did I luck out?"

They both laughed and baby Aoibhell gurgled happily.

"The last of the leprechauns." James repeated as his Buick rolled slowly down the sweeping curves of Box Canyon.

"The last of the little people." He stated out loud and laughed at the description of his friend, young Wayne Higginbotham. Whether he was truly the last of the little people or not, Wayne did have amazing magical powers as he had proved back in Finaan and in Dublin and of course, he had the ears. Mind you, despite all his magic, Wayne Higginbotham would have been burned to a crisp, had James not rescued him from that basement.

James couldn't help but grin like an idiot as he recalled Wayne brainwashing two very aggressive Special Branch cops with no more than a wave of his hand, as they had questioned James in the aftermath of the fire.

"Ah happy days." Malone whispered as the Buick squealed around another tight bend.

No doubt he and Wayne would be laughing about such reminiscences next week when the pointy-eared little devil came to visit.

James grinned.

Well he would certainly have some news for young Higginbotham by then. If all went well at his interview, he would be able to stop working illegally as a bereavement counsellor and become a fully-fledged reporter on the San Fernando Courier.

"Confessions a specialty." He laughed.

Life just seemed to get better and better for James Malone.

Four

"I don't know how things can get much worse." Doris Higginbotham moaned as she stared at her half empty tea-cup in the "Lite-Bite" café on Shepton's busy, bustling High Street.

Margaret Houghton–Hughes raised her eyebrows as she sipped her tea, the little finger of her right hand poised, erect and pointing away from the handle of her china cup:

"In what way do you mean, Doris dear?"

Doris took a paper tissue from the pocket of her coat and sniffed loudly:

"Well what with our Frank gone and our Wayne jiggering off to America and then all this University business, or whatever it is. I'm going to be left stuck all on me own, up there on Greenwood Avenue. I mean, I would never have moved up there if our Wayne had told me he were going to be going off and leaving home so soon."

Margaret, Doris' younger sister frowned:

"He'll come back, when he's done his degree, won't he? Anyway, I thought you liked it up there? It is much more suitable for you than that house on Cavendish Street."

Doris glared at her sister as she plonked the cup and saucer noisily on the Formica- topped, café table.

"Well, I didn't have much choice, did I? I mean what with the house being almost burnt to the ground and we couldn't have stayed with you lot forever, could we?"

Margaret sighed, recognising the covert accusation in her sister's apparently innocent statement and despite the rhetorical nature of Doris' question, answered as sincerely as she could manage.

"You know, dear, you could have stayed with us as long as you wanted, our Doris, both you and Wayne."

She paused momentarily:

"And anyway, Doris dear, you'd already moved back into Cavendish Street, before you went and moved up to Greenwood."

Doris sniffed.

"Aye! I know." She mumbled.

"Our Wayne insisted that we move. Too many memories, he said. And he said that I couldn't keep on walking down two flights of stairs to the bathroom. Not as I got older anyway."

Margaret took a sip of tea.

"Well he was right there, dear." She said, pursing her lips.

"He's a good lad, your Wayne, you could have done a lot worse and, our Doris, you have said yourself that you couldn't have gone on living in that house, not without your Frank."

"Aye, it's alright for some. Some have still got their husband." Doris mumbled indignantly.

"I beg your pardon." Margaret snapped.

"Nowt. I were just talking to meself." Doris replied with a feigned air of nonchalance.

"Trevor wouldn't have gone off and left me. He was a lovely baby, our Trevor was, always smiling."

Margaret flinched at the venom in Doris' statement. She had never really accepted Wayne as an adequate replacement for that first, failed adoption.

Despite the clamour of the busy café, an awkward silence descended on the sisters' table.

Doris and Margaret had been engaged in prolonged spats of jealousy ever since they were little girls in the nearby village of Carelton.

Doris was the more volatile of the two and as the elder sister by several years, had always considered herself to be Margaret's superior. Doris had always had the better clothes and the most handsome boyfriends, while Margaret had had to be content with hand me downs. Once in their twenties, however, Margaret had managed to marry well and her husband Stanley Houghton-Hughes had become a bank Manager, which eventually made the Houghton-Hughes family very middle class; a position Margaret was determined to live up to.

Doris had already been married for several years by the time that Margaret met Stanley. Doris had met her husband Frank in the latter stages of the Second World War, when he had been home on leave. He had been decorated for bravery and had been considered quite a catch, tall, good-looking and ever so smart in his uniform. Since he had left the army, however, he had worked for most of his life in a small factory in the nearby town of Barlickwick, putting thingummys onto widgets and then placing them in boxes.

Frank Higginbotham wasn't an ambitious man and didn't have a competitive bone in his body, an aspect of his personality that totally infuriated Doris. That had been why the Higginbothams had lived in a tiny, stone, terraced house on Cavendish Street, while the Houghton-Hughes lived in almost palatial splendour in a large, imposing, detached house on the Ripon Road; the most desirable address in town.

It was a sign of how stuck-up Margaret had become, Doris was oft heard to say, that she had one of them there bidet things in one of her bathrooms.

28

The sisters also lived out their rivalry through their sons. Margaret had been the first to get pregnant and her only son Cedric had been born in late 1961. Unable to conceive naturally, Doris immediately decided to adopt, so that she wasn't outdone by her younger sibling in the family stakes. Her first attempt at adoption had ended in agony, however, as the child, whom Doris and Frank had named Trevor, had been taken back by his natural mother before the adoption could be legally formalised.

Michael Sean O'Brien was the Higginbotham's second chance at matching Margaret's game of happy families, but he had been very much Doris' second choice.

She had wailed all the way home from the adoption agency in London, bemoaning her new baby's awful large, pointed ears, compared to the physical perfection that had been Trevor.

Oblivious to their mothers' sibling rivalry, Cedric and Wayne, as the Higginbotham's had renamed Michael; had grown up as good friends and had both passed their eleven plus exams and attended Shepton's Wormysted's Grammar School. Both boys had subsequently gone on to achieve good 'O' Levels and it had more than delighted Doris that Wayne had scored one more pass than Cedric. It was a very small victory for Doris in her never ending competition with her little sister. Up to that point their sibling rivalry had become something of a rout, with Margaret winning in every single capacity.

Life for the Houghton-Hughes had been on a continuous upwardly mobile trajectory ever since they had got married. Not only did they have the big house on the Ripon Road, but they also holidayed abroad every year, had a large, brand new car and a number of posh new friends, who were frequently invited to dinner. The Higginbothams were never invited.

"We're just not good enough for the likes of her!" Doris would complain with monotonous regularity.

The Higginbothams always seemed to have to struggle to make ends meet, despite Doris doing cleaning jobs to supplement Frank's meagre earnings at the thingummy factory.

They couldn't afford a car, a colour TV, or even a telephone. As for holidays, they were spent in a small inflatable tent, which had a nasty habit of collapsing in the wind and rain.

Two years earlier, life had become even harder for Doris. Frank had gone and got himself killed, knocked off that stupid little motorbike. To make matters even worse, as far as Doris knew, Wayne had got involved with some Northern Irish feud, because of his real family background. A feud that had resulted in the Higginbotham's house being badly damaged. At least that is what that nice Irish man, James Malone had told her.

That was the problem with adoption; you just didn't know what you were getting and what history lay behind that child.

Doris had had to live with the ignominy of staying with the Houghton-Hughes in the weeks after the fire, until their insurance had paid up and the house on Cavendish Street had been repaired.

Doris and Wayne had moved to the house on the Greenwood estate with its incredible views about six months ago.

Then Wayne had gone and passed all four of his 'A' levels.

This time Doris failed to revel in the fact that Wayne had scored one more than Cedric, because he had immediately announced that he had the grades he needed and was going to go off to University.

Doris didn't know anyone who had ever gone to University, except maybe the Doctor.

Cedric had opted to join his Father's bank after his 'A' levels, why couldn't Wayne do something like that?

Why did he need another three years at school, for goodness sake? He wouldn't be starting work until he was at least twenty-one.

There were lots of good jobs going in Shepton that he could have started at eighteen.

Wayne could have been a trainee manager at the big department store in town "Rackmans"; now that was a good job. The managers there wore suits!

Wayne could even have tried to get a plumbing apprenticeship, or something like that, but oh no, he had to go off to do this University thing.

"So when is your Wayne going to America?" Margaret asked Doris, snapping her out of her miserable reverie and breaking the long awkward silence that had descended between the sisters.

Doris sighed heavily:

"He went today. He went off first thing this morning on't train. He were getting a plane from Leeds to London and then flying off to America."

"Must have cost him a bomb." Margaret stated with raised eyebrows.

Doris shrugged:

"I didn't give him a penny, He says he earned it all from his Saturday job and his other savings."

Doris' face hardened.

"I reckon he's not just going to see that Malone chap. The one who saved him in Cavendish Street, you know."

She sniffed and shuffled in her chair, subtly inviting her sister to enquire exactly what Doris suspected

Margaret leaned towards her, conspiratorially.

"What do you mean?"

Doris sniffed loudly again:

"I reckon he's gone to look for his proper father."

Margaret snapped back upright.

"What makes you think that?" She asked; mouth agape.

Doris savoured the moment as her sister waited in eager anticipation of whatever salacious gossip Doris was about to impart.

The sisters leaned in together so that their heads were nearly touching.

"Do you remember what they said about Wayne's real mother and father at that adoption place in London, when we went to pick him up."

Margaret paused for a second:

"They said she was a waitress, wasn't she? She was sixteen and from Ireland, if I remember correctly."

Doris nodded then looked around to see if anyone was listening.

A frail looking old lady sat alone at the table next to them, devouring an enormous Danish pastry. On the other side a young mother was loudly berating two disorderly infants, while trying to feed a tiny baby a bottle on her lap.

Doris sniffed again.

"Aye, well, you remember what that Malone chap said about his Dad being in the IRA and there being a feud, or sommat, hence them trying to do Wayne in." She whispered.

Margaret nodded enthusiastically.

"Well they said at the adoption agency that his father was………."

"American!" Margaret exclaimed, interrupting her sister's explanation in mid-flow.

"They said he was American, didn't they?"

Doris gave one triumphant nod.

Margaret frowned.

"But that James Malone said that Wayne's real Dad had been murdered by the IRA."

Doris sniffed again:

"Well he could have been wrong, couldn't he?"

Margaret mulled over Doris rational for a second.

"What if it's his mother?"

Doris nearly dropped the teacup she was lifting to her mouth.

"What?" She gasped.

Margaret frowned thoughtfully.

31

Doris scowled:

"They didn't say SHE was American at the adoption doodah, did they? They said HE was, his dad."

Margaret sat back in her chair:

"Well we're both just guessing aren't we? It'll all come out in the wash, I'm sure."

Doris sipped the last dregs from her teacup.

"Aye, I suppose so, but I'll tell you sommat for nowt, Margaret love. It wouldn't surprise me if our Wayne has gone for good. Whether it's America, Manchester, or wherever he's going to University. I'll bet you he's going to go off and leave me all on me own."

Doris sobbed loudly and then blew her nose equally noisily on a grubby tissue.

The little old lady at the next table glanced at her, as did the two infants.

"Mummy, that lady's crying." One of the children informed his mother who just nodded.

Margaret Houghton-Hughes grimaced and the thought flashed through her mind that she was glad that Cedric was her natural son. She didn't often feel sorry for Doris, but ever since Wayne had run away when he was eleven, things had never seemed quite the same in the Higginbotham household.

Margaret squeezed her older sister's hand and smiled reassuringly.

"He'll be back. You'll see, love."

Doris smiled sadly.

"He's not been the same, Margaret, not since he ran away that time, just before he went off to that there Grammar School. Our Frank never really told me what went on over there in Ireland, not really. I'm sure sommat important must have happened to him. He didn't go all that way for nowt. You know, I have wondered, from time to time, whether he might have met his proper mother, or father then. I've often wondered if our Frank knew and never said nowt."

Margaret smiled sympathetically:

"I'm sure Frank would have told you, if anything like that had happened."

Doris shrugged again and then stood to leave, Margaret did the same.

"Oh well, it'll be reight, I suppose. One thing is for sure, they can't be rich and famous or he'd have beggared off a long time ago."

Five

The news article about Father Logan was very small. Bishop O'Leary almost missed it as he frenetically scoured the morning newspapers. His eyes had passed over to the photograph of a half naked young actress, which had caused him to dribble his tea as his mouth twitched and his tongue flicked over his extremely plump bottom lip. He was quite unaware why he had glanced back up at the short paragraph, almost lost in a small news item column, maybe he had recognised the name as his eye had passed over it, but somehow his eye was irrevocably drawn to the thick black type that reported the death by suicide of yet another Irish Catholic Priest. This one, a Father Logan, had gone and hanged himself.

O'Leary's mouth fell open. Father Logan had been Bishop Donleavy's assistant and protégé. Donleavy had once described him to O'Leary as a future potential head of the "Order," such was his dedication and promise. The article went on to state how, only two years earlier, Father Logan's boss, a Bishop Donleavy, had been found murdered in St Patrick's Cathedral in Dublin and how he had been traumatised by the incident.

O'Leary suddenly felt very cold as his blood seemed to freeze in his veins and he shivered violently. Father Logan had been the last surviving member of the "Sacred Order of St Gregory" in Ireland, apart from O'Leary himself.

Had Logan's demise been suicide?

Or were far more sinister forces at work?

Since the incident at Finaan seven years earlier, when Father Burke and Father Callaghan had perished and young Father Malone had disappeared, more than twenty Irish Priests had died in mysterious circumstances. Seventeen of them had been members of the "Order" at one time or another, a fact known only to O'Leary. Of the seventeen deaths, eight had supposedly been suicides, three had been accidents and six Priests had died of "natural causes." Fourteen of these deaths had actually taken place since the "Order" had been stood down, two years earlier.

O'Leary shook his head.

Who could be doing this?

The "Order" had been stood down because it had supposedly achieved its goal of destroying all the world's demons. The death of the Finn creature in Finaan and De Feren's success in assassinating Finn's progeny in England had supposedly seen the end of the "little people" as the ignorant liked to think of the immortals. The end of the immortals rendered the prophecy that identified God's assassin and began with the line "A child no mortal man shall sire," irrelevant.

Of course, O'Leary knew that Malone had survived the Finaan incident. He had been despatched by the "Order," a victim of the Banshee Aoibheall.

Could all this be down to her?

O'Leary shivered at the thought of the beautiful young woman who could supposedly drain the life out of a man with no more than a touch. He wondered what had happened to her. She had disappeared without trace after betraying Father De Feren, during his mission to kill Finn's offspring.

She was a demon, no doubt. He had never trusted her, even when De Feren had presented her as his ultimate weapon.

O'Leary hurriedly closed the newspaper and wiped his brow with a clean white handkerchief.

He would be next. He had to be:

"The last surviving member of the "Sacred Order of Saint Gregory" in Ireland.

The words echoed repeatedly in his head.

Nowhere was safe. Not even Rome itself could provide sanctuary. His Eminence, Cardinal D'Abruzzo, the head of the Order in the eternal city, had perished. Supposedly he had suffered a heart attack, but O'Leary knew better than that.

It was surely too much of a coincidence that D'Abruzzo's death had been closely followed by a disastrous fire in one of the Vatican City's basements. A fire, which had destroyed all the records of the "Sacred Order of St Gregory" and its entire fifteen hundred year campaign of ridding the earth of unnatural demons, in order to prepare the way for the return of the Messiah. Poor old father Bianca, the custodian of the Order's records, had survived the fire but had been so badly burnt that he would spend the rest of his life in care. If the mighty stone walls of the Vatican City and the ranks of the Swiss Guard could not protect Cardinal D'Abruzzo and Father Bianca, what could?

O'Leary thought back to that glorious summer day in Dublin two years earlier when the ancient oak door of Bishop Donleavy's office had been blown into a thousand pieces and Donleavy had been killed at his desk.

Why had De Feren gone so crazy?

Surely he should have been happy that his life's work had been achieved.

O'Leary, of course, could not remember what had happened that day, even though he had been there. He must have taken a very heavy blow to the head, as he had developed total amnesia. He had seen the results of De Feren's attack, however, when the ambulance man had brought him round. The deranged Belgian Priest must have used a grenade to destroy Bishop Donleavy's door so comprehensively. Then he had gone and set himself on fire and thrown himself under a double-decker bus. What a fool!

O'Leary took a deep breath.

But what if De Feren hadn't been the killer that day?

What if Bishop Donleavy's killer had been someone else altogether and De Feren had actually been trying to save Donleavy?

O'Leary dropped the newspaper onto the breakfast table.

What if the Garda and everyone else had been wrong about De Feren and whoever it was that had killed Donleavy had been responsible for De Feren's and all the other deaths?

De Feren had been dedicated to the "Order" but he had not been the type to flip at the point of his greatest triumph.

Suddenly it all made total sense. It had to be Aoibheall the Banshee.

So why hadn't she finshed him off that day in the cathedral?

Why could he not remember anything that happened that day?

O'Leary rubbed his forehead. His head was beginning to ache.

He wondered momentarily what might have become of the messiah child in the midst of the destruction of the Order. Cardinal D'Abruzzo had hinted at Donleavy's funeral that the boy had been placed in the care of someone who was a professional in the business of protection. O'Leary crossed himself surreptitiously and issued a quick prayer for the poor child.

His fat frame trembled in his chair as he glanced nervously around the dining room in the small bed and breakfast farm that served as his current sanctuary. An elderly commercial traveller in a shabbily shiny, blue pinstripe suit, slurped a runny egg at a neighbouring table. O'Leary caught his eye and he nodded curtly before returning to his breakfast.

O'Leary stood and made his way back up to his room. He too was wearing a business suit, albeit of much better quality than the salesman's. He was not wearing any items of clothing that would have identified him as a Priest, much less a Bishop. If anyone asked him, he would inform them that he had retired from the civil service and was fulfilling a long held ambition by travelling around his beloved Ireland.

In reality, ever since the Garda had cleared him of any involvement in the murder of Bishop Donleavy, he had been on the run.

O'Leary was now in no doubt that the devil himself in the shape of a beautiful young woman had killed Donleavy and had no doubt been responsible for the rest of the deaths of the members of the Order in Ireland and those in Rome. O'Leary knew now that it had been the trauma of seeing the she-devil that had caused him to lose his memory. That was why his head had shown no sign of injury. The Order's finest assassin, Pierre De Feren, had thrown himself under a bus because of the pain of his immolation, not because he had been mad.

Bishop O'Leary threw his scant possessions into an old battered suitcase and locked it.

The she-devil, Aoibheall, would find him, of course she would, but Bishop O'Leary was going to make sure that it wouldn't be easy. The world was a big place and O'Leary knew of places where it would be easy to disappear and even Sherlock Holmes himself would struggle to find him. Plus he would make sure he was armed and ready. He giggled a nervous, girlish laugh and stepped out of his room.

"Oh yes, I'm not going down that easily." He muttered as he began to plod down the staircase in the bed and breakfast lodging, on the main road into the market town of Clifden, Galway, just a few miles away from the village of Finaan, where the final decline and fall of the once mighty Order had begun, seven years earlier.

"It'll take more than a mere Banshee to kill me!"

Yet his bravado was belied by the palour of his face and the perspiration that covered his forehead.

"Are you alright?" The B&B proprietor asked him as O'Leary settled his account.

"Of course." The Bishop replied haughtily.

"I am merely behind schedule."

The proprietor watched the Bishop's ample frame wobble hurriedly off down his drive and rubbed his chin, suspiciously.

"It looks like he thinks the devil himself is after him." The aged salesman stated as he appeared by the proprietor's side in the hallway.

The proprietor shook his head.

"Something's upset him, so it has. Something very serious I would think."

"Serious indeed!" The salesman nodded and dabbed his egg stained chin with his napkin.

Six

The enormous 747 banked sharply as it crossed the San Gabriel Mountains on its final approach to Los Angeles International Airport. Wayne Higginbotham stared out of the window at the remnants of the clean white snow on the mountain tops, contrasting with the azure blue of the Southern Californian sky. He marvelled that the snow was still there, even after a blazing California summer. Wayne watched as the long, straight streets and boulevards of the metropolis slowly emerged through the wispy, thin streaks of cloud and then a gasp at the sight of a silver flash, as the Pacific Ocean came into view. This was Wayne's second visit to Los Angeles, but no matter how many times he came, he was sure he would never tire of that first glimpse of the distant shining sea.

He smiled. How different it was to the dark, cool of the early Yorkshire morning he had left so many hours before.

So much light. So much life.

A new world, fresh and shiny, steel and glass, sun, sea and sky; compared to the damp, mossy, grey stone, black clouded, tomb like atmosphere of home.

He could see swimming pools reflecting bright sunlight in almost every back yard, palm trees lining the roads and as the plane descended, humungous shiny cars and pick-up trucks crawling along the incredible web like network of freeways.

"God bless America!" Wayne whispered, his nose pressed to the thick glass of the aeroplanes's window.

It was James Malone who met him in the main body of the terminal:

"Hey, look at you, man." He grinned as he gave Wayne a friendly hug.

"You get bigger every time I see you. If you keep growing like this you'll be playing for the Lakers in no time."

Amidst the vast crowd of people meeting and greeting and hugging and kissing, Wayne was relieved just to see a familiar face.

"I think my growing days are over." Wayne laughed.

"Well it's a relief to see you like that! I wasn't quite sure who I'd be meeting. I was half expecting Clint Eastwood." James grinned, referring to Wayne's shape-shifting antics in St Patrick's Cathedral, Dublin two years earlier.

"But even though you're you, hell, you've changed!"

"And you're sounding more American by the minute, Father Malone." Wayne countered with a friendly poke in the older man's ribs.

"It's your hair, it's gotten so long. Is this a part of the getting ready to be a student pose?"

James asked as he took the heavy bag off James and plonked it on a trolley.

Wayne yawned:

"I didn't think it was that long, just a bit thicker."

James laughed again and shook his head:

"Now how the hell am I going to convince anyone that my buddy is one of the little people when you can't even see his pointy ears?"

Wayne made a sarcastic face as the two friends crossed the concourse and headed out onto the busy road at the terminal gates. Taxis, buses, cars, all jostled for position at the side walk as James escorted the clearly shattered Wayne across the pedestrian crossing towards the car park.

"Still got the old Buick then?" Wayne teased James as the former Priest climbed the concrete stairs to the second floor of the car park.

"I do still have the old girl, so I do." James replied, suddenly sounding very Irish again.

"But I would swap it in an instant for a good ol'Moggy 1000 like I had back in Finaan."

"Really?" Wayne gasped in astonishment.

"No!" James replied quick as a flash, as he opened the trunk of a huge black car and dropped Wayne's bag in.

"Now let's get out of this smog and up to the Canyon, where I think my darling Carrie might just have a few cookies and a nice cold beer. You are eighteen now aren't you? We'll pretend we're in Ireland, or even England, instead of California, where you're officially stuck on soda pop until you hit twenty-one."

"That sounds absolutely marvellous." Wayne mumbled as he climbed into the Buick.

As soon as the car started to move, his eyes closed and he immediately fell into a deep dreamless sleep.

The man was dressed entirely in black. His long velvet cloak shifted eerily, yet there didn't seem to be any sign of a breeze.

His blond hair tumbled carelessly around his shoulders, yet despite the fact that he was standing so close, Wayne could not make out any distinct facial features.

Just the eyes: cold, clear, merciless, bright blue eyes.

The man, if man he was, oozed spiteful malevolence.

"So you are the "Slanaitheoir mor?" He almost spat out the words as he sarcastically and deliberately mispronounced each syllable.

"Gaelic Irish, such a primitive tongue." He laughed.

"So you are the one, who the immortals have sent to try and stop me. You are their...."

He paused, as though desperately seeking the appropriate word.

"Champion?"

The word was elongated, as though nothing could sound more ridiculous and the tone made it more of a question than a statement.

The man's voice was rich, deep and unbearably arrogant.

They have sent me a whelp, a boy who has only been shaving his chin fluff for a few paltry seasons. I expected a warrior of note. I, at least, expected a man. But they have sent me..."

Again he paused and Wayne felt his leer as he leaned in closer to the terrified teenager:

"You!"

The man's mocking laugh sent shivers down Wayne's spine.

His stomach tightened, as though his gut had tied itself into knots. He tried to come up with a witty and sarcastic riposte, but his mouth just flapped open and he found he could not make a single sound. He swallowed hard to try and lubricate his throat, but he was so terrified that he could not even think straight.

"The immortals must have hidden themselves away for too long on that remote overgrown damp rock in the Western sea. The cowards retreated into their caves and burrows and hid like children playing infantile games. Did they really think that my forces would not hunt them down one by one, until we had cleansed the Earth of their stench?

Did they truly think that we would not travel to the very ends of the earth to find them and root them out, one by one?"

The man pulled himself away from Wayne and stretched to his full height.

"I have waited an eternity for this day. This day; when the very last memory of their existence is wiped away like a putrid stain. The day I crush their very last hope. The day when instead of sending a champion to match me, they send a victim to try and placate me."

The man roared with laughter.

Wayne felt himself rising from the ground, as though someone was pulling him up by the scruff of the neck. He could feel his feet dangling helplessly.

The laughing stopped.

"You have led a charmed life, boy, but it ends now!"

The man sounded a bit like Wayne's old Deputy Head Master at Wormysted's Grammar School in Shepton, Dai Davies.

"Did you think it would be easy, boy?"

The man hissed then laughed again.

No, that wasn't Dai Davies.

Dai Davies never laughed like that.

Dai Davies was hard, but fair, this laugh was that of evil incarnate.

"Die now whelp and with you die the dreams and hopes of your people."

"Here we are, Wayne. Box Canyon at last, safe and sound." James Malone's voice woke Wayne just as he felt his throat tightening.

"Man that 405 was a nightmare, damn rush hour. It lasts four hours either side of the day here to be sure."

"Oh!" Wayne gasped as the evening sunlight shone reassuringly red through the trees.

"That was quick!"

Wayne shivered as he remembered the crux of the nightmare he'd been having as James' Buick had been speeding along the Freeway.

"Quick for you maybe, but Jeez. Hey, you OK?" James asked, his face betraying his concern as the car crunched to a halt on the gravel outside James house.

"Yeah, just....I guess I'd fallen into quite a deep, deep sleep." Wayne stated flatly, his voice a little bit tremulous. He was still shaking as he clambered unsteadily out of the car.

"Hi Wayne, how are you?" Carrie's voice wafted through the warm evening air.

James' beautiful, blonde American wife approached the car while nestling a tiny baby in her arms.

"Great, yeah, great, thanks." Wayne gasped.

James pulled Wayne's bag out of the trunk as Carrie kissed him on the cheek.

"Good flight?" She asked. "You sound, like, totally shattered."

Wayne nodded eagerly.

"Yeah, it's been a long day, I guess. I just went into a really deep sleep in the car."

Carrie took him by the arm, cradling the baby in the crook of her other elbow.

"Jet lag sucks." She laughed.

"Stop your chatter wife, the man needs an ice cold beer." James shouted good naturedly as he entered the Spanish style cottage that had been Carrie's before he had met her.

40

Carrie grinned:

"There's more to life than beer, James Malone. James is a cultured young man. Anyway he's not twenty one yet."

James Malone stuck his head out of the kitchen door just as Carrie and James reached it.

A cold, bottle of beer was thrust into Wayne's hand.

James Malone laughed:

"While Wayne is with us, Box Canyon is an outpost of the British Empire and subject to the laws thereof. And drinking is legal in good ol' blighty at eighteen. Is that not true Mr. Higginbotham?"

Wayne grinned sheepishly.

"Guess so." He shrugged as he twisted the top off the bottle and took a huge draft of the cold clear amber liquid.

"Oh that's good!" He declared with a sigh.

Carrie laughed:

"Men, you're all the same!"

James winked at her:

"Don't be insulting our guest, wife of mine. He's no man, he's one of the little people, so he is."

Wayne grinned:

"Half!" He declared as he was ushered speedily through the well-equipped kitchen, where something was bubbling in a pan that smelt delicious.

James took Wayne into the lounge where he bade him to sit down. Carrie handed James the baby while she stepped back into the kitchen.

"You hungry Wayne?" Her disembodied voice echoed around the corner.

"Starving." Wayne lied. He'd eaten well on the plane, even so whatever Carrie was cooking smelt just too good to refuse and Wayne would have felt it impolite to refuse anyway.

James plonked the baby on Wayne's knee and laughed at the youth's horrified expression.

"Sure, she won't bite." He exclaimed:

"Wayne Higginbotham, meet Aoibheall Malone!"

Wayne looked at James in astonishment.

"You named her after...?"

James laughed:

"Ah, she wasn't so bad and I loved her name even if she was a million year old crone with malicious and murderous intent."

The next few days passed so quickly that Wayne felt he had no sooner arrived than he was placing his bag back into the Buick's trunk. He walked back from the car towards James and Carrie's house on a beautiful, hot Southern California morning. He stepped into the yard and walked up to the bougainvillea-lined fence and looked out at the incredible view over the San Fernando Valley that greeted his friend every morning. Behind him he could hear water tinkling merrily, as it cascaded down the fountain that was the main feature of James' yard.

He had spent many happy hours over the past few days doing nothing but sitting in the yard talking, drinking beer, eating barbecued burgers, hot dogs and steaks. Mmmm, talking of food, Wayne's mind flashed back to that meatloaf that Carrie had presented him with on the night he had arrived. Now that had been fantastic. And why were the barbecued steaks that James seemed to live on, so much better than the ones that Doris bought at the butchers in Shepton? He licked his lips at the thought of that sweet, tender meat.

"You ready then, buddy?" James' voice brought Wayne back to reality with a bump.

"Yeah, I'm ready." Wayne grinned as he turned from the stunning vista that never failed to intoxicate him. The long straight boulevards, the steel and glass towers in the distance and the snow capped peaks beyond and the endless shimmer of the heat haze and smog.

Wayne took a last look at the wall of the canyon, up behind James house.

James had told him on his last visit that they used to make the Roy Rogers movies up in those rocks.

"Ah I was addicted to watching those cowboy movies on our little telly when I was growing up in Dublin." He had stated fondly, his Irish brogue making a sudden and unexpected return:

"It shocked the hell out of me when I got here and saw that they weren't really black and white."

The sandstone boulders and spiky cacti certainly made it look like a western set.

James Malone was clearly a very happy man. He was about to embark on a new and exciting career in journalism, he had the house of his dreams in a wonderful place; he had a beautiful wife and a beautiful baby girl.

Wayne smiled. James Malone deserved it. He only hoped that he would be as lucky.

A shiver ran down his spine as he thought back to the nightmare that he had had in James car when he had arrived in L.A.

It seemed to Wayne that he had seen a harbinger of his own doom.

Wayne was suddenly aware of Carrie hugging him and the chill melted.

"It's been so awesome having you stay with us again." She gushed:

"Next time you gotta stay longer, we could do Disney and all that stuff."

Wayne smiled and kissed her on the cheek.

"Thank you ever so much for having me." He whispered before bending down to plant a firm kiss on baby Aoibheall's head.

"You got quite used to her, eventually." Carrie teased him, kindly.

"Yeah, well, guess I'll have my own one day." Wayne laughed.

"I hope, but not for a while yet."

"Come on Higginbotham!" James bellowed from down by the Buick.

"Anyone would think you were sad to be leaving."

Wayne grinned.

That was true. He wasn't leaving California yet, not for another few days. His next stop was 2145 Coldwater Canyon Boulevard in Beverley Hills and some quality time with the famous movie actress Terri Thorne, Wayne's real Mom.

So why did he feel so uneasy?

Seven

Lucy Hetherington just wanted the damned tourists to go away. She could hear them whispering loudly in the knave somewhere behind her, then laughing and talking as though they were on the street outside. Did they not know that this was a holy place? Did they not know how to behave respectably? Had they never been taught any manners, or decorum?

Lucy just wanted peace and quiet as she sat, head solemnly bowed, in the pew near the lectern of Christ Church Cathedral, Oxford. She wished some fire and brimstone preacher would climb up, grasp the edges of the wooden lectern and hail torrents of righteous abuse down upon their ignorant, fat, loud, ugly, touristy heads.

She hated the tourists when they came to Jersey, her home island. They were always so awful, so badly dressed, so loud and utterly common. They gawped at her house from the lane as they drove past in their silly little rented cars. They drove too fast past her, when she was out riding and frightened her horse Flick. When she glowered at them to show them her displeasure, they would shout at her, call her names and make rude signs at her. Sometimes, especially in the summer, Daddy couldn't even get a table in their favourite restaurant in St.Ouen, her local village, because it was full of tourists.

They were just the most tiresome, unutterably frightful people. Why couldn't they stay in their little houses on their little estates and watch moronic TV, like they did all the rest of the time?

Lucy Hetherington was angry. She was confused and angry. No, she was confused, frightfully upset and very bloody angry indeed. In fact Lucy Hetherington was devastated. She took a tissue from a small packet in her pocket, unfolded it and quietly and discreetly blew her nose into it.

It was all Daddy's fault. Or was she being unfair? Was it Mummy's fault?

Well, whoever's fault it was, her life had been totally ruined. Nothing would ever be the same again. Absolutely nothing!

Lucy had been so looking forward to this weekend too. Mummy and Daddy had brought her over to the mainland to take her to Oxford and get her settled into her college, where she would spend the next three years reading classics. First, however, they were going to spend a couple of nights in London, do a little shopping and enjoy the finer things that the City had to offer and then Daddy had simply ruined it all. He had drunk too much wine, of course. Daddy often drank too much wine, nowadays.

"Poppet," He had slurred over dinner at Claridges' on the Saturday evening. "Darling poppet, there is something I have to tell you, before you go up to Oxford. It is something I've been meaning to tell you for two years."

The whole appalling saga had started just over two years earlier, when she had had the most vivid and terrifying nightmare while at Boarding School. Her mind seemed to have been invaded by someone claiming to be her brother, her twin brother. That in itself had been ridiculous. She didn't have a brother, let alone a twin. He had said that he was trapped in the basement of some house on some street, somewhere up in the English North country. The details had seemed vague to her even then, but over two years later she couldn't remember any of the specifics at all, except that the voice she had heard, even in her dream, had definitely had a Northern accent. Yorkshire seemed to ring a bell. Anyway, she had been found by the housemistress on the dormitory payphone, long after lights out, as she completed the calls that the voice had asked her to make. She presumed that it had all been a nightmare and that she had been sleepwalking; that was until the school informed her parents about her late night shenanigans and her daddy had been forced to admit to her that she had been adopted and that it was possible that she did have a brother.

A child nearby began to scream.

"JUST GO AWAY AND LEAVE ME ALONE, WILL YOU!"

Lucy wasn't quite sure whether she had actually shouted the words or not, she was sure she had just thought them, but she was suddenly aware of a couple of families of affronted looking tourists quickly scurrying for the Cathedral exit.

Lucy sighed and bowed her head again; at least it was quiet now. Only the seemingly distant sound of the busy Oxford traffic permeated the ancient stone walls and ornate stained glass of the cathedral.

On Saturday evening, at Claridges, after ensuring that he had taken enough Dutch courage, Daddy had confirmed what she had been expecting to hear ever since he had told her that she was adopted.

"Look poppet." He had whispered as he held her hand tightly:

"No time is a good time for this sort of thing, but we really did mean to tell you this when we told you about the adoption, but I suppose I lost courage when the news seemed to hit you so terribly hard."

Lucy's mother had gone to the powder room. She knew she just couldn't bear to see her daughter's reaction after the horror of the original announcement, when Lucy had fainted on the spot.

"I do have a twin brother, don't I, daddy?" Lucy had interrupted her Father.

He had smiled sympathetically.

"Yes poppet, you do, in fact, have a twin brother."

This time Lucy did not faint. She seemed to consider the news for a moment and then asked:

"Do you know anything about him? Where he is? What his name is?"

Rupert Hetherington shook his head.

"Nothing at all, I'm afraid, poppet."

Lucy bit her lip.

"Why were we separated?"

Rupert sighed and sat back in his chair as his wife returned to the table. Lucy recalled the raucous laughter from a party at a nearby table and wondered how they could be so happy when every day seemed to bring news that brought her world closer to collapse.

Rupert cleared his throat:

"It was the way it was, back then. It was the Sixties, The Beatles and all that. In fact wasn't it Larkin who wrote that "sex began in 1963?" He looked to his wife for confirmation but she just shrugged, smiled weakly and dabbed her eyes with her napkin.

"Anyway, the sexual revolution had started and all of a sudden there were lots of babies available for adoption. It seems, however, that the people who adopted your brother did not want twins and for some reason the agency split you up. He had already gone, up North I believe, when we got you."

Lucy shook her head.

"That's inhuman, how could they split up twins when so many single babies were available. I mean they wouldn't even do anything as appalling as that in the Soviet Union, or communist China. Would they? Excuse me, please."

Lucy stood, her bottom lip quivering and marched off towards the powder room, leaving her parents in emarrased silence at the table.

When she returned the subject was ignored and was not mentioned again all weekend. Now her parents had returned to Jersey and Lucy's new life at Oxford had begun.

She stood and left the silent sanctuary of Christ Church and stepped out into the fresh September air. As she strolled along "Dead Man's Walk" by the old town walls and Merton Field, she found herself doing what had become quite a habit recently. She was looking at every single boy of a similar age to herself and not appraising their good looks, or sex appeal, but trying to see if they bore any physical resemblance to her.

One or two grinned at her, evidently getting the wrong idea. She ignored them. Lucy Hetherington was capable of looking quite witheringly haughty when she so wished.

Lucy was one of the first students to take up her rooms in Queen's College. Most undergraduates would arrive at the beginning of October for Fresher's week. So the walk was quite quiet, almost bucolic. Just beyond Merton Field, across the Broad Walk by the corner of Christ Church Meadow, the willow lined, infant Thames slowly slid past. The sunlight made everything look so romantic. Lucy was already in love with Oxford and the atmosphere of the warm late summer day just made everything seem so idyllic.

The buildings all seemed so pristine. The "dreaming spires" stretched up into the cloudless sky, like so many arms reaching out into the heavens.

"Per Ardua, ad Astra." Lucy remembered one of the Latin mottos she had learned, "by hard work, to the stars," was that the R.A.F.? She couldn't remember, but it certainly seemed applicable to Oxford.

By the time she had crossed Merton Street and had avoided a couple of kamikaze cyclists along Logic Lane, Lucy had forgotten her melancholy and was looking forward to the supper that she had arranged with Toby Pendleton, an old Etonian from back home in St. Ouen, Jersey, who was just starting his third year.

Yet, as the light began to fade and Lucy stared into the mirror in her rooms, whilst brushing her dyed long blonde curls, the thoughts returned.

If she wasn't really Lucy Elizabeth Charlotte Hetherington, who was she?

Where was her birth mother?

Who was her real father?

Why had she been separated from her twin brother?

Where was he?

Who was he?

What was he doing right now?

What were the circumstances of their conception?

Love?

Why hadn't they married like normal, decent people?

Rape?

Eeewww, just too awful to contemplate.

Maybe her mother was out there, thinking about her all the time. Wondering what had become of her.

Maybe her mother was lying, gin addled, in a council flat somewhere with several snotty nosed brats pulling at her apron string. Eewww again.

Maybe her mother had been a prostitute? A drug addict?

After all Lucy had been born in the Sixties.

Maybe her mother had kept her twin brother and just had her adopted?

Maybe she was just a plain old reject.

Maybe her real family were all sitting down to supper right now, oblivious to her very existence.

Maybe they were all dead.........

Lucy pulled a tissue from the box on her dressing table and wiped the tears from her eyes.

She wondered how she had managed to get four A grade 'A' Levels and a scholarship to read classics at Queens, when for two years her thoughts had been totally dominated by the circumstances of her adoption. And now she had a twin brother to wonder about too.

She stared and stared at her reflection, so what if she was late. Toby would wait. He was a gentleman.

Lucy wondered if others thought of her as being really good looking. Of course, mummy and daddy said she was beautiful and most of her old boyfriends had said she was simply ravishing.

Was she?

Would her mother have been as pretty as her? Probably not if she was poor. Poor people were rarely pretty.

Lucy was quite aware that she turned heads. She had decided that a new look was needed before she started her new life in Oxford and so she had had her hair expensively dyed.

Even before she had gone blonde, she had had thick, luxuriant brown hair with enough of an auburn tint for people to think her a redhead in the sunlight.

Now, she knew she looked fabulous.

Lucy was reasonably tall for a girl at five feet, seven inches but not tall enough to scare boys off.

She was fashionably thin and had never had to bother about her weight.

She had a fair, fresh complexion and had never been bothered by more than the odd spot.

She had gorgeous, big, blue green eyes.

Well that's what Henry St.John Brocklehurst had told her.

Mind you, he had turned out to be a cad.

It was strange really. She had just one feature that she hated. Just one thing that had always made her wonder about her ancestry, even before the shock of finding out she was adopted.

Daddy didn't have it.

Mummy didn't have it.

Nanny and Gramps Hetherington didn't have it.

She didn't know about Mummy's parents because they'd died in a car crash in Rhodesia, so one of them may have had it, but no one had mentioned it.

Lucy pulled back her newly blonde tresses. She had always worn her hair long, ever since she had been tiny. Ever since some nasty, common boy at her first riding school had called her a Pixie.

Lucy stared at her reflection and the two extremely pointed ears, that she wore her hair long to cover.

At least they didn't stick out now. Daddy had paid to have them pinned back when she was twelve, before she went off to board at Roedean.

She wondered if any of her real family had been cursed by such monstrous appendages.

Rupert Hetherington stared down at the island of Jersey as it came into view through the plane's small window.

"Melinda, darling, how do you think Luce reacted to the news about her brother?"

Melinda Hetherington sighed heavily.

"Better than I expected really, it was the why were they separated question that upset me."

Rupert grimaced:

"I know, I know."

He squeezed his wife's hand as his mind flew back eighteen years. He could still see the Nun's face as she reached into the cot:

"These are the twins." She had smiled as she picked up the boy.

"This gorgeous fellow is Michael."

The Hetheringtons had flinched at the sight of the boy's ears.

The Nun had put the baby boy back in the cot and picked up the girl:

"And this lovely little lady is Charlotte. Isn't she lovely?"

The Hetheringtons looked at one another:

"Well darling?" Rupert had asked his wife.

"The ears are definitely smaller and the fact that they stick out can be fixed, you know."

Melinda Hetherington had hesitated.

"I really don't think I could manage two." She had whispered, her face vividly betraying her disappointment.

"I always wanted a little girl and you are right, the girl's ears aren't as bad as the boy's. She is such a darling thing."

"Look, I know it would be rather bad form, but, well, is there any chance that we could split them?" Rupert had asked hopefully.

The Nun had looked horrified.

"Well really, we would rather keep them together." She had blustered, envisaging every single prospective set of parents refusing to take the twins with their strange auricular deformities.

The Hetheringtons had looked at one another.

The Nun panicked.

"I could ask."

"We'd be terribly grateful, of course, and we would be able to make a reasonably substantial donation, to the Charity, of course. The girl would have a way beyond average standard of living. It would be such a shame for her to lose out on this opportunity, just because…er."

"Yes, I understand." The Nun had replied.

Rupert rubbed his forehead as the plane circled the island.

"Do you ever feel guilty?" He asked.

"About the boy?"

Melinda put her head on to his shoulder.

"Every day darling. I mean I presume he's OK. They can work miracles now with plastic surgery."

Rupert rubbed his chin.

"I do sometimes wonder what ever became of him?"

Eight

It was a very strange thought that crossed Wayne Higginbotham's mind when he first introduced James Malone to Terri Thorne.

"Wouldn't it be wonderful if they, sort of, you know, hit it off?"

They hadn't met on his last visit because Terri had sent a driver to collect Wayne from Carrie's house on Box Canyon, while she had completed a filming assignment.

Wayne loved Carrie and knew that James wouldn't do the dirty on her, but in the same respect it would be great to have one of his best friends as his step dad.

It would definitely be better than having Dean Vitalia, his mother's slimy manager and agent, who she had married just a few years earlier.

As Wayne had guessed, James and Terri got along tremendously. After all, they were both Irish, they were both in their early thirties and they were both very attractive people.

James was tall with thick, dark curly hair and big brown eyes. He had a dark, almost Mediterranean complexion.

"Ah sure, someone in my family tree was an awful lot darker than the average Paddy." He had once told Wayne when he had questioned him about his dark features, then he had roared with laughter:

"The true Celts were dark people, you eejit!"

Terri Thorne was not dark at all. Her skin was very white, her complexion almost porcelain. Her hair was dyed blonde, but very expensively and well. Her eyes were big and blue and her face remarkably unlined for a woman of 34. Her figure was still very, very good, despite the fact that she had borne four children in her short lifetime.

"So you're the Priest who saved my son's life?" Was her first question to James when Wayne had first introduced them and the initial hugs and kisses had been dispensed with.

"I've heard so much about you and all of it good."

The last words were spoken in a mock expression of shock.

"Ah, young Wayne, I mean Michael, has been telling his fairy stories again has he?"

James replied with a grin, suddenly sounding very Irish again.

"When this young fellow visited Blarney, he didn't just kiss the stone, so he didn't, he took a huge bite out of it and swallowed the bloody thing."

51

James, Terri and Wayne all laughed easily as Terri guided the friends into her house.

"Oh and by the way," James continued, his voice taking a more sober, serious tone:

"It was Wayne, I'm sorry, I mean Michael, who saved me, not the other way round and not just once but twice. Seven years ago when he was knee high to a grasshopper it was Wayne, I mean, Michael and his adopted dad who defeated the "Order's" assassin when I was lying in a useless heap on the ground, with me arm snapped under me and two years ago it was…" He paused.

"Michael's quick thinking that stopped the both of us getting killed in Dublin."

Terri smiled proudly.

"Why do I not find that hard to believe?" She stared admiringly at her son.

"My you've grown again, Michael." She gasped as she found herself looking up to Wayne, who was now a good couple of inches taller than his mother. She put her hand on his cheek in a gesture of maternal tenderness and smiled warmly.

"I've missed you." She whispered.

Wayne smiled back and stared into his mother's eyes, which he had so obviously inherited.

"I've missed you too, Mom."

He was finding it easier to call his natural mother "Mom."

It had seemed weird when they had first been reunited all those years earlier. Wayne had a "mum," even if she was a pain in the backside and his adoption of the American term had seemed somewhat contrived. Now it seemed almost natural.

Wayne had been totally amazed by his mother's house when he had first visited Los Angeles. Nestling on the lower Southern slopes of the Santa Monica Mountains, the modern white single storey structure didn't have quite the view that James' house had from its lofty perch over the San Fernando Valley, but its outlook over some of the most expensive real estate in the world: Beverley Hills was spectacular in itself.

It was certainly a far cry from Cavendish Street, or Greenwood Avenue in Shepton. The pool alone made Wayne's mouth drop open and the only thing he had been able to say on his first visit was "wow."

Terri bade Wayne to put his bag in the guest room and then show James the pool whilst she checked on Conchita who was minding the children. She quickly grabbed a beer and a can of Soda from the fridge and passed them to James.

"I'll be with you in a couple of minutes." She stated as she disappeared off towards her small nursery room.

James grinned:

"Looks like you get the soda, Wayne. You have a good law abiding Mom."

Wayne ripped the can open and shrugged.

"As long as it's cold." He gasped between slurps.

James laughed mischievously:

"I'm only kidding, just don't tell the cops. Anyway, I'm driving."

He took the soda off him and passed him the beer.

Wayne took an appreciative swig from the bottle.

"It's so much hotter than the last time I was here."

James laughed.

"That's because it was January the last time you came! You eejit! They do have seasons here, even if they are all better than the best summers at home."

The pair strolled to the fence at the end of the yard. Endless long, straight, palm-fringed boulevards stretched away into the distance until they disappeared in the haze. The towers of downtown L.A. could be seen in the distance, floating on a sea of smog.

"It feels like I live in the country compared to this." James sighed.

Wayne snorted.

"Feels like I live in the bloody stone age."

Behind them they could hear tiny footsteps as little Marco, Wayne's half brother toddled towards them by the pool.

"Miko, Miko." He shouted excitedly as he pointed at his grinning big brother.

Just a few paces behind, a concerned looking Terri watched Marco's every step as she cradled her daughter Marina in her arms:

"Mind the water Marco, don't go near the pool." She ordered, gently, but firmly.

Wayne swept his little brother up in his arms:

"Hello Marco!" He laughed as the infant squealed with delight.

Terri smiled proudly as he pointed at Wayne and turned so that her latest child could see her firstborn:

"That's your big brother, yes, isn't he handsome?" She cooed.

Wayne smiled at his first sight of his new sibling and laughed as she covered her face shyly and nuzzled into Terri's shoulder.

"Hi Marina." He whispered.

"I'm Michael."

Terri felt a surge of pride. For the first time three of her children were together with her.

Behind her smile, however, a very small shadow passed over the sunshine of her happiness, as she wondered if she would ever have all four together like this.

"Well I'm going to leave you guys to play happy families." James grinned.

He took Wayne's hand and shook it vigorously.

"I'll see you soon, Wayne." He grimaced and gave his young friend a hug:

"Either I'll be over in the ol'country soon and I'll visit you in England, or you get yourself back here as soon as you can."

"I will." Wayne promised.

"Thanks for letting me stay."

James shrugged.

"It was a pleasure and good luck at that University. Be good and if you can't be good, be brilliant!"

Wayne laughed as James said his farewells to Terri.

"I'll see you, Wayne." James shouted as he disappeared into the house.

"Yeah, see ya, James!" Wayne shouted back.

"He's so nice." Terri stated with a smile.

Wayne nodded and smiled sadly.

"Yeah, he's cool."

Terri smiled:

"Dean won't be back until Sunday morning, I'm afraid. He's in Vegas with his brother doing some deal or something."

"Oh that's a shame." Wayne blurted as sincerely as he could possibly manage.

Terri twisted her mouth and frowned. She looked really annoyed.

"Do I take it, Michael, that you don't like my husband?"

Wayne gulped.

"Er..."

Terri laughed.

"Hey I'm a better actor than I thought and you are a good judge of character."

Wayne let out a huge sigh of relief.

The last time he had visited his mom, Dean had only made a brief fleeting appearance and had been just about civil to his stepson. Wayne had not liked him at all and had been convinced that the feeling had been pretty much mutual. The thought that he would only have to put up with Dean for a maximum of twenty-four hours, or so, filled him with glee.

"We're having a party for Marina's birthday on Sunday and to celebrate you being here, of course. It should be so neat." Terri said with a huge smile.

Wayne wondered how she got her teeth so white.

"In the meantime we're gonna have so much fun. Yes we are...."

She cooed to her baby daughter.

Wayne Higginbotham watched his mother twirl around her yard with the baby Marina in her arms. He had only seen her as happy as this when they had first met and then they had both been so riddled with nerves and sheer exuberance.

Wayne was in heaven. He could feel the heat of the Southern Californian sun burning his back.

The water of the glistening pool lazily lapped the edges and in the distance he heard a train's whistle echo mournfully in the mountains.

The scent of flowers filled his nostrils and he had to screw his eyes up against the intensity of the light.

At the age of eighteen, he was no longer a lonely, only child, stuck up in a semi-detached, ex-council house on the edge of a cold Yorkshire moor, or in a squalid, stone, terraced house with a loo in the basement.

He was in a swish house in Beverly Hills with his beautiful, famous actress mother and his adorable little brother and sister, standing by a swimming pool.

So, why did he feel a sense of foreboding?

Why was there a nagging doubt at the back of his mind that this was all just too good to be true?

He had had the dream again, while staying in James' guest room.

The dream with the black-robed, faceless figure, with the piercing, merciless, blue eyes. Again the figure had mocked Wayne and his claim to be the "Slanaitheoir mor:" The prophesied offspring of the union of the immortal "Tuatha de Danaan" and the ancient Royal line of Ireland.

Wayne laughed as his mother played with his baby brother and sister by the pool. Maybe Dean wasn't all bad. He had given Terri something she had been longing for ever since she had had her first babies adopted. Was he the reason Wayne felt nervous?

He hadn't felt like this when he had met him the last time he had visited his Mom.

Wayne shook his head to try and dispel the nagging gloom and happily accepted the cold beer that his mother passed to him.

"Don't let the cops see you." She grinned.

That first day passed all too quickly.

Once the little ones were in bed, Wayne was able to talk with his mother in peace as they both tried desperately to fill in all the gaps that existed between them. They had missed so many years together.

By the time he went to bed, Wayne was totally exhausted. Despite the air conditioning the room seemed unbearably hot. Wayne tossed and turned for what seemed like hours, before he finally drifted off to sleep.

"Hello again, whelp." The deep arrogant voice rumbled as those cold blue eyes bored into the very core of Wayne's soul.

Nine

And so it came to pass, that in the middle of a grey, swirling, green mist, the great and the mighty of the Tuatha de Danaan, or as some called them, the men of Dea, assembled together in the great Hall of Judgment in the netherworld of Tir Na Nog.

There present was the Dagda and Angus Og, his first born son, Nuada, the silver hand, Lir and his son, Manannan. Lugh of the long hand and his father, Tuireann and Fionnbharr, father of Aillen and all the Kings or Princes of the mighty Tuatha de Danaan.

Eire and Fodla and Banba, daughters of the Dagda and Brigit, the poet were there too, for women warriors were as famous as their male counterparts in the armies of the sidhe.

There had been no greater gathering of the Tuatha, since they had passed out of the physical realm of mortal man, long, long ago.

Yet their concerns were now located in that realm, that none of the Tuatha had set foot in for so many years, none, that is, except for Aillen Mac Fionnbharr.

Aillen Mac Fionnbharr, until his recent demise, known to the inhabitants of a corner of County Mayo as Mickey Finn, had called the gathering, for the time was nigh. The time when the final confrontation between good and evil would take place on the lush green grass of the mortal world.

The hall resembled a great barn, wooden, with a thatched roof and piles of rushes on the floor. The interior was smoky and dark, yet the hall's lack of substance would have been betrayed to the mortal eye by way the light inside shimmered and shifted; and by the way the occupants of the hall themselves created the light.

"The time has come." Aillen bellowed, over the clamour made by the boisterous shades of the immortal sidhe, while banging his drinking horn on the table.

"To end the threat that the dark ones have held over us for so many long years. The "Slanaitheoir mor" has been born and the cursed agents of the "Order of St.Gregory," have finally been defeated."

The hall rang with the cheers of the gathered warriors and the triumphant banging of horns and stamping of feet.

Aillen held up his hand and waited until the gathering had quietened, so he could make his voice heard again.

"It is but a hollow victory thus far my friends, for the "Order" did not pass without first fulfilling part of their purpose."

There was an audible moan and a great deal of muttering.

Aillen waited for a moment to allow the enormity of what he had just said, sink into the minds of the assembled men and women of Dea.

"Aye, the "Order" allowed the king of demons himself, to be born and even now, in his infancy, he prowls the world of mortal man like a wolf cub, waiting for his moment to strike."

The hall erupted with noise, as everyone seemed to want to ask questions of the last Prince.

Aillen raised his hand again and the hall quickly fell silent.

"It was foretold that my half-blood son, the "Slanaitheoir mor" would have to pass three great tests before he would truly overcome the dark powers that plague us all. He has passed two of these tests, even before his seventeenth summer."

The hall erupted in shouts, cheers and whoops of delight as well as banging ale horns and stamping feet.

Aillen waited for a modicum of quiet to descend again before continuing:

"The demon must still pass through the childhood stages of mortal man and will be weak for a short time to come."

Nuada stood, his prosthetic silver hand glowing in the twilight of the hall.

"The "Slanaitheoir mor" must carry out his mission without delay, before the whelp and his guardians have time to realise what is happening. He must strike now and strike fast."

The hall exploded into wild applause and shouts of agreement.

The first King of the Tuatha sat down, nodding sagely at the wisdom of his words and the way they had been received.

"I agree, Nuada!" Aillen bellowed.

"But the "Slanaitheoir mor" will need our help. That is why you have all been summoned here, this day."

The assembled Tuatha de Danaan went very, very quiet.

Aillen looked at his audience, studying each face in turn. Some of the most beautiful people on the earth had passed when the Tuatha left the world of men and never would their like be seen again.

"The "Slanaitheoir mor" needs our help." He repeated plaintively.

"Name it...Mac Fionnbharr." Lugh shouted brusquely from the back.

Aillen nodded and once again appraised his audiences.

"The boy needs to be able to use the sacred treasures of the Tuatha de Danaan."

The collective gasp of the throng was like a breath of wind.

"He has some shards of the great stone, has he not?" A voice queried from the back of the hall.

Another voice growled.

"No mere mortal can wield the treasures of the Tuatha de Danaan."

Another hissed:

"He is born of mortal woman's womb."

Aillen nodded and held up his hand:

"The demon my son shall face is greater than any single warrior of any host that we ever faced, even in the years of our greatest triumphs. And my son stands alone. Remember, the last drop of our noble blood runs in his veins. My son is the grandson of mighty Fionnbharr. His blood is the blood of Nuada. My son is no mere mortal whelp. He is descended from the mightiest of Kings!"

Old King Fionnbharr stood abruptly, his full red beard bouncing uncontrollably. He removed a huge ring from his little finger. He took a dagger from his belt and dug a stone from the centre of the ring. He held it aloft to show the assembled Tuatha.

"This is one of the last shards of the "The Lia Fail." He bellowed:

"Many here have similar stones. Give them as I give this to my grandson, through my son Aillen. The Christians possess some others in Rome. The boy will have to get them himself. When the very last shards are found, the stone will reform. It will be whole again for the first time in more than three thousand years of mortal men. There, that is the first of the treasures that he shall have."

The gathering issued a collective gasp and then erupted in cheers and the stamping of feet. Several stones were passed to Fionnbharr.

Aillen held up his hand to quieten the audience.

"I thank you my Father. The Lia Fail, once reformed will give our champion the strength of a host of warriors, if the last shards can indeed be found. Yet it will not be enough alone to defeat the demon. I wish for the "Slanaitheoir mor" to have also the great spear of Finias, that Lugh threw in anger in the days of his youth. The spear that never misses, once it is thrown in battle."

"It is his." Lugh bellowed, standing and waving his fist:

"It is hidden in the cave of the bear, by the great wall of the sea. I will show you Mac Fionnbharr, so that you can guide the boy to it."

The audience cheered heartily and Lugh's back received many slaps of support and gratitude.

Aillen bowed, his gratitude etched all over his face.

"There is one other treasure that the boy will need. One other great weapon that will render him nigh invincible and will make the life bane tremble, like a new born lamb before the knife. I would beg the mighty Nuada, for the sword of Gorias."

Nuada who was sat at the front of the company stood, slowly.

He was very tall and his long black shaggy mane and his beard gave more him the appearance of a giant grizzly bear than any sort of man.

"I would be glad to offer the boy this treasure, son of the Fionnbharr." Nuada shouted.

A great cheer erupted.

Nuada held up his silver hand.

"But the sword that swept off the heads of our enemies at Magh Tuireadh, like a scythe mows the heads of corn and which won a thousand other battles, is no longer mine to give as I will."

A low hum of muttering broke out amongst the assembly.

Nuada bowed his head:

"I was a fool, my friends. I hid the mighty sword of Gorias, in the burial mound of my kin. I must tell you now, that after lying in peace for thousands of mortal years, the grave of my father has been desecrated."

A great collective moan echoed around the hall.

Nuada turned to the company, his voice cracking with anguish.

"This happened in recent days. A party of weak eyed mortal men, the sort whose necks would have been wrung in our day, those who wear windows of glass on their noses, came to the burial mound of my father. They used magical tools to show them where my treasure could be found and they dug up and stole my sword, my torc and my cauldron."

The shock and anguish at the outrage of such a brazen act of grave robbery caused a disbelieving murmur around the hall.

"The mighty sword of Gorias, now lies on a silk cushion, in a cage of glass."

Nuada almost spat the words in contempt.

"Where lies this glass cage, my Lord Nuada?" Aillen demanded.

Nuada shrugged:

"My sword is in one their halls of stone, in the City that grew by the Black Pool."

The hall's company roared with anger.

Aillen smiled and the assembly slowly settled.

"Then my son will have to pay a visit to that Dublin museum. It will further his education."

He picked up his drinking horn and filled it from a flask of ale.

"Here's to MacAillen." He shouted.

"To the "Slanaitheoir mor" of legend and prophecy. May his destiny soon be fulfilled."

The roar of the assembly of the Tuatha de Danaan echoed in the hills like a rumble of thunder.

Jack Robson had been fishing on the Irish Loughs most of his adult life. He preferred the Loughs even to his own upper Tyne. Jack was a soccer coach by profession and quite a successful one at that. His team had finished sixth in the English second division only last May. It was rumoured that one of the big clubs in the First Division was looking at him as a potential replacement for the incumbent manager. One day, he hoped, he might even realise his dream and manage Newcastle.

His day on Lough Nafooey had been just great, so far. Three huge silver pikes lay in the bottom of the boat and he had just felt another tug on his line.

"Away man." He shouted at his companion, Padraic O' Flaherty.

"It looks like we've got another bonny one, wor lad. If we play it canny man, it'll be me best day ever."

Padraic was a very experienced fisherman. He had found it much more lucrative to accompany wealthy tourists out on the Loughs than to continue in his old job as a postman.

Sure some of them were painful, but he knew Jack well and had accompanied him on Nafooey before as well as on Loughs Mask and Corrib and Jack certainly tipped well.

"Hold on tight there, Jack." He advised needlessly.

"Sure this one's the size of a whale."

Padraic took his hip flask from the breast pocket of his Donegal tweed jacket.

"Keep it tight Jack, just keep it tight."

He gasped, as he took a huge swig from the flask. He carefully placed the flask down on the bench in front of Jack and slowly took the rod slowly from his charge.

Jack picked up the flask and slurped a huge draft of the fine Irish whiskey.

"Ah man, that's var nigh perfect." He gushed, wiping his mouth:

"I'll..." Jack stopped in mid sentence, his mouth agape, like one of the dead pike in the bottom of the rowing boat.

"Did you hear that, it sounded like thunder?"

No, I was too busy with this." Padraic whispered through gritted teeth:

"Ah come on me beauty, come to papa." Padraic chortled as he slowly began to reel in whatever was on the end of the line.

61

"Errrr…." Jack mumbled.

"Do you want to be taking it and reeling her in yourself Jack?" Padraic asked enthusiastically.

"It feels like a monster."

Jack didn't move. His mouth was wide open and his eyes staring up into the sky above the mountains behind Padraic's back.

Padraic frowned and turned to see what his Geordie companion was finding so interesting.

The steep bank climbed away from the lough behind the boat and at about twenty feet, met the road, which sloped diagonally up towards Finny. Above that the green mass of the mountain climbed almost vertically to the broad flat summit and above that nothing but the leaden, grey Irish sky.

"What is it Jack?" Padraic demanded, impatiently,

"If you don't shape yourself, we'll be losing this Moby Dick and it won't be my fault."

Jack Robson seemed to snap out of it.

"What the hell did you have in that flask, Paddy man?" He asked aggressively.

Padraic pulled on the line and turned the reel gently.

"A fine Tullamore, so it was, just to warm the cockles of your heart."

Jack Robson took off his flat cap and scratched his largely bald-head.

"I'll never touch whiskey again." He whispered, as he turned the flask upside down over the side of the boat and poured the amber liquid into the Lough.

"What the hell are you doing?" Padraic demanded angrily.

"I've just seen a bloody great barn like building, floating up over the top of that mountain. A bloody great barn, like, I tell you man. I saw it with me own eyes."

Jack's voice was flat and monotone.

"And then it just sort of turned into a cloud and blew away, like."

Padraic held the rod and reel tightly.

"Take the rod Jack, it's your catch." He urged the tourist, gently.

"It wasn't the whiskey."

Padraic shivered, turned and looked nervously over his shoulder, making the Stations of the Cross as he did so.

"That would have been the fairy hall, Jack Robson. You're not the first to see it, but you are the first in my lifetime."

Jack Robson never touched a drop of alcohol ever again.

Ten

His Eminence, Cardinal Pietr Warzowski heaved a deep and heavy sigh as he slumped into the wooden chair behind the simple wooden desk. He clasped his hands together as if in prayer, but then grimaced and tightly gripped both arms of his chair as his exasperation surfaced. The irritating sound of the masses of chattering tourists in the nearby piazza filtered through the open window of his Spartan office. The incessant noise made the Cardinal even more annoyed. The deep reds and oranges of the late summer setting sun stained the plain white walls. A single crucifix cast a long dark shadow across the plaster:

"I just don't understand it." He suddenly exclaimed as he stood up again, knocking the chair backwards. It crashed noisily on the wooden floor and the sound echoed around the room.

"Fifteen hundred years, scores of priests, several Bishops and even a number of Cardinals and we didn't even know they existed?"

Father Abraham Reichmann averted his eyes from the broken chair and shook his head:

"With all due respect, your Eminence, they were an incredibly effective secret society. We weren't meant to know anything about them. That was the whole point. Yes, there were rumours, hidden whispers in quiet corridors, but the "Sacred Order of St.Gregory" had plenty of experience in making themselves invisible."

The old grizzled grey-haired Priest's eyes twinkled as he chuckled.

"Not even the Holy Inquisition knew that much about them, in their day, although they did work together on occasion, hand in red velvet glove as it were."

The Cardinal picked up his damaged chair, sat down, and ran his hand through his thinning grey hair.

"So how do we know who is, or who was, a member of this "Order?" How did they, or do they become members?" He asked, his face a picture of exasperation and pained disbelief.

The Priest stroked his stubbly chin:

"Like all the best secret societies, it seems membership was by invitation only. Once upon a time, it seems the "Order" was almost as universal as the Roman Catholic Church itself. At its peak, over one thousand Priests, of all ranks, were members of the "Sacred Order." In more sophisticated times, as superstitions died out, so the need for such a secret society faded. They operated where they were perceived as being needed, hence why the last major theatre of operations was

Ireland. I am told there were less than thirty operatives a decade ago. More than half of those were in the Republic of Ireland."

The Cardinal shook his head:

"But there have been deaths outside Ireland." He insisted.

Father Reichmann acknowledged the Cardinal's statement with a shrug.

"Yes, a number of deaths have occurred in Eastern Europe and South America, but Ireland was where the "Order" was last recorded as having been a functioning organisation. Elsewhere they were just an association of simple, like minded clergymen, usually old, old men: the remnants of a different age of Catholicism. Superstition and a belief in the existence of supernatural monsters was the reason behind the foundation of the "Order" and the entire reason for its existence to the present day."

Cardinal Warzowski sat in silence for a moment.

"So why is this secret order now suddenly tearing itself apart so violently? Why is it haemorrhaging so much blood? Why are so many Priests, devoted men, once committed to the Holy See, men who believe in the words of the Holy scriptures, engaging in acts that will condemn them to perpetual damnation, to an eternity of burning in purgatory?"

Father Reichmann snorted and shrugged his shoulders:

"The only member of the "Order" that I have been able to speak to is unclear on this matter. Although he did allude to some major misfortunes that the "Order" had successfully covered up, until now, that is."

The Cardinal cursed under his breath.

"Father Bianca?"

Father Reichmann nodded.

The Cardinal took a deep breath:

"Well unless we act quickly, the entire world will soon know about these misfortunes. All these deaths have had the authorities in several countries sniffing around mother Church like excited bloodhounds. The press are even worse. They are like flies buzzing around a rotting corpse. Media speculation is getting totally out of hand."

Father Reichmann nodded and smiled grimly.

"More than Twenty Roman Catholic Priests have now committed suicide around the world over the last three years. The largest grouping has been in the Republic of Ireland. No less than six Priests have committed suicide there in the last two years alone. There have also been many other unexplained fatalities…."

"And all of these suicides and the other deaths have definitely been linked to this "Order of the Sacred St. Gregory?" The Cardinal interrupted the old Priest.

Father Reichmann nodded:

"According to Father Bianca, just about every single one of them was a member of the "Sacred Order of St Gregory" at some point in their clerical career."

The Cardinal threw his hands in the air:

"I still don't understand. What exactly was this "Order" all about? What was its purpose?"

Father Reichmann smiled patiently.

"It seems it was an elite unit of devoted Priests. A specialist unit set up by the blessed Pope Saint Gregory, to rid the Earth of the servants of Satan wherever they might exist and in whatever form they manifested themselves. This was in order to prepare the pathway for the eventual second coming. It is all to do with a prophecy."

"Of course! There's always a prophecy!" The Cardinal muttered, shaking his head.

Father Reichmann shrugged:

"Father Bianca knew the prophecy by heart. I took great care to write it down."

The old Priest reached into the inside pocket of his jacket and pulled out a pair of small round spectacles which he placed carefully on the end of his nose. From his trouser pocket he pulled a tatty, crumpled piece of paper, which he unfolded. He cleared his throat and in a clear deep voice that belied his aged features, he began to read:

"A child no mortal man shall sire
By mother's blood Royal line acquire,
Shall suckle he no milk white breast,
Shall rise in exile, unwelcome guest,
Shell learn to change his form at will
His shape, his face, his ways to kill
Unseen, unheard, his telling blow,
His doom to lay The Messiah low,
Shall tears then flow and kings shall fall
And darkness take us, one and all"

The Cardinal shook his head.

"And the meaning of this is?"

Father Reichmann folded the piece of paper and tucked it back into his pocket.

"It refers to one who the "Order" called: "God's assassin.""

The Cardinal shrugged.

"I have not heard of this "God's assassin." Does he assassinate on behalf of God? Or does he attempt to kill God himself?"

Father Reichmann nodded and grinned.

"Your Eminence. For fifteen hundred years the "Order" has believed that the lines refer to a demonic individual, a servant of Satan, whose sole purpose will be to murder Our Lord when he eventually returns to Earth in the second coming, thereby, leaving Satan alone free to inherit the Earth. The line about no mortal man doing the siring of this creature, led His Holiness, the Blessed Pope Gregory to believe that this assassin would not be human, hence the foundation of the "Order" and its mission to elimate all unnatural creatures."

"Unnatural creatures? What on earth would they be?" the Cardinal blustered.

The old Priest ignored the interruption and continued, his motions getting more animated as he delved deeper into the information that Father Bianca had given him.

"Vampires, werewolves, witches, demons, immortals, all were considered potential sources of God's assassin so the "Order" simply set about eliminating anyone that they believed fell into those categories."

The Cardinal sat back in his chair:

"But surely such creatures never really existed outside storybooks and fairy tales?" He asked uncomprehendingly.

"Ah, maybe, maybe not, but that was the "Order's" raison d'etre. Those were very different times, your Eminence." The old Priest stated.

"And many people have suffered and died over the years it seems, having been accused of falling into one of those unnatural categories, whether at the hands of the Holy Inquisition, or by the silent blade of the "Order.""

"Surely we are talking about what happened hundreds of years ago?" The Cardinal suggested hopefully.

"Witches were burned, drowned or hanged all over Europe, irrespective of the ideology of the Church."

Father Reichmann grimaced and shook his head:

"It seems the "Order" carried out its last official assassination just seven years ago, your Eminence, and it seems that even just two years ago a hard core were still actively engaged in field operations as they described them."

Cardinal Warzowski buried his face in his hands.

"If this gets out, the Holy Roman Church will be a laughing stock. We will never live it down."

Father Reichmann nodded his agreement.

"I know it sounds perverse, but it appears that the evidence of the "Order's" existence is already being covered up for us, your Eminence. Not only is the membership decreasing, both naturally and unnaturally, as we are discussing, but there does seem to be other actions taking place to erase the "Sacred Order" from the face of the Earth. Father Bianca's injuries were caused by a fire in his library. He was very lucky indeed to escape with his life. The library was totally destroyed. That library was the complete record of the "Order." Every scrap of information regarding the "Order" and all of its activities over fifteen centuries was destroyed, there and then."

The Cardinal pursed his lips.

"Do you think there was any chance that it was an accident, or that Bianca himself was responsible?"

Father Reichmann shook his head vigorously.

"Father Bianca assured me that the burning was an act of sabotage and attempted murder. It occurred on the very day that the good father noticed a key file was missing from his desk. A file that contained the name and location of every last surviving member of the "Sacred Order of St. Gregory." It would appear, Your Eminence, that someone is eliminating the remnants of the "Order" one by one."

The Cardinal raised his eyebrows.

"Who could do such a thing? This "God's assassin?""

Father Reichmann shook his head.

"I have no idea, Your Grace. As you said earlier there is doubt about the very nature of the term "God's assassin." It appears that His Eminence the Cardinal D'Abruzzo was experiencing a great deal of doubt at the very end of his life. There is one vital piece of information that I have not told you, yet."

The Cardinal sat forward, his interest piqued.

"It seems that about seven years ago, the "Order" thought that they had eliminated the very last potential source of this prophesied "God's assassin". There was a rather untidy incident in the far West of Ireland."

The Cardinal gasped.

"Finaan."

Father Reichmann nodded grimly.

"Four Priests perished."

The Cardinal scowled.

"If my memory serves me correctly, three Priests from that community died tragically in separate incidents over a period of twenty four hours."

Father Reichmann smiled.

"It seems that one Father Francisco Pizarro, a key member of the "Order" also disappeared that night. He was the "Order's" chief assassin no less. It also just happens, that all of the Irish Priests who disappeared that night reported to his Grace, Bishop O'Leary."

The Cardinal raised his eyebrows.

"The Bishop who also disappeared recently? The one who was with Bishop Donleavy when he was so brutally murdered in the sanctuary of his own Cathedral?"

Father Reichmann nodded.

"Did I tell you that His Grace, the Bishop Donleavy was the head of the "Order" in Ireland?"

Cardinal Warzowski blew out his cheeks.

"This all just gets worse and worse. All this comes from poor Father Bianca? Is his mind still sound?"

Father Reichmann nodded eagerly.

"I have not got to the best bit yet, Your Eminence."

The Cardinal fell despondently back in his chair again and waved his hand imploring the aged Priest to continue.

"Just after the incident in Finaan, His Eminence Cardinal D'Abruzzo, the supreme head of the "Order" here in the Vatican, had a Nun brought up to Rome from Sicily. She was a virgin, of course."

The Cardinal's mouth fell open as he anticipated what Father Reichmann was about to say.......

"Don't tell me: she gave birth to a child." He stated incredulously.

Father Reichmann clapped his hands together.

"Exactly, your Eminence. A boy."

Cardinal Warzowski stood and walked slowly to the window, his eyes closed as he contemplated the implications of what he was hearing.

"And where is this child now?" He whispered.

Father Reichmann shrugged.

"No one knows. Father Bianca says that he was here in the heart of the Vatican City until just before His Eminence Cardinal D'Abruzzo died, but that the boy simply disappeared, along with his mother. The good father is of the belief that His Eminence died of a broken heart."

"It seems that death is a common factor in this sorry tale, Father Reichmann." The Cardinal sighed.

"We must find out what is going on and we must find out very, very quickly. You must raise a team, two or three young Priests from here in the Vatican. Find the best, most trustworthy individuals you can, search every seminary. We must trace this child and his mother. We must also try to find Bishop O'Leary, if he still lives. I feel he might have useful information for us."

Father Reichmann stood and bowed.

"I will do my best, Your Eminence."

The Cardinal tried to smile but managed no more than a grimace:

"This must not, I repeat; must not enter the public domain, Father."

Father Reichmann looked offended.

"Of course, Your Eminence."

"Secret Societies, assassinations, murders, suicides, the scandal would rock the very foundations of Saint Peter's itself." The Cardinal whispered as he held the door open for the Priest.

Father Reichmann scurried busily out of the Cardinal's office.

"Good day, Your Eminence." He said as he walked out into the corridor.

"I will keep you fully informed of my progress."

Cardinal Warzowski nodded and whispered.

"God be with you, Father." Then he turned, walked slowly back across his office and took his seat behind his simple desk.

If the "Order" had been just a bunch of fanatics and the suicides and inexplicable fatalities the result of internal feuding, then there was a chance that the whole affair could be brushed under the carpet, with maybe just a few salacious stories being allowed to enter the public domain in order to provide a smokescreen to cover the more serious issues.

There had already been speculation about the disappearance of Bishop O'Leary in several downmarket tabloids in Britain and Ireland.

Maybe the Nun had been D'Abruzzo's secret mistress and the child was the son of the late Cardinal. That could also potentially be released. There would be a scandal and the child and his mother would suffer a degree of infamy, but such scandals soon become yesterday's news.

Cardinal Warzowski bit his lip. He had known D'Abruzzo and he did not seem like the sort to engage in a clandestine affair. Then again, he had seemed too level headed to be involved in ridiculous secret societies.

Maybe the child was the second coming of Jesus Christ.

Maybe the "Order" had been over confident and facilitated his return too early, only to suffer a massive defeat themselves and leave the Holy infant at the mercy of God's assassin.

Maybe the Lord Jesus Christ himself had already been assassinated. Scandal was one thing. The Church was used to scandals.

The death of God, the proximity of judgment day and the end of all things, were different matters entirely.

Eleven

The soft, blurry, blue light was such a relief for Wayne as he dived beneath the surface of the pool to escape the searing heat and glare of the Californian morning sun. If it was this hot so early in the morning, what was it going to be like in the middle of the afternoon when the party would be in full swing? The roaring, rushing sound of water passing by filled his ears as he pulled back his legs and kicked powerfully, blocking out the city noise above and for a moment Wayne, his senses numbed, wished that he could stay in the cool sanctuary of the pool forever. Streams of sunlight penetrated the water like searchlights scouring the pool to find him. Wayne swam between them, savouring every second of his morning exercise.

He closed his eyes. Tomorrow he would be back on the plane and by Tuesday morning he would be back in Shepton, back to reality. Why couldn't his week in California have been a month? Why couldn't it have been forever?

He felt the intense heat of the sun as soon as his face broke back through the surface of the pool into the inferno that was Terri's back yard. He gasped for breath and took in a huge lungful of air that felt like it was coming out of the end of a hairdryer. Wayne pushed back, closed his eyes again and floated lazily as though sunbathing. The intense light penetrated his closed eyelids and he smiled, enjoy it now, he thought to himself, you won't be feeling heat like this for a while.

The last few days had been brilliant, his mom shared his sense of humour and it seemed like they were getting to know each other better and better every time they met. If only those times occurred more frequently.

Wayne felt a pang of guilt as an image of Doris flashed involuntarily through his mind. Poor old Doris, life hadn't dealt her the best of hands had it?

The poor woman had absolutely no idea that Wayne had been very happily reunited with his real mother. Wayne grimaced at the prospect of her discovering the truth about his relationship with Terri. That would kill her.

He opened his eyes and gazed up at the palm tree that towered over the pool. It would be the last time he would be able to study a palm tree for a while. Wayne turned onto his stomach and then pushed his arms and legs and in two powerful strokes was by the aluminium ladder, which he grabbed and pulled himself up out of the pool.

Wayne dried himself and slumped down on a poolside chair emitting the heaviest of sighs as he contemplated his return to Yorkshire. That wasn't the only thing weighing on his mind, however. He had had the same dream again last night. The figure in black with the vivid blue penetrating eyes had tormented him and mocked his claim to be the "Slanaitheoir mor." For reasons that he could not explain, the dream had chilled him to the very marrow of his bones. It was far more worrying than his impending return to the grey, dreary dampness of Yorkshire, even though that prospect was very real and the figure in black merely a figment of his imagination. Wayne shook his head and slowly, over the course of the rest of the morning, the chill that had swept over his body was brushed aside by the Californian sunshine and a cup of his mother's delicious coffee.

By mid afternoon nothing could have been farther from Wayne's mind than dark faceless figures and icy chills. Wayne's baby sister's first birthday party was in full swing. His Mom and her agent husband had sure gotten acquainted with a considerable number of the beautiful people during their time in Hollywood and most of them seemed to be at his sister's party for some reason. Wayne couldn't help but notice a distinct lack of fellow one year olds celebrating Marina's birthday with cakes and ice cream, or whatever babies ate.

"Oh we're having a little bash for Marina next Saturday, you know, when all her little friends will come round. This party was meant to be a joint celebration, for Marina, for your being here and because Dean just wanted a good excuse for a party." Terri had explained earlier that morning. Wayne had just nodded. If the party had been partly for him it would have been nice if James had Carrie had been invited, but it seemed that Dean was in control of the guest list. Wayne was more than a little surprised that he had been invited to what was supposedly, partly, his own party, given his lack of a relationship with his stepfather, an emotion that he had made the mistake of articulating to Terri. His mother's response had been no more than an admonishing glare, yet Wayne knew that he had more than overstepped the mark. No matter how much Wayne felt his relationship with his birth mother was normalizing, there were obviously still some areas where her life was not open to his opinions or criticism.

The lack of infants at Marina's party was quite a relief for Wayne in reality, he had never been comfortable with small children and his few days with his younger siblings Marco and Marina had reinforced that impression. While Marco was going through the early stages of the terrible twos, Marina never seemed to stop whining. Poor Terri had seemed quite exhausted at points, despite Conchita's help. The fact that the party wasn't an infantile affair meant lots of good food and drink, which Wayne found much more enjoyable than sausages on sticks and birthday cake. What could be better on a blistering hot Californian afternoon than a cold beer, or a well mixed Margherita?

What was even better, as far as Wayne was concerned; was that many of the guests seemed to be young, female, unattached and incredibly beautiful. He knew that they were only there at the behest of his stepfather, but hey, for once he did not mind that Dean Vitalia was an untrustworthy, despicable, slimy toad. He was something of a mover and a shaker in Hollywood casting and that brought the would-be actresses out in their droves.

"Oh-my-God, are you English? I just love your accent. It is soooo cute."

The tall, tanned, leggy blonde gushed as she heard Wayne ask another tall, tanned, equally leggy blonde if she would like a drink. The fact that the first girl had said exactly the same thing just seconds earlier, merely made Wayne smile. It must have been the fifth time that a stunning girl had commented on his voice in the last fifteen minutes and that had never, ever happened in Shepton.

"Do you know Rudy Giano? He's a friend of mine from my High School and his folks moved to London, His Dad was in the army or something, you know?"

The girl gabbled excitedly. Wayne smiled politely; he had never seen anyone with such a perfect smile. Everyone in Los Angeles seemed to have absolutely perfect, straight, dazzling white teeth, but this girl's smile could only be described as devastating.

"London's a very large city and I live quite a long way away." He mumbled, suddenly becoming very conscious of his own dental shortcomings.

The girl grinned.

"I am sooo sorry, that was like, such a stupid thing to say."

Wayne smiled, his lips clamped together as if by glue.

The girl held out her hand.

"I'm Julia."

Wayne smiled back then rubbed his hand over his mouth.

"I'm...er, Mike." He mumbled, taking her hand and shaking it gently.

The girl looked around nervously.

"Do you know whose party this is?" She whispered, leaning in towards him conspiratorially.

"I just came with a girlfriend. She said that a famous agent lived here, you know; and that if I ever wanted to get a break in to the movies then this was the sort of place to come. You know, the sort of place to get noticed."

Wayne grinned, forgetting this time to hide what he considered to be his hideous, crooked yellow teeth.

"Actually it's my sister's party. She's one."

The girl gasped.

"Oh-my-God, I am so sorry, I mean oh-my-God, I have crashed your sister's party. Please don't have me thrown out. I need..."

Wayne held up his hand.

"Hey, don't worry, I won't tell anyone you crashed. As a matter of fact, I'm rather glad you did."

Wayne could hear his accent getting more plummy and English by the second.

The girl blew a sigh of relief and then flashed that beaming smile again.

"That's just sooo, like, me, you know." She screwed up her nose in self-mockery.

"Dur, like hi host, I just, sort of, crashed your party."

Wayne laughed.

"I'm not the host, Julia; that would be my stepfather, Dean Vitalia. He's due to arrive very soon. You'll recognise him when he gets here. He looks like a Mafia Don."

Julia's mouth fell open.

"Like Al Pacino? Oh-my-God, did you see that movie the Godfather, I just sooo love that movie."

Wayne smiled and listened politely as Julia told him about all her favourite movies and actors and actresses.

Suddenly she seemed to notice someone over Wayne's shoulder.

"Oh-my-God, is that Jack Green over there? Excuse me."

Julia brushed past Wayne and moved down the yard through a throng of people.

Wayne hadn't noticed that many more guests had arrived while he had been spellbound; listening to Julia's lists of likes and dislikes.

Unfortunately, the majority of the new guests seemed to be male; tall, tanned males who all looked like American football players. Their teeth were every bit as white as the girls.

It all made Wayne feel quite inadequate, even the smallest of the newcomers was probably almost a foot taller than his five feet nine inches and had more muscles than a Charles Atlas "After" picture.

"You OK honey?" He heard Terri's voice behind him.

"Yes, fine, thanks Mom." He nodded.

"Are you enjoying yourself?" Terri asked before smiling the same sort of dazzling smile that the young wannabe actresses used.

Wayne smiled back, his lips clamped tightly together. Terri seemed reassured that her son was having a good time, then she turned back to whoever she had been talking to.

Wayne suddenly realised that in the midst of so much beauty and glamour, he was way out of his league. Yes, he wasn't bad looking and his long, corkscrew hair hid his ears, but compared to the people packed into his mother's back yard he was a pale, scrawny, small, spotty youth with crooked yellow teeth. Worse than that, he was now visibly sweating. He felt a drop of water drip off his eyebrow, then another ran down his nose.

The temptation to disappear into the house and re-emerge, as someone altogether more glamorous was overwhelming, but Wayne remembered what had happened the last time he had mixed shape-shifting and alcohol. The two did not sit well together.

The disco music thumped repetitively and Wayne edged through the people by the poolside back towards the house.

Perhaps he'd had too many beers and Margaritas, or maybe it was the heat, but Wayne began to feel a little light-headed. The general clamour of conversation seemed to be getting louder, as though people were competing to be heard. It was as if being heard would get them noticed.

Wayne noticed Julia walking towards him with a smile that seemed as false as it was wide. He smiled back at her politely, then quickly turned and made for the cool, security of the kitchen.

Once inside Wayne leaned against a kitchen unit and took a deep breath. Only a couple of guests had sought the cool air-conditioned sanctuary of the kitchen. Conchita was busying herself preparing plates of party food.

Wayne decided that he should lie down for a few minutes to regain his composure.

He had never felt so weird, so out-classed. Generally, Wayne Higginbotham was comfortable in any circumstances, unlike Doris who had an enormous chip on her shoulder, especially when it came to her posh sister Margaret. Wayne had always felt that he could hold his own in any company, yet here he had begun to feel like a scabby, mangey, donkey in a pasture full of unicorns.

"Michael!" He heard his Mom's voice shout from the yard, just as he was leaving the kitchen to lie down for five minutes.

"Mikey, where are you?" She repeated as she entered the kitchen.

"Erm, here." Wayne replied, smiling weakly.

His mother perused his face, a look of maternal concern etched onto her features. She wiped a bead of sweat off his forehead.

"Are you sure you're OK honey?" She asked.

"It is hot out there today, way above a hundred."

Wayne nodded.

"Yeah Mom, I'm fine. I just needed a little shade for a minute."

Terri nodded understandingly.

"Dean's just arrived." She stated with the slightest hint of a grimace, he's brought his cousin and his cousin's little boy. Come and meet them."

Wayne felt sick.

"Yeah, Ok." He murmured as his mother took him by the elbow and guided him out into the blinding light and blistering heat of the crowded yard.

"Dean likes you, you know." She was whispering. "He's got no choice anyway, you're my son and I'll never lose you again. I know I almost lost you, just before Marco was born and I will never, ever let anything like that happen again. I swear. Career or no career."

Wayne noticed a young girl with her back towards him wearing a very short dress which displayed her long legs and slender figure to perfection. Her hair was long, blonde and unbelievably shiny and silky. She was engaged in an earnest conversation with someone, whilst playing with that perfect hair in the way that Wayne had read that girls do when they are flirting with someone.

He heard his mother's voice call Dean's name as the girl turned and smiled that dazzling smile. It was Julia who had been talking to Wayne's stepfather, Dean Vitalia.

Dean was cuddling Marina in one arm, while Marco clung to his other hand.

Wayne couldn't help but notice that Dean's perfect white smile was almost reptilian as he approached him.

"Hey Mikey …. how you doin?" Dean gushed as he had pulled his hand away from little Marco's. He gave his stepson a slight hug then rested his hand on Wayne's shoulder and stared into his eyes.

"You're looking good, Michael. You got your Momma's good looks. Maybe you oughtta consider a career in the movies." He punched Wayne's shoulder playfully.

"So you havin' fun in my house?"

Wayne nodded and gulped.

"Yes, thank you very much. It's been great so far."

Dean laughed and turned back to Julia.

"Don'cha just love the English, all so polite and so proper."

Julia laughed sycophantically.

"Hey Mikey, there's somebody you just gotta meet."

Dean handed Julia a card.

"Call me!" He stated, almost dismissively.

Wayne noticed Terri shift uncomfortably, as she picked up the whimpering Marco.

Julia glanced at the card and that thousand-watt smile lit up her face.

"Oh-my-God, thanks, Mister Vitalia." She gushed flirtatiously, before turning back towards the side of the yard where there was an agreeable amount of shade, under a number of strategically placed garden umbrellas.

Wayne just caught her glance as Dean took his shoulder and guided him down a short path towards a table by the pool.

Julia looked ecstatic. She grinned and winked at him triumphantly.

Wayne couldn't help but feel sorry for her. It had been like watching a snake hypnotising its prey. He wondered how long it would be before Dean took her to bed, which was his obvious intention. Tall gorgeous leggy blondes were ten a penny in this neighbourhood.

Wayne knew that Dean had several stunning blondes on his books, why would he need another one?

Wayne wouldn't have trusted Dean had he been the last man on earth, yet unfortunately Dean Vitalia was his mother's husband and the father of his little brother and sister.

Wayne shrugged, maybe he was just jealous. Julia was the most beautiful girl he'd ever seen by a million miles and was so far out of his league that getting together with her would be like Liverpool F.C. being paired with Shepton Bulldogs in the F.A. Cup. Hell, Stephanie Fleming back home had been out of his league, that was why he'd had to invent Mickey Finnegan, the alter ego that had almost lead to his doom.

Wayne was suddenly conscious of two figures standing before him. One was a large fat man with slicked back, jet black hair. He was wearing a ridiculous John Travolta-like white suit and was sweating profusely. He wiped his brow constantly and ostentatiously with a white silk handkerchief. The other figure was a small boy of about seven standing with his back towards Wayne, looking out over the view of Beverley Hills. His hair was very blonde and even curlier than Wayne's. It looked so perfect that it must have been a perm.

"Aurelio, this is the guy I told you about. This here's my stepson: Michael, all the way from London, England. Wayne this is my cousin, Aurelio, prospective Senator of these here United States."

The fat man held out his hand, which Wayne grasped. It was sweatier than the man's forehead and felt cold, clammy and greasy at the same time. The man's grip was also very light and the handshake limp and half hearted.

"I'm very pleased to meet you, sir." Wayne stated mechanically.

The fat man grunted.

"Ha! The English, always so polite. I just love you guys."

He grasped Wayne's cheek between his thumb and forefinger and gave it a slight twist.

"You're right Deano, he does look a bit like his Mom." He laughed as he ruffled Wayne's hair as though he was about six years old.

Wayne scowled in annoyance, but the fat man was too busy mopping his brow to notice.

"So, howdya like the United States of America, Michael?"

"It's fantastic." Wayne responded, trying to sound eager for the sake of politeness.

"You should go out East, it's too damn hot down here. Howdya live like this Deano?" He grunted at his cousin.

Dean Vitalia laughed.

"It's no hotter than Sicily, Aurelio. Our Grand pop, would have had it like this all the time. You've just gotten used to the cold up there in Boston."

Aurelio whistled through his teeth.

"Ain't this too hot for an English guy like you?" He asked Wayne before puffing out his cheeks and blowing. He shook his head as though he found the heat incredulous.

"I heard it's always cold and foggy in England." Aurelio added.

"When it ain't raining." Dean chipped in with a sarcastic laugh.

"No it's……….." Wayne began before Aurelio interrupted him.

"Foggy, cold, wet and God damned grey. That's what I hear. Everybody always out on strike. The trains don't work, the cars fall apart and nobody ever sees a dentist. England, that's some place huh? At least you got Maggie Thatcher over there now. She'll sort out all those Pinko-communists that you Europeans seem to breed. Hey, my stepson's European too. His Momma's Italian. Lucien, come over here, meet Mikey, he's come all the way here from London, England."

Wayne bristled with anger as the boy with the curly blonde hair turned slowly away from the fence. How dare fatso be so rude about England. It wasn't always raining, nor was it foggy and………….

The boy looked up, straight into Wayne's eyes.

Despite the heat, Wayne felt as though he'd just plunged into a pool of icy water. It was as though the blood stalled in his veins and a violent shiver ran through his body from head to toe.

Wayne Higginbotham was looking right into the same ice-cold, steely blue eyes of the black robed figure from his nightmares.

The boy smiled and Wayne's heart froze.

Twelve

Tick, tock, tick, tock, tick tock. Ticka, tick, ticka, tick, ticka tick.

All Doris Higginbotham could hear was the sound of her life slowly ticking away, as the several clocks that she kept in her living room marked each and every passing second. She was sat in her usual armchair, strategically placed by the gas fire, but with an excellent view of the TV.

Yet, for once she had not activated the remote control. She didn't feel like watching the rubbish and the repeats that constituted the general afternoon fare. She didn't feel like doing anything much.

Doris had passed her morning in the town, as usual, doing a little bit of shopping at the Co-Op supermarket, as usual and having a coffee at the Lite-Bite café, as usual, before catching the bus back home at precisely five past eleven, as usual.

It had been an even more boring trip than usual.

She would often bump into someone she knew while pushing her basket around the aisles of the store, or while strolling up Shepton's ancient cobble-stoned High Street. She nearly always met someone she knew in the Lite-Bite, quite often her sister Margaret would meet her there. Yet this morning there had been no one. No friendly faces, no chat, no salacious gossip, nothing.

Doris pursed her lips and glowered at the blank TV screen, catching her reflection in the grainy-grey glass. Was this it then? Was this the pattern of her life now? Loneliness, stuck inside the same four walls.

Somewhere, outside, in a nearby field, a sheep bleated. She heard a car slowly rumble past the front garden of the house. Then silence, except for the tick-tocking of the clocks.

"Aye, this is what it comes to in the end." Doris muttered as she perused the cheap ceramic ornaments on her mantelpiece.

"Nowt!"

Doris sniffed and gripped the arms of her chair as she felt a sob rise in her throat. She swallowed hard and bit her lip. Crying wouldn't help!

When she had married Frank, she had expected that they would have a large family, four or five kids maybe and that they would all live happily ever after. The boys would get good jobs, plumbers, builders, electricians maybe, while the girls would marry well and they'd all live nearby and provide lots of grandchildren. Then the kids would look after Frank and Doris in their old age. A week's holiday in Blackpool every year, maybe a little car that Frank could pootle around in. She'd never wanted much.

The rich tapestry of the life she had seen herself living, had begun to unravel with her first miscarriage. Several more over a ten-year period finally convinced the Higginbothams that they would never be able to have children of their own. Her sister Margaret had also struggled to conceive, but had finally been blessed with a healthy son.

This had been the last straw for Doris. She had always competed with her younger sister, almost obsessively. She had been delighted when Margaret had married the weedy bank clerk, Stanley Houghton-Hughes, who had attended the town's Grammar School, Wormysteds.

"It'll never last." She had informed anyone who would listen.

"He's too posh for her."

However, the marriage did last and Doris' other claim to superiority over her sister was negated when Stanley began to slowly rise through the bank's hierarchy. Soon Stanley's bank salary overtook Frank's meagre wage at the thingummy factory. Doris had reacted by accusing her sister of putting on "airs and graces." The birth of Cedric Houghton-Hughes had been like rubbing salt in the wound.

Doris glowered at a back and white photograph in a brass frame on the window sill. It showed Cedric, probably aged about two and a half, holding a toddling baby Wayne's hand. Doris and Frank had immediately applied to adopt a baby when she had heard that Margaret was pregnant. The Roman Catholic Church had been very supportive, thanks to Frank's family's excellent churchgoing record and a baby boy had duly been supplied from the "Crusade of Rescue" in London. He had been so cute, smiley and handsome that Doris had fallen in love with him immediately. His birth name had been John Albert Watson, but Doris and Frank had agreed to change his name to Trevor. The four months that Trevor spent in the Higginbotham household were the happiest months of Doris' life. In her mind, he was the perfect baby. Tragically, he then became ill; seriously ill. Trevor was whisked to hospital with suspected meningitis, which would have been bad enough on its own, but at the same time, Emily Watson, his mother decided that she could not go through with the adoption procedure and with the help of her mother, took over the nursing of her baby John. It was as though Trevor had died.

The "Crusade of Rescue" did their best to find a replacement baby for the Higginbothams as quickly as possible and that was how Michael Sean O'Brien had ended up in Frank and Doris' family. As cute as he was, he was no Trevor. Poor Michael had huge pointed ears, like some sort of pixie. Poor Doris had cried all the way home from London at the prospect of raising such an ugly baby.

Doris bit her lip again. Well now that ugly baby was eighteen and galavanting off in America and would be going off to University almost as soon as he got back.

Frank was dead, so Wayne, as they had named Michael, was all she had.

What if he didn't come back from University?

What would happen to her if he didn't get a good job?

Who would look after her?

Would she always be alone, like this?

Doris didn't even have her cleaning job at the "Junction Inn" anymore; she had had to retire due to her worsening health.

Was listening to the clocks ticking the countdown to her death all that was left for her?

No!

Wayne might not have been as perfect as Trevor, but he hadn't been a bad lad. He'd gotten to that Grammar School and had passed all his exams and he'd done better than Cedric Houghton-bloody-Hughes. Plus his ears hadn't seemed quite so freakish as he'd got older.

Doris didn't understand why he was going off to this University. Why didn't he just get a job like Cedric had done? Cedric had a good job at the bank where his dad worked. What could Wayne do that was better than that? What would he get from this University?

He wouldn't be starting work 'till he was twenty-one. Frank and her had both been working by the time they were fourteen.

Doris shook her head.

"Aye, they don't know they're born, these days."

She climbed stiffly out her chair and crept through into the kitchen. She filled her kettle with water and lit a gas ring, placing the full kettle on top of the roaring blue flame with a grunt of effort.

"No he'll come back, our Wayne. He'll probably end up working in the solicitor's office, or sommat."

Doris' self-reassurance made her feel much better. In fact she couldn't help but smile wryly when she thought of Margaret's reaction if her Wayne became a solicitor one day.

Maybe he'd get a house up on the snobby Ripon Road, near Margaret's and he'd take his mother in to live with him. She could look after her grandchildren while Wayne and his wife went out to work.

As she sat back down in her armchair, clutching her mug of tea, Doris Higginbotham felt much better. In fact as she pressed the button on her remote controller, to switch on the TV, her reflection in the screen was definitely smiling before it exploded into a million coloured pixels.

Thirteen

Far, far away from the grey-green hills of the Yorkshire Dales, Maria Vitalia sat in her own armchair, staring out of the open French windows at the magnificent lush, green lawn that sloped away down to the ornamental lake at the bottom of the garden. An ornate fountain took pride of place at the lake's centre, a marble statue of a naked woman sat astride a sea-serpent, which sent a jet of water four feet into the air from its raised, open mouth. Maria hated the statue. It was vulgar beyond belief. Aurelio, her husband had said it would remind her of her home in Italy. All it had actually succeeded in doing was to remind her of her husband's gross bad taste.

Huge ancient oak trees lined the drive that was just visible, off to the left. A white picket fence denoted the border of the paddock where four stunning thoroughbreds gambolled in the late summer New England sunshine.

A warm breeze caressed her cheek as a butterfly flew briefly into the shade of the room and then fluttered back out into the sunlight.

Maria sighed heavily. So much luxury, so much wealth, yet she had never been more miserable in her young life. Soon her husband's black Lincoln would be rolling slowly up the drive and things would get even worse. She reached over to the exquisitely carved coffee table and picked up the glass of clear liquid, placing two white tablets in her mouth before taking a sip. She flinched and screwed up her face in disgust at the taste in her mouth, but then took another large gulp before carefully placing the glass back on the table.

Maria hadn't always been so miserable. Just eight years earlier something had happened that had made. Maria Francesca Giardina, then an eighteen year old novice at the Convent of the Blessed Virgin, in the Sicilian town of Bagheria, the happiest girl in the world.

She had been an exemplary postulate and the thought of taking her vows and becoming a Sister within the Dominican Order and a fully-fledged Bride of Christ, filled her with unbridled excitement.

She had always known she was going to be a Nun, ever since her local Priest had told her that he could see the light of Christ shining in her eyes, when she had been very, very small. She had known from that moment on that Christ had chosen her to be his special one and that her life would be totally dedicated to his service and his service alone.

Her parents had been baffled. Maria's father was a simple farmer; he raised sheep, a few cattle and sold a few olives. He wasn't particularly religious but, like his peers and predecessors, he was a nominal practicing Catholic. Maria's mother had been very religious and although disappointed that her only daughter would not give her grandchildren, she had come round to the fact that Maria knew what she was doing.

When she was eight years old, Jesus had tested Maria. Her mother had announced that she was going to have a little brother, or sister. Maria had been ecstatic and counted the days until her little baby sibling was born. Tragically, her mother died while giving birth to Maria's little brother, Antonio. The boy had survived for a few days, but had been very, very weak and had eventually passed away in Maria's arms.

Maria knew that Jesus had taken her mother and her baby brother to test her resolve, but she knew that she would meet them again in paradise, so she had not even slightly wavered in her determination to serve her Lord.

When she had reached the age of twelve, Maria had noticed that the village boys were taking an interest in her. She therefore cropped her luscious raven hair and took to wearing voluminous dresses that totally hid her burgeoning adolescent figure. No mortal male would ever match the perfection of her Saviour and the Light of the World, so she would cut herself off from them.

Maria entered the nearest convent as soon a she left school, much to the annoyance of quite a few of the local lads who thought that she was incredibly beautiful, despite her cropped hair. Her large brown eyes, button nose and perfect rosy red lips could not be hidden away, nor could her flashing smile, even if it was a rare sight. The demure way she looked at boys, then the way she slowly averted her eyes, just as they tried to catch her gaze, drove them wild. Yet Maria remained totally and obstinately oblivious.

She had only been in the convent for just over a year and had just become a novice when, as part of the choir, she was invited to sing before Cardinal D'Abruzzo.

The Cardinal was known as one of the most senior officials in the Vatican City itself and his visit to the small provincial, backwater had been greeted with great excitement both inside and outside the Convent. The Mother Superior had been manic in the months preceding the visit, ensuring that everything was perfect, that the Convent was spotless, that the correct local dignitaries, both religious and secular had been invited and that the choir was note perfect.

Unknown to the sisters, however, Cardinal D'Abruzzo was the head of "The Sacred Order of St. Gregory" and he had a very special and specific reason for visiting the modest Sicilian Convent. He needed a mother for the Messiah.

Cardinal D'Abruzzo had no idea what would constitute a suitable vessel for the second coming, but the disembodied voice that guided his actions had insisted that a suitable girl would be found in the Convent of the Blessed Virgin in Bagheria.

D'Abruzzo knew better than to disobey the voice and as soon as he saw the young novice singing her heart out in the front row of the choir, he knew he had found the new Virgin Mary.

Maria remembered the way the Cardinal had stared at her. Every time she glanced in his direction she felt his eyes burning into her, so she was not surprised to be brought before the Mother Superior after the service. The Cardinal introduced himself and asked her outright, in front of the Mother Superior, if she was still intact.

"Of course!" She had responded indignantly, her dark eyes flashing dangerously.

"Then God has great work for you." The Cardinal had whispered. He had seemed almost intoxicated, transfixed by the girl's beauty, almost in a state of euphoria.

Maria did not know how the child subsequently entered her womb.

She remembered being taken to Rome, which for a girl who had never left Sicily was a great adventure.

She remembered being introduced to a few very important Bishops and Priests and being pampered and fawned over. She remembered being shown into a beautiful chamber in a luxurious apartment that was described as being her new cell.

She even thought she remembered drinking the sacrament from what she was told was possibly the Holy Grail.

Yet she would never forget the feeling of sheer exultation she felt, when she was told that she was pregnant, that she was still a virgin and that she would be bearing the Messiah.

That feeling that she had always had, that she was special, that she would be Christ's alone, had come to pass.

People would remember Maria Giardina as the very reincarnation of the Blessed Virgin Mary.

Maria smiled sardonically at the thought: "The reincarnated virgin Mary, Ha."

She exclaimed aloud.

She took a large swig of the clear liquid and scoured the driveway to see if there was any sign of her husband's car. Trees swayed in the warm breeze and one of the horses gave an excited whinny.

It had all gone downhill from there.

The child had duly been born and Maria had never thought that such pain would be possible to endure. Yet survive she did, but only to become a prisoner within her chambers. The restrictions placed on her made the convent seem unbelievably relaxed.

It was for her own good she was assured. Imagine the reaction if the second coming was announced to the media in an increasingly cynical world. She was not allowed to show the child to anyone, nor was she allowed to see anyone except a Doctor and two or three Priests.

The child and his mother had to be protected until the time was right.

She would be allowed beautiful new clothes, fine food and anything she wanted as long as she cooperated.

Maria was told that something out there was the sworn enemy of her child and would stop at nothing to destroy him. This creature was the spawn of the devil and could change its shape and fire energy from its hands like the people in comic books. As hard as she found this to believe, Maria accepted the protection of "The Order."

The child had helped her get through her confinement.

He had seemed so perfect.

She named him Lucien, to denote that he was the "Light of the World."

Up until the age of about four he had seemed like any other child, albeit beautiful beyond belief with his cherubic features, peachy complexion, his clear blue eyes and curly blonde hair. He could not have been more of a contrast to his dark haired, brown-eyed mother.

Yes, he had walked early and talked early but Maria put that down to her own skills as a mother and to the child's divinity.

From the child reaching the age of four, however, she had begun to realise that the baby that she had presumed to be the new Jesus was more petulant and domineering than she would have expected for someone described as meek and mild.

Sometimes he would even use an adult's voice to tell her what to do, but then he was a deity and he did seem to love her very much.

She soon learned to fear his temper, however. One day, in a fit of pique, he used his mind to incinerate a pigeon that had the misfortune to land on the chambers window sill, just because his mother would not let him have a cookie.

Another time he had knocked her onto her back with no more than a contemptuous glance, because she refused to pick him up.

Maria had often found herself doing things that she could not remember initiating. It had soon become clear to her that the boy could control her mind.

By the time the boy had reached the age of five and was being introduced to various representatives of "The Sacred Order of St Gregory" as the new Messiah, Maria was having serious doubts about the true nature of the child she had given birth to.

Was it only just over two years since I was safely ensconced in the Vatican? Maria wondered as she took another gulp of her drink.

That was when D'Abruzzo had burst into her chambers one day, full of excitement. He had asked to see the child alone. He had been hopping from one leg to another like an excited little boy while Maria had fetched young Lucien from his own room. She did not know what had been said, as she had been dismissed, but Lucien had seemed in an extremely good mood when she had been allowed to return to him.

"They've killed the baddie at last." He had announced gleefully.

"The Order" has finally fulfilled its purpose, this time!" Maria had smiled at him indulgently.

"That's great, my special one." She had gushed.

For a few days all had seemed well. Lucien had behaved angelically; even the generally taciturn Cardinal had appeared to be in a good and benevolent mood. Maria, who had grown quite imperious during her confinement in the Vatican had begun to dream about her role as the mother of the Messiah and about how the Church would soon have to venerate her in place of the original Virgin Mary. Maria Francesca Giardina would be more powerful than any Queen, or Empress had ever been, in the entire history of the world. Soon, Maria had believed, even the Holy Father himself would have to prostrate himself in front of her.

Maria smiled sadly as the sound of a horse whinnying brought her back to the present.

How could she have ever been filled with such hubris? It is said that pride comes before a fall, but how could a young girl, who had been such a model of modesty, humility and devotion have become such a egomaniacal monster?

She took a sip from her glass and shook her head.

Everything had seemed to change overnight. It had been late September, 1979 when Cardinal D'Abruzzo had once again burst into Maria's chambers, this time however, his face had been taut and gaunt, his forehead creased in a worried frown, his eyes downcast.

He had asked for an audience with Lucien, once again and after just a few minutes had left, seemingly in a state of extreme agitation.

Maria had rushed into her son's room to find him sitting grim faced on his bed.

"My Darling, what has happened?" Maria had asked as she reached out to cuddle the boy.

The child raised his right hand.

Maria had been lifted gently through the air by an invisible force. It was as though a giant had picked her up and set her down several feet from her son. He glowered at her:

"Sorry Mama, but this is not the time! Leave me alone for a few minutes."

"But" Maria had begun to protest.

"Leave!" The child had uttered more forcefully and Maria had been forced back towards the door by what had seemed like a powerful gust of wind.

Maria had paced up and down her chambers, wringing her hands frantically:

What could have gone wrong?

Had the "Order" failed to achieve what it had claimed?

Was Lucien still in danger?

The boy had emerged after several minutes and had smiled at his mother.

"Momma, would you like to get out of here?" He had asked, innocently.

Maria had smiled:

"Well maybe it's early yet. Maybe we should wait until you're a bit older."

The boy's face had clouded:

"Pack your things mother. We are leaving here tomorrow. You are going to take a husband. I will find you a suitable man and I shall have an earthly father at last. Do not worry you will still live in luxury, I will ensure that and I will ensure our protection. These churchmen aren't the only ones who are good at that. Indeed, I believe we can do much better than these beskirted fools."

Maria had frowned:

"A husband?" She had whispered incredulously.

"Yes, it's time someone who looks as good as you experienced the pleasures of the flesh." The boy had grinned impishly.

Maria had blushed a bright shade of crimson. Her mouth had dropped open in shock and disbelief.

"But I, but…"

"You will do as I say, mother." The boy's tone, no longer childlike, had broached no argument.

Back in New England, Maria shook her head at the memory.

She should have known then that she had been used. If she was honest, she probably did know, but just hadn't wanted to admit it.

It had all been down to her pride, her ego and of course the machinations of the sycophantic Priests and lackeys who had served her every need.

She had been only too ready to believe that she was the mother of the saviour of the World and thereby as near to a Goddess as was possible.

Lucien had asked her to summon D'Abruzzo the very next day. He had arrived and Maria had been summarily dismissed again. The Cardinal's audience with the boy lasted no more than two minutes. Maria distinctly heard raised voices. The Cardinal left Maria's chambers extremely quickly, his face as white as a ghost's. He glanced at her for a moment as he was leaving. His eyes were full of panic; it was as though he was pleading with her to help him or to follow him. Then he had shaken his head and scuttled away down the ornate corridor with his robes flapping around him.

When Maria had turned round, Lucien was stood in the middle of the room with their bags on either side of him.

"Come mother. It's time to go." He had smiled.

Maria had panicked:

"But where? How?" She had exclaimed; horrified at the prospect of stepping out of their Vatican sanctuary with no money and no idea what awaited them in the wicked world outside.

The child had just smiled that beatific smile.

"Trust me, mama, just trust me."

Maria drained the glass and then let it drop onto the plush, deep carpet of the exquisitely decorated room. Oh yes, he had promised her luxury and he had kept his word, Lucien was good at that. He had promised her a husband and he had been as good as his word.

They had simply walked out of their chambers into the Vatican City, straight past St. Peters, straight past the armed yet archaically uniformed Swiss guards, straight through the Piazza St. Pietro under the gaze of all those stone saints and straight into a taxi.

"Tell him to take us to the Hotel D'Inghilterra." Lucien had whispered.

Maria had complied, although she had no idea how they would pay.

When the taxi stopped, Lucien had given his mother several bills from a huge wad of lira, which he had pulled from his small backpack.

"Courtesy of the Cardinal." He grinned.

Maria couldn't understand why "the Order" had simply let her go so easily, after being so insistent on protecting her and her son for so long. Why had D'Abruzzo not intervened? Why had the Swiss Guard not stopped them from leaving?

She had waited a couple of days before she had even dared to ask Lucien his opinion.

"The "Order" has been dissolved." He stated calmly.

"I ordered it when D'Abruzzo informed me that they had achieved their final victory." They had been watching TV in their hotel room when Maria had finally broached the question.

The boy had then twisted his face.

The child had smacked his fist into his hand.

"I smelt fear in D'Abruzzo. He was uncertain about me. I could see it in his eyes. There was a distinct lack of faith."

The boy had smiled.

"A lack of faith is a terrible thing do you not think momma?"

Maria had gulped and nodded enthusiastically.

The boy had continued.

"D'Abruzzo was beginning to doubt my, authenticity. So had others in the "Order.""

Maria had shaken her head. The words the boy used seemed so innocuous from one so young.

The boy shrugged as he continued.

"That tiny element of doubt meant that he and his entire organisation had failed me. I can not afford to take any risks and D'Abruzzo, despite his assurances and his honeyed words, was becoming dangerous to me."

The boy had paused again and had stroked his chin. He had sat on the bed, his lips pursed.

"Faith is not true faith, unless it is absolute." Lucien declared pompously as he eyed his mother.

Maria, not for the first time, had been afraid of her own son.

"Now I am growing and getting stronger every day. Soon there will be no power on earth, no matter what the prophecies say, that will be able to stop me, but not yet. I recognise that I am still a child and I still need some form of protection. However, I no longer wish to hide behind the skirts of incompetent Priests. There are others who are just as skilled in the arts of protection. I have arranged everything."

He smiled his beatific smile at his mother.

"I'm going to make sure they look after you too, Momma."

Maria had smiled weakly and nodded.

"Thank you, Lucien. What are you going to do about the "Order?""

Lucien had grinned and pointed the remote at the TV to turn up the volume:

The sombre looking news presenter was just in the process of announcing the sudden and unexpected death of the much-respected Cardinal D'Abruzzo, one of the Vatican's most senior figures and a world-renowned expert on the occult. It had been diagnosed as a heart attack.

Just a couple of days later, while Lucien and his mother enjoyed an ice cream in the hotel lobby's snack bar, the boy had seen Aurelio Vitalia approach the hotel reception desk.

"Ah, your future husband has arrived at last, mamma." The boy had grinned, mischievously pointing at the fat, sweating American.

Maria had actually laughed.

"No way. Luca!" She had exclaimed: "He's too old, he's too fat, he's too sweaty and he's far, far too ugly."

"I know." The boy had grinned: "Nevertheless, soon he shall be sharing your bed."

His cold, blue eyes had looked into hers and Maria knew he was not joking.

Back in her palatial home in New England, Maria sighed again. Had she ever have a choice in the matter?

Had she tried to stop the boy's machinations, would he have harmed her?

Of course, the boy had been right all along. As much as Aurelio Vitalia had initially disgusted her, he had started to sweep her off her feet that very afternoon. She had never been as flattered as when he had suddenly appeared with the largest bouquet of flowers she had ever seen.

Had it all been just Lucien controlling her mind?

His mind too?

Did she still have any free will left at all?

She had been married now for two years and Lucien must have stopped controlling her mind when it came to Aurelio, because the very thought of him touching her, pawing her, groping her body with his big fat stubby fingers made her skin crawl.

She hated his fat belly, his sweaty head, his disgusting odour.

She hated him shouting at her, as if she was stupid.

She hated him hitting her.

She hated him lying to her.

She had been tricked.

She had been lied to.

She had been used.

She was not the reincarnation of the Blessed Virgin Mary; she was not even a virgin any more.

She was a fool. A stupid, ignorant peasant girl from the back end of nowhere.

Was that why they'd chosen her?

Why her? Surely there were plenty of other girls out there, bad girls who wouldn't have minded being used.

Maria Giardina had been a good, devout Christian girl who had only ever wanted to serve her Lord Jesus Christ.

And Lucien was not the second coming of Jesus Christ. She knew that now.

He was not the Messiah and he was an awful lot more than just a very naughty boy. Outside, Maria Vitalia heard the scrunch of gravel as the black Lincoln entered the driveway.

Aurelio and Lucien returning from their business in Las Vegas and from his slimy cousin Dean's place in LosAngeles.

Maria reached under the chair and picked up the Colt pistol that she had stolen from Aurelio's bedside cabinet drawer.

She felt Lucien's presence as he sought out her mind.

She knew that he knew what she was planning to do.

The vodka and the all the sleeping tablets she had taken made her feel a bit fuzzy.

She liked the feeling. She knew that Lucien couldn't reach her in time.

Maria knew that suicides didn't usually go to heaven, but she might be allowed special dispensation.

She had done everything she had done in the interests of the Lord and after all, the Priest had said that she had the light of Christ in her eyes.

She put the barrel of the gun into her mouth.

She heard car doors banging, shouting and the sound of running feet.

She heard Lucien's voice in her mind.

"Mamma, I command you: Noooooooooooo!"

She smiled.

"Too late, Luca, my son!"

She pulled the trigger.

Fourteen

Wayne Higginbotham woke with a start as he felt the bump of the Jumbo jet as it touched down onto the tarmac at Heathrow airport. He looked out of the tiny window at the rain streaking across the glass and the voluminous amounts of spray that the aircraft created as it sped along the runway.

"Good morning Ladies and Gentlemen and welcome to London Heathrow, where it is Tuesday morning and the time is now ten thirty am. The temperature outside is a pleasant sixty degrees and the forecast is for drizzle, clearing slowly from the West. We hope you have enjoyed flying with us at British Airways this morning and that you will consider travelling with us again. Those with connecting flights should contact a member of our ground staff in the terminal building and on behalf of the crew; we wish you all a safe onward journey. Thank you!"

As the chief stewardess issued the warning about passengers remaining seated until the aircraft came to a stop and about smoking regulations, Wayne took a deep breath and relaxed in his seat. He was home, well nearly home and the nightmare figure had not reappeared in his dreams since he had seen the boy at the party. Wow what a party that had been, Wayne smiled, the Beach Boys had been right, how he wished they all could be Californian girls. The thought of Julia's body made him close his eyes as he tried to recall every single detail of the time he had spent with her, yet it was the boy's eyes that came immediately into his mind.

Wayne opened his eyes and grimaced, surely it was too much of a coincidence for the boy to be the dark messiah and for him to be related, albeit distantly and only by marriage, to the man charged with his destruction.

Perhaps he was being totally ridiculous, apart from the eyes the child could not have looked any less like a dark Lord. Indeed, the boy had looked positively Angelic. Yet the eyes had been exactly the eyes of the dark robed faceless figure of Wayne's dreams: Light Blue, clear, cold and merciless.

Wayne smiled; maybe he'd just described the eyes of every single blue eyed, blond haired Scandinavian.

Yet, he had been certain that at the very moment of their meeting, he had felt the tentacles of the boy's mind attempting to reach out into his head, momentarily, as the child had looked up into Wayne's eyes. To

Wayne it had seemed like the boy had been probing, pushing to find out absolutely everything about his new "second cousin" even though their eye contact had only lasted milliseconds, before some vacuous blonde girl had disturbed the boy by ruffling his hair and squeaking:

"Oh my God Dean, is this your nephew? Isn't he just so adorable?"

The Child had frowned, furiously, as he had turned away from Wayne and appraised his new admirer, while Wayne had smiled politely at Aurelio and Dean, blurted an apology and a reference to the bathroom and rushed off back towards the sanctuary of the kitchen.

The giant plane slowly came to a halt and people immediately jumped up to try and retrieve their possessions from the overhead lockers. Wayne watched the melee and wondered why people were always so desperately eager to grab their stuff when it would be another five minutes at least until the doors were open for passengers flying "cattle-class."

His mind wandered beck to Sunday's party and his strenuous efforts to avoid the boy for the rest of the afternoon.

"Michael, are you sure you're OK?" Terri had asked him at one point, her face aghast as he had almost fallen into the pool simply because he was too busy trying to locate his potential nemesis amongst the revellers.

"Have you had too many Margheritas?" She asked, sounding somewhat amused.

"Er, no." Wayne had stammered. "There's er, just someone I'm desperately trying to avoid."

His birth mother had laughed.

"Only one, Mikey? I've got at least forty or so of those here."

Wayne had smiled back at her before noticing that the child had been looking in his direction from a point on the far side of the pool. He had turned quickly and walked back towards the house.

Wayne had squeezed past the beautiful Julia's back as he had made for the kitchen. He had heard her telling a tall, bronzed, disinterested looking hulk that she just sooo like loved the British band The Cure. Wayne had smiled. Oh well at least he had something in common with one of the Hollywood glitterati. He grabbed a cold beer and sat on a rock under a palm tree near the back end of the yard where he could observe the interplay of the guests at his little sister's party and would get plenty of warning should the child approach him and decide to continue his mental interrogation.

As the evening had begun to fall, Wayne had watched as people had moved around like social butterflies, taking names, swapping phone numbers, all looking for someone who might be useful to their careers.

Everyone seemed to be talking; no one seemed to be listening. Then he had noticed Aurelio talking animatedly to Dean and Terri. Wayne had been wondering what was going on when he was suddenly conscious of someone sitting down next to him.

"Jeez, partying is so like, such hard work." He heard a familiar voice declare, an edge of frustration in the soft melodic voice.

"Hi Julia." Wayne had muttered, trying to sound as cool and nonchalant as possible.

The beautiful young, actress had turned her smile on to full beam as she caught Wayne's eye.

"You know, I'm really beginning to think your stepfather is trying to avoid me." She had complained with an exaggerated pout.

"Oh, he'll play hard to get while my Mom's around, but wait 'till he's on his own."

Julia smiled.

"Don't worry, he's not my type, I mean he's sooo old. He must be at least forty. Anyway, whatever, I'm getting just a bit bored."

"Really?" Wayne had asked, doing his old favourite Sean Connery voice before continuing:

"So many people to meet, so much good…" He rolled his eyes sarcastically, "…music. Anyway you seemed to be having quite a good time with the man mountain over there and he's not old."

He had pointed towards the man that he had seen her talking to, earlier."

Julia had gasped and clasped a hand over her mouth.

"No way." She had squealed.

"Are you jealous, Michael?" She had teased Wayne, licking her glossy, moist, red lips coquettishly, then she had started to laugh:

"You really shouldn't be, you know. He would be like sooo much more interested in you than he would be in me. Believe me!"

Wayne had blanched.

"What, you mean………."

Julia had giggled hysterically:

"You mean you really can't tell? Man, you are sooo gonna really struggle in this town. You better stick close to me. Anyway what sort of music are you into?"

Wayne shrugged.

"Punk, you know, a bit of the gothic stuff, the Cure, Siouxsie and the Banshees. That sort of thing."

"No way! Oh my God, I just love the Cure." Julia had exclaimed excitedly, running a hand through her silky blonde hair and then toying with the fringe.

Wayne had just smiled, weakly.

Then Julia had stood sharply and held out her hand.

"I need a beer." She had exclaimed.

"Come with me. We can find somewhere a bit quieter and you can like, tell me more about England, Robert Smith and the Cure and all that stuff."

She had flashed that million-watt smile again and Wayne had forgotten all about the boy.

Wayne was suddenly conscious that the people in his row were now beginning to bumble slowly down the aisle, so he stood and grabbed his backpack from the overhead locker.

He wondered if he would ever see Julia again.

He would certainly always remember her.

He had travelled to America a boy, now he returned, a man and this time he had not used any magic, or shape shifting trickery. He felt his chest swell up with pride as he struggled towards the exit of the plane, bumping his bag on the back of every seat he passed.

It had been quite late when he had emerged from his Mom's guest room, leaving Julia to fix up her make up and so on. He had bumped into his Mom in the kitchen.

"Hi! Where've you been?" She had asked, with the hint of a mischevious glint in her eye.

"Oh I was just a bit tired." Wayne spluttered.

"So I just had a little lie down, for a few minutes." Terri glanced down the corridor just as a still slightly dishevelled Julia emerged from the guest room. Terri grinned knowingly.

"Mmm, looks like you weren't the only one feeling a touch fatigued. Must be contagious."

Wayne had grinned back at his mother and couldn't help but wonder how Doris would have reacted in similar circumstances.

"Oh by the way, you missed one hell of a tantrum." Terri had laughed as she took a sip of a Margherita:

"Your cousin, the delightful Lucien, suddenly decided that he needed to get home to his mommy in Connecticut, right away. Aurelio wasn't happy but Lucien just threw this enormous and I mean enormous tantrum and it seems he got his way. They left about an hour ago. I just can't believe Aurelio let him get away with it."

"So they've gone." Wayne had not been able to conceal his glee.

"And Dean?"

Terri had shrugged.

"Oh he's still chatting up some starlet young enough to be his daughter. But hey, I've just got my own kids for breakfast tomorrow."

She had given her first-born son a hug as Julia had crept sheepishly past, casting Wayne a conspiratorial wink that Terri had turned just in time to see.

"Just be careful, my beautiful, handsome son."

She had whispered into Wayne's ear, a knowing smirk on her lips and a glint of pride in her eyes.

The last day in Los Angeles passed in a blur. Wayne had retired early after his "rest." The party had still been in full swing but Wayne had lost interest and had suddenly realised that he was really tired. The next morning there had been no sign of Dean. Terri had stated that he had said that he had a real busy day lined up and had left real early. So Wayne had spent the time before he was due at the airport in the company of his mother and his young siblings. It had all passed too quickly.

Yet, as he emerged into the terminal building at Heathrow that Tuesday morning, to catch the connecting flight to Leeds/Bradford airport, Wayne Higginbotham couldn't help but grin like an idiot.

Fifteen

Father Reichmann arrived in Ireland in the middle of the heaviest downpour Dublin had seen in many years. Yet the old German Priest had more important things on his mind than inclement weather, despite the fact that he was soaked to the skin within two minutes of leaving the terminal. His first major concern was getting hold of a taxi. On such a miserable day they were in very short supply, but within another couple of minutes he found himself sitting in the back of a Ford Granada, which he directed to a police station on the Port Laoise Road. His second concern was the message he had received from one of his young charges, Father Declan Doyle, who had been swiftly despatched to Ireland following Reichmann's meeting with Cardinal Warzowski. The message had been extremely encouraging. A rotund man in late middle age, fitting Bishop O'Leary's description, had handed himself in at a Garda station claiming indeed to be the missing Bishop. Father Reichmann could hardly contain his excitement as the taxi slowly struggled through the congested city roads.

If the man did in fact prove to be the erstwhile Bishop of Knock and one time deputy head of the "Sacred Order" in Ireland, then a great many questions could, hopefully, be answered.

Father Doyle met his older German colleague in the reception area of the Garda station. Father Reichmann decided that the young Priest looked extremely miserable for a man who had achieved a rather miraculous objective so quickly and efficiently.

"And how are you, Father?" Doyle asked as the older Priest held out his hand in greeting.

"I am very well indeed, my young friend." Father Reichmann gushed as he enthusiastically pumped Doyle's hand.

"I am all the better for hearing of your success in finding our elusive colleague so quickly. It looks like our Blessed Lady has smiled upon us."

Father Doyle shrugged and grimaced.

"It is definitely His Grace, the Bishop, Father, but I don't know how much sense you'll be getting out of him. He's as mad as a March hare."

Father Reichmann frowned disapprovingly.

"Now, now Declan, don't be disrespectful. His Grace is still a Bishop, ordained in the name of Our Lord. Can I see him?"

Father Doyle blew out a sigh and nodded.

"Of course, Father. He is not under any charge or anything. Come this way."

A Guard nodded respectfully and escorted the Priests into the back of the station where four cell doors stood on each side of the corridor. The Guard opened a steel slot in the door and peered inside the cell:

"I have some visitors for you, Your Grace." He shouted.

"Tell them to go away. I don't want to see anyone." A disembodied voice almost screamed from behind the heavy door.

"No one! Do you hear me? No one!"

Father Reichmann tapped the guard on the shoulder.

"Is he under arrest for anything?" He asked, politely.

The guard shook his head.

"No, Father. He just walked in off the street and asked to be put in a cell. He says he is being hunted by a errr......"

The policeman took off his cap and scratched his head. His face affected a bemused expression.

"Well Father, it's better that he stays here for his own safety. He claims he is being hunted by a Banshee."

Father Reichmann nodded as the Guard rolled his eyes and pointed to his head.

"I'll let you in, but, I think you'll not find a great deal of coherence in there..." He let the words hang in the air as he drew back the thick steel bolt and swung the door open.

"No, no, no!" A pathetic voice squealed in the darkness.

The guard switched on a light and the Priests were greeted with the sight of a man of around 300 pounds in weight squatting on the cell bed hiding his head under his arms.

"It's them. They've come for me." He screamed.

"It's her, she's in disguise. She's going to kill me like all the rest. Don't leave me Officer. Don't leave me!"

Father Reichmann turned to the guard and nodded.

"He'll be OK in a minute. Just let him calm down a bit."

The guard shrugged, nodded, turned and left the cell. The ominous clang of the bolt being drawn echoed in the close confines of the bare cell.

"Listen to me, Your Grace, you are quite, quite safe." Father Reichmann whispered reassuringly.

"We are here to protect you, to help you."

The Fat man turned away from the Priests, his head still totally hidden.

"I know who you are. You're the Banshee Aoibheall. You've come for me. You've killed the rest now you want me. She comes into my

100

dreams. She invades my head. She is all in black like death himself. She has these eyes................."

Father Reichmann sighed heavily.

"You will stop this nonsense immediately, Herr Bishop. I am a Roman Catholic Priest, not a creature from a Child's storybook. Pull yourself together immediately!"

He shouted, his German accent emerging clearly as his anger overtook him.

Bishop O'Leary turned slowly. His eyes peered out from under his chubby hands.

"You're not her?" He whimpered pathetically as he slowly dropped his arms and faced the two Priests.

"No, I assure you, Your Grace, that I have never been a female, nor a fairy, either good or bad." Father Reichmann stated calmly.

Father Doyle tried to suppress a laugh, which emerged as a snort. He covered his mouth and turned away from the Bishop who now sat forlornly on his bed, his forehead covered in beads of sweat.

"Are you...are you with the "Order?"" He whispered tremulously, his eyes still wide with terror, flicked from Priest to Priest and then to the door, then back to the Priests. Before Father Reichmann had a chance to answer. The Bishop stood and with an agility that belied his weight sprang to the door and tried to peer through the slot.

"If you're with the "Order" then we're all in danger. She's killing us all."

"This Banshee?" Father Reichmann suggested sceptically.

"Yes, she's working with "God's assassin." They're killing all the "Order" and then they'll kill the child."

He turned to Reichmann and grabbed him by the shoulders.

"He's here. Our Lord is here. He walks among us again. They don't want that, they want him dead. Then we'll all be damned. There'll be no salvation for anyone. Just darkness, eternal damnation and darkness."

His voice got higher and his words came faster as panic overtook him.

Father Reichmann calmly pulled the Bishops hands off his shoulders.

"We are not with "The Sacred Order of Saint Gregory," your Grace. I am here on behalf of Cardinal Warzowski, the Head of internal investigations in the Vatican." His voice dropped to a whisper.

"I am investigating the suspicious deaths of several of your colleagues and acquaintances in this "Sacred Order of St. Gregory.""

Bishop O'Leary stepped back towards his bed and crossed himself; then he dropped to his knees and began to pray in Latin. After several moments, with a sigh he climbed back onto his feet and sat on his bed, breathing deeply, his eyes closed.

"Can I ask you some questions, Your Grace?" Reichmann asked. His voice was back in its usual quiet tone, totally devoid of accent.

The Bishop opened his eyes.

"Cardinal Warzowski?" He repeated. Reichmann nodded.

"Internal investigations?"

Reichmann nodded again.

Bishop O'Leary blew out a sigh of relief.

"Of course, Father." He stated as he slowly regained his composure.

Father Reichmann sat on the bed next to the Bishop, while Father Doyle leaned against the cell door.

"Tell me about the incident at Finaan, seven years ago."

Father Reichmann asked gently.

"It would appear that all the unfortunate events we are now seeing, seem related in some way to that particular incident."

Bishop O'Leary shrugged.

"I've spoken about those dreadful accidents, so often…………."

Father Reichmann reached into his bag and took out a Bible.

"I do not have time to waste, Your Grace. You will swear on this Bible to tell me the whole truth and nothing but the truth. I know all about Pizarro and the mission to kill the last demon, or whatever it was. I want to know what really happened, who this demon was, not the lies that have been told previously. If we are to stop these killings and protect this child that his Eminence, Cardinal D'Abruzzo believed to be the second coming of Our Lord, then we must act now."

His voice had once again gained a Germanic accent, which made his words sound all the more threatening. The Bishop's eyes grew round again.

"Y,y,yes, of course." He stammered, then took a deep breath.

"We thought we had eliminated all of the demons in Ireland, years ago."

"What form did these demons take?" Reichmann interrupted.

The Bishop shrugged.

"Here in Ireland, there is a legend, a tradition that a mighty race of beautiful and terrible immortals once lived here, long before the word of Our Lord was brought to these shores, by the Blessed Saint Patrick. This race was called the "Tuatha de Danaan" meaning the tribes, or people of Dana. We do not know what Dana was, a Goddess? A country? Anyway, where was I? Ah yes, these people were eventually superseded by other invaders, the Celts and so on, so, it is said, they took refuge in barrows and deep underground. In effect they became the little people of Irish folklore: the sidh, or fairy-folk."

Bishop O'Leary paused momentarily. He looked up to see if the German Priest and his young Irish colleague were listening, or whether they were just staring at his ramblings. They both appeared to be listening intently. Father Doyle was nodding knowingly.

"Please continue." Father Reichmann whispered.

The Bishop smiled weakly.

"I was asked to join the "Order" by Bishop Donleavy long before I was sent to Knock. He was a good man." For a moment the Bishop lost his thread and he looked haunted again. Then, just as quickly, he continued.

"At first I thought the sidh were just the stuff of legend. Then I was shown things. I saw things that science couldn't explain. I was shown the true nature of evil."

Father Reichmann raised his eyebrows.

The Bishop grinned manically.

"I once saw an old woman turn into a cat, right before my eyes. It didn't do her any good. We burnt the witch alive in her cottage." He chuckled gleefully, his many chins wobbled uncontrollably.

Father Doyle coughed but Reichmann merely glanced, his eyes admonishing his young colleague.

"Please continue your Grace, please tell me about Finaan."

Bishop O'Leary glowered at Father Doyle.

"You may think I'm mad young man, but I know what I saw. The sidh really did exist. Even so, we thought we had killed them all by the end of the Sixties. Then one day in 1974, a young Priest brought to my notice a creature calling himself Mickey Finn, living in the hills of County Mayo, who brazenly claimed to be one of the little people. I told His Grace Bishop Donleavy and after quizzing this young Priest, a Father Malone of Finaan and at the advice of Father Burke, a great operative with years of service in the "Order," we called in the "Order's" chief rat-catcher: Fr Francisco Pizarro."

The Bishop coughed.

"I must have a glass of water if I am to continue." He gasped.

Reichmann nodded at Doyle who banged on the door. Moments later the Bishop had a glass of water, which he sipped sparingly. Then he took a deep breath and continued:

"Pizarro confirmed after a brief reconnaissance mission, that this Finn was a indeed a sidh. He went ahead and planned the mission, he had killed many demons in his time and as far as I can tell this should have been a straightforward kill. I don't know all the details of what happened that night, but things began to go wrong even before Pizarro set out to destroy Finn. Poor Father Callaghan, who had briefly served the "Order" years earlier, committed suicide the night before the operation. I presume he must have lost his nerve.

The operation went ahead anyway. I really do not know what went wrong. The creature's cottage was destroyed, burned to the ground, so we must presume that he was killed. I am certain Pizarro did not fail. Pizarro himself was never seen again and poor Father Burke was found dead in the wreckage of his car nearby. It appears he had been speeding away from the cottage. Father Malone also disappeared for a few years..."

Father Reichmann, whose face had been a mask of concentration suddenly snapped into life:

"You mean he didn't kill himself? His clothes were found on a riverbank, the day after the cottage burning. The church still believes him to be dead."

Bishop O'Leary smiled, a thin humourless smug smile.

"Oh he is dead now. The Banshee saw to that two years ago when we eliminated Finn's half breed offspring."

Father Reichmann prompted the Bishop to continue.

"Oh yes, we found out that the dark magic was still being used. There was no hiding place from the "Order." We called in Pizarro's successor: Father Pierre de Feren to hunt down the one who was using magic. He was a fool. He thought he could fight fire with fire. He tried to use a "tame" Banshee to find whoever wielded the magic, which she did, but then she absconded from his care."

"What about this Fr Malone?" Reichmann asked, slightly impatiently.

The Bishop shrugged.

"The fool came back to Ireland. He'd been hiding in America. We caught him of course. No one escapes the "Order." He was brought to my office. Father De Feren, His Grace Bishop Donleavy and I all tried to persuade him to tell us what he knew about the events at Finn's cottage, but he wouldn't talk. De Feren used Aoibheall, the Banshee to search his mind and find out what he knew. That's when we found out about the boy, Finn's son.

Once Aoibheall has been in your mind there isn't much left. His body was thrown in the Liffey."

Father Doyle gasped.

"You murdered a Priest?"

Reichmann turned and put a single finger to his lips.

"It was for the greater good." O'Leary blurted.

"We couldn't allow "God's assassin" to grow up and kill Our Lord. We had to defy the prophecy."

"Prophecy?" Father Reichmann asked raising his eyebrows.

O'Leary nodded eagerly and began to recite the prophecy like a schoolboy facing a test:

"A child no mortal man shall sire
By mother's blood Royal line acquire,
Shall suckle he no milk white breast,
Shall rise in exile, unwelcome guest,
Shall learn to change his form at will
His shape, his face, his ways to kill
Unseen, unheard, his telling blow,
His doom to lay The Messiah low"

Father Reichmann nodded.

"Yes, I've heard that before. So, what happened to the boy?" He asked as he rubbed his forehead. He was getting quite a headache.

"De Feren burnt him alive in his hovel, the way we always deal with such vermin."

The Bishop shrugged.

"Now we need to find Aoibhell and to kill her before she eliminates the rest of the "Order.""

Father Reichmann pursed his lips.

"Exactly what did happen at St Patrick's, the day His Grace, Bishop Donleavy died."

The Bishop shrugged again.

"You know as much as I do, Father. I must have taken a blow to the head when De Feren burst into Bishop Donleavy's office. He must have used a grenade. The good Bishop's door was blown to smithereens."

Father Reichmann rubbed his temples:

"You say this Banshee can strip minds? Do you not think she may have been involved with De Feren and might have betrayed him then? After all, the murder of His Grace was the start of the current series of unusual deaths of members of the "Order." She might have stripped your mind of the day's events."

Bishop O'Leary's eyes opened as wide as saucers.

"I never thought of that, Father. Yes, yes you're right. That would explain everything. De Feren must have lied about her absconding. I saw how he looked at her. I saw the naked lust in his eyes. He must have been seduced by her. She must have used him to get to us, to attack us in the heart of our own church. Yes, now it all makes sense. Then she must have betrayed him and set him on fire, maybe he saw the error of his ways and she decided to rid herself of him. Witnesses said he was on fire when he ran out of the cathedral onto the road and under the bus."

Father Reichmann nodded.

"So as far as you are concerned, Your Grace. We must find this Banshee if we want to stop the "Order" from being wiped out and then much, much worse?"

The Bishops head wobbled as he nodded his agreement.

"Yes, it is imperative that we find her and eliminate her as absolutely as soon as possible."

Father Reichmann stood.

"Will you come with us, Your Grace? I am sure the Guards would not mind you leaving."

Bishop O'Leary blanched.

"No, no. I will not leave this cell. She could be just out there, waiting to finish me off. I will leave here when she is dead."

As he was speaking he was climbing back on to the bed.

"Just keep her away from me."

Father Reichmann grimaced.

"I think that's enough for today." He stated cheerfully.

"I think I now have a fair idea of what happened at Finaan and in St Patrick's Cathedral, your Grace. Thank you for all your help." He kissed the Bishop's hand and waited for Father Doyle to do the same.

O'Leary grinned at the two Priests:

"Make sure you find the Banshee, but do not forget she is very, very dangerous."

Fathers Reichmann and Doyle agreed that they would.

Father Doyle knocked on the cell door and a guard let the two Priests out:

"Will you not be taking him?" The Guard asked Father Reichmann.

The old Priest shook his head.

"He feels safer in your care." He rolled his eyes.

"Not quite a full shilling, as they say."

The Guard laughed.

"So, what do you think?" Father Doyle asked as the pair left the garda station.

"As mad as mad can be." Reichmann's response was quick and honest, but then he shocked young father Doyle.

"Yet, there is an awful lot of truth in what he has told us. I do not believe in fairies, personally, but that is not to say categorically that they do not exist. What shocked me was that Father Malone did not perish all those years ago, but was murdered in cold blood by men of the cloth, so recently."

Father Doyle grinned.

"Ah well, I might be having some good news for you there, Father."

Father Reichmann peered at his young colleague quizzically.

Father Doyle looked around the street carefully to make sure he could not be overheard then leaned towards the older Priest and whispered.

"I met Father Malone's mother's Priest yesterday."

Father Reichmann almost burst.

"Yes...and?"

Father Doyle smirked.

"I didn't want to say anything in there to contradict His Grace but..."

"But what?" Father Reichmann interrupted impatiently.

The young Priest looked around again, enjoying the old Priest's annoyance.

"I really had to dig deep and make promises and swear on the Bible and all that but...."

Father Reichmann did explode this time.

"For the sake of Our Blessed Lady Declan, will you bloody well tell me what you know?"

Father Doyle laughed.

"You better keep your passport handy Father. Father James Malone is alive and well and living incognito in California."

Sixteen

Terri Thorne was furious. Worried, yes, concerned, yes, upset, yes; but most of all, she was furious. She had tried to ring Dean at least five times since she had received the call from Aurelio. He wasn't answering his private number, the general line to his office had either dialled out, or on her last call some lackey had promised to get him to call back. That had been twenty minutes earlier and she still hadn't heard a thing.

Once again his phone went straight on to his answering machine message. Terri swore and slammed the receiver down in annoyance.

For goodness sake, Aurelio had sounded absolutely grief stricken. The news that his beautiful new wife had committed suicide had obviously come as a great shock and he needed his cousin to support him in such a time of crisis. Terri made up her mind, she would have to go to his office, get past his over protective staff and drag him out of whatever meeting he was hiding in. She asked Conchita if she would mind looking after the children for an hour or so and then jumped into her silver Porsche 924 and drove off up the Coldwater Canyon road towards Mulholland Drive and then on to Dean's office in North Hollywood.

The traffic was surprisingly light and once she had got past the section where she had been forced to do five quick "California stops," the drive became totally enjoyable.

Terri loved her babies but she had to admit that she had almost forgotten how much she enjoyed the freedom of just driving through the Santa Monica Mountains in the glorious sunshine. By the time she pulled in to the parking lot she had quite forgotten her bad mood and by the time she got to Dean's office she was actually singing the old Eagles hit "Hotel California."

"No Ma'am. He is not here." Earl, the African American security man at the reception desk repeated.

"You don't have to lie, Earl. I know he's here and he just doesn't want to be disturbed." Terri insisted forcefully.

Earl shook his head.

"I ain't lyin' Miss Vitalia Ma'am. He ain't been in the office since half past eight this morning. Said he had an important meeting down on Sunset. Look, I've called Suzi down to tell you."

Earl pointed at the elevator door, which had just opened to reveal Suzi, Dean's altogether far too gorgeous to be real, blonde secretary.

"Hi! Mrs Vitalia. " Suzi stated mechanically as she slinked seductively across the marble floor, her high heels clicking and echoing noisily in the cool, cavernous lobby. She was chewing gum in that slow bovine like way that suggested total disinterest in anyone, or anything.

Terri wondered if she was actually any good at performing any of her secretarial duties.

Her unnatural, pneumatic cleavage was certainly an impressive sight. No wonder Dean had employed her.

Suzi stopped right in front of her boss' wife and raised one solitary sceptical eyebrow.

"Didn't Dean tell you he was going to be out interviewing today? Mrs Vitalia."

Her voice suggested that she was bored in her role as a secretary and that she was merely passing time until she got that first big break on the silver screen. Terri wondered what Dean had promised her?

Terri shook her head.

"No! No, he didn't." She sighed.

"Look, Suzi this is really important."

Terri insisted; her mannerisms becoming increasingly frantic.

"Dean's cousin's wife has just committed suicide out east. Are you sure he's not in one of his "do not disturb" meetings, upstairs?"

Suzi shrugged.

"No, really, I mean, I know he's out, Mrs Vitalia."

Terri groaned.

"Oh well, if he comes back, tell him to call me. If you could just let him know that it's real important, ok?"

Suzi almost smiled:

"Sure, I'll let him know, Mrs Vitalia."

Terri turned with a grimace. She couldn't help but notice poor Earl's eyes almost popping out of his head as Suzi strutted her way back to the elevator in her very tight, knee length pencil skirt.

"Bet she can't even type; let alone do shorthand." Terri grumbled under her breath.

Her mood had definitely deteriorated by the time she drove back out onto the Hollywood Freeway. She had decided to head home via Sunset Boulevard and to take the Santa Monica Boulevard all the way back to Beverley Hills.

Despite the radio, the sun shining and the palm trees swaying, Terri couldn't recreate the exhilarating feeling of freedom that she had experienced on the way to Dean's office. Instead she felt positively angry again by the time she stopped at the traffic lights at the head of Highland Avenue. For some reason, as she waited for the lights to change, she had happened to glance into the parking lot of the Hollywood Highlands Motel. The blood froze in her veins. Dean's Black Porsche 911 was parked in a bay by one of the rooms, its familiar polished metal gleaming in the California sun.

At first Terri jumped to the conclusion that the Porsche must just have been a similar model and once the lights had changed she drove on for a few blocks regardless. Black Porsches are ten a penny in Beverley Hills, she thought to herself as she shrugged and concentrated on the road ahead. A nagging doubt, lurking in the back of her mind, however, began to chip away the foundations of her certainty and within a couple of miles she had convinced herself that the only way to eliminate any lingering suspicion would be to go back and check. She indicated and swung left, using the L.A. grid system to drive back to the motel. This time she drove directly into the parking lot and checked the Porsche's registration plate. It was definitely Dean's. Terri's knuckles whitened as she gripped the steering wheel of her car. What was Dean doing in a motel in the middle of the day? Terri took a deep breath. There could be a multitude of reasonable explanations, she thought to herself, but the same doubt that had brought her back to the motel continued to gnaw at her optimism. Terri winced as she climbed out of the cool of her air-conditioned sports car into the intense heat of the day. She walked to the reception building as slowly as someone walking to the execution chamber.

Dean had always cheated on her, she knew that. It was the cheapness of the situation that really annoyed her.

A low grade motel? In the middle of the day? How could he?

Before she knew it she was stood at the desk, without a clue what she was going to say or do. She felt such an idiot as she stood there opening and closing her mouth like a goldfish in a bowl.

"Can I help you Ma'am?" An acne-ridden teenager asked her eventually through a mouthful of gum. Terri closed her eyes:

"Er............I'm looking for a Mr.Vitalia." She stated more confidently than she had believed possible.

The teenager took a couple of minutes to scan the register.

"Nope...no Mr.Vitalia has checked in, today, yet." She mumbled over her constant mastication.

Terri pointed outside into the parking lot.

"The black Porsche, do you know who that belongs too?"

The teenager shrugged.

"I think it's the couple in number four." She suggested as she peered at the car.

"That's the room on the first floor above that bay. Mr and Mrs Smith, if I remember correctly."

Terri smiled sweetly.

"How original, thankyou."

She walked out of the reception and cut through a bare stone archway, past a soft-drink machine and an ice-box.

A concrete staircase led up to the first floor. She strolled up to room four and, ignoring the "Do Not Disturb" card hanging on the door handle, knocked firmly on the plain blue door.

"Room Serveece!" She called in her best Mexican accent.

Nothing happened for several seconds, then abruptly the door was opened by a man, wearing nothing but a towel wrapped round his waist.

"God-dammit can't you............"

Dean Vitalia's eyes rolled back in his head as he let out a deep long sigh that tacitly acknowledged the game was up.

"Oh that's just great." He muttered under his breath.

Terri's mouth went dry as she peered into the gloom of the fully draped bedroom. A blonde girl was sat up in bed, holding a sheet up over her chest to hide her naked body.

"Hi honey!" Dean suggested ironically. "Didn't really expect to see you here."

Terri shook her head.

"Obviously." She whispered quietly.

"How did you...?"

Dean began, but Terri had already turned away and was marching briskly off along the landing, leaving her husband to watch her disappear down the stairs and out into the parking lot.

"Who the hell was that?" The blonde girl asked.

Dean shook his head as he pulled off the towel and started to climb back into bed.

"Room service, I guess." He shrugged nonchalantly. "She didn't see the sign. Anyway where were we?"

Terri Thorne drove home very slowly indeed. Her eyes were too misted to see the road ahead clearly, but she refused to stop, just as she was refusing to cry.

So Dean was a no good two timing rat. That wasn't news. What was new was that she'd actually caught him in the act as it were. This time she couldn't sweep it under the carpet like she'd always done before, nor could he.

As soon as she got home Terri packed a bag for herself and had Conchita pack one for each of the children. Within an hour the huge electric gates were swinging open again and the silver Porsche 924 was crunching off the gravel onto the smooth hot tar of Coldwater Canyon Boulevard. Terri Thorne didn't really know where she was going, but that didn't really matter. She had no more than twenty bucks in her purse, but she did have the two good things that Dean had given her in their few short years together, Marco and Marina and at that moment, that was all that mattered to her.

Seventeen

Wayne Higginbotham didn't have the dream again for many weeks. For one thing, he was too busy settling into the life of a University of Manchester fresher and by the time he got to bed he was too tired to dream. The other thing was that he was desperate to have the dream again and dreams never happen when you want them to.

He had rehearsed his lines over and over and over again, so he was convinced he would remember them in the dream. He would wait until the faceless black figure insulted him, calling him an insignificant whelp, or whatever, then he would launch into an attack, saying that he knew who the black robed figure was and that it was he who was no more than a whelp, indeed, he was no more than a snotty nosed kid. Not only that, but Wayne would say that he knew where the kid lived and was just biding his time before he would fulfil his prophesied destiny, by destroying the little squirt. So of course, the dream didn't happen.

Weeks turned into months and it seemed like no more than five minutes after he had started student life, that the first term was over and Wayne was packing to go home for Christmas.

The thought of going back to live with Doris in Shepton didn't please Wayne one little bit. During those first ten weeks Wayne had more than enjoyed that first heady taste of freedom and independence that University life had given him, even if the formal Hall of Residence that he had chosen, with the only other Wormysted's boy to go to Manchester, John Lancaster, had been a disappointment.

Wilton Hall had been designed to cater for students who had attended posh, single-sex boarding schools and was just like everything Wayne had ever heard about public schools: Plummy boys, formal dinners, wearing collar, tie and gowns, spoon banging and frequent bouts of food fighting. That bit had been so immature.

Despite Wilton Hall, Wayne had John had made the most of the big city life and had been out almost every night, attending concerts in town, or at the University student union. Frequenting pubs and student bars and going to loads of new wave discos. The good thing about Wilton Hall was the fact that everyone had a private room and security wasn't that strict, so sneaking girls in wasn't too difficult. By the end of that first term, Wayne had had more than one "girlfriend."

The other good thing about University was the diversity of the student population. Wayne made quite a number of friends from all over the country, different ages, different sexes, different races and colours. As far as Wayne was concerned, it was the real world he was living in now, free of the shackles of small town routine and the cosseting, monasticly mundane Grammar school.

Even the work hadn't been too arduous. It certainly hadn't got in the way of Wayne's social life. Wayne was reading for a degree in History and Politics. He had always loved history at Wormysted's and had been reasonably good at it. At University, however, the study of history was a revelation. It wasn't just reading textbooks and regurgitating the narrative in different words as an essay. It was about doing real research, scouring libraries for source material, arguing points in tutorials and listening to differing views and opinions in lectures. There were no right and wrong answers, just different interpretations of events. As for the Politics option, which Wayne had been offered as a subsidiary subject, that was just as inspiring. The study of Marx and Engels, Thomas Payne, J.S.Mills and Thomas Hobbes fired Wayne's imagination. By the end of term he was telling anyone who would listen, that he was now a committed Utopian Socialist.

The Wayne Higginbotham that climbed into John Lancaster's little Fiat car for the drive back over the Pennines to Shepton was quite a different character to the boy who had left the small Yorkshire market town just ten weeks earlier. The changes ran far deeper than the black leather biker's jacket with the evocative white lapels that he had blown half his student grant cheque on. They were deeper than the long dyed-black corkscrew hair that covered his large pointed ears and the copious amounts of eyeliner that now seemed to permanently surround his eyes.

Mrs Elizabeth Ball, Wayne's mentor at Gas Street Primary School, the lady who had galvanised the search for the younger Wayne when he had run away to London and then on to Ireland, would certainly not have recognised the youth, who, after saying his farewells to John, despondently trudged up the path to 49 Greenwood Avenue, his hold-all slung over his shoulder. She would have remembered a shy, incredibly polite boy. Doris' strict disciplinary regime had produced an individual who had known his place and would not have dared transgress any boundaries.

The discovery of his magical heritage and his prescribed destiny had given Wayne some degree of confidence, but while he had lived under Doris' roof that had always been suppressed. Life at Wormysted's Grammar School had also been extremely regimented. Discipline had been very strict under the watchful eye of the fearsome Dai Davies and Wayne had always been terrified of getting into trouble. He knew that not only would he have to face the terrifying Welshman if he ever broke the rules, but also Doris when he got home.

The one and only time that he had done something that would have led to at least a detention, he had used his magical powers to disappear. That had been the time when he had sneaked into the Chemistry lab with Dino Giardano to get enough sulphur to make a small number of stink bombs. Dai Davies had caught poor Dino, but Wayne had walked straight out of the lab, as invisible as the air he was breathing. Wayne Higginbotham's entire school career therefore, had passed without a single disciplinary blemish on it.

Wayne's individuality had never really been allowed, or indeed encouraged to blossom in the confines of Shepton. Going off to University had provided that liberation. Wayne had blossomed. He had allowed the confidence that emanated from the feeling of being special, a chosen one, to flourish and he had not had to use his magical prowess once.

The Wayne Higginbotham who opened the door of 49 Greenwood Avenue and shouted:

"Hi mum, I'm home," now oozed confidence and a mature self-assurance. What Wayne had yet to learn was that confidence could sometimes be interpreted as arrogance.

It was later that first night home that Wayne's new-found self confidence first manifested itself. He had already had two rows with Doris since his arrival back at Greenwood Avenue. The first had been about his lack of visits home and phone calls since his departure for Manchester way back in October. Wayne had simply shrugged and promised to ring more.

The second row had been about the fact that he had intended to go out to the pub on his first night home. Wayne had ignored Doris' protests and had gone out anyway, his self-justification that he needed to catch up with what had been going on in Shepton since he had left.

By the time Wayne staggered home, Doris had already gone to bed in a foul mood.

"At least that spares me any more of her rants." Wayne thought contentedly as he stumbled up the stairs as quietly as he could manage. He knew Doris was awake, he could imagine her sitting up in her bed with her arms crossed over her ample bosom, her false teeth out and her fiercest scowl on. He couldn't help stifling a giggle as he sneaked past her bedroom door.

"Shhh" he whispered to himself in the darkness as he opened his bedroom door, which let out an annoying squeak. He closed the door behind him and let out a huge sigh of relief:

"Ahh, my own bed at last." He grunted as he began to carelessly disrobe. The last thing he had wanted, as the room began to spin slightly before his eyes, was for his bedroom to fill with a familiar, albeit now rare, green mist.

"Hi Dad." He slurred as the spectral figure of Aillen Mac Fionnbharr strode through the mist and materialised in Wayne's bedroom.

"You are drunk, my son." The ghost stated, its voice laced with disappointment and a level of disgust.

"It is not seemly for a warrior to drink to excess, unless he has faced his mortal enemy in battle and vanquished him, or to soothe the nerves before battle."

Wayne shrugged.

"Look dad, I'm a student, not a warrior." He responded, his voice slurring the words as he struggled to get undressed.

Aillen frowned. "You are more than just a warrior, my son. You are the "Slanaitheoir mor.""

Wayne nodded: "Yeah, yeah, I know."

Aillen sighed.

"I have good news for you. The High Council have agreed to furnish you with three of the magical treasures of the Tuatha de Danaan. No warrior could wish for more.........."

Aillen's voice trailed off as he glanced at Wayne's wall and noticed the poster, depicting a female tennis player scratching her naked bottom.

"By the beards of the Celts, she has no shame."

Wayne grinned at his father's reaction to his poster.

"Cool isn't it. I got it at the Athena store in Manchester. I've got one on my wall there too."

Aillen shook his head and turned back to his son.

"What are your plans for the despatch of the demon? Would you like to hear about the mighty treasures of our people and how you might use them?"

Wayne pulled back his bed covers.

"Yeah, I'd love to know about these treasures, dad, but I'm a little bit drunk right now and very, very tired, so if you don't mind?"

He climbed under his covers and was asleep before his head hit the pillow.

Aillen Mac Fionnbharr was furious.

"Never have I been treated with such disrespect. We shall discuss this night tomorrow, my son!"

With that he turned angrily and disappeared into the mist, which evaporated almost instantly.

Wayne spent most of the next day studiously avoiding Doris and the million questions she seemed to have prepared for him.

"So what do you eat at University?"

"Who are your friends?"

"How are your lessons?"

"What are the teachers like?"

"Are you washing your hair often enough?"

"Are you changing your underpants?"

"Have you got a girlfriend yet?"

"Mum, for Gods's sake!" was his despairing response to most of Doris' questions, which only seemed to serve in further firing her curiosity.

Once again, by the time the evening came around, Wayne was desperate to seek the sanctuary of the pub. To his horror, however, when the time came for him to announce his departure, he found that his wallet was completely empty.

The thought of asking Doris for a loan was unthinkable. Doris would happily have lent him some money, but he would never have heard the last of it and the leverage that she would take from such a situation was just not worth the hassle. He would have to visit the bank the next day, but as the banks were now closed, he could not afford to go out. Wayne was trapped in the house with Doris for an entire evening.

"So, do you have a shower everyday at that college?" Doris asked him as he sat on the sofa in the small living room reading a battered copy of "Das Kapital."

Wayne sighed and looked up at her, his eyebrows arched in annoyance.

"No!" He whispered, before immediately turning his attention back to his book.

Doris sniffed and turned back to the flickering television.

"You're not taking any of them drugs are you?" She suddenly demanded as the show she was watching paused for a commercial break.

"They say all students take drugs, nowadays." She continued, pursing her lips disapprovingly.

"And why have you taken to wearing make-up? You're not one of them, are you?"

Wayne slowly and deliberately closed the book.

"No, mum, I am not one of them, as you call gay people and I do not take drugs. I wear eyeliner because it's what people who like the sort of music that I like, wear. It's fashionable." He sighed.

"Anyway I have some work to do for next term, you know, some research. So I'm going up to my room to read this." He brandished the battered book.

"I'll see you later." He muttered as he stood and stalked off up the stairwell.

Doris shrugged her shoulders.

"Aye well, that's what happens when they go to these posh places. They get too big for their boots." She moaned as some underdressed girl standing in a field, suggestively bit into a cylindrical chocolate bar on the screen in front of her.

Almost as soon as Wayne entered his room, the green mist began to swirl by the window.

Wayne heaved a heavy sigh. He knew that Aillen MacFionnbharr was not going to be a happy bunny after the previous evening's events. Sure enough, as soon as his spectral form began to take shape in the mist, Aillen's face was a mask of fury.

"Am I permitted an audience with the celebrated "Slanaitheoir mor" this evening, or is he perhaps too tired? Or ale blathered, to take my counsel?" Wayne's father hissed sarcastically as he stepped into the room.

"Er, I don't suppose an apology would suffice." Wayne suggested with a half-hearted smile.

Aillen grimaced.

"I have never been as disappointed in anyone, as I was with you last night, my son. Your insult would once have caused you to be dismissed from my sight and banished from the Court of the Tuatha de Danaan for many years."

Wayne nodded despondently.

"I know, I'm sorry."

Aillen stroked his chin and the merest hint of a smile creased his lips.

"It is fortuitous for you that you are so important, my son."

Wayne nodded sheepishly.

"Now, to business." Aillen declared with an imperious wave of his arm.

"As I said yesterday, the The High Counsel of the Tuatha have agreed to furnish you with three of the four great magical treasures of the Tuatha. The great and mighty Lugh has agreed that you shall be allowed to bear the great spear of Finias; that he threw in anger in the days of his youth. Once thrown this spear never misses its target. The wondrous and celebrated Nuada of the silver hand, the first king of our people to step onto the island of Erin, has agreed that you may bear the sword of Gorias. The sword that once unsheathed renders the warrior who bears it invincible. And all are agreed that you should have the whole stone of Falias, most of which you already have in your possession."

With that Aillen reached into his robes and brought out several small grey rocks, which he handed to Wayne.

"It is our belief that the last pieces of the stone lay in Rome, in the hands of the cursed "Sacred Order of Saint Gregory." You must go there and find them."

Wayne raised his eyebrows sceptically.

"Oh that shouldn't be too much trouble then. Step into the lion's den and whip one of its teeth out."

Aillen frowned.

"First you will find the sword and the spear; that will render even the "Order" powerless against you. You must act fast, while the demon is still a child. Go to Rome, get the last shards of the stone and then kill the child."

Wayne sat dejectedly on his bed and held up his hands.

"Dad, look, with all due respect, this is 1981. You can't just waltz off to Rome on British Airways with a bloody great sword and a spear. Anyway, what do you mean: find? Have you not got them there?"

Aillen's frown intensified.

"We know where they are. You will have to get them as soon as you can. As for getting to Rome, there must be alternatives to flying? What about the train?"

Wayne shrugged.

"Trains are expensive. I've passed my driving test but I don't have a car, and I wouldn't even make it onto a coach carrying weapons. Anyway, the demon you're going on about isn't in Rome."

Aillen frowned. "You have my treasure, you can not be poor."

Wayne shrugged. "It's not about being poor. I have planned my finances carefully and going off to Rome would cost a bomb, plus it's Christmas."

Aillen's eyes grew wide and his mouth dropped open in amazement.

"You're not frightened, are you?" He gasped.

Wayne snorted, "what? Of a snotty nosed seven year old? I've met him and he's such a kid. It wouldn't be right to kill a kid."

Aillen's mouth dropped even more open.

"You have met the demon?"

Wayne grinned, it was the first time he had ever seen his father less than totally and completely assured.

"I met him the last time I was in L.A."

Aillen shook his head in disbelief.

"What? How do you know this?"

Now it was Wayne's turn to frown. He looked vaguely in the direction of his bedroom window:

"For ages I've been having this dream. This figure would approach me. It was dressed entirely in black yet it didn't seem to have any face, you know, any features at all. What it did have were eyes; horrible, cold, dead eyes. Eyes that burn into me, you know, that like can see right through me. It would taunt me about being weak and a whelp and so on. Then when I was in L.A., my mother's slimy husband introduced me to his cousin and his cousin's new stepson. It was definitely him. The eyes were the same and trust me, I'd recognise those eyes anywhere."

Aillen rubbed his chin thoughtfully:

"Did he recognise you? Did he know who you were?"

Wayne shook his head.

"No, I don't think so, anyway. I think he got distracted. The moment I met him though, I could feel his eyes burning right into mine, just like in the dreams, even for the few seconds he was looking at me. Oh yeah, I ought to tell you. My stepfather's cousin met his new wife in…"

Wayne paused for dramatic effect:

"Rome!"

Aillen put his hands on his hips and started to laugh.

"By all the Gods! My beloved Theresa has gone and married into the family of the guardian of the darkest denizens of hell itself."

Wayne scowled.

"Do you think she's in danger?"

Aillen stroked his chin again.

"Of course she is in danger. If the demon has chosen this family to raise him to physical maturity then they must be as evil as any family that has ever existed. Yet, it is the demon that is in the greatest danger as long as he did not recognise you. By the grace of outrageous good fortune, the most difficult part of our task has already been achieved. We know who the demon is and where he is. We only need to gather our tools and we can eliminate him before he gets old enough to do any damage."

Wayne grimaced again.

120

"By we, you mean me! And how am I supposed to get these "tools" on a plane? Have you thought about that one yet? And where exactly are this sword of Numpty and the spear of Lugs?"

Aillen stopped chuckling.

"The sword of Nuada and the spear of Lugh are both in Ireland. You must go, tomorrow. I will guide you."

Wayne shook his head.

"No, I'm sorry Dad. I can't."

Aillen looked perplexed:

"What do you mean?"

Wayne sighed heavily and slumped on to his bed. He turned his head to stare out at the slate grey Yorkshire sky.

"Father, I can't go anywhere. My mum, Doris, will go insane if I go off again. It was bad enough at the end of the summer holidays when I went off to the States."

Wayne turned back towards Aillen.

"Anyway, like I said, it's Christmas in a couple of days."

Aillen closed his eyes. His head dropped.

"My son! We have such a chance now to nip this evil in the bud. Such an opportunity may not arise again."

He whispered sadly.

Wayne shrugged, stood and leaned his elbows on the windowsill and cupped his chin in his hands dejectedly.

"I'll get him, don't worry about that. We need a cast iron, waterproof plan though. We need to get the weapons to the States, safely and before that we need to get me trained to use them. I am not exactly Errol Flynn, you know. Anyway, I'm going to be busy this vac, I've got three essays to write."

Aillen Mac Fionnbharr clenched his teeth.

"So the "Slanaitheoir mor" has stories to write that are more important than saving every living soul on this world. Are you sure you are not frightened? Are you sure you are a man?"

Wayne shook his head and turned back towards his father from the window.

"It's not like that and..........."

The last wisp of green mist slowly disappeared into thin air.

"Bum!" Wayne gasped and he slapped the windowsill in exasperation.

"What is it with everyone? Why does no one want to listen to what I have to say?"

He heard Doris' voice shouting up the stairs:

"Wayne, Wayne. There's sommat I need you to do."

121

Wayne rolled his eyes and bellowed that he would be down in a minute.

Would the demon invade his dreams that night he wondered?

Would he be able to deliver the speech he had practised so many times?

When it came down to it, would he ever be able to kill someone even if it was the most evil thing on earth?

Wayne Higginbotham suddenly realised that being the "Slanaitheoir mor" was not quite as easy as it had once seemed.

Eighteen

A narrow shaft of sunlight beamed into the bedroom through a gap in the heavy royal blue curtains. The ornate lace curtain behind the heavy drapes caused the sunlight to shift and shimmer playfully. A small circle of sunlight danced on the expensively decorated wall. The small boy sitting on the bed, with his knees tucked up to his chest and his arms wrapped tightly around his shins glared at the brazen beam of light and stuck his bottom lip out even further. He hated the sun, hated light, hated joy. He scowled across the room at the reflection in the mirror on his dressing table. The reflection he could see was pathetic: a small blond haired boy with bubbly curls and rosy cheeks. The boy's nostrils flared in annoyance. Here he was; the most powerful entity on the planet, trapped in the body of a mere petulant child. Why did humans take so long to grow? He had been trapped in the body of a child for nearly seven years now, imprisoned in a body that he couldn't fully control and didn't understand. The boy's body was a shell, a vehicle for an entity of unimaginable power, yet it still had the irrational emotional responses of a normal human.

Why did he still mourn the passing of the child's mother? It had been weeks since the stupid woman had blown out her brains, but he still couldn't help feeling sad. He had been so sad that he had even stopped hunting down the insects that had masqueraded as the "Sacred Order."

It annoyed him that he had felt slightly guilty when he had caused D'Abruzzo his heart attack. The Cardinal had been useful, for a while. The boy almost missed him. At least he was cultured, unlike the fat slug Vitalia, who he now called father. The boy smiled for the first time in weeks. At least there was no residue of goodness in Vitalia's heart and he was dumb, easy to manipulate and provided cast iron protection.

It had been ages since he had sought out his rival too. The last surviving offspring of the race that had once occupied the planet: the so-called Tuatha de Danaan. The boy sneered, released his legs and fell back onto his pillows. How he hated the Tuatha de Danaan. His own kind had been worshipped by primitive men, but the Tuatha had taught the primitives how to be self sufficient. Eventually primitive men had not needed the gods of dark places anymore. They had invented their own gods and goddesses and the spirits of his own race had declined and disappeared. Not him though! He had stayed around long enough to see the primitives turn on the Tuatha de Danaan, He had watched gleefully as the immortals had declined and had been hounded into the dark corners of the world, until they had to eventually cede the whole surface of the earth to the furless apes. That made him smile.

He had waited, biding his time until the chance came for him to return. He had grown powerful, more powerful than any member of his species had ever been. He had fooled the "Sacred Order" into believing that he was the pathetic Israelite pacifist that the Romans had crucified and whose followers believed that he would return. It had been so easy. For centuries he had guided the "Order," moulded them and through them eliminated the last remaining relics of the only power that could possibly stand against him. All that was left of the once high and mighty Tuatha de Danaan was one half-breed boy.

It had been easy to find him. The Tuatha existed in more than one spiritual dimension and because the boy had performed magic, his aura could be seen in the same dimension in which the powerful one existed. No features or anything, but enough to show that the last hope of the Tuatha de Danaan was no more than a whelp. He had enjoyed tormenting him. The boy smiled as he thought about their next encounter. Should he reveal his name to the whelp yet? Make him pee his pants when he found out whom he would soon have to face? No, not yet.

The limitations of the body of the human child made such a taunt too dangerous. It was, however, definitely time for him to stop mourning the bitch that bore him. This night he would hunt down the last of the "Order." Their part in his resurrection would be forgotten and their very existence expunged. The few slaves and pets that he would decide to keep when he destroyed mankind would have no knowledge of his origins, or of those that had seen him as anything less than a veritable god.

The boy climbed off his bed. Yes, he definitely felt better now. The fact that he had not been powerful enough to stop the woman killing herself was all but forgotten in the anticipation and glee that he felt at the prospect of sending another stupid Priest into the abyss. The boy took a sheet of paper from his desk and ran his finger down a list of names. His bottom lip stuck out when he realised he was down to just two potential victims. Ah yes, it was time for the fat Irish Bishop to die!

The boy grinned and fell back on his bed, the demon inside travelled through time and space and emerged in the mind of Bishop O'Leary, cowering in the corner of a cell in an Irish Garda station.

It was strange, however, for a fleeting moment the demon was hit by two serious doubts and its delight in the demise of O'Leary was tempered by two thoughts that crossed its mind.

One: the thought that it had missed a real opportunity to eliminate its enemy, yet it was totally unclear to the demon when such a moment could possibly have arisen.

Two: that the whelp might not be alone, something else had briefly emerged into the magical dimension, but had disappeared so quickly that the demon had had no chance to even remotely discern an aura.

The child awoke in the middle of the night, tears of frustration rolling down his cherubic face:

"DADDEEEEEE!" He bellowed.

Nineteen

Christmas in Los Angeles is a strange time. The weather is usually warm and pleasant, the skies blue and the scent of exotic blooms hangs in the air. Yet almost every house is richly adorned in Christmas decorations. Fairy lights twinkle conspicuously, while life-size nativity scenes are displayed in people's front yards and a million Santas cling precariously to rooftops. It was still an alien sight for James Malone. He just couldn't associate Christmas with weather that was better than any midsummer he had ever experienced in Ireland. He stared at the outlandish scenes that people had created as they tried to make balmy Southern California appear wintery and seasonal as he drove home from the college in Tarzana, where he was taking a part- time course in journalism. He rubbed his forehead. The headache was getting worse. Working on the Chatsworth Courier at the same time as studying reporting techniques was proving to be extremely taxing. He was certainly looking forward to the few days vacation he had booked over the Christmas holiday.

James' Buick scrunched on the gravel as he turned into the driveway of the house in Box Canyon. The prospect of a cup of Carrie's delicious coffee, a hug from his beautiful daughter and an advil made him sigh with relief. He climbed out of the car and stretched his aching body before grabbing his briefcase from the backseat. His relief at his arrival home was short lived. James frowned as he noticed a strange black Ford sedan parked next to Carrie's car.

"For the love of Jesus, I hope we don't have visitors." He whispered as he trudged suspiciously up to the front door and opened it with a swiftly growing feeling of dread.

Carrie was pouring a mug of coffee from a flask as he walked into the kitchen, concern etched on his still handsome features. Her eyes darted towards his, nervously.

"Hi honey." She whispered. "I thought you might need this." Carrie handed James the steaming mug.

"You bet I do!" He gasped. "Do we have any advil?"

Carrie nodded, turned and opened a cupboard.

"Who's is the?............" James started to say at exactly the same time as Carrie stated:

"You have a visitor, James."

He cocked his head to one side questioningly. Carrie nodded towards the living room and passed him a couple of small white tablets.

"He's waiting for you in there."

Her eyes were wide, concerned, maybe even afraid. James scowled, took a sip of coffee and swallowed the tablets.

"Better not keep him waiting then, had I?" He flashed his wife a reassuring grin, then turned and walked into his living room.

The black robed figure sitting on Carrie's old sofa stood abruptly.

Every single hair on the back of James Malone's neck stood up and his stomach seemed suddenly empty. The figure held out a hand.

"Ah, Father Malone I presume, we meet at last."

James took the proffered hand and shook it unenthusiastically.

"I'm Father Abraham Reichmann, James, of the Holy See. I have been looking for you for quite some time, young man."

James recognized a German accent. The Priest still pumping his hand was quite elderly and had a kind look about him which confused James.

In his heart of hearts he had always known that the "Order" would catch up with him one day. It was just that he hadn't expected it to be so soon.

The old Priest appraised the younger man with a concerned frown.

"You seem very nervous James. Don't be! I am not with the so-called "Sacred Order of Saint Gregory." Indeed as far as I am aware, that organisation has ceased to exist, since the sad passing of poor Bishop O'Leary."

Father Reichmann's mouth cracked into a benign smile.

"I am, in fact, investigating their, erm, activities over the past few years."

"Ah!" James uttered his first sound since entering the room.

"I, er…"

Malone sank slowly into his favourite armchair.

"O'Leary? He's dead?"

The old German Priest nodded sadly as he eased himself back on to the sofa.

"The poor man hanged him self in a Garda cell a few days ago, convinced to the end that a vengeful Banshee was on his trail."

James Malone whistled softly.

"Maybe he did have a soul after all."

Father Reichmann smiled grimly.

"For a Roman Catholic Priest of whatever rank, to be moved to take his own life, must mean that something very serious is happening. Yet, no less than twenty-one priests have now perished, most by their own hand, over the past seven years. The common factor is that all were members of this "Sacred Order of St.Gregory," at some point."

The Priest clapped his hands together and gave James a beaming smile.

"Of course, one of that number has miraculously come back to life, it seems, and more than once. Even Our Lord couldn't manage that."

James looked confused.

"I was told that you had committed suicide after the Finaan debacle, but had, on the contrary survived, only to become a victim of the chief suspect in all these suspicious deaths, the banshee of Bishop O'Leary's nightmares."

James grinned, ran a hand through his hair and took a deep breath.

"I very nearly was, no thanks to His Grace, our late Bishop."

Carrie carried two mugs of coffee into the room, casting a nervous glance at James as she placed the mugs on the small coffee table that was positioned between the two men.

"It's OK, honey. I don't think he's come to finish me off." James reassured her with a pat of her hand.

"Oh my, far from it, Father!" Fr Reichmann exclaimed in horror.

"Cardinal Warzowski, the head of internal investigations in the Holy See, has asked me to solve this mystery and hopefully put an end to what has become a severe embarrassment to mother church. That is why I am here James. I need to know exactly what happened all those years ago in Finaan and who, or indeed what, is behind the annihilation of the "Order." Thank you for the coffee my child." The old Priest smiled up at Carrie.

James nodded, took a deep breath and related the story of everything that happened in Finaan since he had met the strange old farmer Mickey Finn in the hills above Lough Mask over seven years earlier, being extremely careful, however, to leave out the part played by young Wayne Higginbotham.

Nearly an hour later, Father Reichmann was still sitting transfixed as James described how, five years after the events in Finaan, he had escaped the banshee's attempt to kill him in the icy waters of the River Liffey in Dublin and had fled back to California.

"So you do not know what became of this, for want of a more scientific term, banshee?" Reichmann asked resignedly.

James shook his head.

"And you know nothing about Father Pierre De Feren and the murder of His Grace Bishop Donleavy. The tragic events that occurred in Dublin, two years ago."

"No Father."

James shook his head again, but studiously avoided eye contact with the older Priest.

Father Reichmann frowned and pursed his lips.

"Father Malone. What do you know of "God's assassin?""

James grimaced and shrugged:

"Protecting Our Lord from "God's assassin" was supposedly the entire raison d'etre of the "Order." And by the way Father Reichmann, I haven't been a Priest for seven years. Please, just call me James."

Father Reichmann sighed and smiled sadly.

"Once a Priest, always a Priest, Father Malone. Only Our Lord can relieve you of that duty and obligation." He smiled again and shook his head.

"You know, the deeper I dig into this whole "Order" affair, the more confused I get. Has Our Holy Father returned to Earth? Or something else, something entirely evil?"

James shrugged again.

"Believe me, Father, I am stunned by what you have told me about the demise of the "Order." Although I will admit that I am not too sorry. The murder of innocent people in the name of whatever cause, is something I object to, very strongly indeed. You know, I think the "Order" really thought they were doing the right thing, but then, so did Hitler."

Father Reichmann nodded and smiled sadly.

"I am afraid I know only too well what you are saying. My own Father died in the concentration camp at Buchenwald. He was a good Catholic, but was caught by the Gestapo, helping Jews to escape the gas chambers. My mother herself was of Jewish stock, hence my name Abraham. She died in Auschwitz. "

James murmured his condolences.

"I'm sorry Father, I didn't mean…"

Father Reichmann held up his hand and smiled again.

"Do not worry! I know you did not mean offence. How were you to know? Yes, I agree with you. We once thought the Holy Inquisition was doing the Holy work of our Lord. We now know better. The "Order" thought they were doing God's Holy work. Yet your experience suggests less than Holy methodologies. Unfortunately, we cannot now hold them to account. There are, as far as we are aware, only two surviving members of the entire organisation now and one of them, a certain Father James Malone was a victim of the "Order" himself, missing, believed dead, at least as far as Rome is concerned."

James frowned.

"I was never in the "Order" personally, Father. I was just asked to help. No, forced to help would be a better way to put it."

The old Priest nodded.

"I understand, but be careful, Father Malone. The only other survivor is in hospital in Rome, suffering from third degree burns to most parts of his body. Whatever, or whoever it is that is eliminating the "Order" is desperate to expunge every single trace of their existence. Did I mention that the "Order's" office in the heart of the Vatican City was burned to the ground?"

James grimaced.

"No, you didn't."

The old Priest nodded, absent-mindedly.

"Mmm, everything was destroyed, of course, absolutely everything. It is as if the "Order" had never existed."

James exhaled a small whistle.

"Whew, surely there must be some other references to the "Order" in the Holy See?"

Father Reichmann twisted his mouth.

"Not a thing. They were very successful at being a secret society. Did you hear that His Eminence Cardinal D'Abruzzo also died a couple of years ago? He was the head of the organisation it seems. It is a strange business, but he died swearing that the Messiah had been reborn. He even swore on his deathbed that judgment day was soon to be upon us."

The old Priest stood up slowly and painfully.

"I have taken enough of your time, Father Malone."

He arched his back painfully.

"I am getting too old to be playing the detective, Father." He laughed.

"Just call me James, please Father." Malone insisted as he too stood up.

"Thank you for your hospitality." Father Reichmann called to Carrie in the kitchen. She smiled back at him as he walked out of the door. James followed him out onto the porch.

Christmas lights seemed to be twinkling everywhere in the warm darkness of the Californian evening. The valley below shimmered, myriads of lights, both seasonal and regular, created a carpet of light that danced joyfully as far as the eye could see. The noise of crickets was almost deafening.

Father Reichmann took a deep breath of warm musky air as his eyes shifted over the valley.

"I have seen a great deal of evil in my life, James. Things that still give me, an old man, such nightmares that sleep has become something that I abhor. I am afraid, no terrified of closing my eyes, James, for fear of the horrors that lurk in my subconscious mind."

The old man coughed then turned towards James Malone.

"Cardinal D'Abruzzo truly believed that he had seen our Lord Jesus Christ reborn, James. He was absolutely adamant that he had witnessed the second coming, the second resurrection of Our Saviour. According to the late Bishop O'Leary, Cardinal D'Abruzzo covertly raised the Holy child in the heart of the Vatican City, until the boy was five years old. If it really was the Christ child that we had in our midst, then I fear that the forces of evil may have already triumphed, for the child and his blessed mother have disappeared without trace. If that is the case, then we are all doomed, James. Darkness shall surely take us."

The old Priest touched his silver crucifix.

"Yet, old fool that I am, I still have faith."

He heaved a heavy sigh and grimaced.

"I believe the "Order" started out with honourable intentions. I knew His Eminence, the late Cardinal. He was a devout Christian, James, a good pious man. I believe that most of the "Order's" members were good Christians who truly believed that just as only fire can fight fire, only evil can truly defeat evil. Yet I now believe that they failed in their valiant attempts to destroy the dark forces of evil, James. I believe now, from what I have heard from Fr Bianca in Rome, who still clings to life by a thread and from the late Bishop O'Leary, is that somehow, by trying to use evil to combat evil, they allowed something to come into the world that has devoured those who tried to control it. I am beginning to think the late Cardinal may have been mistaken."

James nodded his agreement:

"I saw things in Finaan that I would never have believed in a million years, Father.

But I assure you that Pizarro and De Feren were two of the most evil people I have ever met. The "Order" was not exactly a gathering of Saints and angels. As for Aoibhcall the Banshee, she was not exactly an altruistic egg either, but she was not pure evil like those two. In any case, as far as I am aware and I cannot tell you how I know this, but I am certain that Aoibheall the Banshee perished two years ago. I am sure that she is not responsible for the massacre of the "Order.""

Father Reichmann smiled his sad smile, his blue eyes twinkled despite his age and the horrors he had seen.

"Then there must be someone else out there with murder in their heart. Bless you James Malone. Take care, I will pray for you."

The old man turned and disappeared into the night.

James was about to turn back into the house when he had the sudden urge to reassure the old Priest that things might not be as bleak as the old man had feared. He felt the need to tell him everything about the "Slanaitheoir mor" and Wayne Higginbotham and…….

"Father Reichmann!" He shouted.

"Wait a minute!"

He stepped onto the gravel drive area. He could see the outline of the Priest standing in the darkness by the black Ford. The sound of crickets was almost deafening.

"I will tell you this. There is someone out there who is our side. All things balance and yes, I do believe the "Order" allowed a power of unimaginable darkness into the world, but maybe God, maybe something else, I don't know, got there first. We have a powerful ally, Father. A very, very powerful ally."

He heard the old Priest laugh.

"Excellent! So you still have the true faith in Our Lord, James. You see, you are still a Priest."

The figure climbed in to the car, which, lights ablaze backed out into Box Canyon.

James Malone stood momentarily in the darkness, slapped the palm of his hand to his forehead and blew out a sigh of relief.

"Thank goodness he misunderstood me. Why did you nearly have to go and blow it all Jimmy big mouth?" He whispered into the darkness.

James Malone turned back towards the light of his kitchen, walked up the path and closed the door behind him. He was greeted by Carrie throwing herself towards him.

"What the hell was all that about? I thought he was one of those "Order" dudes here to kill us." Carrie burst into tears in James arms.

"Hey…" James soothed her, stroking the back of her head, her silky blonde hair soft to his touch.

"The "Order" can't touch me now."

Carrie pushed back and her eyes glared into his.

"What do you mean?" She whispered.

James took a deep gulp of air.

"They're all dead, every single last one of them. Well nearly!"

Carrie's eyes flicked from left to right, trying to catch anything reassuring in James eyes. "Isn't that a good thing?" She implored.

James' mouth was suddenly very dry.

"I think so, honey, I sort of hope so, but, believe it or not, I'm really not sure."

Twenty

It was the last night of the Christmas vacation and Wayne Higginbotham had decided to stay home, for once. His bags were packed and John Lancaster had arranged to collect Wayne at two pm on the Sunday afternoon for the one-hour trip over to Manchester.

Wayne wasn't being entirely altruistic in his decision not to go to "The Junction Inn" on that Saturday night. Even though he had convinced himself that he was staying in to please his adoptive mother, Doris. The sad fact was that Wayne was bored with life in Shepton again.

He had suddenly realised, on the previous Friday night, why he had been so eager to escape the small town environment that was, until recently, all he had known. It wasn't just the stifling routine of life in 49 Greenwood Avenue: Doris' incessant questioning and constant, irritating and increasingly irrelevant, inane chatter. It was the town itself. Wayne felt that he had outgrown the tedium of the usual football and girls discussions over pints of Yorkshire ale, supped in the confines of "The Junction Inn," the pub Doris used to clean on the corner of Cavendish Street.

A series of schisms seemed to have developed between the boys who had gone off to different Universities and Polytechnics and their old schoolmates who had stayed behind in the town. Once the novelty of catching up on gossip had worn off in the early heady days of the vacation and the jollity of the holiday festivities had passed. Wayne didn't seem to have much to say to his old mates and they very little to him. Entire evenings seemed to pass with the Lads simply staring into the creamy white frothy heads of their smooth pints of Yorkshire ale, muttering the occasional philosophical "Aye" and smacking their lips. This was, of course, punctuated by frequent, seismic belches and the rumble of competitive farts.

The occasional forays to "The White Horse" on the High Street on the pretext that all the fit girls in town hung out there; did nothing to alleviate the monotony. The brief flurry of excitement that Wayne had experienced one evening, when he had caught sight of Stephanie Fleming in the "White Horse" was all too quickly tempered by the sight of Martin Berenger putting his arm around her. Stephanie had been the object of all of Wayne's affections way back when he had been in the fifth form. He had used his shape shifting skills in a futile attempt to seduce her, an action that had almost got them both killed when the

"Order's" assassin Fr De Feren had attacked Wayne and the girl that Wayne had presumed to be Stephanie. Fortunately it had been the Banshee Aoibheall that had perished, not the gorgeous Miss Fleming.

Wayne's attempts to make her his girlfriend had foundered on the rocks of his own incompetence and inexperience, even in the guise of an older sophisticate and due to the fact that Stephanie was enamoured by the Oxford undergraduate, Martin Berenger. Wayne had been quite surprised to see them still together, until someone had explained that they were now no more than just old friends. Martin had graduated and was already "something in the City," while Stephanie worked in the local Building Society Head Office and was now engaged to a builder from Bradley.

Above and beyond all of that, Wayne had encountered a fair degree of animosity from the "local" lads. The unfortunate youths who had not attended Wormysted's Grammar School and subsequently gone on to get good jobs, or escape to University. The young men whose lives had been largely mapped out by their failure to pass the eleven plus and who had mostly attended St. Swithin's Secondary Modern School, leaving at sixteen to take up menial jobs and manual work.

Wayne had been the only boy in his year at Gas Street Primary School who had passed the eleven plus exam and some of his old acquaintances had made great sport out of baiting him at any opportunity. Indeed, any Wormysted's boy was considered fair game.

Wayne had always ignored such juvenile behaviour while he had been at school. Ever since his life-changing encounter with Baz Thompson when he had been eleven, Wayne had tried to avoid fights and physical violence. Not that he was frightened; it was just that Wayne knew what he was capable of. Baz Thompson had never recovered and although Wayne did not feel any sympathy for him, he did not want anyone else to end up the same way. At least five times while Wayne had been out over the Christmas vacation, he had been taunted and challenged by a succession of brainless thugs, picking on his dress sense, his mascara, or just the fact that he didn't look like one of them. The last time he had been out, which just happened to have been the previous night, a shaven headed hooligan had asked him if he was a "poofter" as he was wearing make-up and did he want a kiss? Wayne had merely stared at the skinhead and used his mind control technique to convince the thug that attacking him wasn't a good idea. Even so, Wayne knew that sooner or later someone would try and beat him up and would receive the full force of the power of Tuatha magic, just like Baz Thompson, Francisco Pizarro and Fr De Feren.

It was strange, but Wayne had never encountered any hostility in Manchester. Maybe it was just a small town thing and anyway there were ten thousand students in Manchester, so there was definitely safety in numbers.

So it was that that Saturday night Wayne watched "The Generation Game," a variety show and "Match of The Day," while Doris waffled on in the background about her aches and pains and who in the town had died in the past few weeks.

"Lucky old them." Wayne had muttered under his breath at one point.

It therefore came as something of a relief to her son when Doris declared that she was tired and was going to go to bed. Wayne informed her that he was going to watch a horror film on BBC2 and that he wouldn't be too late up, which he wasn't. The film turned out to be quite boring and totally lacking in the gratuitous nudity that usually filled horror films of the period, so Wayne had yawned, stretched and turned off the TV before grabbing a glass of water and trudging upstairs.

Sleep came quickly and Wayne's subconscious mind drifted off to California and a young girl called Julia, or was she Stephanie, or was she Emma, a girl at University that Wayne fancied from afar. The night progressed with a number of strange dreams, all involving the same girls. Sadly all the dreams were as un-erotic as the horror movie he had wasted his time watching. In all of the dreams, the girl was in trouble and Wayne was totally powerless to act. Then came the worst dream of all. One of the girls was screaming, Wayne couldn't decide which girl it was, whomsoever it was, she was screaming for dear life.

Then Wayne was with her, the black robed figure entered the corridor where Wayne and the faceless girl seemed to be trapped, an endless corridor of locked doors. No matter how fast they ran they didn't seem to be able to move. Then, suddenly, the girl was gone and Wayne was left to face the phantom alone.

Even asleep, Wayne felt his hackles rise as the faceless creature lifted its head and stared right at him. The hairs on the back of his neck stood up and he felt a cold sweat breaking out all over his body, His very flesh seemed determine to slip off his body and find sanctuary somewhere. Those same cold lifeless blue eyes burned into Wayne's.

"So whelp, are you ready to die?" The deep, mocking voice filled his head.

"Are you ready to join all the cursed Priests who thought they could manipulate and control their creation and guarantee their first class ticket to the afterlife?"

Wayne knew that he had been waiting for this moment. He knew the words he wanted to say, but in his dream-state he just couldn't make his mouth move.

"I have left them all so terrified, that they have taken their own lives, rather than face me in the flesh. I have yet to decide if I shall show you such mercy."

The phantom laughed at Wayne.

"Look at the champion of the once might race of immortals: A trembling child who wants to hide behind his mommy's skirts. A baby, who is going to wet his pants should I so much as raise my little finger, oh how I shall delight in watching you gasp your last breath and how I shall relish my final victory over a race who were little more than childish conjurors. Their weak magic amused me. As for you, your pathetic magic is cursed. Any magic you perform will result in heartbreak and pain. This is my curse that shall follow you until I put you out of your misery."

"SILENCE!"

The booming voice seemed to come out of nowhere. Much deeper than that of the phantom.' It seemed to surround and permeate everything, like an enormous clap of thunder that made even the ground resonate.

"YOU DARE TO CALL ME A WHELP, WHEN YOU ARE NO MORE THAN AN INSIGNIFICANT INFANT, BARELY PULLED SQUEALING OFF YOUR MOTHER'S BREAST?"

With a start Wayne realised the voice was his own. The words the speech he had been rehearsing for weeks.

The phantom fell back, confusion and pain obvious in the merciless eyes.

"I KNOW WHO YOU ARE, LITTLE MASTER VITALIA. I KNOW WHERE YOU ARE, YOU SPOILED LITTLE TANTRUMING BRAT AND I KNOW HOW TO DESTROY YOU AND TRUST ME, WHELP, I AM GOING TO DESTROY YOU!"

The eyes were now wide open, terrified.

"How? How do you know me?"

The voice had now lost its imperious arrogance. It was now the whine of a small and frightened child.

The dream Wayne smiled and advanced on the phantom.

"That's for me to know and for you to fear." He heard himself whisper menacingly.

The phantom screamed. A piercing, shrill scream that filled Wayne's head and made him cover his ears and start screaming himself.

Wayne Higginbotham sat up in bed, sweat rolling down his face. For a moment he didn't know where he was. He was totally disoriented, was he at home, in that corridor? Had it been a dream? Wayne's breathing was shallow and fast, he was almost panting. Had he really been screaming or was that just in the dream? Had Doris heard?

Wayne reached over and turned on his bedroom light. Outside, an owl screeched loudly. Wayne nearly jumped out of his skin. That's the scream he had heard he thought to himself.

Wayne took a sip of water and then remembered the voice, his voice, saying some of the things he'd practised. He fell back on to his pillow and slowly tried to compose himself. Then he smiled.

"Well, that all seemed to go well!" He whispered as he closed his eyes.

In a very large ornate country house, somewhere in New England, a seven-year-old boy sat up in bed, his eyes wide, round and terrified, tears poured down his face:

"DADDEEE!" He bellowed.

Twenty-One

Pierre de Burgos' party was turning out to be a frightful bore. The host, Pierre, was probably the most affected student in the entire City of Oxford. Everyone knew he had left his hometown in Hampshire as plain old Peter Burke. That name just hadn't been prestigious enough for one of the stars of the Philosophy, Politics and Economics course, so Peter had soon reinvented himself as Pierre and his Irish ancestral name of Burke had reverted to its Hiberno-Norman root: De Burgos. Along with the name change, Peter had camped himself up massively. Every pronouncement was made in the most theatrical manner possible, with melodramatic language and overly expansive gesticulation.

Peter's accent had suddenly become what could only be described as cut glass, with perfectly enunciated vowels and properly pronounced words. One of his other acquisitions in his quest to be perceived as no less than a doyen of high society was an upper crust girlfriend. His own "prime-top-totty," as he described her.

Lucy Hetherington was fed up with being regarded as a piece of "top totty" and she was very bored with Peter Burke and his pretentious alter ego: Pierre de Burgos. To that end she had already decided that tonight was the night she was going to end their relationship. She didn't even really know how she had ended up going out with Peter, apart from the fact that she had got really awfully drunk one evening just after Toby Pendleton had dumped her and Peter had been kind enough to help her home. He had pestered her quite a lot after that and they had started going out just after Valentines Day. Now it was March and the relationship had more than run its course. She was determined that she would not be accompanying Peter to the May Ball, which would follow the end of the exams in June.

Lucy sipped her Chablis while politely pretending to listen to a third year girl describing her fabulous life in London and how she couldn't wait to escape the small town constraints of Oxford, to do something exciting up in town, like her boyfriend. Lucy appraised the tall handsome young man standing next to the girl. He also looked bored.

"Oh yah," the annoying girl opined, really the only thing I could imagine worse than being in Oxford is having been brought up somewhere appallingly provincial like poor Martin here.

The boyfriend shrugged.

"It wasn't that bad." The boyfriend muttered, looking slightly annoyed.

"And where were you raised, if you don't mind my asking?" Lucy asked the girl's boyfriend. The girl glowered at her menacingly.

The boy smiled.

"Shepton, it's a small town in the Yorkshire Dales." He replied, his voice betraying just a hint of flat northern vowels.

"Very boring, but not half as bad as Fi makes out."

The girl grabbed her boyfriend's arm and steered him away from the much prettier Lucy.

"Must mingle!" she chirped with as much sincerity as she could muster.

"Shepton, Shepton, Shepton." The word reverberated in Lucy's mind. Why did the name of a town she had never heard of resonate so profoundly in her head? Had she heard it somewhere before? She sat perplexed on one of Peter's leather armchairs.

"Are you alright, old girl?" Peter, in his best Pierre persona enquired.

"You do look rather piquey."

Lucy shook her head.

"No, no, really. I'm fine. Pierre. Does the word Shepton mean anything to you?"

Pierre de Burgos put his finger to his lips and rolled his eyes thoughtfully.

Then he smiled a deliberate condescending smile.

"It's a Building Society darling, on the High Street as you head towards Blackwell's on the corner of Cornmarket Street. One of those silly little bank type things, based in ricket-ridden northern mill towns and frequented by the proletariat. They save their pennies there if they are lucky enough to have a job, so that they can buy their little ticky-tacky, chintzy terraced houses."

Pierre flounced off, puzzled by the apparent random nature of Lucy's question.

"Shepton, Shepton, Shepton."

Lucy was concentrating so hard that she began to feel quite faint.

The background noise of traditional jazz played on Pierre's old hi-fi, gentle chit-chat broken by occasional braying laughter and tinkling glasses seemed to flood Lucy's mind. She put her head in her hands.

"Shepton, Shepton, Shepton."

"Are you alright?" The soft northern voice asked.

Lucy looked up, her eyes wide. The annoying third year girl's boyfriend towered over her.

"Yes, I'm...er." Lucy gasped.

The boy crouched down to Lucy's level.

"Have you overdone it a little?" He asked, sympathetically.

"I'm Martin Berenger by the way." He held out his hand. "I did PPE here, graduated last year. I miss it like hell actually, hence why I'm back. Fi thinks it's because I miss her."

Lucy took the proffered hand and shook it.

"Lucy Hetherington. I'm very pleased to meet you."

"Can I get you anything, Lucy?" Martin asked.

Lucy shook her head:

"No, this is going to sound really stupid, but I'm really not drunk, it's just that the name of your town, Shepton, means something to me and I really can't think what."

Martin let his mouth fall into a lopsided smirk.

"Shepton? It's Ok. It's a very pretty Yorkshire Dales market town with a castle and all that stuff, unfortunately it's also a bit of a Yorkshire mill town so it has its fair share of industrial scarring."

Lucy rubbed her forehead.

"Look this is going to sound really weird, but I think I once had a dream about it."

Martin grinned.

"You actually dreamt about Shepton? Hell, for most folk down here that would constitute a nightmare."

Lucy shook her head again.

"No it wasn't like that. It was really weird. It was while I was at school. I had to ring somebody. I got up, left the dorm and used the house payphone. There was a fire, that's right, a fire." She looked up excitedly and sat up rigidly in the armchair.

"There was a fire and someone asked me to ring the fire brigade and than someone else."

She paused and put her hand over her mouth as if in shock.

Martin frowned.

"Are you definitely sure you're OK?" He asked, cocking his head to one side to try and see her eyes.

"You haven't taken anything weird, have you?"

Lucy gripped the arms of the chair.

"Name me some hotels in Shepton."

Martin raised his eyebrows.

"What? OK, Well, erm, there's "The White Horse, The Lion, The Unicorn, erm ......"

Lucy shook her head and grimaced.

"No, it wasn't one of them, but there was a hotel."

Martin pondered the question a little bit longer, then shook his head.

"No, that's about it, except for the one by the station, erm, yeah, The Midland."

"THAT'S IT!" Lucy shrieked.

Martin and Lucy were suddenly aware that all eyes were on them, including Pierre's and the annoying girl, Fi.

"Erm Martin, are you here with me?" The annoying girl demanded as she approached Martin and the room settled back into the rhythm of gentle chit-chat, muted laughter, clinking glasses and jazz.

Martin shrugged.

"Yeah, I'll be with you in a minute Fi."

The annoying girl turned away huffily.

"I'm sorry, looks like I've got you into trouble." Lucy smiled, sympathetically.

Martin grinned sheepishly.

"Never mind. It's been nice talking to you." He stood upright.

"Wait!" Lucy asked plaintively.

"There was one other thing...."

Martin smiled expectantly as Lucy put her fingers back to her forehead:

"There was a street, er Cavanagh, Caveau...ermmm."

Martin shrugged.

"Cavendish?"

"Yes, Cavendish Street." She gasped, "Cavendish Street. Thank you, thank you so much."

Martin shrugged again, his face bearing a slightly disappointed look.

"Pleasure." He replied.

"I was wondering, erm, could I..."

"Martin can we go now? I'm bored." The annoying girl interrupted her boyfriend.

Martin nodded and gave Lucy a wistful glance, but Lucy Hetherington was looking at the floor, deep in thought, her thumb and forefinger paused at her lips.

"There was a number and a name but I..."

She looked up, but Martin was nowhere to be seen.

"Oh! "Lucy gasped, then under her breath she muttered.

"Damn!"

"Lucy, darling!" She heard Pierre's effete voice calling her as he approached her chair, champagne glass in hand.

"Dear, dear Lucy, Why on earth were you talking to that frightful northern oik?" He chirped.

Lucy sighed and stood up to look her boyfriend in the eye.

"Because Peter, he was a million times more interesting than you will ever be. Consider yourself absolutely and unequivocally, dumped." She shouted almost at the top of her voice and then softly.

"Just like me, I think you need to find yourself a nice boyfriend."

Lucy Hetherington stormed out of Pierre's rooms in Brasenose College and headed back towards the sanctuary of Queen's offering a cheery goodnight to the porters at both colleges.

In the jazz-backed silence that followed Lucy's outburst, the only words that were uttered for several long seconds were Pierre's.

"My goodness, how intolerably and incredibly rude!"

Twenty-Two

Doris Higginbotham snorted with derision as she unceremoniously budged an overweight woman out of the way as she struggled along the crowded High Street.

"Bloody tourists!" She muttered as the woman glowered at her furiously.

Doris was late. She had arranged to meet Margaret at the Lite-Bite at eleven o clock, but the bus from the Greenwood estate had been delayed due to the heavy market day congestion and the High Street was packed with shoppers and day-trippers.

"I was beginning to think you weren't coming." Margaret announced as Doris finally slumped into the plastic chair.

"Tea?" Margaret asked, one eyebrow raised quizzically, as she lifted the steel teapot over Doris' cup.

Doris blew out a huge exasperated sigh and nodded.

"Aye, thanks Margaret love. I were beginning to think I was never going to get here meself."

"Has he gone back then?" Margaret intoned as she finished pouring her elder sister's tea.

"Who?" Doris pursed her lips as she splashed milk into the cup.

"Your Wayne." Margaret snapped. "Who did you think I meant?"

Doris sighed again.

"Aye, I'm on me own again. Just me and the four walls."

Doris sniffed.

"I don't know what's come over him at that college. He's taken to wearing make up you know."

"I know!" Margaret gasped.

"I saw him on Christmas day there, don't forget."

Doris and Wayne had spent Christmas day at the Houghton-Hughes house, much to Doris' chagrin. Margaret had insisted that it would have been just too sad for them to be alone at Christmas.

Doris shook her head resignedly.

"I don't know what to do." She muttered.

"He's got long hair now, just like a girl and he's wearing make up."

"You don't think he's, you know......." Margaret suggested while making a limp-wristed gesture with her left hand.

Doris shrugged her shoulders and her eyes welled up with tears.

"He's had girlfriends, our Margaret. He had that one when he was at Wormysteds; Stephanie, I think her name was, but I couldn't get anything out of him about whether he has one in Manchester or not. In fact I couldn't get anything out of him at all. When I got to see him that is. He were always out over the Christmas holidays and when he wasn't out, he had nowt to say. He's got right big headed you know. Eeeeh, I don't know what our Frank would have made of him now."

Margaret sniffed.

"You don't think he's on drugs do you?"

Doris took a sip of tea and then bit her lip.

"I asked him outright if he were taking drugs. He said not, but you don't know, do you!"

Margaret shook her head.

"You know Doris, I'm so glad our Cedric didn't go off to University. He's doing really well at the bank, according to our Stanley anyway and we can keep an eye on him while he's living under our roof."

Doris scowled a deep angry scowl that made her look much, much older than her fifty-four years. There was a long awkward silence as the sisters contemplated their respective sons. Doris' misery was completed when Margaret touched her arm conspiratorially and smiled her smuggest smile.

"Our Cedric's got a girl now. He introduced us last Sunday."

She pursed her lips and nodded as if to say: "take that!"

"Oh aye." Doris feigned interest.

"Oh yes," Margaret smirked.

"He brought her for lunch. Lovely girl! She's a Doctor's daughter from Grassingdon."

Doris clenched her teeth.

"Posh then." She hissed through a barely discernable and insincere smile.

"Oh yes." Margaret gushed.

"She's very well spoken and very pretty. I don't know whether anything will come of it or not, so I wouldn't go getting a hat yet, our Doris, but you never know."

Margaret Houghton-Hughes was almost in heaven. The look on Doris face was an extremely satisfying mix of embarrassment, rage and envy.

Doris Higginbotham was in an incredibly foul mood by the time she left the Lite-Bite.

"After all I've done for him." She muttered as she barged through the throng on her way back to the bus station.

"Taken him in, brought him up, fed him, clothed him and this is the thanks I get. I knew I should have turned him down, I knew I should have waited for another, one more like our Trevor. I knew he wasn't right as soon as I saw them ears!"

A man in a suit glanced at the strange woman muttering to herself as she crossed the road to the annoying beep of the pelican crossing.

"What you looking at?" She growled aggressively.

The man raised his eyebrows and wisely kept his counsel.

What was the world coming too when even grannies were turning into hooligans?

Twenty-Three

The Spring term seemed to pass in a flash for Wayne. No sooner had he got back to Manchester than he seemed to climbing into John Lancaster's car again, facing the short trip back over the Pennines. The prospect of spending the Easter vacation in Shepton with Doris was even worse than it been over Christmas. At least then everyone from school was back in town with news about their Universities, or Polytechnics and there was Christmas to look forward too. Easter promised absolutely nothing!

Even worse, Wayne had recently met someone that he found extremely interesting and the four-week vacation seemed like an eternity, especially after a sudden disclosure the previous evening had left him reeling.

Four weeks, wars had been fought and won in less time than that!

Wayne and John had gone to a party in the Student Union building on the Oxford Road the last Saturday evening before the end of term. The organisers had promised lots of New wave and new romantic music, all in aid of "Rock against Racism." Unfortunately the party had proven to be a crashing bore. The thumping music was proving to be mainly Seventies disco-funk, which Wayne hated and boys outnumbered girls by a margin of about three to one. Wayne had eventually drained his plastic glass of lager and had leaned lazily on a column, his hands in the pockets of his tight black jeans, his eyes closed and he had yawned expressively.

"Is it really that bad?" He had heard a female American accent ask. He opened his eyes to a vision of loveliness, but was in such a bad mood that he snapped:

"It's worse, much worse and do you mind, I'm trying to pose here."

Instead of turning away, insulted by Wayne's rude riposte, the girl had laughed, turned to her less attractive friend and shouted.

"At last, somebody interesting."

Wayne had been flattered enough to grin at the girl, his bad mood miraculously dissipating, despite the music.

"Let's go somewhere more interesting." The girl had suggested before holding out a hand and drawling:

"Hi, I'm Sabine and this is my friend Kim."

Wayne had taken the hand and had shaken it firmly:

"Wayne!" He had declared and then with an imperious wave of his hand towards the approaching John Lancaster who was tightly clutching two pint glasses as though his life depended on not spilling a drop.

"And this sad specimen is Johnny Lanc."

"The girls had giggled."

"What?" John had asked, bemused, as he handed Wayne his beer.

"Nothing!" Wayne had responded with a grin.

"Come on, drink up. We're getting out of here. This is Sabine and Kim by the way."

He waved an arm vaguely in the direction of the two girls.

"They're coming with us." He had informed his friend nonchalantly as he put the plastic glass to his lips and greedily guzzled the amber liquid.

John glanced at the girls, both still giggling at him and scowled.

"What's wrong with staying here?"

Wayne had grimaced.

"Do I really have to tell you?" He had groaned, twisting his mouth sarcastically as the repetitive monotone beat of yet another appalling disco hit boomed out over the hall speakers.

John had shrugged. He clearly hadn't been enamoured with the prospect of pairing up with Kim, but Wayne had already moved towards the exit and Sabine had followed him, her head cocked towards his as she listened to him joke about the poor quality of the beer.

Wayne watched the bleak, industrially scarred landscape of Rossendale pass by as John's Fiat trundled towards Shepton. Sabine had turned out to be from New England. Her father was a visiting professor at a University in the Midlands and she had decided to do her degree in the UK rather than at home in the United States.

Wayne had been transfixed by her as soon as he had seen her. As far as he was concerned she was the most beautiful girl he'd seen in Manchester, or anywhere else for that matter. Her hair was blonde, but cut short and fashionably spiky, her voice husky and deeply sexy. Her hazel eyes had an indescribable mischievous quality. She also did that thing that Lady Diana did with her eyes, looking up demurely from under thick dark lashes.

Over the last week of term he'd met up with her almost every night and as far as he had been aware they had got on tremendously well.

They had even kissed a couple of times, which is why Wayne had not been prepared for the bombshell that she had released the previous evening. Wayne had been moaning about returning to Shepton the following day and how much he hated the prospect of four weeks of boredom, living half way up a Yorkshire moor with Doris. He had even done an impression of his adoptive mother, which had had Sabine rolling with laughter. As the laughter had subsided, however, Sabine had taken a deep breath and announced that she thought her boyfriend from back home, might be on the verge of proposing to her over the Easter vacation.

Wayne's entire world had collapsed around him: Boyfriend? Proposal?

He had known Sabine a whole week and nothing had been mentioned about a boyfriend, or marriage, or anything like that.

Wayne had been stunned into a long awkward silence, which had only ended with a barely audible gasp of: "Oh!"

Sabine had then made matters even worse by describing her boyfriend to the stunned first year student.

"He's called Jim, he's twenty-two, six feet, three inches tall and a biker, although not the grimy kind. He was at Yale after all. He's real cool."

Wayne had grinned pathetically.

"Oh!" He had repeated, before adding "great" which had sounded more like a growl than a word.

Only then did Sabine realise that she had mortally wounded her new friend.

"Oh my God, did you think? I mean, oh no, Wayne…………"

Her sympathetic tone had been like a knife twisting in Wayne's gut. He had smiled weakly and had proceeded to deny that he had fallen head over heels for the girl, but both he knew and she knew that he was lying. The night had come to a rather swift close after that.

Wayne rubbed his eyes as the first spots of rain hit the Fiat's windscreen.

"Great!" Wayne muttered: "Four weeks in Shepton, in the rain."

His mood had not been improved by the letter he had received from Terri, his real Mom, the day before he was due to go back to Shepton. In it, she had described how she had walked out on Dean with the kids and was staying with Wayne's auntie Annie in a place called San Clemente. The fact that she had left that Italian slime-ball pleased Wayne immensely, especially as it provided greater distance from Dean's cousin and the devil-child. On the other hand, he was sure going to miss that house with its view of Beverley Hills and that incredible pool.

John had laughed:

"At least we can have a few beers at the Junction."

For Wayne Higginbotham, the prospect of a few beers at the "Junction Inn," the pub on the corner of Cavendish Street, a few doors from the house in which he'd spent most of his first sixteen years, was not an attractive prospect. He wanted to escape, to get away. All he could think about, apart from Sabine, was going to help his Mom in the warm sunshine of California: the blue skies, the palm trees, the cypress trees. That pool! Oh well, there would be no pool any more but hey, on the bright side, no more Dean either. For some reason, the thought of cypress trees made him think of Rome. Wayne scratched his head.

"Rome? Didn't he have something to do in Rome? Just before he had died, Bishop Donleavy had mentioned a Priest in Rome that Wayne had needed to see. A Priest who had some more pieces of the Stone of Fail, locked away in a vault somewhere deep within the Vatican City. The name sprang back into Wayne's mind: "Father Bianca."

The dying Bishop had given Wayne a ring to show Father Bianca, to prove that he was truly acting at the Bishop's behest. Aillen had slso gone on about him going to Rome. Wayne smiled as John began to hum a Joy Division song.

That's what he would do with his Easter vacation. He would go to Rome and get Father Bianca's bits of the stone. It would be warmer than Shepton and Wayne loved Roman history so he would enjoy it immensely. It would also help him to forget all about Sabine for a while.

The fact that he was doing something towards the cause of eventually destroying the demon would also please Aillen Mac Fionnbharr and would get him off his back.

The only downsides were that Wayne knew that Doris would be furious, when he informed her that he would be going off to Rome and the fact that he would be putting his head right into the lion's mouth if the "Order" were still operating.

"So what are you doing next week?" Wayne heard John's voice over the sewing machine whine of the Fiat's tiny engine.

"I'm going to Rome." Wayne replied. A smile creased his lips.

"I've got a vacation assignment, for my history course, in Rome."

Twenty-Four

Terri Thorne chewed her expensively manicured fingernails nervously as she waited for the phone to ring. The motel room was plain, but clean and had been adequate accommodation for the last few nights. The bill, however, was going to be much more than she could afford. She had cut up her credit card and tossed the pieces into the trash at her old house in Coldwater Canyon Boulevard. Terri had not wanted Dean to be able to trace her using credit card transactions as the scent in the hunt. Unfortunately the $20 that she had had in her purse had been spent on food.

Terri watched her children, Marco and Marina, as they watched the TV in silence. Marco was going to be a very handsome boy. His hair was very dark, like his father's, but his eyes were a stunning light blue. Marina, who was still only a baby and who was sucking on her pacifier rather than paying any real attention to the TV was blond and brown eyed. Funny how parental traits mix and merge in their offspring Terri mused as she smiled at the gurgling infant. The phone shook Terri out of her reverie as it rattled angrily on the cradle.

"Hi Colm?" She asked hopefully, then sighed with relief as her brother's Irish brogue, now inflected with a sharp New York edge, greeted her.

"Well now little sister, how are you?"

Terri couldn't help bursting into tears as she relayed the details of Dean's infidelity to her big brother.

"Why the little schmuck, I oughtta ring his scrawny neck." Colm roared so loudly that Terri had the hold the phone away from her ear.

"Is there anything you're needing?" Colm asked after he had cursed Terri's husband a few more times and had dredged the bottom of his barrel of oaths.

"I need money, Colm." Terri sobbed. "And a place to stay, I guess."

"Ah just like the good old days." Colm laughed.

"Sure I've missed your calls begging for a loan of a few bucks over the last few years."

Terri laughed for the first time in days. The natural warmth of her brother being so welcome after the studied insincerity of her husband and the dismissive platitudes of her supposed friends.

"Well you know Annie is renting a place near San Diego?" Colm suggested with a hint of reproach in his voice. Terri had been out of touch with her family for some weeks and even before that had been getting increasingly distant. The problem was that she had been loath to play the big shot Hollywood actress and had hated to brag about her life and the successes, yet the less she contacted her brothers and sisters, the more they suspected that she had grown aloof. It hadn't helped that Dean had hated her Irish family and had made it quite clear that none of them were welcome in his home.

"I didn't know, Colm." Terri sighed sadly. "I know I haven't been in touch as much as I…"

"Ah forget it. I know what it's like. Two kids, a career and a dirtbag of a husband. Look, tell me how much you need and I'll wire it to Annie. Have you got enough gas in your car to get you to San Clemente?"

Terri tried to remember how much gas she'd had in the Porsche and then recalled that she'd filled it just before she'd found Dean in the motel.

"I guess so…" She mused while picking a pen out of the motel desk drawer to write down her younger sister's address and phone number.

Some four hours letter, just as the needle on the Porsche's fuel gauge nudged empty, Terri Thorne found herself outside a white Spanish style condo overlooking the ocean in the town of San Clemente.

Before she even got a chance to ring the apartment door bell, Annie rushed out of the ornate colonial front door to greet her older sister and her nephew and niece in a shower of hugs and kisses:

"How are you?" She gasped as she gripped Terri's shoulders and stared deep into her eyes.

"He hasn't hit you has he? Colm will murder him if he's so much as laid a finger on you."

Terri laughed:

"No I'm fine, but how are you? What are you doing here? I didn't even know you were in California."

Terri's voice had switched from her usual Californian drawl back into an Irish lilt as soon as she had seen her sister. Annie almost carried her and Marcus and Marina into the condo and regaled her with the tale of how she had engineered her move from New York where she had been staying with Colm, the girls' eldest brother and the proud owner of one of New York City's best Irish bars, to L.A. She had not contacted Terri because, as she explained over a fine cup of tea, she had not wanted to be seen as a parasite, "using" her famous big sister's name as a leg-up. As it was, Annie O'Brien was doing pretty well as a psychiatric nurse anyway.

"I mean what better place could I have found to practice my chosen profession in than La-La land." Annie laughed as the sister's caught up on each other's news:

"I mean, just about everyone here is a nutter!"

The sisters laughed freely, Annie at the pure joy of seeing Terri again, Terri at the relief of having somewhere to stay where she would be safe with the children.

The main topic of conversation was the catching up on family news. Annie relayed all the latest gossip about Colm, his wife Maria and their family, their other sisters, Molly back in Ireland, Siobhan in Australia, the younger brothers, Sean, farming in New Zealand and Liam who now had his own bar in Boston and then the youngest, Katie, who was now twenty five and living with her boyfriend in the small town of Westport, on the West coast of Ireland, from where she could keep a careful eye on the patriarch of the family, Tom Mick a John O'Brien.

Terri sighed wistfully: "Now I've escaped that schmuck, I must go home and see the old man before he goes and dies on us all. Dean hated me having anything to do with any of my family. He even managed to get me to give up on Michael at one point."

Annie caressed her sister's hand sympathetically.

"How is Michael?" She asked. Terri nodded:

"He's good, he's a quite the young man now. He came over during the summer. He's at University, in Manchester. I am so proud of him."

Annie frowned as she prepared to broach a difficult subject.

"Terri, what are you going to do now? You know, with Dean and the kids?"

Terri shook her head and clasped her mug of tea so tightly that Annie thought it might break.

Terri's eyes filled up as she stifled a sob.

"I don't know. Dean loves Marco and Marina. I guess he'll fight me for custody. I just don't know."

Annie bit her lip.

"Da thinks he's got mafia connections."

Terri snorted.

"How would he know stuck up there in the hills, five thousand miles away? Although Dean does have a cousin, a lawyer out east, who looks like a proper Mafioso."

Terri grinned.

"If I do disappear, get the police to check that I'm not holding up a bridge somewhere."

Despite the laughter, Terri's demeanour over the following days did betray her concerns.

She jumped nervously every time Annie's phone rang. Every ring of the doorbell was greeted by Terri's gathering the children together and fleeing into the sanctuary of Annie's spare bedroom, which had become Terri's refuge.

Annie noticed that although she was meticulous in her care and attention to the children, Terri seemed to be neglecting herself. The one time Hollywood actress had stopped wearing make-up and the dark roots were now definitely visible in her long blonde hair.

One evening, after Annie had returned home from the hospital, she found Terri sitting on her bed crying as the children played on the floor nearby.

"Terri darling, what's the matter?" Annie asked putting her arm protectively around her sister's shoulder.

"I've made a mess of everything." Terri sobbed.

"I've got no money, no prospects, no husband. What am I going to do, Annie?"

Annie knew it was not the time for insincere platitudes.

"You've got two choices Theresa Vitalia nee O'Brien. You either surrender and slope off pathetically back to Ireland to live with Da, leave the kids with Dean and try and start again over there." Terri's eyes opened wide in horror...

"Or" Annie continued: "Terri Thorne pulls her finger out, gets herself together, gets her hair done, gets herself a job and starts living the American dream again."

Terri gulped.

"But how? I owe Colm a thousand dollars, I..."

Annie shrugged:

"Ah Colm has more money than Rockefeller, he'll not miss a few bucks. How much is that worth?" She nodded her head at the window, outside of which Terri's Porsche gleamed in the California sunshine.

Terri gasped then slowly, her mouth cracked into a smile.

"I never thought of that."

Annie pursed her lips:

"That would certainly buy you a first class ticket back to Shannon."

She gave her sister a mischievous glance.

Terri clambered off the bed.

"You always were a bossy little devil, Annie O'Brien! That thing is a going to become an old chevvy, a new hairdo and some retail therapy. I still have a few contacts that aren't part of the Vitalia Empire. You're not shipping me back to the woods little sister!"

Within a week Terri Thorne had a new job, modelling clothes for the catalogue of a small fashion retailer in Hollywood. Marco and Marina were soon roped in. As a glamorous Mom, with a familiar, if not universally recognised face, two beautiful and photogenic children and a hunger for hard work, the modelling contracts soon rolled in. By Easter, Terri Thorne was earning almost as much as she had during her days as an actress.

It was inevitable, however, that by placing her head above the parapet, she would soon be seen.

It was Easter Sunday afternoon when Annie's doorbell rang. Annie was working at the hospital, Marina was taking her afternoon nap and Marco was watching cartoons on the TV. Terri had been sat at the breakfast bar; she closed her magazine and sauntered to the door.

"Who is it?" She shouted. There was no answer. She opened the front door a couple of inches but before she had even noticed who was there, she was then thrown back into the room as the door burst open.

"I was always telling you to use the safety chain." Dean Vitalia sneered, as he stood silhouetted in the doorway.

"Can I come in and maybe see my children." He growled menacingly as he advanced into the condo's front room.

Terri nodded, terrified.

Marco jumped up.

"Daddeee" He shrieked as he ran towards his father who swept him up in his arms.

"Hey, little guy." Dean grinned and playfully ruffled his son's hair.

"You've grown. You'll soon be playing quarterback for the Rams at this rate." He glowered at Terri.

"Where's my girl?" His voice was little more than a whisper, but it oozed menace.

"In there, asleep." Terri indicated the spare room with a nod.

Dean smiled and strolled into the spare room. He glanced down at his daughter who was snoring gently.

"Hey little lady." He whispered as he kissed his finger and then placed it gently on Marina's cheek.

"Where've you been daddy?" Marco asked as Dean carried him back towards his mother.

"Did Mommy not tell you?" Dean grinned as he placed his son down and then crouched on his haunches.

"Daddy's been real busy trying to find Mommy, because Mommy's been playing hide and seek. But Daddy's won because he's found Mommy and the games over now."

He stood and gazed into Terri's eyes.

"Pack your things." He whispered.

Terri shook her head.

"It's over Dean." She whispered back, her bottom lip trembling with fear, her eyes wide.

Dean gently reached out and gripped her chin between his thumb and his forefinger.

"I said pack your things. You're coming home." His whisper was now a threat. His eyes had hardened and were little more than slits.

"You cheated on me." Terri gasped. "I'm never coming home. I want a divorce."

She felt Dean's hand tightening on her chin and then his fingers slipped down to her throat. Terri tried to move backwards but found herself blocked by the breakfast bar.

"Did you really think you could simply take my kids and just disappear?" Dean growled.

His fingers tightened around Terri's throat.

"I could snap your pretty little neck like a dry, dead, twig." He hissed; his nose only an inch from Terri's. She could smell alcohol on his breath.

"But I wouldn't do that to my kids. I wouldn't take away their mommy. Not unless she ever tried to steal them away from me again."

His eyes burned into Terri's.

"Ok! Ok! You can have your divorce, you Irish bitch, but I will have equal custody of the children. Total equal custody and if you ever, ever try to deny me access................."

Dean's fingers tightened again and Terri began to struggle for breath. Just as she was sure she was about to lose consciousness, Dean released her and swept towards the front door.

Terri coughed and gulped for air as she almost collapsed. She gripped on to the breakfast bar as Dean turned back towards her.

"I know where you are now. Do not leave this place thinking you can hide again. Those are my kids too. Next time I won't be so sympathetic. Oh and you are finished in Hollywood lady. Don't think you'll ever be seen in another movie as long as you live.

Nobody crosses a Vitalia."

Dean swaggered back over to Marco who had watched wide eyed and horrified as his father had threatened Terri.

"You be a good boy for mommy." Dean whispered gently. "Daddy will see you soon."

He turned and walked out of the front door, without another glance in Terri's direction, straightening his jacket as he went.

"Did Daddy hurt you Mommy?" Marco asked as he walked over towards his mother, who slowly slipped down on to her knees.

"No, honey. Mommy and Daddy were just playing." Terri lied. "Mommy and Daddy were just fooling around."

Marco twisted his face into a small angry mask.

"I don't like daddy." He spat!

Twenty-Five

Rome, the Eternal City. It was everything Wayne Higginbotham had ever dreamed of and more. Wayne loved ancient history and few subjects could excite and animate him as much as the study of classical Rome and Greece. The Colosseum, the Forum, the Capitoline Hill had all been much better preserved than he could ever have imagined and the Pantheon had been the highlight of all them. A vast domed church now, it would have been recognisable in its current form while the Legions of Rome ruled most of the known Earth.

Yet for all his joy at having seen such wonders, Wayne Higginbotham felt totally and utterly deflated.

First of all he had been correct in his assumption that Doris would blow a gasket when he had announced almost immediately upon his arrival home, that he had a history assignment to do over the vacation which would take him to Rome for five days.

"And what about me?" She had bellowed indignantly:

"What about all the jobs I've got lined up for you? I've nobody but you to do owt for me now."

Wayne had felt a degree of guilt about abandoning Doris for his Roman holiday. However, his adoptive mother's outburst had hardened his resolve.

"It's only five days, I'll be back by Saturday."

Doris had had other ideas about Wayne's vacation time and the prospect of his being gone for five days infuriated her. She had not forgiven him for galavanting off to America for a week, just before he'd gone off to University.

"I've plenty of jobs here for you to do." She had blustered, folding her arms defiantly across her chest.

"I want the window frames outside painted for a start and there's the back garden to be done."

Wayne's mouth had dropped open incredulously.

"What?" He had gasped.

Doris had been getting into her stride and had decided to tell her son a few home truths.

"Oh aye, I know all about you lazy students. It were in t'paper how you do nowt but drink, take drugs and have sex. All of it paid for by proper working folk's taxes. Then you have the cheek to go out and protest about war and stuff. That's what you lot need, a decent war.

Putting you all in t'army would do you a world of good. I mean look at you, you're wearing bloody women's make up!"

Wayne had aggravated Doris by actually laughing at her statement.

"I think you should read a different paper, Mum," he had laughed.

"I don't do drugs and I don't know who's getting all the sex, but it isn't me. Plus a touch of eyeliner does not make me a raving transvestite."

Doris had twisted her face contemptuously:

"You've been nowt but a big head ever since you passed for that Grammar School. You and your big words and your fancy, nancy talk. Well you can forget about jiggering off to Rome and you can get some proper work done here for me."

Wayne had heard enough and had responded equally as furiously.

"Oh, so I'm just your odd job man now, am I? Painter, decorator, gardener, labourer and probably plumber to boot, no doubt."

Doris had wagged an admonishing finger at Wayne while spittle had gathered in the corners of her mouth.

"And don't you talk to me like that. You're not too big for a thick ear." She snarled.

"Those are the sorts of jobs you should be looking for, not all this posh stuff. It'll all come to nowt, you mark my words."

Wayne had shaken his head despondently.

"You really don't have a clue, do you?"

Doris had resorted to her usual fallback position, which she had been using for as long as Wayne could remember:

"Eeeeh! I'll tell you what I do know Mr. fancy pants. If I'd known then what I know now, I would never have adopted you. I can tell you that for nowt. If I'd known you'd just up and leave as soon as you'd finished at that Grammar school, I'd never have bothered. Our Trevor would never have done this to me."

Wayne had been apoplectic with rage. The Trevor card had been produced by Doris once too often. Doris' adopted son was no longer the shy mild mannered boy who she had managed to intimidate throughout his childhood.

"It's always about Trevor with you isn't it? Perfect little Trevor, with his perfect lovely little smile and his perfect lovely little ears. Well mum, the bad news is, Trevor didn't make it. You got me instead. Little big ears, me and all my faults. Me and my mascara!"

The look of abject horror on Doris' face did not assuage Wayne's fury. His face was contorted with rage and his finger aggressively jabbed the air in front of Doris' nose.

"Maybe you should have left me in London. Somebody might have adopted me who would have appreciated me and you could have got yourself another little slave, with a perfect smile and normal cute little ears. Somebody who would have done everything you told them and got a nice little job on the bins in Shepton, so that they could look after you into your old age and do all your little jobs for you!"

Wayne's adoptive mother's mouth dropped open and for once, Doris Higginbotham was lost for words.

"And by the way, I'm going to Rome in the morning whether you like it, or not!"

Wayne had roared before turning and stomping off upstairs to his room. He could have used mind control on her and she would have accepted his going with good grace and a smile, but Wayne had had enough! It was time she knew how he felt!

Doris stood transfixed, no one had shouted at her like that since she had been a little girl.

Eventually she had attempted to compose herself with a nice cup of tea, but by the time Wayne had re-emerged a couple of hours later, she was still in no mood to even so much as look at him, let alone speak.

Wayne had left early the next morning without another word being exchanged between them.

Now here he was, loitering with pathetic intent in the Piazza Pio XII, under the shadows of all the saints, with just one day left before he would have to face Doris again and he had failed miserably to find any trace of a Father Bianca.

Wayne wondered how he could have been so stupid. Had he just expected to turn up at St Peter's with a ring and expect everyone in a cassock to know of Fr Bianca's whereabouts? He had read that the Vatican City had less than a thousand inhabitants, with a daily population rising to nearly four thousand with all the lay workers and so on, but he had forgotten to take into account the masses of pilgrims and tourists who flooded the Vatican, many of whom were clergymen or Nuns themselves.

He had spent two whole days fruitlessly wandering the streets and gardens of the Vatican, asking almost every clergyman he saw if they knew of a Fr Bianca. He knew he had been taking a risk and that any one of those Priests might have been in the "Sacred Order of St Gregory", but it wasn't as though the Vatican had a telephone directory detailing a Father Bianca's whereabouts. Every Priest he had spoken to, however, had looked at him as though he was a madman, recoiling in horror at his punkish lined eyes, long hair, leather jacket and white drainpipe jeans and had merely shrugged and professed ignorance of any Fr Bianca.

Faced with another day of pointless investigation, Wayne strained his brain to try and think of a different tactic that might offer better results. Suddenly he clenched his fist in triumph; a brainwave of tsunami proportions had just flooded his mind. Maybe, he thought, I should use the Vatican police to find Father Bianca, pretending that I am a relative bearing a family heirloom. After all, they don't know whose ring this is.

Wayne's spirits brightened. All he had to do was to find the offices of the Corpo della Gendarmeria, the Vatican police force and ask them the whereabouts of the elusive old Priest. It didn't take him long to find the Barrack of the Papal Gendarmes. He marched confidently into the ornate building and approached a front desk manned by an officious looking moustachioed policeman in a splendid uniform.

"Excuse me, but parla Inglese?" Wayne asked as politely as possible.

The Gendarme looked up from the paper he was studying and grimaced at the apparition standing before him. He wasn't used to kids, looking like they should be in a pop group, approaching him in the confines of the barracks.

"A little." He replied suspiciously.

"I'm looking for a Priest who lives here in the Vatican."

The policeman smiled sarcastically.

"Si, we have a few here." He answered with that smug look that Wayne knew was rooted in the Gendarme's feeling of total superiority.

"A Fr Bianca, to be precise." Wayne stated with a humourless smile back.

The Gendarme visibly bristled.

"A moment." He almost shouted over the desk before picking up a telephone and jabbering excitedly in Italian.

"Please take a seat." The Gendarme suggested pleasantly as soon as he had replaced the receiver. He pointed to a chair stood backed up against the whitewashed wall.

Wayne shrugged and sat down. Maybe he was going to get a result after all.

After about five minutes, another gendarme appeared and approached Wayne. This one was older than mustache, his uniform more ornate, his hair grey and he was very tall.

"You seek Father Bianca?" He proposed as soon as he stood before Wayne.

"Yes, sir." Wayne replied politely as he stood, his head inclined upwards even though he was now at his full height.

"May I ask why you seek Father Bianca?" The policeman frowned as his eyes ran up and down Wayne's clothing, halting with a slight look of disdain as their eyes met and the older man noticed the eyeliner.

"He's my great Uncle and my Grandma had a ring that she said I should pass to him. It's a family heirloom, you know."

"Ah, a family heirloom." The Gendarme nodded knowledgably.

"Please, follow me." He turned smartly, his shiny leather boots squeaking on the marble floor tiles.

Wayne did as he was obliged and followed the Papal Gendarme out of the barracks and across a square. The gendarme walked quickly and Wayne was almost running to keep up with him. The gendarme entered an austere looking door on the side of an enormous palace-like building. Wayne had no idea where he was being taken, as he followed the tall policeman down a succession of corridors. Finally, just as Wayne began to get the stitch from having to almost run to merely keep up with the long legged giant, the gendarme stopped at a plain door and knocked.

"I have young man with a gift for Fr. Bianca." The gendarme announced in English as he waved Wayne into the room. It was a spartan office: plain white walls bearing a few nondescript photographs and a simple crucifix on the wall behind the cheap looking desk. A white haired Priest stood up from behind the desk as Wayne entered.

The gendarme smiled at the Priest and then saluted smartly, he said something in Italian that Wayne didn't understand and then left, closing the door gently behind him.

"Father Bianca?" Wayne asked, somewhat timorously.

The Priest smiled:

"No my son. I am not Fr Bianca. Fr Bianca is in hospital, waiting patiently to pass from this life and to then enter the kingdom of heaven. I am Fr Abraham Reichmann, a mere vassal in the service of the Holy See, but the most important question is, who are you?

For I know for an absolute fact, that poor Father Bianca had no family whatsoever."

The Priest's German accent had totally bemused Wayne. He had not been expecting the Gestapo, but that was what the old Priest sounded like. He even looked like the evil Nazi -interrogator that Wayne had seen in a recent TV Second World War drama series, with his little half moon specs and his slicked back grey hair. All he needed was a leather raincoat.

"Have you come to finish the job?" The Priest asked, still sounding almost pleasant.

Wayne had seen too many movies about World War Two to be taken in by the German's friendly, parochial demeanour. Soon it would be a leather glove slapped across the face and "Ve have vays of making you talk Tommy!"

Wayne could have slapped himself. He had walked into the heart of the "Order" like a willing sacrificial victim and now here he was, facing losing all his fingernails.

"Have you come here to finally wipe any trace of the "Sacred Order of St Gregory" off the face of the Earth, by murdering Fr Bianca?"

Wayne sneered and glowered at the Priest defiantly.

"I am not here to murder anyone. I'm not like your bloody "Sacred Order of Saint bloody Gregory." I am here to give something to Fr Bianca and I believe he has something for me."

The Priest smiled, almost benignly. He waved an arm towards a wooden chair by the desk:

"Please sit. I think we may have much to discuss, young man."

Wayne sat down, slowly and deliberately. He had spun the chair before sitting so that the chair back faced the desk and provided a barrier between him and his interrogator. He remembered Steve McQueen once doing something similar in a movie.

"If I was a soldier, I would give you my name, rank and number, but as I'm not a soldier. You get nothing." Wayne sneered, tossing his long, curly hair back in a gesture of defiant nonchalance.

Father Abraham Reichmann raised his eyebrows and a half smile crossed his lips.

"Young man, we have many ways of loosening your tongue."

For a brief moment, the thought crossed Wayne's mind that facing Doris Higginbotham, even in her worst mood, would be a much better proposition than being in his current predicament.

Twenty-Six

The editor of the Hollywood Sentinel stuck out his bottom lip and glowered at James Malone. His hands were clasped together tightly on the desk in front of him and he was leaning forward aggressively.

"So you've got six months experience on the San Fernando Courier and a college diploma in journalism?"

James nodded enthusiastically.

"Before that you were a bereavement counsellor and before that a Priest in Ireland?"

James nodded again.

The editor sat back against his huge black leather chair and chewed on his expensive Mont-Blanc pen. His office in the tall steel and glass skyscraper building was full of green plants, modern sculptures and modern steel and glass furniture. The intense sunlight only just penetrated the darkened glass and the room was cool, chilled almost to the point of being cold by an extremely efficient air conditioning system. The office could not have been more different than the chaotic open plan inky sweatbox that constituted the editor's office and journalist's floor at the San Fernando Courier.

James rubbed his hands together nervously.

Eventually the editor leant forward, glowered at James again and jabbed a finger in his general direction:

"That is without doubt the worst C.V. of any sucker who has ever walked into this office. You've broken no major stories. You've got no real experience. Man, you don't even look like a hack. Tell me why the hell should I employ a schmuck like you, when a potential Pulitzer prize winning professional journalist with legs up to her neck, might walk through that door in five minutes time, begging me for a job?"

James grinned the amiable boyish grin that he was still capable of.

"I don't have legs that go up to my neck and I stopped wearing skirts when I left the Priesthood, but what makes you think that I'm not a Pulitzer Prize winner?"

The editor sank back again.

"Because you don't look like one." He snarled.

James grinned again.

"Do you think William Randolph Hearst looked like a great journalist? Did Bob Woodward, or Carl Bernstein look like they were going to bring down Nixon?"

The editor was silent for a moment.

"My mother's from the old country. She told me to always be good to Priests. You know?

She said they'd put a good word in for me, which just might be the deciding factor in my getting through those Pearly Gates."

James laughed.

"Or not, as the case may be."

The editor leaned forward again:

"Tell you what, I like you. You got six months, Irish. Six months to come up with a front-page story that'll knock my socks off! Do that and you got a permanent position on the Hollywood Sentinel. Now get outta here before I change my mind."

James stood and proffered his hand.

"Thank you, sir. You'll not regret it."

The editor shook James' hand for a brief instant, without even looking up from the scatterings of papers on his desk.

"See my secretary. She'll pass you to the deputy editor who'll give you a place to work, a typewriter and all that stuff. You start Monday."

James decided that discretion was the better part of valour and so made a quick exit before the editor had a chance to change his mind.

That night, however, after spending a lovely evening celebrating with Carrie, James found sleep hard to come by.

Working on the Courier had been easy. It had been Court reports, traffic incidents, school fetes and college football. Finding front-page headlines would be a different kettle of fish.

The editor had been right. It would take more than confidence and the gift of blarney to get James Malone a front-page story. James knew, of course, that his tale of the "Sacred Order of St Gregory," clerical assassination squads, a supposed second coming and the existence of real life "little people," would not only guarantee him a Pulitzer prize but the front page on every newspaper in the world. Yet it was the one story he couldn't use. Who would believe a story like that? He would end up getting locked away in a secure facility somewhere. So what was he going to do to get a front-page headline?

After a night of tossing and turning James awoke to the smell of Carrie's wonderful coffee. It was a Saturday and James only plan was to play with Aoibheall, his daughter in the back yard. By the time he had wandered into the kitchen to get his coffee, it was already nearly 90 degrees outside.

Carrie, dressed in tracksuit bottoms and a running vest appeared at the door, perspiring freely. Her hair wet and slicked back on her head:

"Oh man!" She gasped. "I just ran all the way down to the mailbox and back. I am soooo out of condition."

Carrie dumped several envelopes onto the work surface near the sink as she turned on a tap, poured water into her cupped hands and then threw it over her face.

James took the envelopes and picked one out, putting the rest down on the breakfast table. He examined the envelope closely while holding his mug of steaming coffee in the other.

"Is Aoibheall awake yet?" Carrie asked through her short staccato breaths.

James shook his head.

"No, fast asleep still, sleeping like a baby as they say."

He put down the mug and ripped open the envelope.

"Who's that from?" Carrie asked as she put her hands on her hips and swivelled the top half of her body from side to side.

"Mmmm?" James responded with a murmur as he read the hand-written letter.

"The mail, who's it from?" Carrie laughed as she breezed past her husband and snatched the letter playfully out of his hands.

"Hey give that back!" James protested, half-heartedly. "It's from Wayne."

"I can see that." Carrie taunted him, waving the letter mischievously.

She tossed the letter back to him with a grin.

"I'm going in the shower. Listen out for Aoibheall waking."

James shook his head.

"Mad as a hatter, so she is."

He sat down and continued to read the letter from the point where Carrie had disturbed him. The first bit consisted of the usual pleasantries. Wayne wondered how the Malone family were doing and what life was like in California. He went on to say how University life was great fun and described a beautiful American girl he had met, but how unfortunately, she already had a boyfriend. Wayne also described his horror at the prospect of a long Easter vacation with Doris. He was, in fact, hiding in his bedroom as he wrote, trying to stay out of her way. James raised his eyebrows when Wayne described how he intended to go to Rome the very next day after he had written the letter, to follow up on something that Bishop Donleavy had told him during the "Battle of Dublin."

"Are you mad, Wayne Higginbotham?" James whispered under his breath as he turned the page.

The next paragraph described Wayne's confusion at some news he had received from his birth mother, the actress Terri Thorne. She had written to Wayne telling him that she had left her husband and the father of her children. Wayne had been delighted about his Mom leaving that "Italian slimeball" as he described him in the letter, but upset that he wouldn't be able to stay at that fantastic house in Coldwater Canyon anymore.

James raised his eyebrows.

"A bit selfish there, master Higginbotham." He muttered.

The letter petered out into the usual pleasantries and James placed it down on the table.

Had Wayne gone mad? Why was he going to Rome for goodness sake? Talk about putting his head in the lion's mouth. James shook his head.

"Well, he's a big boy now, I guess." He said as he wandered into the kitchen to refill his coffee mug.

Carrie emerged around the corner of the kitchen doorway rubbing her hair vigorously with a towel:

"So what's happening in Wayne's world?" She asked.

James shook his head again.

"The eejit is going to Rome." He whispered, still amazed at Wayne's decision.

"I mean, right into the heart of the Holy See just to grab a few bits of stone. I really hope for his sake that the "Order" really is disbanded."

Carrie frowned.

"Well I guess he's not a kid anymore." She carried on rubbing her hair.

"Did he have any other news?" She asked as she put the towel around her neck and took a mug from a cupboard on the wall.

James shrugged:

"His, Mom, you know, the actress, has left that husband that Wayne didn't like."

Carrie pondered the news for a second:

"The mafia dude?"

James frowned:

"Mafia?"

Carrie laughed:

"Yes, remember, Wayne described him as a real Mafioso type. In fact he said he was convinced that's how he did so well in Hollywood."

The germ of an idea began to seed itself in James' mind.

"I remember now." He muttered, distractedly, as he wandered into the living room.

"Hey, was it something I said?" Carrie shrugged as she poured her own coffee, gazing around the suddenly empty kitchen.

James Malone was imagining a front-page headline in thick black type:

"HOLLYWOOD AGENT IN MAFIA SHOCK"
"MY LIFE WITH A GANGSTER BY ACTRESS"

James Malone grinned. Maybe not Pulitzer prize winning stuff, that would have to wait until he could describe the events in Finaan and Dublin and maybe whatever came next.

It would get him a front-page, however, and that permanent job in one of the most prestigious newspapers in Southern California.

Twenty-Seven

Lucy Hetherington shivered and pulled her expensive camel cashmere coat tighter around her. The wind howled and whistled as it gusted down the long terraced street, cutting between the ranks of plain, grey, stone houses. It was as almost as though the late Victorian industrial dwellings that bordered both sides of Cavendish Street had formed a topless wind tunnel, deliberately channelling the wafts of cold air, which cut straight through Lucy's coat, chilling her to the bone.

At the far end of the street Lucy could see the immense grey edifice of the Belmont Mill, its smokestack chimney soaring high into the sky like a humungous, single finger pointing heavenwards. It was only one of several smokestacks that she could see. They looked less like the steeples of mighty industrial cathedrals, than dark satanic Northern mockeries of the spires of affluent Southern varsity towns.

Lucy couldn't help but think of George Orwell's: "The Road to Wigan Pier" and how the Old Etonian had described the plight of Northern industrial workers in the pre-war years. King Cotton had once ruled here too and his reign looked as though it had been particularly cruel and savagely autocratic.

Lucy had never been North of Oxford and although the City of "Dreaming Spires" had rows and rows of terraced cottages, they certainly looked more welcoming and much cosier in their warm red bricks than these cold, grey stone worker-ant barracks.

Lucy shivered again. It was difficult for her to imagine that she was over three weeks into Spring, if March the twenty-first was taken as the first day of Spring. How could this possibly be her Easter vacation? It had been warmer in Jersey in January, before she had gone back down to Queens. It felt like winter still had a very firm grip on the North. Even in Oxford she had already managed to totally dispense with her coat for the last couple of days of term.

She also found it hard to imagine now, why she had ever wanted to visit a small Northern Market town, just because she had once had a vivid dream about some boy being her brother and this was the town he supposedly lived in. Maybe the brother had turned out to be correct but this Shepton thing could be the result of nothing more than having read something about the place or seeing it on TV, or something.

Martin Berenger had described Shepton as an attractive market town. It certainly wasn't from where she was standing. To her right there was a small pub, which quite simply looked like several terraced houses knocked together. It was called "The Junction Inn," presumably because there was a huge railway goods yard behind her. To her left there was a small ice cream factory: "Ice Villa Creamery" with a couple of gaudy yellow and white ice cream vans parked outside. Lucy couldn't think of anything worse than ice cream in such freezing cold weather. She wondered how such a company could possibly stay in business, or even thrive in a place that reminded her of Narnia: "always winter and never Christmas."

Lucy had had plenty of time to think on the train on the journey North. Yet the more she thought about the circumstances of her adoption, the more confused she got. The situation was more incomprehensible than ever to her now. She had been adopted soon after her birth by mummy and daddy, but her twin brother had already been chosen and taken. Lucy shivered again, but it wasn't the cold this time, it was the sheer indignity of having been rejected. Why had the people who had taken her brother not taken her as well? Had she been so ugly? Deformed? Maybe mummy and daddy had had surgery carried out on her when she had been a baby and they hadn't told her about it, just like they hadn't told her about the adoption. They were such kind and nice people that they would have adopted her no matter how hideous a baby she had been. Oh, but that would be just too awful. Lucy refused to contemplate such nonsense.

"Pull yourself together, old stick." She had commanded herself: "You're behaving like a fool."

She had arrived in Shepton bearing a huge sense of foreboding. Her mood had matched the weather: grey, overcast and cold.

"No good can come of this." She had repeated to herself as she had waited on the station concourse for a Taxi. She had seen the Midland Hotel opposite the station. A vague memory of ringing someone there lingered in the back of her mind.

Now, standing on the corner of Cavendish Street, Shepton, Lucy was obviously glad that the people who had adopted her brother had left her behind. Imagine having to grow up in such a frightful place. Even so, it did seem awfully unfair that they had taken the boy and left the girl. As far as Lucy was concerned, such things only ever happened in the third world. She pouted her lips in annoyance. Stupid people, look what they missed out on and how lucky had she been? Rupert and Melinda were the best parents in the world. She felt a pang of sympathy for her brother. Imagine if Rupert and Melinda had managed to adopt both of them, his life would have been so much better.

Another icy blast cut through Lucy's coat. If she stood here much longer she would die of hypothermia. It was time for Lucy

Hetherington to snap into action. She marched smartly across to the Junction Inn and walked straight into the bar. The smoke was so thick in the bar area, that Lucy's eyes immediately began to smart and water. The noise of chatter and raucous laughter was deafening. A fruit machine was playing an annoying, repetitive electronic melody, punctuated by the frequent jangle of coins tumbling into the tray. The ceiling and windows were yellowed by nicotine and every inch of wall space seemed to be covered in pictures and photographs of ancient steam trains. Lucy approached the giant of a man behind the bar, pulling a tall pump handle backwards, forcing dark brown frothy ale into a pint glass.

"Excuse me." She trilled.

The barman didn't even glance at her. His huge arm just kept pulling the handle until with a satisfied grunt he lifted the pint glass on to the bar.

"There y'are Fred, and a half for Rio?"

A small, wiry old man with skin like wrinkled prune and wearing a flat tweed cap that had seeen many better days stood beside Lucy at the bar.

"Aye, and an ounce of Golden, Jack."

The barman nodded, pulled a half-pint glass off the shelf behind him, grasped the pump in his mighty fist and began pulling again.

The wiry man turned to face Lucy, looked her up and down from head to toe and then winked at her.

"Is tha looking for me, love?" He grinned from a mouth almost bereft of teeth.

Lucy visibly flinched before she desperately took a deep breath and regained her composure.

"Unfortunately, not." She replied, trying her best to smile sincerely.

There was a huge explosion of laughter and Lucy flinched again. Her relief was palpable when she realised that she was not the source of the amusement, but that a huge fat fellow, who was laughing more than anyone else had just told a filthy joke.

Lucy almost jumped out of her skin when a dark booming voice from somewhere up above her head asked:

"Now then, what can I get you, young lady?"

Lucy turned to see the barman towering over her.

"Pint of best, is it?" He laughed, much to the amusement of the nasty, little wiry man.

"No!" Lucy declared.

"Actually, I'm looking for someone."

The barman looked around the room. Lucy realised that it had suddenly gone quite quiet."

"Tha's looking for somebody, is tha love? Well I can tell thee tha can have any one of this lot, with looks like that."

The barman boomed and almost every man in the bar roared with laughter. Lucy tried to calm herself, although she could feel her cheeks reddening. She knew all eyes were upon her. She coughed.

"Does anyone here know if there's a young man of about nineteen, living on this street?"

The fat man who had told the joke was the quickest to respond.

"Nay love, tha doesn't want to go messing wi'bits o'lads when tha could have a proper man."

There was another explosion of laughter. Lucy's entire face was now burning.

"I think he lived in a house in this street, where there was a fire, probably about three years ago."

The barman leaned down towards Lucy.

"I think tha might be looking for young Wayne Higginbotham. Doris' lad. He'll be about nineteen now and there was a fire at number eighteen but............."

"Thank you." Lucy blurted and ran out of the bar as fast as her legs would carry her.

The last comment she heard was some wag shouting:

"She were too skinny to be t'stripper anyway."

And then more laughter.

The barman shook his head as he watched Lucy quickly disappear.

"But they aren't there any more, love." He murmured to no one in particular.

Lucy found some semblance of relief in the biting cold wind as it cooled her blazing cheeks. That was the most humiliating experience of my entire life, Lucy thought, as she scurried past the identical dwellings, with their tastelessly bright front doors. The freshness of the air was a blessing compared to the choking, smoky atmosphere of the pub. Her chest was still heaving and her heart beating so hard and fast that she imagined it would crash out through her ribcage if she didn't calm down, quickly.

Lucy Hetherington had always imagined herself as being quite adept at public speaking and she had quite a bit of debating experience, both at school and at Oxford. She had even imagined herself standing as a Tory MP one day, as she had never lacked the confidence to stand in front of a crowd.

Lucy now realised that her confidence had been rooted in the comfort of her own environment, amongst her peers, people like her. She had never experienced anything as intimidating as "The Junction Inn." Even the most raucous Rugby Club disco on Jersey had seemed much less of an alien environment than the Junction.

By the time she found herself standing in front of the door of 18 Cavendish Street, Lucy Hetherington had reduced herself to little more than a gibbering wreck. She had convinced herself on the journey up, that she had been separated from her brother as a baby, because she was deformed in some way. That feeling of rejection had now been joined by a sense of total humiliation. How could she ever hope to go into Politics if she was going to be so intimated by her inferiors?

Lucy took a deep breath and knocked twice on the green, glass panelled front door.

She saw a shadow move behind the glass and the door inched open.

"Hello!" Lucy called, in her friendliest, most endearing voice, trying desperately to ignore the feeling that her heart was trying to jump up her throat and escape through her mouth.

"If you're giving away the watchtower, you know where you can stick it." A gruff female voice rumbled from behind the door.

Lucy flinched again. The door started to close.

"No, wait…" Lucy almost shrieked.

The door opened a little wider and a middle-aged woman with a cigarette hanging from her mouth eyed the girl suspiciously.

"You're not one of them bloody morons, are you?"

Lucy frowned.

"Erm no, I'm not a moron, I don't think, actually I'm………"

"I can't stand 'em. Always spouting religion and then marrying loads of wives. Dirty devils! They should stay in America where they come from, not coming bothering decent, hard working folk like us."

Lucy's eyes were almost popping out of her head. This was all just too surreal to be true.

The woman continued with her tirade:

"And as for them Osmonds, well they should be shot, using pop music to indoctrinate kiddies. Toothy, grinning devils they are."

Lucy took another deep breath:

"Excuse me, madam, but I think you mean Mormons, one of which I am not. I am actually looking for someone who I believe lives at this address."

The woman glowered at her. She took the cigarette from her lips and flicked a long column of ash on to the pavement, just missing Lucy's shoe

"You're not from round here are you, love? Who is it you're looking for?"

Lucy hesitated:

"Look, I know this sounds awfully stupid, but the man at the pub said his name is Wayne Higginbotham and he's the same age as me."

The woman screwed up her nose.

"Do you know who you sound like? That woman on't telly. Reads the news. Eeeh she's right posh, just like the Queen."

The woman took a long drag on her cigarette:

"Nobody here by that name love, sorry."

She began to close the door.

Lucy heaved a huge sigh and was just about to turn away when the gruff voice suddenly exclaimed:

"No, hang on a minute. Higginbotham, that's them as lived here before t'fire. We bought the house eighteen months ago, once it'd been done up. Aye, Higginbotham they were called."

Lucy brightened immediately.

"Do you know what happened to them, where they might have moved to?"

The woman shook her head:

"No, sorry love. They didn't leave a forwarding address. Some post came for them, but I just binned it."

"Thank you." Lucy gushed, "thank you so much."

Lucy tried both neighbouring houses. Number sixteen did not answer the knock on the door, maybe they were out, but at number twenty, a little old lady timorously opened the door and peered at Lucy over a safety chain.

"Excuse me, I'm awfully sorry to bother you, but you wouldn't happen to know where the Higginbothams moved to, would you, by any chance?"

The little old lady cocked her head to one side.

"You'll have to speak up love. I'm deaf in that ear."

Lucy repeated her question. The little old woman stared at her blankly. Then:

"Oh you mean T'igginbottoms, love. Aye. I don't know where they went when they moved. Up over Greenwood, I think. Poor Frank died you know, three years ago. Killed on't road he were, knocked off his motorbike. I see Doris in't town now and again. Lad went off to college somewhere. He were a nice lad, right clever, went to the Grammar school. They adopted him you know."

Lucy smiled:

"Yes, I know."

Lucy spent the rest of the day wandering around the town. Quick searches in the library and in the Parish church proved fruitless. Lucy walked all the way to the Grammar School: Wormysted's, but it was closed for the Easter holidays.

The High Street was handsome, with its wide setting and its cobbled, tree-lined setts in front of the shops. The Parish church stood at the end of the High Street and a pretty castle loomed behind. Moors surrounded the town and once one crossed the canal and escaped the industrial part of town, it really was quite bucolic. Maybe Martin Berenger had been right after all.

There was little else that Lucy could do. She now had a name and a school and she knew that her brother had grown up and like her, was now in further education. Did she need to know more?

As the train rumbled south and Lucy reflected on her trip to Shepton, one thought began to play on her mind. The dream really had been real. She really did have a twin brother. There really had been a fire, nearly three years ago, in a house on Cavendish Street, in a Northern town called Shepton and a boy of her age, called Wayne Higginbotham, had survived it. Indeed, the year of the fire had indeed been an unfortunate year for Wayne, if his adoptive father had died the same year.

Had she really saved her brothers life by making those calls from the dorm that night? And if so, how had he contacted her?

The more answers Lucy got, the more questions seemed to emerge.

Twenty-Eight

A myriad of possibilities flooded Wayne's mind in an instant. He could feel a surge of power welling up inside him, just like it had way back, when he had blown Baz Thompson through the air like a rag doll, just like when he had blasted Francisco Pizarro in Ireland and De Feren in Dublin. Wayne Higginbotham knew that he could just blast his way out, knocking the Nazi Priest right out through the wall if he wanted to. Then again, he probably wouldn't get far, even if the Papal Gendarmerie and the Swiss Guards didn't get him, the Roman Carabineri probably would. Even with his powers he couldn't fight an entire country.

Maybe he could just use his mind to brainwash the Priest, like he had sort of done to Doris in the past and to others when he had felt threatened.

Or, maybe he could just turn himself into something so scary that the Priest would be too terrified to do anything but let him go, just like when he'd used Darth Vader to scare off Aoibheall the Banshee when she had confronted him in his bedroom. Wayne licked his lips nervously, what the hell was he going to do?

For nearly three years, ever since his confrontation with the demented Belgian Priest, Pierre De Feren in St Patrick's Cathedral, Wayne had tried to be sparing in his use of magic. Bishop Donleavy had told him that the "Order" had disbanded, but it had been his careless use of his powers back in Shepton, that had led De Feren right to Wayne's front door and almost cost him his life. As for now, however, desperate times called for desperate measures.

Wayne glanced surreptitiously around the room to ascertain the best viable exit. The only window was high up to his right and small, the only door was behind him.

Wayne prepared to stand and take whatever action first came into his mind, but his feverish planning was interrupted by a most unexpected sound. The sound of an old man pleasantly chuckling:

"Ve have many vays of making you talk. That is what they always say in your English war movies don't they? I presume you are English by the way? Your accent is Northern, Yorkshire, if I am not mistaken? I am quite the Anglophile you see. I have travelled much in your country. I have seen your funny Basil Fawlty and his "you started it, you invaded Poland" sketch. Don't mention the war."

The old Priest was peering at Wayne over his spectacles and his chuckling was far from the evil sneering Nazi laugh that the youth had been expecting.

"You English can never forget the war, can you? Name, rank and serial number, indeed."

Fr Reichmann imitated Wayne's earlier statement in a fairly admissible Yorkshire accent.

"You do not look like a soldier." He stated then with an admonishing frown and in his best Gestapo accent he added:

"You look more like a spy and we shoot spies, don't we?"

Wayne blanched slightly, as the old Priest stood and clasped his hands together behind his back. He looked up at the crucifix on his wall and shook his head sadly.

"Personally, I am only too happy to forget the war." He sighed.

"That crucifix was in the chapel in my prison camp. I was in the German army, the Wehrmacht, the chaplain for a Bavarian division. In other times they would have been farmers, labourers, workmen, teachers, lawyers. They were not evil men, just normal people trying to survive in what were extraordinary times. I spent three years on the Russian front, then six years in that Soviet Prisoner of War camp. That crucifix was all we had to remind us of our humanity. We hid it after every clandestine service. Six years!"

Fr Reichmann sighed as he turned back towards Wayne. He removed his spectacles and dabbed his eyes with a tissue.

"When I did finally get home and believe me, I was very much in the minority in surviving that camp, I found that my parents had both died in Nazi concentration camps. My father for helping Jews, my mother for being descended from one."

The old Priest suddenly looked much older and less threatening.

"So!" He continued: "Or as the Nazis in the movies always say: Ach so! You see, not all Germans are Nazis, Gestapo, or SS men."

Wayne disguised his enormous relief by feigning disinterest and shrugging nonchalantly.

"My dad was in the war. He was a hero."

Fr Reichmann perched himself on the corner of his desk as Wayne straightened his back and continued:

"He was in Monty's Eighth army. He was there when they chased Rommel right out of North Africa. When he was in France, he blew up a German tank, single handed."

Wayne's expression was almost challenging the German Priest to be less friendly.

Fr Reichmann responded by raising his eyebrows and slowly nodding his head.

"Ya, some people do heroic things in war, some people do cowardly things. Some people commit acts of unimaginable evil, while others show degrees of compassion above and beyond the realms of comprehension. Believe me, young man, I hated the Nazis every bit as much as your father must have done."

The old Priest wiped another tear from his eye with a grubby looking handkerchief, which he'd pulled from a pocket in his black cassock. He blew his nose loudly, pushed his spectacles back up to the bridge of his nose and then peered myopically at Wayne.

"Do you believe in God, young man?"

Fr Reichmann's question and his sudden change of direction took Wayne quite by surprise.

"Er, no." He stammered, then after a brief pause.

"Well I didn't, definitely didn't, but now maybe I'm not quite so sure."

Fr Reichmann pushed his spectacles back up his nose and smiled benignly.

"What has caused this change?"

Wayne shrugged again:

"I've seen things that, well things that I once wouldn't have believed. I used to be so certain, but now..."

Fr Reichmann chuckled again.

"Ignorance and blind certainty are the roots of all extremism, my son. When a man has absolutely no doubt about the righteousness of his actions, then he no longer rationalises those actions. He no longer balances his decisions on the scales of morality. Rights and wrongs become irrelevant. That man knows that whatever he does, he is doing the right thing. An ignorant man will follow him, because he knows no better and does not think about morality anyway.

When a man is uncertain, he uses his brain, his wisdom to try and make the right decision. Because he is thinking, he weighs up his actions on those moral scales and any actions that follow will hopefully, have been fully rationalised. It is much more likely therefore that those actions will be right, rather than wrong."

Wayne scowled.

"So you're not sure you believe in God?"

Fr Reichmann grinned.

"I am as certain as any man ever can be, my son. I too saw things when I was a young man, however. Things that would shake anybody's faith and to this day I find myself wondering how a benevolent God could ever have allowed such things. Sometimes it is easier to believe in the devil, than it is in God."

The old Priest's voice trailed off into little more than a whisper.

Wayne put his fist to his mouth, coughed and cleared his throat.

"Were you talking about the Nazis, or the "Sacred Order of St Gregory" when you were talking about extremism?"

Fr Reichmann smiled pleasantly.

"Both!"

Wayne cleared his throat again:

"So you, you're not, you're not one…?"

Reichmann interrupted him.

"No my son. I am not in the "Order." Praise the Lord! For, as far as I am aware, there is only one actual survivor of that confounded organisation still living. The rest have all been murdered, had curious fatal accidents, or have committed suicide. My current task is to find out what they did, why they did it and who has been killing them. The reason you are here, sitting in my office, is because you asked for that sole survivor by name. Very few people know he still lives."

Wayne blew out a huge sigh:

"They're all dead. Every single one of them?"

Fr Reichmann nodded as he retook his seat behind the desk.

"Ya, every one of them, except our dear Fr Bianca. So, young man! Who are you? And why did you really want to see him?"

His tone was much more formal, but despite the German accent Wayne didn't feel quite as threatened as he had before. There was something trustworthy about this Priest. His eyes were gentle and kind, his smile quick and warm. Wayne's only problem now was how much to tell him. What parts of his history with the accursed "Sacred Order of St Gregory" should he divulge?

Wayne sighed and then with an ironic grin and a shrug of his shoulders began to speak:

"My name is Wayne Higginbotham. No rank, no serial number."

He grinned and felt mildly reassured when the old Priest grinned back.

"You were right," he continued: "I'm from Yorkshire. I have come across the "Order" twice before in my life. Eight years ago they killed someone very close to me and had it not been for my dad, they would have killed me and a good Priest too."

Fr Reichmann held up his hand bidding Wayne to stop for a second, as there was a brief rap on the door.

"Come." Reichmann shouted.

A younger black robed Priest stuck his head around the door.

"Is everything alright?" He asked, a look of concern etched on his features as he appraised the black and white, eye-lined young Punk, sitting before the old German Priest's desk.

Fr Reichmann nodded eagerly and glanced at Wayne:

"Would you like some tea?"

Wayne nodded and turned to the young man at the door:

"Yes please, white, two sugars."

Fr Reichmann laughed:

"Why do the Irish and the English like their tea so much? Father Doyle would you be so kind?"

Fr Doyle gave the older Priest an inquisitive look, frowned as if confused, then shrugged.

"Sure, won't be long." He said chirpily, before disappearing and quietly closing the door.

"Now where were we?" Fr Reichmann prompted Wayne.

"You were telling me about the "Order" trying to kill you and your father coming to your rescue."

Wayne nodded eagerly.

"My dad leapt over this huge wall, right out of nowhere and chinned the "Order's" assassin with a real Mohammed Ali style right hook."

"Chinned?" Fr Reichmann intoned, evidently unfamiliar with the word.

"My dad punched him right on the chin." Wayne stated proudly.

"It didn't knock him out, but it totally stunned him."

Fr Reichmann frowned, took off his spectacles and wiped them on a cloth he had produced from a drawer in the desk.

"Do you know who this assassin was?"

Wayne's mouth cracked into a satisfied half smile:

"They called him Francisco Pizarro and he was barking!"

Reichmann replaced his spectacles on the end of his nose.

"Barking? What like a dog?"

Wayne grinned.

"No, it means he was mad, insane, you know, like a mad dog. He was a loony!"

"Ah!" The German nodded.

"What happened then?"

Wayne thought about his options. If he admitted seeing Pizarro fall back into Mickey Finn's burning cottage, then he could have been accused of being an accessory to murder.

"I don't know. I passed out." Wayne lied convincingly.

Fr Reichmann nodded.

"And then…"

Wayne stroked his chin thoughtfully.

"My dad took me home. There had been another Priest with the "Order" there. I was told he died in a car crash trying to get away. There was a good Priest as well. He helped us, but I can't remember his name."

Reichmann nodded thoughtfully.

"So that was your first encounter with the "Sacred Order?""

Wayne nodded and then blew out a sigh before continuing:

"Three years ago the "Order" sent someone to kill me and my dad, I think."

Fr Reichmann sat back in his chair.

"Why did the "Order" want to kill you and your father?"

Wayne shrugged.

"Because we were there when they'd lost Pizarro, I suppose. Maybe they knew my dad had punched his lights out. They sent a weird Belgian Priest to kill me and he would have succeeded but for a good friend of mine. My dad wasn't so lucky. Although the police said it was an accident, I think they managed to knock him off his motorbike."

There was another tap on the door and Fr Doyle brought a mug of steaming tea into the room, which he passed to Wayne with more than a little temerity.

"As requested, Father, milk, two sugars."

He glanced nervously at Fr Reichmann.

"You're sure everything is alright, Father? You don't need me here?"

Fr Reichmann smiled.

"No, Fr Doyle. I will inform you later about what has transpired today."

Fr Doyle departed in a flurry of cassock, looking slightly crestfallen.

"Fr Doyle is as keen as mustard, as they say. He is desperate to get to the bottom of this whole "Order" mystery."

The German Priest stated by way of an explanation for the younger Priest's apparent dismay, while Wayne took a welcome slurp of tea.

"Aaah that's good." Wayne muttered before taking a deep breath:

"The assassin this time was a nasty little Belgian freak called De Feren."

Wayne spat the name contemptuously, spraying tea onto Reichmann's desk.

"Oops Sorry!" He muttered, trying to wipe away small splashes with his hand.

"Anyway, once my dad was out of the way! He tried to burn me to death in my cellar, along with my girlfriend, but we were lucky. We managed to get out."

Wayne altered the facts slightly to increase the credibility of his account. He had made a decision when he had decided to talk, that the Tuatha de Danaan, Banshees and magical powers, in fact anything supernatural, were best left out of the tale.

Reichmann's eyebrows were raised almost to his hairline.

"You are sure about all this?" He gasped incredulously.

"Do you think I'd make this stuff up?" Wayne responded indignantly.

Reichmann sighed and waved his hands submissively.

"No, no, please continue."

Wayne took a deep breath:

"I couldn't leave it there. I had to know who wanted me killed. So I went to Ireland. I visited the "Order's" office in Dublin and confronted the head man, Bishop Donleavy."

Reichmann gasped audibly.

"Was it you that killed him?"

Wayne shook his head:

"No way. Do I look like a muderer? It was the crazy Belgian, De Feren. He was shooting at me, but he missed and hit the Bishop. I guess the guilt was too much for him. He set himself on fire with a bottle of brandy and then ran out into the road, straight under a bus. It served him right!"

There was along silence, interrupted only by the sound of Wayne slurping his tea.

Finally Fr Reichmann took off his spectacles and rubbed his eyes.

"So why do you wish to see Fr Bianca, Wayne Higginbotham?"

Wayne grimaced.

"Before he died, Bishop Donleavy told me that the "Order" had declared victory, as soon as they found out that Pizarro had succeeded in killing his target, even if it had cost him his own life. As far as they were concerned, they had killed the last threat to the Second Coming of Jesus Christ. He told me that the "Order" had effectively ceased to exist from that moment on. Mission accomplished, as they say."

Reichmann crossed himself as Wayne continued.

"Unfortunately, as the good Bishop informed me, the child that had then been summoned into this World, seemed more akin to being the son of Satan than a rebirth of Jesus Christ."

Wayne took the ring that Donleavy had given him from his pocket and handed it to Fr Reichmann.

"Just before he died, he gave me this."

The German Priest studied the ring for a few seconds then nodded.

Wayne continued:

"He told me to find Fr Bianca, show him the ring and that Fr Bianca would give me some stones that he was keeping safe in a vault, somewhere in the Vatican."

Fr Reichmann rubbed his forehead.

"Stones, you say. Do you know what the significance of these stones might be? How they could be used?"

Wayne bit his lip.

"No, I supposed they were some sort of special relic, a totem, you know!"

He lied again.

Fr Reichmann took his spectacles off and fiddled with the frame.

"The events you describe in Ireland, eight years ago. That was near the village of Finaan, wasn't it?"

Wayne nodded and screwed up his mouth, in a gesture that suggested that the German Priest perhaps knew more than he had let on.

Fr Reichmann continued:

"A most tragic event. One Priest committed suicide, one died in a car crash and one disappeared, presumed dead at the time. As for the events in St, Patrick's Cathedral, three years ago, there was no mention of anyone else having been there in the Dublin police report, except for De Feren, Bishop Donleavy and the recently deceased Bishop O'Leary who seemed to have conveniently lost his memory."

Wayne shrugged.

Reichmann looked the youth straight in the eye:

"Swear to me now, Wayne Higginbotham! Swear on the Holy Bible, that you are innocent of any crime."

The German Priest passed a Bible over the desk to Wayne.

Wayne raised his eyebrows, leaned forward and stared directly into the German Priest's blue eyes.

"I swear on this Bible that I am innocent of any crime, but as you know, I am agnostic at best now, so I will swear on something far more important to me. I will swear on my own eternal soul that I am innocent of any crime."

Wayne felt the Priest's eyes burning into his own for what seemed an eternity. Then the older man slumped back with a satisfied grunt.

"I have seen a great deal of evil in my life, young Wayne Higginbotham."

Fr Reichmann spoke slowly and clearly, his hands clasped together and his gaze still concentrated on Wayne's eyes.

"I have seen men act far worse than any animal. I have seen such atrocities that would make that curly mop of hair of yours even more twisted. I have also seen acts of such nobility that I have been moved to tears even just remembering them. I have also seen many people at the point of death and it is then that one truly learns how to read a man's eyes. Few are brave enough to lie as the last breath of life seeps out of their lungs. Even though you are not at the point of death, I know that your eyes speak the truth, although I am convinced you are being somewhat, let's say "economical" with some elements of your tale."

The old Priest smiled empathetically:

"As I probably would be in your situation."

Wayne nodded knowingly.

Fr Reichmann blew out a huge sigh.

"What you have told me pretty much matches the story your friend James Malone told me."

Wayne tried to suppress any sign that he recognised the name, but Reichmann grinned triumphantly.

"Your eyes are the window to your soul, Wayne Higginbotham. I saw the flicker of recognition. He was the Priest who helped you in Finaan, wasn't he?"

Wayne merely raised his eyebrows.

"You will be glad to know that he didn't perish in the aftermath of those terrible events in the West of Ireland, but that he fled to America. I saw Father James a few weeks ago. He is well, although he now claims to have forfeited his ministry and has married a beautiful young woman and had a child. He told me about the "Order's" belief in the supposed second coming and the possibility of they had released a great evil into the world. He was also very keen to assure me that there was a balancing force to that evil. Do you know what, or who, he might have been referring to?"

Wayne smiled sadly.

"No, Father Reichmann. I haven't a clue. I think I've told you all I can at this stage."

Reichmann nodded appreciatively.

"I think that underneath your demonic dress sense, you are a very important young man. If the "Order" took it upon themselves to send an assassin to dispose of you, then you must be a significant player in whatever endgame is about to begin. I wish you well, young master Higginbotham. I wish I could help you with the stones that you seek, but Fr Bianca is still too unwell to talk and I, personally, know nothing about them."

Wayne nodded, although he could not help a grimace of disappointment.

Fr Reichmann smiled again:

"I shall continue to investigate the circumstances of the "Sacred Order" and the veracity of this supposed child, be it for good or evil. Do not judge the "Order" too harshly Wayne, for they were mere victims of their own certainty."

Both men stood, the older Priest escorting the eye-lined, punk student to the door.

Fr Reichmann held out his hand:

"May God go with you, Wayne Higginbotham. I am certain our paths will cross again, one day. Oh, by the way, you better have this back."

He handed Wayne Bishop Donleavy's ring.

Wayne shook his head.

"If Fr Bianca is not going to be well enough to give me the stones, there's no point me having it. It belongs to you lot, you know, the Church."

Fr Reichmann nodded:

"Thank you my son." He whispered. "Oh, just one last thing, do you know anything of the prophecy?"

Wayne shook his head.

"No, what prophecy?"

The priest grimaced.

"Just a moment." He uttered as he trotted behind his desk, picked up a pen and quickly scrawled several lines of spidery handwriting on a piece of paper.

He folded the paper and handed it to Wayne:

"This was the "Order's" raison d'etre, as it were. Read it sometime, young man. It may mean something to you. Then again, it may not."

Father Reichmann proffered his hand once more.

Wayne shook the old priest's hand and with an audible sigh of relief walked out into the corridor, closing Reichmann's door behind him and carelessly placing the folded paper in his pocket. He had survived his journey into the heart of the hornet's nest but had failed in his mission to get the shards of the Stone of Fail. Never mind, what he had still seemed to generate enough power for him even if the stone wasn't complete. That left just the sword and the spear of the magical treasures of the Tuatha De Danaan that he would need to get hold of before the apocalyptic battle. He would have to travel to Ireland if he was to purloin them and that would have to wait until the summer.

For Wayne Higginbotham the rest of the Easter vacation would have to be spent painting window frames and mowing lawns.

Twenty-Nine

It was a glorious early May morning, the sky was cloudless and blue, the air pleasantly warm in the absence of any breeze. The normally grey hued moors that surrounded the town of Shepton took on a glorious emerald appearance in the bright spring sunshine. The yellow daffodils by the roadsides had been replaced by an abundance of gaily-coloured tulips and the leaves on the trees were almost full grown, green, lush and heavy. Birds darted from tree to tree in a frenzy of nest building and coupling, exuberant birdsong filled the air.

Yet, Doris Higginbotham was not happy.

Doris had not been feeling well for days. It had all started soon after Wayne had returned to Manchester for the summer term. Doris had been taking her usual constitutional into town when her ribcage had suddenly seemed to tighten and her breathing had become laboured. Pains had shot across her chest and her mouth had dried up. Convinced that she had been having a heart attack, Doris had been forced to lean against a wall until her breathing had returned to something like normal and the pain had subsided. She had reached the Lite Bite that morning, but had vowed not to over extend herself by walking so far again. She had decided to abandon her old favoured haunt and had started to use the café in the Co-op supermarket.

"Well it's closer t'bus station." She explained to Margaret, that glorious morning as the sisters met for their usual weekly tea and chat.

"I can't seem to get beyond the Post Office before me wind cuts off." She explained.

"The Lite Bite is such a long walk, when you're not feeling right."

Margaret had nodded her head sympathetically.

"Have you thought about losing a little bit of weight?" She asked, as diplomatically as she could manage.

Doris' eyebrows shot up her forehead.

"Why, do you think I'm fat?" Doris exclaimed, incredulity etched on her features.

"I weigh no more now than I did ten years ago." She stated indignantly, pursing her lips in an expression that conveyed the full amount of her unequivocal annoyance at her sister's effrontery.

It was a lie, of course. Doris had ballooned since Frank's passing. The boring monotony of her lonely life at home was only alleviated by constant snacking, while she sat watching mindless rubbish on the TV.

Chocolate bars, cream cakes and cookies were all devoured with indecent frequency and in ever increasing quantities.

"Any road up," she sniffed, "what if I have put a bit of weight on. I've only once to die. There's nowt in my life to look forward to now. I might as well take what pleasure I can, before I kick the bucket."

Margaret, quite aware and covertly delighted, that her comment had riled her older sibling, shook her head sadly:

"That's no attitude, our Doris. You really shouldn't be talking like that. You're only fifty-five years old for goodness sake. You have Wayne's wedding to look forward to, when he, you know, if he decides to get a girlfriend and then there'll be grandchildren."

Doris detected more than just a slight hint of sarcasm in Margaret's optimism about Wayne's future prospects. Her sister's wry smile hadn't helped in convincing Doris of her sincerity either.

"Has he got a girlfriend, yet?" Margaret asked innocently.

Doris scowled:

"Not that I know of." She grumbled: "I don't know what he gets up to at that University. That's the trouble when they're not your own. You don't know how they are going to turn out."

Margaret shrugged.

"I know a lot who'd say the same about their own, Doris. It's just the fashion I think. Although I must say I'm pleased our Cedric is so straight-laced."

The look on Doris' face persuaded Margaret to change tack very quickly.

"Anyway, you ought to get yourself to the Doctors with that breath shortage thing.

It could be the start of heart trouble, angina, or something."

Doris sipped the last of her tea.

"Aye, well. It'll be right. Like I said I've only once to die and I don't suppose I'll be missed much."

There was a long silence as the two sisters watched the world go by from the Co-op café's window. It was a Wednesday, a market day, so the town was packed with Farmers and their jolly rosy-cheeked wives, making the most of the lovely weather after a long hard Yorkshire winter. The hustle and bustle of the busy Market town persuaded Doris that she should take the bus straight back home. She couldn't deal with crowds now, not in her current condition.

Later that afternoon, sat alone in her armchair, with "Emmerdale Farm" flickering on her TV, Doris broke a large piece off a chocolate bar and considered her ill fortune.

Margaret had married Stanley, who was a Bank Manager and very much alive. She had married Frank who had put thingummys onto widgets in a factory and was now dead. Margaret had her own child, while she had been forced to adopt a baby and had been forced to accept her second choice even then. Margaret's son had stayed at home and was working locally. Her adopted son had escaped at the first possible opportunity and left her on her own.

Margaret's son was going to marry someone rich and posh. Her son would soon be wearing a dress if he carried on the way he was going.

Margaret was still a size ten, while she..........

Doris Higginbotham's bottom lip began to quiver and tears started to roll down her face.

She bit a huge lump out of the piece of chocolate.

"What did I do wrong?" She moaned.

"Eeeeh Frank, what did we do to deserve this? Trevor would never have left me on me own like what he's done. Where did we go wrong?"

Thirty

Terri Thorne had been quite surprised to receive a phone call from Michael's friend, James Malone. She knew him; of course, he had delivered Wayne to her house in Coldwater Canyon the previous summer. He must have got Annie's number off Michael. She had conveyed her gratitude to him then for what he had done for Michael, when he had saved her son from the burning basement in England. He had seemed like a nice sort of guy, his Irish sense of humour was very much the same as hers, even though he was a Dublin City boy, while she was from the remote far West of Ireland. Now they had both probably become much more Californian than Irish, but their green roots were deep. He was even a similar age to Terri and although she found it difficult to admit, quite attractive, although Terri knew he was very much in love with his Californian wife Carrie. Michael had told her that.

So when the phone had rung in Annie's condo and Terri heard James' voice she had been convinced that there was a problem with Michael.

"No, no. It's not about Michael." James had insisted in response to her initial exclamation of fear. It's about Dean."

"Dean?" Terri had gasped: "What about him?"

"I think it's best if we meet." James had insisted:

"What about the Radisson, near Burbank airport, Friday morning?"

Terri had hesitated:

"I have a photo shoot on Friday morning."

"Friday afternoon then?" James had persisted.

"OK." Terri had finally agreed after a long pause.

So now she was sitting in the front lobby of the Radisson Hotel near Burbank airport, wondering what on earth Michael's friend wanted to know about Dean. Was he doing it on Michael's behalf? She looked at her watch. He was late. The Diet Coke she had ordered was brought to her table by a young waitress. Terri gave her two dollar bills and told her to keep the change. She was just looking at her watch again when she caught sight of James walking into the dimly lit lobby through the heavily tinted glass doors. A blast of light and heat flooded in with him. As summer approached, she was glad of the air-conditioned comfort of the lobby, she could tell James was too. She could see the sweat marks under the armpits of his jacket.

"Man, it's hot." He gasped by way of an introduction.

"I'm sorry I'm late. The traffic was awful. I don't know about you, but on days like this I almost wish I was back in Ireland."

He held out his hand, which Terri shook.

"I never wish I was back in Ireland." Terri stated in her most businesslike voice.

"So, James, you told me you want to talk about Dean?" She asked as she re-took her seat, smoothing her short black skirt under her legs as she did so.

James looked around the busy reception area and beckoned a young Hispanic waiter over to their table:

"Would you like a coffee, or something?" he asked Terri.

She directed a glance at her Cola on the table and shook her head.

James' eyes followed hers.

"Ah!" He exclaimed before glancing at the waiter and placing his order: "I'll just have a regular coffee, white, no sugar."

"Decaff? Large? Small? Creamer, Cream or milk?" The waiter asked in a voice that betrayed boredom and annoyance.

James clarified his order and turned back to Terri.

"I'm sorry to drag you over here like this." He gushed, while placing a card on the table in front of Terri.

"But Wayne has told me a few times that he believed that Dean was somehow related to the Cosa Nostra. I don't know how he has come to this conclusion, but I thought you would know better than anyone else and you know, well, you've got to use any resources that you can. I'm doing a piece on the mafia in Hollywood and …"

He jerked his head in the direction of the card. Terri picked it up.

"So, you're a reporter now? For the Hollywood Sentinel no less. Bit of a change from being a village Priest in County Mayo, isn't it?" She raised her eyebrows and smiled sardonically, as she returned his press card.

James grinned, a wide, white, toothy grin. Terri couldn't help but respond in kind.

She had set out with the intention of being slightly frosty to James, in the belief that it was actually Michael that he had come to discuss. Michael had told her in the past about what a great guy James Malone was, but she was running low on trust as far as men were concerned, especially attractive men.

James' blushed slightly. Terri Thorne was undeniably a very beautiful woman. Her white silk blouse was displaying a generous amount of tanned cleavage and she had just crossed her legs, so he had glimpsed a very shapely, bronzed thigh. Despite his fidelity to Carrie, her smile had awoken boyhood inhibitions. He cleared his throat nervously.

"In a recent letter, Wayne told me that you'd left Dean. So I figured you might be able to fill me in on his activities, as it were."

Terri smiled a bright white Hollywood smile.

"I still can't get used to you referring to my son as Wayne." She stated with a shake of her head.

"It's such a weird name, don't you think? Who would call a boy, Wayne? It's a surname, like John Wayne, isn't it? Anyway, as you're my son's friend, I'll say this about Dean Vitalia."

James had placed a small cassette recorder on the table, which he was just about to set to record when his coffee arrived. Terri waited for him to sort out the payment and to add his cream to the coffee before she continued. James pressed the two piano key buttons that started the recording machine.

"Dean Vitalia is a schmuck, a liar, a cheat, a no good husband, a no good father, a philanderer, a letch, a flatterer and a skinflint, but I do not think he's involved in organised crime in any way."

James couldn't disguise the disappointment in his response.

"Oh." He gasped.

Terri took a sip of her soda:

"Aurelio Vitalia, Dean's cousin out East on the other hand, despite the fact that he is now sooooo involved in Republican politics and is such a good friend of the Catholic Church, is definitely involved in the Mafia."

James' mouth dropped open. Terri continued:

"The press have referred to him as the Holy Don on several occasions. Dean found that funny: "Ain't nuthin' Holy 'bout Aurelio." He used to laugh. When he was a lawyer he would always be defending villains who were so obviously Mafioso. Dean used to get really upset: "If he goes down it will kill us all," was one quote I particularly remember."

James rubbed his forehead.

"And you don't think Dean is capable of running the West Coast for his cousin?"

Terri shrugged dismissively.

"Dean has a one track mind. Unless it was prostitution, or pornography, Dean wouldn't be in the slightest bit interested. That much I can tell you."

James nodded encouragingly.

Terri, suddenly aware that what she was saying was potentially dangerous, glanced around the hotel lobby. It had quietened down since the couple had sat down together.

A family, two adults with two pre-teen children were stood at the reception desk, while a man in a beige linen jacket wearing a pair of Ray-Ban aviators was sat at a table at the far side of the lobby. When she next spoke, Terri's voice was little more than a whisper.

"Aurelio got married. Dean told me the woman had been a Nun in Italy. Can you believe that? The woman shot herself late last year. She blew her own head off, so they say. Aurelio didn't seem in the slightest bit upset. He now has a stepson and he is the creepiest child I have ever seen in my life. When he looks at you it's not just that he strips you naked, he strips your very soul bare too. I really felt like I was in the presence of pure evil when he came to visit us. Michael, I mean Wayne, met him too."

James sat back in his seat.

"So, you don't have anything that I could use in my report about Dean, except his cousin?"

Terri shook her head. She glanced at the Ray-Ban man. He was staring directly at her, but turned away quickly when she caught his eye.

"No." She whispered.

"If I was you James Malone, I'd be very careful in the way you deal with this story. Dean may not be a gangster, but I'm sure that whether through Aurelio, or not, he knows people who are."

James flashed his electric smile again.

"Ah, I'll be fine. If the "Sacred Order" can't kill me, I sure don't think the mafia will succeed."

He took a sip of his coffee, then turned off the tape recorder and placed it in his soft leather briefcase:

"By the way, you have a remarkable son, Terri."

"I have two remarkable sons." She replied, flashing a slightly admonishing glance from under her long dark eyelashes.

"And a remarkable daughter."

The two Irish exiles stepped into the oven like heat of the Los Angeles afternoon. James shook Terri's hand and thanked her for her time.

"He's destined for great things, your son. You ought to be really proud of him."

Terri smiled politely:

"Thank you, Mr Malone and remember what I said. Be careful."

She jumped into her little Chevvy and turned the starter motor twice before the old car started. Oh how she wished she still had that Porsche. She saw James Malone's shiny black Buick leave the parking lot as she reversed out of her space. Across the lot she saw Mr Ray-Bans glancing in her direction as he hurriedly ran towards and climbed into a small European coupe.

The Chevvy bounced out onto the Boulevard like a racing car, with a squeal of burning rubber and in a cloud of exhaust fumes. Terri veered on to the left hand lane and immediately swept past a couple of lumbering trucks. She heaved a sigh of relief as the Chevvy swept through a light just as it turned to red. She peered into her rear view mirror. The coupe was way back, only just leaving the hotel's parking lot. Terri flicked her car past a van and swerved wildly up a side road, tucking the Chevvy into a parking space outside a bungalow and there she waited. Sure enough the coupe flashed past the road end within a few seconds, going at quite a speed.

Terri waited a while longer and then proceeded to re enter the boulevard, driving at a much more leisurely pace. She had only travelled half a mile or so when she saw the flashing blue and red lights of a police patrol car, pulled over by the sidewalk ahead. Another few yards and she could see the coupe, stopped just ahead of the police car. Terri Thorne laughed out loud when she saw Mr Ray-Ban with his hands pressed hard to the hood of his coupe as one Highway Patrolman scratched details in a little notebook and another frisked him for weapons.

The following morning, Terri arrived at her old house in Coldwater Canyon to hand Marco and Marina over to Dean. They had agreed to share the children, but due to his commitments, Dean soon turned out to only be available on certain weekends and this was one of them. Conchita rushed out to meet her old mistress as Terri walked up to the front door. The Mexican maid hugged Terri and in floods of tears, expressed how much she missed her, then she picked up each child in turn and spun them around and around with joyous abandon. Dean, in contrast, skulked moodily in the shadows.

It was only when Conchita had taken the children up to their rooms, Terri having given both of them a tearful kiss, that Dean finally emerged into the light and approached Terri.

"Thanks for bringing them." He muttered as Terri turned to climb into the old Chevvy.

Terri grimaced.

"It's a pleasure." She replied acerbically.

Dean, kicked at a pebble at his feet. His hands were stuffed deep into his pockets and his head downcast.

"So, you seeing anybody?" He demanded.

Terri opened her car door and heaved a disgruntled sigh.

"Not that it's any of your business, but no, you?"

Dean ignored the question as it was thrown back at him.

"So who was the guy at the hotel?"

Terri climbed into her car and glared up at her soon to be ex-husband.

"Hotel? What Hotel?" She responded angrily and incredulously.

Dean took a hand out of his pocket and rubbed his chin. He looked down at his wife.

"Radisson. Burbank. Yesterday." He spat each word out as if it was a distasteful morsel of food that had lodged in his throat.

Terri smiled sarcastically.

"So I was right, mister Ray-Bans" was tailing me. Dean, that was so cheap."

Terri's erstwhile husband shrugged.

"Not as cheap as a seedy hotel…" He suggested irately.

Terri was more than ready with an adequate riposte.

"Well it certainly wasn't as half as cheap as the Hollywood Highlands Motel, Dean Vitalia and I certainly wasn't in bed with anyone else at any point. The man I was with is a very good friend of Michael's, actually."

Dean snorted with derision.

"Do you really expect me to believe that?"

Terri slammed her car door shut and leaned out of the window.

"To quote one of your favourite movies, Dean: "Frankly, my dear, I don't give a damn.""

There was a squeal of tyres and a scrunching of gravel, as Terri sped away from what had been her home. Dean stepped back to avoid the ensuing massive cloud of exhaust fumes and dust.

"Friend of Michael's, huh?" Dean repeated Terri's claim whilst nodding calculatingly.

"We'll see, honey. We'll see."

He turned and went back into the dark interior of his house.

For a moment a dark cloud swept ominously over the face of the LA sun.

Thirty-One

The ocean was as pewter grey as Welsh slate, reflecting the sombre tones of the early morning sky. Random flecks of white appeared as waves tossed, rolled and broke against one another. The mournful calls of seagulls echoed against the sheer, vertical walls of the cliff face, rhythmically punctuated by the roar of crashing surf, far, far below.

"I must be mad, totally, absolutely and completely barking mad." Wayne Higginbotham muttered as he fastened the chin-strap of his mountaineering helmet. He winced as he caught a piece of loose flesh in the plastic locking clip.

Aillen Mac Fionnbharr stared out from his cocoon of grey-green mist.

"You know exactly which cave the spear head is in, Mac Aillen?" He asked, for what to Wayne seemed like the twentieth time.

"Yes, father." Wayne sighed. "You have pointed it out a million times. Anyway, how did Lugh get it down there in the first place?"

Aillen shrugged:

"He turned himself into a swan and flew down, of course." Aillen responded as though the answer would have been totally obvious even to the biggest idiot.

"Of course he did!" Wayne muttered sardonically.

Aillen frowned.

"I still do not see why you do not do the same thing?" He suggested, folding his arms impatiently:

"It would be far quicker and far less risky than this absurd rope trick that you are about to perform."

Wayne tugged hard on the safety rope, which he had anchored with a bow-line knot to a post on the fence that was meant to prevent people inadvertently falling over the edge of the cliff. Then he checked his descent rope, which he had tied to the same post, for probably the fourth time.

He silently thanked the staff at the Dales Outdoor Centre in Shepton who had guided him in his purchase of climbing equipment.

"Because, Father, you advised me some time ago to not go using my abilities willy-nilly for fear of betraying my existence to the enemy. We still don't have all of the shards of the stone, remember?"

Aillen twisted his mouth.

"You are right, my son. I shall leave you to your task, as it is now light. It would disturb the minds of men if I was to be seen like this.

Good luck!" He called cheerfully and with a wave of his hand Aillen Mac Fionnbharr disappeared. His surrounding mist swiftly drifted out over the sea.

Wayne clasped a carabiner to the safety harness he was wearing and for the third or fourth time, checked that his laces were tight on his thin rubber, climbing boots. He attached the safety rope to the carabiner; then checked that he had correctly looped the descent rope through his special solo-belaying device.

"Your life will depend on using this properly, laddie." The big bearded Scotsman in the shop had warned him as he had demonstrated for the umpteenth time how to thread the rope through the device.

"If you fall it will lock." He had assured the nervous student.

"I hope it's guaranteed." Wayne whispered as he tugged at his belay gloves.

Finally, when he had satisfied himself that he had checked and double-checked all his equipment Wayne took a deep breath.

"Ah well, here goes nothing." He said as he tossed the bulk of the descent rope over the edge of the cliff. Then he climbed over the fence, turned his back to the sea and began his slow and laborious descent of the Cliffs of Moher.

Wayne slowly and carefully fed the rope through a figure eight descender, just as he had been shown, using the belay device as a safety back up.

"Spiderman, spiderman, does whatever a spider can…"

He sang timorously, as he slowly found footholds. Sometimes he just placed the thin rubber soled boot flat against the stone cliff face and found that it gave him just as much purchase. As his confidence increased, he began to descend almost in a sitting position:

"Batman, diddle, diddle, diddle, diddle…" Wayne sang, then suddenly his right foot slipped, swiftly followed by his left and he slammed ignominiously into the rock wall. All the breath was knocked out of him, but the belay device did its job and locked the rope.

Wayne took a deep breath and waited, dangling uselessly until he felt confident enough to pull his feet up and start to descend again.

All the time Wayne was conscious of his effort not to look down at the angry, swelling, swirling maelstrom of water below him. He looked back up to the cliff edge. He had probably descended no more than thirty feet. He could feel spray in the air and the sound of the tumultuous waves crashing over rocks into the cliffs filled his senses.

"Only another fifty feet to go." Wayne chirped with a confidence that he certainly wasn't feeling.

"Don't worry." He muttered to himself. "At least if you fall you can turn yourself into an albatross."

He pulled at his safety rope to make sure it was still tightly bound to the fence post. If he did fall and his belay device failed then at least he would only drop the hundred feet, or so, that his safety rope allowed. That is, unless it snapped, or was cut on the rocks, of course.

Wayne licked his bone-dry lips and desperately tried not to look down.

The rubber boots gripped the sandstone again as, slowly, carefully, Wayne resumed his descent. He knew he had a good couple of hours before any tourists would arrive at the cliffs, but he still faced the long climb back up.

"Less haste, more speed." He thought, as he slowly let the rope slip through the figure of eight. He looked up to his left where O'Brien's tower peered out over the wild Atlantic to the Aran Islands. The cliffs at that point towered over seven hundred feet above sea level, even where Wayne was descending, the sea was six hundred feet below the cliff edge.

To pass the time and in an attempt to allay his nerves, Wayne's mind flicked over to other things. The Ford Escort he had just bought back home. How great would it be to take that back to University in the Autumn!

He thought about his building Society account and how the car and all the equipment he had bought for this expedition had nearly emptied it. Going to America the previous year and Rome at Easter, hadn't come cheap and Frank had only allowed him a small amount in his account from Aillen's treasure horde. Of course, Wayne still had a few trinkets of jewellery hidden at home. One piece, which Wayne had given to James Malone's brother Dan, to fund an earlier expedition to Ireland, had fetched nearly half a million pounds. Wayne, not being of age at the time to use such an amount of money, however, had allowed Dan Malone, who was a lawyer, to put that money into a secret account in London, so as not to alert Doris that anything in the slightest bit unusual was going on. The rest of the fortune from Aillen's horde was being held in trust until Wayne reached twenty-one. Oh well, Wayne was sure that Dan would access him some funds, if he needed them.

Wayne thought about Doris and how she had exploded yet again when he told her he was going to Ireland to do some fieldwork as soon as he had arrived home at the end of term.

"First it was America, then Italy, now it's Ireland. You'll do owt to get away from here, won't you?" Doris had yelled.

Wayne had thought for about half a second and had then simply said:

"Yes," with an extremely ironic grin, before fleeing to the sanctuary of his bedroom to avoid the ensuing torrent of abuse.

Most of all, however, Wayne thought about Sabine and how he had spent the entire summer term trying, unsuccessfully, to woo her. What Wayne didn't understand, was why, when she knew that he was mad about her, did she spend so much time with him? He had even met her boyfriend, Jim a couple of times. He had flown over to visit Sabine during the summer term in Manchester, as he hadn't managed to get over during the Easter vacation and had been out and about with her.

Unfortunately, not only was Jim Hampshire as tall, cool, erudite and handsome, as she had said, but he had also turned out to be a really nice guy. Even the handsome American alter-ego, Mickey Finn, that Wayne had created to woo Stephanie Fleming, looked like a total dork compared to this guy. So why had Sabine introduced him to Wayne? Was it an attempt to make Wayne jealous and miserable? If so, it had certainly succeeded. Wayne had been forced to concede, by the end of term, that the delightful Sabine was a lost cause. She would never dump Mr Yale for a Yorkshire geek with pointy ears.

The only positives that Wayne had been able to draw from what had been a largely disappointing summer term, had been the fact that his lack of a social life had enabled him to knuckle down and do well in his first year exams and the fact that Jim hadn't proposed to Sabine, yet.

A flash of colour off to his right caused Wayne to look round, just in time to see a brightly billed puffin fly past him towards the cliff top. He also noticed that he had slightly overshot his target: The small cave in which "Lugh of the long hand" had hidden the point of his spear.

The cave was little more than a fissure in the sandstone face of the cliff. Wayne pulled himself back up to the hole and fastened his belay device. He reached into the fissure, but recoiled immediately as an angry squawking gull flew out of the fissure, just missing his face. Wayne's heart seemed to stop as he pushed back in panic, flying, arms flailing desperately, back into thin air, but the belay device worked again and held the rope in place. Wayne swung and spun helplessly for a minute then flattened him self to the cliff face, gasping for breath. He took several deep breaths then reached into the tiny cave again, this time, right at the end of his fingertips, feeling something solid. Wayne pushed his face right up against the cave and stretched his fingers as far as they would go, after failing to make any contact for several seconds, he finally managed to grab, between two fingers, what felt like wet, cold skin. He pulled his arm back and dragged the object out of the fissure. It was a folded, oiled cloth, yellowed with age and covered in guano. Wayne breathed a sigh of relief. He had what looked like one of the four great treasures of the "Tuatha de Danaan" right there in his hand. All he had to do now was to climb the seventy or eighty feet back to the top. Wayne tucked the oilskin into his jacket, took off his abseiling gloves and then began to climb like Batman, back up the cliff-face.

As he used his safety rope to gratefully pull himself up over the cliff edge nearly an hour later, Wayne felt a surge of pride and an overwhelming sense of relief. In the distance he could see a car pulling into the car park next to his Auntie Katie's Ford Fiesta. He was just in time; it was illegal to climb on the Cliffs of Moher and the arrival of the first of the days many tourists would have been disastrous if he had still been dangling over the cliff edge. The cliffs were, after all, the most popular tourist destination in Ireland, despite not being as tall as the Slieve League cliffs in Donegal.

Wayne pulled off his helmet, wiped the sweat off his face and then slipped himself out of his harness. He quickly untied the bow-line knot from the fence post, rolled up his rope and placed his equipment in the rucksack. In the distance a couple of people with a dog were walking up the path while a second and a third car pulled into the car park. Wayne pulled the rucksack on to his back and began to stroll nonchalantly down the path. A sliver of sunlight slipped between the grey clouds as he reached the couple with the dog.

"Morning." Wayne greeted them as he skipped jauntily by.

Once in the car, Wayne unwrapped the filthy, ancient oiled cloth. A rusted spearhead fell out onto his knee, leaving a brown stain on his jeans.

"Oh well, that's really state of the art weapons technology." Wayne grumbled disappointedly.

"I mean, I could take out a Chieftain tank with a rusty bit of scrap, couldn't I?"

He prodded the spear-head dismissively, expecting it to crumble to dust at his touch. An involuntary surge of energy seemed to rush out of his index finger as it struck the rusted relic. His finger stuck to the metal, almost like Wayne was experiencing an electric shock. After just a few seconds, Wayne managed to pull his finger away and instinctively stuck it in his mouth. The bronze spearhead on his knee now shone like burnished gold.

Wayne gulped:

"Whoa, treasure number one, in the bag."

Thirty-Two

Father Reichmann tried to avert his gaze from the horrific scene unfolding in front of him, but he was powerless to resist his own morbid curiosity. Starving, emaciated figures, naked, or dressed in loose rags, crawled towards him, beckoning him, silently beseeching him to help them, but he could do nothing. He was standing on the other side of the razor wire, just staring at them, frozen, unable to move.

The mocking sound of laughter filled his ears as two grey uniformed Nazi guards appeared and kicked out at one skeletal figure, who rolled over and tried to shield his shaven head with his hands. Somewhere an alarm bell was ringing. The Nazis kicked the pathetic figure again. This time one caught his head with a heavy jackboot. The skeletal man went limp and did not move again. Fr Reichmann wanted to scream at the swaggering, laughing guards, but no sound would come out of his mouth. The alarm bell kept ringing insistently, as the Nazis started to shoot at the withered, gaunt wrecks that had once been human beings, with submachine guns. The only sounds he could hear were the rattle of the gunshots, the laughter of the guards and the alarm bell. There were no screams, no cries for mercy. It seemed to Reichmann that death was being greeted as a welcome release, by the pitiful, scrawny victims. They actually looked grateful.

The ring of the telephone jolted him back into reality with a start. That had been the alarm bell in his dream. Fr Reichmann blew out a long sigh of relief. The nightmares had been a part of his life for as long as he could remember. Even so, that did not help him to get used to them, nor did it make waking up any less of a relief. He swung his legs out of bed, wincing as his feet met the cold stone floor, then glanced at his clock as he grabbed the receiver. Who could possibly be ringing at five in the morning? He wondered.

"Father Reichmann?" The voice asked. Reichmann replied in the affirmative before raising his eyebrows in surprise.

"It is Doctor Mancini here from the teaching hospital. Father Bianca is awake and lucid, this morning, although for how long, we do not know. It might be wise to come as soon as you can."

"I'll be right there." Father Reichmann assured the specialist who had been looking after the frail old custodian of the "Sacred Order of St Gregory's" library. No one, not even the most optimistic of the medical professionals had expected Fr Bianca to ever regain consciousness, so bad had his injuries been. Yet, here he was, awake and lucid.

Fr Reichmann had asked Doctor Mancini to notify him if there was any change in the old Priests condition. As the curator of the "Order's" history and the last survivor of the core leadership, any testimony from Fr Bianca could be crucial to Fr Reichmann's enquiries.

He couldn't help but feel a frisson of excitement as he replaced the receiver on the cradle.

Fr Reichmann washed and dressed as quickly as possible, before ringing Fr Doyle and arranging to meet him by the old Priest's bed.

Half an hour later, Fr Reichmann was sitting by the bed of the badly burned Priest, with Fr Doyle standing behind him.

"So I am the last?" The Fr Bianca whispered in a voice as thin as a reed.

Fr Reichmann nodded, sadly.

"As far as we know, every other member, from the lowliest country Parish Priest, to Cardinal D'Abruzzo himself has perished. Father. Bishop O'Leary was the last. He took his own life in Ireland. All the records have been destroyed, Father. The "Sacred Order of St Gregory" no longer exists. It is as though every single trace of it has been carefully, deliberately and systematically erased. Have you any idea who might be behind such an act?"

Fr Bianca nodded feebly. He beckoned Fr Reichmann closer.

"I am sworn to secrecy, Father. The "Order" carried out God's most important work."

The old man coughed, his singed mop of white hair wobbled as his chest heaved.

Reichmann passed him a glass of water, which he sipped.

Fr Bianca closed his eyes as Reichmann and Doyle exchanged worried glances.

After a few moments, the old man's eyes opened again, he beckoned Reichmann to return to his former proximity.

"I can not tell you, what we achieved, but we made the worst possible enemy in fulfilling our Holy quest and he has made us pay. He has made us pay in our very life-blood. Will you give me the Holy Sacrament, Father?"

Fr Reichmann nodded.

"I know all about the child, Father." The German Priest whispered.

Bianca's eyes lit up.

"You Know? How? How is that possible?" His voice was strained and Reichmann could hardly hear him even though his ear was turned to the "Order's" archivist's lips.

Fr Reichmann slipped the ring that Wayne Higginbotham had given him onto his finger as Fr Bianca closed his eyes momentarily.

"Father Bianca." The German Priest whispered.

The old Priest opened his eyes again. Fr Reichmann lifted his hand and showed the old Priest the ring that had belonged to Bishop Donleavy, the "Order's" chief in Ireland and second only to Cardinal D'Abruzzo.

Fr Bianca's eyes almost popped out of his head.

"So you are one of us?" He whispered.

Fr Reichmann put his finger to his lips.

"Then all is not lost." The older Priest sighed contentedly.

"But you said I was the last?"

Fr Reichmann smiled:

"Let us hope the enemies of the "Order" are of the same opinion." He whispered into the old man's ear.

Fr Bianca tried to lever himself up, his face became animated, his eyes desperate.

"The child must be protected at all costs." He croaked as he grabbed Reichmann's sleeve.

"By the blood of the Blessed Virgin. He must be protected. There has been a demon invading my dreams, a faceless demon, telling me that we have failed and that the "Order" was deceived. I know we did not. The demon tells me he will kill the whelp who could save us."

The old Priest closed his eyes again.

Fr Reichmann made a comforting hushing sound.

"All is not lost, Father. I have faith. I…"

Fr Bianca waved his hand, interrupting the German Priest.

"There is so little time." Fr Bianca muttered: "There is a key in the drawer there."

He indicated a bedside table unit,

Fr Reichmann opened the drawer and removed a small gold key.

"I expected trouble." Fr Bianca almost chuckled. "So I had some of the more important relics that the "Sacred Order" had gathered over the centuries, put into a common vault in the main Vatican museum."

He paused and took a few rasping breaths before continuing: "Lorenzo, the caretaker, knows where they are." He coughed again. This time it racked his body and it seemed like he would convulse for a moment. Then he settled back again, every breath seemed to take a huge amount of effort.

"Go and get the Doctor!" Fr Reichmann commanded Fr Doyle, who nodded and scurried off down the ward.

"Please Father," Fr Bianca whispered: "Give me the Sacrament for my time is nigh and I can join my brothers in the "Order" joyously, knowing now, that all is not lost."

Fr Reichmann performed the last rites over the old Priest, who was now struggling to breathe.

Finally, Fr Bianca made a huge effort to sit up. He grabbed Fr Reichmann's hand.

"You must make sure the child is safe." He gasped desperately.

"For he is our salvation, our only hope of eternal life and.........."

His eyes seemed to pick out a single point on the wall and freeze, while a final long rasping, wheeze from his chest signalled the dying breath of the last member of the once mighty "Sacred Order of St Gregory".

He slumped back on to the pillow of the hospital bed.

Father Reichmann crossed himself and began to murmur a prayer for the deceased, as Fr Doyle returned with Doctor Mancini and two nurses.

Dr Mancini strolled over to the bed and felt Bianca's wrist:

"I knew his passing was imminent." He stated philosophically, as he smiled sympathetically. He thanked the two black robed Priests for helping the old man pass with dignity. The nurses covered Fr Bianca's face and lowered the hospital bed in order to wheel him off to the mortuary.

"It was amazing, miraculous even how long he lasted. His lungs were very badly damaged in the fire. For him to wake up at all was a true miracle. God rest his soul."

The Doctor shook his head and raised his hands in a gesture of baffled amazement.

"Amen." Both Priests muttered.

Fr Doyle cleared his throat as he and Fr Reichmann walked slowly down the corridor, leaving the medical staff to deal with Fr Bianca's body.

"Did I understand correctly what happened there, Father?"

He asked quietly.

Fr Reichmann turned to face the Irishman, his face a picture of benign innocence.

"What do you mean, Father?" He replied curtly although the glint in his eyes betrayed his good humour.

"Well obviously I couldn't hear much, but did you just masquerade as a member of the "Sacred Order of St Gregory," before a dying man?"

Fr Reichmann looked exceedingly shocked.

"Whatever gave you such a ridiculous idea?" He rebuked the younger Priest with an amused, hissed whisper.

"I merely showed him a token that encouraged him to open up, a little."

The two Priests wandered out of the ward doors. Fr Doyle frowned.

"So that's the end of the "Sacred Order of St Gregory," then. Fifteen hundred years and it all ends here, on a hospital ward, smelling of bleach, antiseptic and soap."

Reichmann shrugged.

"It is the end of the "Order" as such, but what they set out to achieve, has been achieved to all intents and purposes. As far as we know, they have destroyed the non-human races that according to the prophecy, supposedly constituted the threat to the Messiah and they have succeeded in bringing a baby into being, that will define the future of all mankind."

Fr Doyle looked confused.

"So do you think the child that was born here in Rome is the actual messiah?"

Fr Reichmann shook his head sadly.

"I have not met the child, but I have heard enough to have some very serious doubts."

Fr Doyle scratched his head:

"So do you think the child is evil, Father?"

The two Priests stepped out of the hospital into a beautiful Roman morning. The streets were packed with rush hour traffic and the sidewalks thronged with commuters walking from the station towards their offices.

Fr Reichmann gripped the key to Bianca's vault tightly in his pocket.

"Something, or someone, has destroyed the entire "Sacred Order of St. Gregory," an organisation that has existed since the time of the Roman Empire. It has survived the fall of Empires, pestilence, wars and inquisitions. Yet, in the space of little more than eight years it has disappeared off the face of the earth, every member, every record. Whatever it is that has done this, is more powerful than I dare to imagine and more terrible than even my darkest nightmares. Let us hope that good men like his Grace Bishop Donleavy, his Eminence Cardinal D'Abruzzo and dear old Fr Bianca, did not die in vain."

Thirty-Three

Lucy Hetherington sat on her bed in her college room, with her knees tucked under her chin and her arms wrapped round her legs. She glanced at her watch. Her daddy would be arriving soon to take her home for the long summer vacation.

Lucy was confused; she should have been feeling deliriously happy at the prospect of returning to Jersey, seeing her mummy and her horse, Flick and the crazy retrievers, Spick and Span. She had missed them all terribly while she had been down in Oxford.

Yet, somehow, she felt strangely disorientated. The trip up to Yorkshire, to the market town of Shepton over the Easter Vacation, had not answered any of her questions. Indeed, it had only opened up a potential can of worms.

She had found out that her brother had lived in a tiny terraced house on a grimy industrial street in a place that was half Northern industrial mill town and half bucolic, country market town.

She now knew that he had been raised under the name Wayne Higginbotham and had attended the local Boy's Grammar School. Somehow the name Wayne Higginbotham conjured a picture in her mind of a small boy in a flat cap, filthy Victorian clothes and wearing enormous clogs.

She had so wanted to ask Martin Berenger, who had attended Wormysted's Grammar School in Shepton and who had attended Pierre's awful party, if he had known a Wayne Higginbotham, but she didn't see him all term. It was hardly surprising; he had graduated the previous year. Lucy had bumped into the girl who had accompanied him to Pierre's party, Fi, but she had sniffily informed Lucy that she had dumped him at the end of the Easter Vacation and had absolutely no idea where he was.

Lucy also knew that, somehow, three years earlier, her brother had managed to communicate with her telepathically. There really had been a fire in that frightful little house.

Over the long weeks of the summer term, despite the conflicting demands of exams and her increasingly complex social life, Lucy had found herself thinking about her lost sibling more and more. Her exam performance had undeniably suffered because of the distraction that Wayne Higginbotham, whoever he was, had provided.

She had spent many long, sleepless nights concentrating on finding him using nothing more than her mind, yet no matter how hard she had tried, she couldn't reach him like he had her. It had all been so frustrating. She had lost so much sleep that one of her tutors had actually been audacious enough to ask her if she was taking drugs. Lucy had been mortified at the very suggestion and had told the unfortunate Don exactly what she thought of her.

The whole thing had even ruined the post exam May Balls, when gaiety and frivolity were meant to be the order of the day. Lucy had rejected several offers from extremely eligible young men, just because she felt too depressed to show her face in public.

Lucy looked out of her window. It was a muggy, overcast day. She could see some of her friends sitting on the grass in the courtyard, laughing and talking as they waited for their parents to come and collect them and take them away to wherever they lived their real lives over the summer. They were all so carefree, so privileged. Lucy considered getting off the bed and going down to join them, but she wasn't in the mood for girlish gossip, so she just slumped back onto the bed.

The half-hearted search for her brother had also been the catalyst for the release of a whole gamut of emotions about the circumstances of her adoption. A million questions had flooded her mind, as the dam of disinterest that she had deliberately built to protect her sanity when Daddy had told her about her adoption, had burst. She had found herself wondering about her birth mother and father. Who had they been? Were they still alive?

Were they together? Why had her mother been in such a desperate situation that she had given away a pair of twins? What was her mother like? Where was she from? Was she alive? Did she resemble her?

Lucy Hetherington was in floods of tears by the time Roger, the porter, tapped gently on her door.

"Miss Hetherington, your Father is here Ma'am. Shall I send him up?"

Lucy took a deep breath:

"Yes please Roger." She attempted to sound bright and cheery, whilst swiftly jumping off the bed to repair her mascara in front of the mirror.

One thing was for certain. Daddy was going to have pay for quite a lot of counselling over the summer.

Thirty-Four

The summer months were passing all too quickly for James Malone. His six-month deadline to come up with a front-page news story for the Hollywood Sentinel was getting worryingly close and so far he had come up with nothing more than rumour and innuendo concerning Dean Vitalia's supposed mafia involvement. Sure, Dean was a philanderer, an unfaithful husband and a poor excuse for a father, but he did not seem to be involved in any sort of illegal mob activity. As far as James knew, Dean hadn't seen his rotund, East-Coast based cousin, Aurelio in nearly a year, nor had he been seen in any of the more notorious mob haunts in Las Vegas. If he had wanted to run a story on how many starlets had complained about Dean's casting couch techniques, or how many unfulfilled promises of fame and fortune he had made, then James would have been able to fill the entire newspaper. In Hollywood, however, such things were the accepted norms and would not have been of interest to anyone.

James sipped his coffee while looking out over the valley, idly tracing the track of the Roscoe Boulevard as it shot through Northridge and headed out towards Burbank and the mountains beyond. One long, straight line disappearing into the smog and shimmering haze of a typical Southern Californian, late afternoon.

With a start James realised he could hear his daughter Aoibheall crying in the house. He had left her asleep in her crib while he had tried to come up with an inspired idea on how to nail Vitalia. All he had managed was to notice just how straight California boulevards were.

James threw the dregs of his coffee onto the grass of his small lawn and caught himself wishing that Carrie would not be out too much longer. He was slightly ashamed of himself as he picked his daughter out of her crib and cuddled her, after all, this was the Nineteen Eighties and enlightened men were meant to be as family-centric as their spouses:

"Mommy will be back from the store soon." James comforted Aoibheall, whilst gently patting her back.

So what was he going to do if he couldn't pin the mafia allegations on to Dean?

He had the biggest story since paper had been first run off Caxton's press, in his possession, but he couldn't use it without the risk of being run out of town as a charlatan and then locked up in an asylum to boot. The story of the immortal "Tuatha de Danaan" and their centuries old battle with their mortal enemy the "Sacred Order of St.Gregory" was a sure-fire best –selling front page. But how could he use it and still be considered of sound mind and body?

James continued to think as he patted Aoibheall's back.

"I saw an eleven year-old schoolboy blasting bolts of pure energy from his hands, or I saw a teenager turn into Clint Eastwood before obliterating a solid oak door. Yes Jimmy, now tell me about your childhood Jimmy."

Aoibheall gurgled contentedly.

"They'd all think your poor Dad was absolutely nuts, wouldn't they baby?" James laughed as carefully placed his daughter into her high chair and put a bowl of chopped fruit in front of her. The ring of the telephone took him by surprise; he marched around the kitchen door to pick up the receiver:

"Hello?" James answered the phone.

"Is that Mr. James Malone?" The deep voice rumbled through the speaker, taking what seemed like an age to say each word.

"Yes, speaking." James responded with a puzzled frown. "Who's that?"

"It don't matter who it is, Mr Malone. You been asking a lot of questions about a friend of mine. A good friend of mine. He don't like it. I don't like it. You understand?"

James snorted derisively.

"Look, I'm a journalist, it's my job to ask questions. Who are you referring to anyway?"

The voice waited patiently for James to finish.

"I think you know who I'm referring to. Being a journalist don't give you no right to go interfering in other people's business. It don't give you the right to go poking your nose where it don't belong. You know what I'm saying?"

James made an irritated clicking noise with his tongue.

"Look, whoever you are. I don't respond to threats and I'll go to the police if……………"

James was suddenly conscious that the receiver had been replaced at the other end. His words were being spoken to a background of buzz.

With a slight clenching of his stomach muscles James replaced his own receiver.

"Maybe Daddy has ruffled a feather or two." He joked as Aoibheall stuffed a seedless grape into her mouth. Even so, he couldn't help but feel that maybe grabbing a second tiger by the tail hadn't been the smartest move, considering he had only just survived his two encounters with the "Sacred Order of St Gregory."

"Ha, once I've defeated the mafia, I might just go and tweak the nose of the IRA." James laughed nervously.

"It's a good job your Da's indestructible Aoibheall Malone, or you might not get to see him as you grow up."

The following day James drove his Buick all the way down the San Diego Freeway to San Clemente. He parked outside an ordinary block of condos, walked up to a door and pressed the bell. Terri Thorne's voice echoed through a recently fitted intercom system:

"Who's there?"

James cleared his throat:

"It's James, Terri, James Malone."

The door opened and Terri stuck her head out, glancing round nervously.

"Come in." She said, but her voice didn't sound particularly welcoming. James walked into a comfortable and well-furnished living room. It looked vaguely Mexican in inspiration. Terri noticed him looking round:

"I suppose Michael gave you the address." She stated.

"I asked him to write me with it." James replied hesitantly.

"Sorry."

Terri shrugged.

"It's OK. It's my sister Annie's place. She's working today. As you can see, I'm not. It seems one or two of my larger contracts have been cancelled for reasons that no one seems to want to disclose."

She waved towards a comfortable looking armchair. James sat down. He had noticed Terri's tight blue jeans and simple white Tee shirt combination. Her blonde hair was tied back in a ponytail. Once again James Malone found himself feeling nervous.

How could this woman, whose son he considered a good friend, be the same age as him? She looked like a teenager cheerleader, fresh home from high school.

"Do you think Dean is squeezing you?" James asked, trying to sound mature and reporter like. Terri shrugged.

"Can I get you drink? A beer? Soda?"

James shook his head.

"Er, no thanks. I'm fine thank you." He realised he was staring stupidly at her, like a lovelorn teenager. He averted his eyes demurely towards the ceiling, remembering how many times he been forced to do that as a blushing young Priest back in Ireland, when pretty girls had tried to distract him. There had been many occasions when he had been forced to gaze heavenwards, as though seeking divine inspiration, when giggling flirty girls had smiled and fluttered their eyelashes from the front row of the congregation.

"I don't know." Terri answered his earlier question, her voice edged with bitterness.

"It wouldn't surprise me. Dean knows a lot of people."

James pursed his lips and looked at the Mexican rug on the wooden floor in front of him:

"I had a phone call last night. Some guy doing his best Marlon Brando in the Godfather impression. You know? I wanna make you an offer you can't refuse, sort of thing. The only Mafia cliché he missed out on was: capiche."

Terri blew out a sigh.

"So you've been warned off."

James nodded and scratched his head.

"I guess so. It sort of confirms my suspicions, but it's not going to make the headlines is it? Journalist threatened by heavy on phone." He laughed as he exaggerated the last few words.

Terri smiled sympathetically.

"I told you to be careful. I really can't tell you anything more about Dean. Not because I'm scared, although I guess I could be scared of him, if I thought about it, but because I really don't know anything. He was hardly ever in the house. It was always work, work, work. He was always in Vegas, out East, going to meetings, screenings, auditions, whatever.

I had my own career too and yeah, he was useful in getting me roles before I had the kids. Then it was like, hey you're a mom now, you stay home, look after da bambinos."

Terri mocked an Italian accent and both she and James laughed freely before Terri continued:

"I got wheeled out occasionally, you know, decoration on his arm for the odd premiere, or party, or whatever and that was the limit of my involvement."

James nodded.

"I understand."

Terri looked at her watch:

"Look, I'm sorry to be rude, but the kids are at a little Montesorri School round the corner. I'm supposed to collect them about now."

James stood.

"I'm sorry to disturb you again. I hope the contracts come back." He held out his hand.

Terri shook his hand and opened the front door.

"Oh, I have ways of persuading my husband to lay off." She laughed, but her face suddenly took on a serious hue.

"I mean what I say when I say be careful, James Malone. Dean could be up to his neck in this mafia stuff and I would never have known. I would hate someone so close to Michael to get hurt."

James grinned.

"Oh, I've been in worse scrapes than this, I can assure you. If anything does happen to me by the way, let Wayne, sorry, Michael know who was responsible."

He turned and walked back to the Buick.

Terri watched him drive away. Why had he said that, she wondered? What could Michael do?

She turned and picked the front door key off a hook around the corner. As she opened the door again to leave, a motorbike edged out of a side road opposite. The rider was wearing a full-face black helmet, which was unusual in California. She noticed him staring in her general direction as he revved the Harley Davidson noisily and then sped off after the black Buick.

Despite the heat of the Los Angeles afternoon, Terri Thorne shivered.

Thirty-Five

The last dregs of the pint of "Old Mysterious" slipped down Wayne's throat, like the proverbial nectar of the Gods.

"Oh my God, that was good." He burped appreciatively.

It was the last night of the summer vacation. Autumn colours were beginning to appear in the leaves and there was a distinct chill in the air as the lads piled out of "The Black Bear Inn" in the Yorkshire Dales village of Potwell. The ancient village pub stood by an even older, small, humpback bridge, which crossed the burbling nascent River Wharfe. Wayne's Ford Escort mark one was parked in a car park adjacent to the village green. He reached into his pocket and pulled out his car keys. He knew he was being silly, he had drunk far too much beer to drive, but he was in a celebratory mood. Tomorrow he would escape Doris and her constant nagging and moaning and her incessant trivial demands and get back to the haven of peace that Manchester provided. He burped again as he climbed into the driver's seat of car. John Lancaster jumped into the passenger seat, while Paul Harland and Liam Riley clambered into the back. Wayne had drunk much less then the others, but he knew that he would be way over the limit if they were stopped by the police.

Wayne had passed his driving test whilst he had been in the sixth form at Wormysted's, but had never possessed his own car until he had seen the souped-up Ford Escort outside a house on Castle Street, at the beginning of the summer vacation. A large hand written sign, displayed in the windscreen of the car, had declared it to be: "For Sale: £300."

It was love at first sight. The eleven-year-old Ford Escort Mexico had been given a new coat of lurid green metallic paint and bore a white "go faster" stripe down each flank. The original wheels had been replaced by a set of sexy five spoke alloys and the tyres were fat and wide. Best of all, once Wayne had contacted the owner, he found that the original engine had been replaced with a new 1800cc injected unit, complete with a raucous sounding wide boar exhaust system. As far as Wayne was concerned the car was "sex-on-wheels."

A quick check on his bank statement had meant that he would be able to afford the car and still be able to make his then projected trip to Ireland in search of the treasures of the "Tuatha de Danaan." Especially as his old school mate, Liam Riley, had managed to get him a job working in the local cheese factory for six weeks, starting in early August.

By the end of the summer vacation, Wayne's confidence behind the wheel had grown and even he would have admitted that he often drove audaciously, bordering on the dangerously arrogant.

As the Escort pulled out of Potwell that night, Wayne's ebullience translated into his driving. He accelerated out of the car park at a speed that had his tyres squealing in protest, leaving a cloud of dust and flying gravel in the darkness and shattering the tranquillity of the quiet Dales village.

The roar of the car speeding up the road under the shadow of the mighty peak, Whernside, echoed through the long elongated valley.

As Wayne and his sleeping companions hurtled under the crag at Kilnsey, a small car slipped unseen onto the road behind him. Eventually, Wayne noticed a pair of headlights some way behind him.

"Hah I'll soon lose him!" Wayne bragged as John Lancaster woke up for a second.

"Try not to kill us all." John muttered as his heavy eyelids closed and the Escort careered around a tight bend on the narrow Dales road. High dry-stone walls loomed perilously as the car screamed by. Startled rabbits' eyes glowed in the bright halogen headlamps as Wayne pushed the car almost to the limits, tearing down the Shepton road as though the hounds of hell were on his tail.

Wayne Higginbotham was James Bond in his Aston Martin. He was Graham Hill in his racing car. Roger Clark in his rally car. He was indestructible, invincible. In later years he would look back and realise he had been totally bloody idiotic, but then, for most youths such a right of passage is an obligatory fact of life.

Wayne had been lucky, although of course, he would have attributed the Escort's safe passage from Potwell, to his monumental driving skill. The headlamps that he had seen in his rear view mirror had indeed been left far behind by the time Wayne and his companions passed the sign that informed them that they were safely back in Shepton.

As Wayne passed the thirty-mile an hour limit sign, he obediently slowed right down to comply with the law.

"Just in case the cops are out." He laughed, as the Escort rumbled down on to the town's broad, tree lined High Street. The laughter froze on his face as he looked in his rear view mirror. Flashing blue lights were rapidly gaining on him. Wayne quickly pulled the car over, hoping against hope that the lights would fly by and that it was someone else that the police were chasing, but his faint optimism was dashed when the police Escort pulled up behind him. Wayne jumped out of the car. A rotund and sweating policeman clambered out of the panda car with some difficulty. Sergeant Bill Hartley was not a happy man.

"Good evening, Officer, is there a problem?" Wayne greeted the sergeant with a pleasant smile that belied the true horror he was feeling. Wayne Higginbotham did not fancy a night in the cells, a huge fine and the loss of his driving licence, less than two years after he'd passed his test.

"Problem?" Sergeant Hartley almost bellowed.

"Is there a problem, officer?" He mocked the polite tones of the student acerbically.

"I'll tell you what the problem is lad, you were driving like bloomin' Jackie Stewart with his backside on fire. What's the emergency?"

Wayne blanched.

"There isn't one, sir. I've only just bought this and I suppose I was seeing how it would go."

"How it would go?" Sergeant Hartley repeated: "How it would go? I think you've just proved that it goes very well haven't you? The last time I saw sommat moving at that speed, it were flying over me head with an RAF pilot in it. I nearly broke me neck three or four times just trying to keep up with you."

The Sergeant blew out an exasperated sigh as he perused the young man carefully.

"Do I know you?" He asked as he frowned, racking his brain to see where he might have encountered the youth standing in front of him before.

"I'm sure I've seen your face before." The sergeant stroked his chin.

"I never forget a face, you know. Are you sure we haven't met?"

Wayne gulped and shook his head.

He had, of course, encountered Sergeant Hartley on more than one occasion, both relating to his encounters with The "Sacred Order of St. Gregory."

Sergeant Hartley peered at Wayne's eyes.

"Are you wearing make up, lad?"

Wayne gulped.

"Yes, officer. Eye liner."

"Eye liner?" The sergeant repeated incredulously.

"You mean women's eye liner?" His face betrayed his disgust.

Wayne shrugged.

"I'm a student, officer. It's the fashion."

Sergeant Hartley stared at Wayne for what seemed like an eternity before shaking his head and pushing his hat back so that he could wipe his brow.

"I don't know what the world's coming to." He declared before waving an accusatory finger at Wayne's car.

"Anyway, lad, did you know your brake light is out?"

Wayne turned and looked despondently at the back of his precious Ford Escort Mexico. Sure enough, only one red light was gleaming in the darkness.

"I'm afraid sir, as a traffic offence has been committed at this time of night, I'm going to have to take a sample of your breath." The Policeman declared officiously, as he puffed up his chest and prepared to carry out his solemn duty of dispensing justice to those who transgressed the boundaries of decent, civilised behaviour, especially if they were puffy looking, young hooligans in tarted-up hot rods.

Sergeant Hartley stepped back to his Ford Escort and picked up a breathalyser from the passenger seat.

Wayne felt that cold chill in his stomach.

"Desperate times call for desperate measures." He whispered to himself.

He concentrated hard on the broken tail-light, which immediately re-illuminated with a brilliant red glow.

Sergeant Hartley's mouth dropped open as he pulled the breathalyser from the car.

"Did you see that?" He asked incredulously as he stared at the rear of the Ford with its two gleaming brake lights.

Wayne stared at the policeman.

"Be nice, be nice." The words filled Wayne's mind.

It had been a long time since he had last used his mind control powers and he was unsure whether he still had the ability.

Sergeant Hartley tossed the breathalyser back on to the passenger seat of his car.

"Well sir, it looks like there hasn't been a traffic offence after all." He declared pleasantly.

"I think it must be a fuse problem." Wayne suggested.

"Aye, lift your bonnet, let's have look. I want to see what makes this beggar go like it does anyway. You've had a pint or two haven't you, son?"

Wayne nodded; a guilty smirk crossed his face.

"Old Mysterious." He admitted as he pulled the bonnet release catch.

Sergeant Hartley cringed:

"Oooh, you'll suffer in the morning." He sympathised before showing Wayne where the fuse box could be found and how to clean them.

"Fine engine." The policeman acknowledged enviously, before slamming the bonnet shut.

"Take tonight as a lesson, son. Drive a bit more carefully in future. Good evening."

A very relieved Wayne thanked Sergeant Hartley then wasted no time in jumping back into the car and driving his flabbergasted friends home, at a very sedate speed.

Doris was asleep by the time Wayne, bumbled, as quietly as he could into 49 Greenwood Avenue. He was almost as relieved about that as he had been about Sergeant Hartley's susceptibility to his mind control and his lucky escape from serious charges.

Wayne settled down into his bed and reviewed his summer holidays.

Wayne had spent a wonderful week in Ireland, staying with his maternal grandfather, Tom Mick a John O'Brien, or Daideo as everyone called him, for a couple of days.

His Aunt Katie had come down from Westport to see him and he had spent another couple of days with his Aunt Molly, Uncle John and cousin, Patsy, who was now a strapping teenager, in the village of Oughterard.

His trip to the Cliffs of Moher in County Clare had been a resounding success. The Spear of Lugh was now safely ensconced in his under-pant drawer, along with his pieces of the Stone of Falias. He could now claim that he had almost got two of the great treasures of his ancestors in his possession.

Aillen had been delighted that his son had found the "Spear of Lugh," although he still couldn't understand why Wayne had risked life and limb, by climbing down to the cave instead of using magic. The key message that Wayne had taken from his father's incredulity was that it was OK for him to use magic again. If his father was fine with him turning into a seagull to retrieve Tuatha treasure, then it would be alright if it was used in other situations.

The third treasure that he had sought, the sword of Nuada, had eluded him. Aillen had told him that the Tuatha believed that the sword had been taken to one of the great museums in Dublin. Nuada had described the sword as being encased in glass in a great building of stone, in the city of the Black Pool. So Wayne had visited the Natural History Museum in Merrion Square and the National Museum on

Kildare Street. The sword that he had found in Aillen's horde at Mickey Finn's cottage was proudly on display in the National Museum, but there was no sign of any other sword of similar vintage. Eventually Wayne had asked a museum guide if he knew anything about such a sword, recently discovered in a barrow in County Galway. The guide had professed ignorance of any such event, but he had said that he knew someone who would know, if a pre-Christian, bronze age sword had been discovered. He had used a telephone mounted on a column to ring someone and five minutes later an old man with a bald head and wearing huge, thick spectacles had appeared from a door marked: "DO NOT ENTER."

Wayne had introduced himself as the boy who had discovered the Lough Mask sword, as Aillen's weapon had become known. The old man, a professor O'Rourke, remembered that an English boy had been involved in the discovery of the sword and the cauldron and had thanked and congratulated Wayne profusely. Although when Wayne had asked him about the newly discovered sword, he too had appeared confused.

A fine bronze-age sword similar to the one Wayne had discovered, had been found in a barrow in County Galway in the Nineteen Twenties, but that had been stolen in a raid on the museum during the emergency.

Wayne knew that by the emergency, the professor was referring to the Second World War. Ireland had maintained her neutrality during that conflict, the President at the time. Eamon de Valera, not wishing to provide the British with any support, whatsoever. Professor O'Rourke then added a new element of intrigue to the saga of the sword of Nuada. A very similar weapon had been purchased from a private collector by a museum in Los Angeles, California. A colleague of O'Rourke's had been asked to verify the authenticity of the sword during the mid–Seventies.

"I think it was the Getty museum. They seem to be able to buy anything. I suppose when you have a billionaire as a sponsor then anything is possible." The old professor had grumbled wistfully.

Aillen hadn't seemed to be particularly perturbed by the lack of the sword:

"The spear shall have to suffice." He declared solemnly.

"The demon is still but a child, you should be able to despatch it even without the full arsenal of Tuatha weaponry.

Up until two nights ago, Wayne had only one problem nagging at the back of his mind.

217

How was he ever going to capture Sabine's heart when he got back to Manchester?

Then he had had the brainwave and it was the thought of the sword that had inspired him. Excalibur had been King Arthur's sword and he had been conceived through magic. If Sabine was not going to dump Jim, then she would just have to see a bit more of him. As he settled down in bed on the night of the "Finn Flyer" incident, as it later became known, Wayne smiled, the "Uther Plan" was coming to fruition in his mind.

As Wayne settled down to sleep, Sergeant Hartley was shaking his head as he filed his report, in the police station in Shepton.

"I couldn't book him for speeding because I didn't have another witness and the radar gun is bust, but I could have thrown the book at him for the amount he'd drunk. I could smell it on his breath. He had committed a traffic offence because the tail-light on his car was out. Worse than that, he was wearing make up. So why didn't I book him?"

The young constable who handed him his mug of tea laughed.

"I think tha's gone soft Sergeant. Maybe you fancied him, with his eye liner and all."

Sergeant Hartley glowered at the grinning younger officer.

"I'll show you who's gone soft. It's another week on nights for you Williams."

"Oh Sarge!" The constable whined. "I was only joking."

Sergeant Hartley cupped his chin in his hands, his face a picture of dejection.

"Maybe I am going soft. I do seem to be losing me memory. Where have I seen that lad before? I never forget a face, never!"

Constable Williams shrugged.

"Maybe he's got superpowers and he brainwashed you telepathically to leave him alone then made you forget all about him by just using the superior powers of his mind."

Sergeant Hartley stared at the younger officer in disbelief.

"You silly bugger." He shouted throwing his cap at the Constable who fled the office giggling.

Sergeant Hartley was sure about one thing. He had come across that lad before and he had been equally as bemused then as he was now.

"Williams." He bellowed: "What's telly pathy?"

Thirty-Six

It was just as James Malone was preparing to throw in the towel and concede that maybe he was more cut out to be a counsellor, or a Priest, than a hard hitting investigative journalist, that Manny Schoenberg came to his rescue.

Manny had been a reporter on The "Hollywood Sentinel" since the late Nineteen Fifties. It was often said in Hollywood media circles that everyone knew Manny and because everyone knew Manny, Manny knew everybody. He would sit in a corner of the news room dabbing the keys of his ancient silver Underwood typewriter with a single, chubby finger, growling and grizzling about some perceived, unspecified injustice, while chewing on a fat Cuban cigar. If any of the other journalists dared to approach him he would glower at them and more often than not send them on their way in the wash of a tidal wave of derogatory expletives. James had found him extremely intimidating and had deliberately stayed well away from the veteran hack, with the volatile demeanour and the daunting reputation.

The Monday morning after James had seen Terri Thorne in San Clemente and had failed to persuade her to divulge any useful information about Dean's underworld connections, a newspaper was thrown onto his desk in the busy pressroom.

James had been concentrating on his typing and had not seen anyone approaching his desk. He looked up and was more than slightly alarmed to see the larger than life presence of Manny Schoenberg glaring down at him.

"Read that, kid! You might find it interesting." Manny declared with a nod towards the old copy of the Sentinel that he had deposited in front of the rookie reporter. The vet turned and walked away without another word, before James had even had a chance to express his thanks.

He picked up the paper and scanned the front page: **"FISH MOVIE: A BIG CATCH"**

The banner headline screamed, out referring to a pre-release press screening of a new movie by the highly rated young director Steven Spielberg. The movie, taken from a book by a guy called Peter Benchley was going to be called "Jaws" and was to be released the following month, but Manny Schoenberg had been given the permission by Mr. Spielberg to review the movie long before the public got to see it and before most his press corps colleagues. James looked at the date of the paper: May 30th 1975. He scowled; why had Manny given him an old newspaper about the movie "Jaws?"

Was he just trying to prove what a big shot he had been in order to intimidate the rookie?

James turned to the second page. A photograph of an extremely well groomed, silver haired man, wearing expensive looking spectacles dominated the page:

"SUICIDE MYSTERY OF AL MONTELLI"

"Hollywood was rocked this morning by the news that Mr Al Montelli, 55, founder and co-owner of the "Studio Starcrafts" agency has been found dead in his car.

"Studio Starcrafts" is a key supplier of young actors and extras to the movie industry and has been instrumental in developing the careers of many well-known personalities.

According to police reports there are no suspicious circumstances.

Dean Vitalia, Mr. Montelli's business partner said that he was shocked and horrified by his partner's death, but it would have been Al's wish, that in the true spirit of Hollywood: "The show must go on."

Mr Vitalia refused to comment further."

James read the article three times before dropping the paper back on his desk.

He had heard that Dean had bought into an already established agency when he had arrived in Los Angeles. According to various people he, like his cousin Aurelio, had started out as a lawyer on the East Coast, but had suddenly changed careers and moved out West. James had heard that Dean's original agency had subsequently grown and swallowed several others, before Dean had re-branded it as: "Veni, Vidi, Vitalia" in 1979.

James took a deep breath, stood and walked over to where Manny sat shouting down a telephone. Manny slammed down the receiver.

"What?" He barked at James while ramming a cigar between his lips.

"Th, Th, Thanks for the tip." James stammered.

"How did you know, I was…"

"Word gets round fast on a press room floor, son." Manny interrupted him, his voice gruff and gravely.

"You gonna have to be careful. Vitalia's a nice guy. He's gotta lotta friends. Funny how he don't have many enemies, ain't it? Al Montelli was a good friend of mine. We arrived in Hollywood at about the same

220

time. He gave me a lotta access to a lotta people. That's how I gotta know these big shots when they were still more than happy to get a toothpaste commercial. Yeah, I knew Al Montelli real well and his widow, Lorna, God rest her soul. I tell you this, son. Al Montelli would not have committed suicide. No way!"

James gulped:

"You think he was murdered?"

"Hah!" Manny exclaimed caustically.

"Hey you ought to be a reporter, you know? You catch on real quick."

Manny took the cigar from his mouth and sighed. He beckoned James closer and then began to whisper.

"Hollywood is like one of your tiny little villages, back home in Ireland, son. Everybody knows everybody and everybody else's business. Everybody sees the stains on your dirty laundry, no matter how hard you scrub. Dean Vitalia came out here in the early Seventies with enough money to buy the Queen Mary.

I tell you it was far more than any lawyer earns. So, he gets to California and he invests in a lotta stuff. "Studio Starcraft" was just one of his investments. Al didn't want him in the business, didn't like him, but Al got an offer he couldn't refuse, you know what I'm saying?"

Manny looked round the noisy pressroom and took a drag on his cigar before exhaling a cloud of smoke that made James' eyes water. Manny beckoned him closer. His whisper was now so quiet that James struggled to hear.

"Dean Vitalia made some other good investments in the early Seventies. The Chief of Police and the D.A. are both real good friends of his. I mean real good! Attended a lot of his parties, you know? There was a lotta talk after Al died. They said he had a gun in his hand and his brains was all over the inside of his car. They found the car in a Canyon over Malibu.

The investigation was over real quick. "No suspicious circumstances" is what they said, pah!"

James nodded. He could feel Manny's eyes burning into him. The old reporter sighed heavily.

"If I were you. I'd leave this story alone." Manny's whisper was still a growl.

"A girl went missing, not long before Al died. They found her body washed up in Paradise Cove. They said she'd drowned. She was a model, a bit part actress on Al's books.

Al told me, before he died, that she'd got real friendly with Dean in the weeks before she decided to take a swim with the fishes. Dean had dumped her and she'd made a big fuss. Al hinted that she'd tried to blackmail Dean."

James felt the skin begin to crawl on the back of his neck.

Manny shrugged.

"There was a well established hack here called Rory Benson. He was a good reporter, I liked him. He decided, after Al died, that there might be a story lurking somewhere under the surface of "Studio Starcraft." You know, starlet drowns, owner puts bullet in his brains?"

James nodded eagerly.

Manny screwed up his face.

"Funny thing happens. Rory Benson came to me one night just before we go home and he says to me: "Hey Manny, this Vitalia schmuck, he's up to his neck in it. I got the biggest scoop in years." Well, I warned him. I says to him, Rory, leave it alone. No scoops worth your life. You gotta wife and kids.""

Manny suddenly stopped speaking. He stubbed the cigar out heavily in a glass ashtray on his desk. He licked his lips and took a second as if trying to compose himself. James maintained a respectful silence. Eventually Manny looked up at him again.

"Rory Benson didn't come back to work the next day. In fact he ain't ever come back to work. Nobody's seen sight, nor sound of him since. Word on the street is that he's helping support a Freeway, somewhere up in the Valley."

James saw that the veteran journalist's eyes were flooded with tears.

"I don't know you, son. I know you've gotta getta scoop real quick, or you're out on your ass. I did hear you gotta wife and kid?"

James nodded.

Manny grimaced.

"I took a phone call last night. A voice says "Manny, there's some Irish guy, claims to be from the "Sentinel," sniffing around, asking a lotta questions about Dean Vitalia. He's bothering Dean's estranged wife, Dean's friends and his acquaintances. Manny, the voice says, warn him off. Tell him Dean is a patient man but his patience is getting thin. You tell him Manny, the voice says. So I'm telling ya, kid."

Manny Schoenberg took another huge cigar from his drawer. He rolled it between his fingers for a minute before snipping off the end and slowly and ceremoniously lighting it. A huge fug of smoke soon enveloped the desk as Manny puffed on the cigar to get it sufficiently alight.

James stood still, stupefied by what he had heard.

Manny shrugged.

"So I've warned you. My conscience is clear. It's up to you, son."

He began dabbing at his typewriter again, peering myopically over his half moon spectacles. The audience was obviously over.

James immediately took himself off to the "Sentinel's" vast archive, down in the concrete basement.

Microfiche machines lined a wall, while box files of old copy filled shelf after shelf.

It didn't take James long to discover that what Manny had told him was true.

The girl had been called Sally Sedona and she had left her home in Iowa, seeking fame and fortune in Los Angeles, just a few months before her body had been found washed up in a beauty spot called Paradise Cove on the Malibu coastline. She was 22 years old.

Rory Benson had been a key reporter on the Sentinel and had almost as much copy at one point as Manny Schoenberg. James decided that Rory's widow would be his next port of call.

Maybe she would have some information that might help him.

James couldn't help but feel incredibly nervous, but that was just part of the job of being a journalist wasn't it?

He had faced the "Sacred Order of St Gregory" and survived. He had survived a car crash on a country lane in Ireland. He had had magical energy blasted at him and survived. He had faced a real life Banshee and survived. He had been cast into the freezing River Liffey, unconscious and survived. He had faced a crazed, psychotic assassin with a knife and he had survived.

James Malone grinned boyishly. That's what James Malone did. He survived!

A quick search of a phone book gave him the late Rory Benson's address.

James returned to his desk, packed a notebook and a tape recorder into his briefcase and was just about to leave the office, when, on a whim, he decided to write four short letters: One to the editor of the "Hollywood Sentinel," one to his beloved Carrie, one to his brother, Dan, who was a lawyer in London and one to Wayne Higginbotham.

He stuck the letters in envelopes and then tucked them into his desk drawer. In the background, above the tumultuous clamour of the newsroom, James heard Manny Schoenberg growling furiously.

"I wonder if I'll be like that one day?" James pondered out loud, a passing pretty female reporter, rushing past his desk laughed:

"You might get to be as ugly, but you'll never be as mean." She quipped with a wink.

Thirty-Seven

Wayne's second year at The University of Manchester began somewhat inauspiciously. Fresher's week had been extremely boring. The intake of students had seemed to be devoid of pretty girls, at least in the venues that Wayne and John Lancaster frequented. The house they were now sharing with two other students, just off Manchester's famous "Curry mile," was a dump. A two up, two down, red-brick terrace. It was reminiscent of the house on Cavendish Street that Wayne had spent most of his first seventeen years in. 18 Cavendish Street, however, had at least had a bathroom, even if it was in the basement. The house in Rusholme didn't even have that luxury. Baths and showers were to be taken in the Student Union building, while the only lavatory in the house was inconveniently located in the back yard.

So it was that it was a fairly despondent Wayne and John Lancaster that had ended up staggering back from the "Friday Night Fresher's Disco" in the Student Union with their two housemates: Ben Johnson and Neil MacNaught.

A plain Ford Granada had suddenly and without warning, hurtled around a corner, tyres squealing, just as the students were crossing the Oxford Road causing the youths to have to leap out of the way to avoid being knocked over.

Wayne had shouted an expletive and made a rude gesture. The car had performed an immediate hand brake turn in a pall of smoke and burning rubber and skidded to a halt beside the unfortunate student. A uniformed Police Inspector had jumped out of the car and grabbed Wayne by the lapels of his leather biker's jacket, pushing him roughly up against a wall and lifting him on to his tiptoes.

"I'm going to do you, sonny, for being drunk and disorderly." The Inspector had snarled angrily.

Wayne noticed as he glanced over the police officer's silver pipped shoulder, several pretty young policewomen giggling in the back seat of the Granada.

"What's your name?" The Inspector had demanded, his face twisted and menacing, flecks of spittle hitting Wayne's face.

"Mickey Finn." Wayne had replied with a sneer.

"Upset your night out, have I?" Wayne could see the other students standing nearby looking aghast as Wayne taunted the officer.

"What?" The police Officer had not been able to believe the way the little, eye-lined pipsqueak was talking to him.

"Trying to impress the girls by pretending to be the Sweeney, are we, Officer?"

Wayne had asked sarcastically.

The police Inspector had lifted Wayne higher off the ground and his eyes blazed, as he looked straight into Wayne's:

"Why you little, I'm going to throw the book at you. I'm going…"

Wayne had felt the anger rising. He had glared back at the policeman, his lip curling in anger. The Police Inspector had looked a little bit surprised and had then carefully and gently placed Wayne back on the ground and dusted off the white lapels of his jacket.

"I'm going to stop pretending that I am Detective Inspector Regan and I promise not to be a silly boy anymore. I apologise profusely for wasting your time, sir. I hope it hasn't been too much of an inconvenience." He had then snapped to attention, saluted smartly, turned and duly climbed back into the unmarked car to explain his actions to the open-mouthed and bemused policewomen.

The other three students had not been able to believe their eyes.

Wayne had grinned.

"I told him I was the Queen's illegitimate grandson." He declared with a practiced level of nonchalance.

There had been no sight of Sabine for the first several days of term. Wayne had grown increasingly restless and worried. He had planned the "Uther Plan" in meticulous detail, but it did all depend on Sabine still being at University and still being together with Jim Hampshire.

The worst possible scenario would have been if Sabine had decided to abandon her studies and return to the States to be with her perfect boyfriend.

Alternatively, the ideal situation would have been if she had dumped Jim, or vice versa. She would then have been free to declare her love for Wayne.

Wayne had laughed out loud when that crazy thought had crossed his mind.

"Dream on!" He had muttered.

The most likely scenario would be that she would come back to Manchester, all lovesick from having spent several weeks with Jim in the States and she would use Wayne as a platonic buddy, like she had in the first year, whilst dreaming about her Yale educated, super-duper, biker hunk, back home.

Wayne had to admit he was beginning to feel a bit bitter and twisted about the whole thing.

He had been somewhat surprised, therefore, to find himself feeling like a lovesick twelve year old on a first date, when he did finally bump into her on the Saturday night in the trendy wine bar in Fallowfield. She had hugged him like a long lost friend and planted a kiss squarely on his lips:

"So tell me all about your summer." She had demanded of Wayne, totally oblivious to Kim and a few of her other girlfriends, who all just shrugged and carried on laughing and drinking.

Wayne couldn't help but feel ten feet tall. He knew he'd missed her but hadn't realised how much. She'd changed her hairstyle over the summer. Instead of the spiky short blonde look, she now had it in a boyish "Princess Diana," style.

"They just love her in the States." She declared when Wayne had complimented her.

Her ears and her eyes were just for Wayne, as he related his tall tales about his adventures in Ireland and about his heroic stint labouring like a proper member of the downtrodden Proletariat in the cheese factory. Oh, how she had laughed. She had laughed until her sides were nearly splitting when Wayne told the story of the hapless, sweaty, fat policeman trying vaingloriously to keep up with the "Finn Flyer" until he had eventually caught them on the High Street, but how the tail light had magically illuminated to render the policeman's contention that a crime had been committed totally invalid.

For about half an hour, the rest of the world was irrelevant, it was just Wayne and Sabine.

Then, of course, Wayne's house of cards tumbled into a heap.

"God, I haven't shut up have I? Tell me about your summer." He demanded with a beaming smile.

Sabine suddenly looked slightly embarrassed.

"Oh, it was pretty boring really." She stated with an awkward, uncomfortable laugh.

"I went back home to Boston and I guess I hung a lot with Jim and............"

She saw Wayne flinch, even though it would have undetectable to anyone else in the bar.

"I'm sorry." She whispered.

"I know you like me a lot and.........."

Wayne tried his best nonchalant shrug:

"Hey it's OK. Jim's a nice guy. He's cool."

"He asked me to marry him." Sabine's eyes had disappeared beneath her long dark lashes.

This time Wayne really did flinch:

"Oh." He said, then after a nervous gulp: "Good."

"You don't really mean that, do you?" Sabine asked; her voice now timorous and emotional.

"Yes, of course I do." Wayne blustered, his voice dropping a couple of octaves in his effort to sound macho and ambivalent about the whole thing.

"I mean you told me before Easter that he was planning it."

Sabine nodded.

"I guess I did, didn't I?"

One of her friends grabbed her arm, come on we're off to "Placemates" in town." The girl shouted.

Sabine glanced at Wayne, leaned over and kissed him on the cheek.

"I can't wait to see that car." She whispered and was gone.

Wayne cried himself to sleep that night. He blamed a surplus of alcohol, but he knew that was just an excuse.

Sabine had broken his heart, again. Well that was it. "Uther" was go!

Sabine Andrews was confused. She had thought she was love with Jim Hampshire. She had thought they would settle down and have a nice little family, maybe buy a place up in Vermont. Buy a white clapboard house with a little white picket fence and a paddock for a couple of horses. Maybe they'd have two, or three kids and life would be just like an old Frank Capra movie. She had thought that a three-year stint in England while her daddy was teaching would test her relationship with Jim, but that they would come out of it stronger.

Now she really wasn't sure.

Jim had done all the right things. He had been to see her daddy, called him sir and asked for his permission to ask Sabine for her hand in marriage. Daddy had said that he thought she was too young, but that the choice was hers and hers alone. They had his blessing.

Sabine's mom had died many years earlier, so there really was no one else to discuss it with.

Jim had taken her to an expensive restaurant in downtown Boston. He had behaved like a proper gentleman and when he had taken her home, he had gotten down on one knee and asked if she would consider marrying him and she had said, no.

She didn't even really know why she'd said no.

Jim had asked her if there was anyone else and she had said no. She just wasn't quite ready to commit, yet.

She had thought of Wayne.

Now that she was back in Manchester, she had to admit that she liked the English guy a lot. She loved his cute Yorkshire accent, his long corkscrew hair, his cool music taste, his fashion sense and those cute, pointed ears that sometimes popped through his curls. He made her laugh. He made her laugh in a way that Jim never could. Jim was so serious, so uptight in many ways. The biker thing was a bit of a joke. Jim wasn't a real biker, he was a straight A grade student with a Yale degree and now a job lined up with one of New York's most prestigious financial institutions. Wayne was a kid, while Jim was a man and that was the whole point. Sabine wasn't ready to put away childish things like laughter and fun just yet. She had liked him even more when she had seen him in the wine bar and he had regaled her with his ridiculous tales about his summer. She had nearly turned her friends down when they had asked her to go into town. She had nearly cheated on Jim. She had nearly cheated on Jim with Wayne and that worried her. She really was going to have to make a choice.

She watched the grey clouds rolling sombrely overhead. She saw the first drops of rain hit the window-pane of her bedroom in the large Victorian student house in Levenshulme that, she was sharing with five of her friends. She heard the doorbell ring. Who could possibly be visiting at half eight on a Sunday evening?

The sound of music thumping through the bedroom wall, told her that her best friend Kim wouldn't have heard the doorbell. As the other three girls who shared the house were all out, she thought had better go and answer it herself. She jumped off her bed walked quickly down the stairs and opened the front door.

A tall figure stood silhouetted against the darkness.

"Jim?" She gasped. "Oh my God, Jim? What the hell are you doing here?"

Thirty-Eight

Doris Higginbotham had not enjoyed the summer one little bit. First of all it had been too hot. Doris liked it warm, but not that hot. It had been ridiculous at points. The thermometer had hit eighty degrees on some days. It had almost been as bad as that awful summer of 1976, when the entire nation had been on drought alert and it had been as hot as ninety degrees, even in Yorkshire. She had really struggled to get into town in the heat and town was Doris' only release from the prison that 49 Greenwood Avenue had seemed to become.

Doris had had many friends on Cavendish Street and in the surrounding area. She'd lived there with Frank for nearly seventeen years when he had gone and gotten himself killed on that daft motorbike. Then somebody had set fire to the basement and tried to kill her Wayne. The police had never got to the bottom of that. That nice young Irish chap. Malone, had said it was the IRA, but Doris wasn't sure. Anyway, that had led to Wayne pushing her into moving into 49 Greenwood Avenue.

"I'd never have bought it if I'd known he wasn't going to be staying." Doris moaned to Margaret in the Co-op café. It was a phrase she had repeated every time she had seen her sister, since Wayne had gone to University. Margaret could have almost quoted the next few sentences, verbatim.

"It's too far out of town! The hills too steep to walk up and there's only one bus an hour. I know it has a proper bathroom upstairs and a telephone and what have you, but I'm stuck up there on me own all day when I come out of town. I mean I'm getting on now and the Doctor says I've got angina."

"Is that why you were struggling to walk?" Margaret asked, knowing full well that Doris now attributed all her health problems to the condition that her GP had recently diagnosed. Margaret could see that her older sister had put on more weight since she had last seen her two weeks earlier.

"Oh aye!" Doris exclaimed. "It right takes me wind away, you know. It's because the oxygen can't get round me blood. That's what the Doctor said. Mind you when he said I had problems with angina, I thought he were talking about down there." Doris guffawed as she flashed her eyes to an area generally below her waist.

"I mean, our Margaret, I'm getting on now. Another few of years and I'll be on t'old age pension, as well as me widow's pension. They reckon angina can lead to a heart attack and then what will I do? Stuck up there on my own?"

Margaret grimaced by way of agreement. If Doris was going to follow her usual script then the next few sentences would be her vitriolic attacks on her adopted son.

"It's like this summer, you know. I had lots of jobs lined up for him, but he'd no sooner put his bag down than he was off to Ireland on some field project doodaa. Mind you, I think he's looking for his real mother. He says he isn't but why else would he keep going to Ireland? I tell you Margaret, he couldn't get out of the house fast enough."

"Dairy." Margaret muttered under breath, anticipating the next moan.

"Then he gets back from Ireland and says I've got a job at the West Marwick dairy, you know, the cheese factory. Well I said to him, I said there's jobs to do here, but he reckons he has to pay for this car he's gone and bought."

"Blackpool." Margaret whispered.

"That's another thing. He's bought this car, now any other son would take their poor old widowed mum out for t'day. Not our Wayne, oh no. He could have taken me to Blackpool for t'day. It always does me good does Blackpool. It's the sea air, you know. He could have taken me to Morecambe, I mean, I'm not fussy, but oh no. Poor Doris gets nowhere."

"Trevor." Margaret murmured.

"Our Trevor would never have treated me like this. Lovely, smiley baby, our Trevor was."

Doris looked sad and wistful, as she always did whenever she mentioned her long lost, first adopted boy.

"Is he still wearing make up?" Margaret asked, as she always did, conscious of the fact that it caused Doris quite a degree of angst.

"Aye." Doris stated tersely, before taking a sip of her tea.

"That's the problem with them these days. There needs to be another depression and a good war. That'd sort 'em out. Let 'em go hungry like we had to. There were six of us lived on a cabbage for a week. Do you remember, Margaret?"

Margaret smiled a sickly sort of smile. She did not wish to remember how she had gone hungry along with Doris and their two much older siblings, Nora and Edna during the Nineteen Thirties."

Doris remained silent for a while. She had finally run out of vitriol.

How's your Cedric and his girl?" She asked her sister.

Margaret smiled one of those "cat that got the cream" smiles.

"Well, he finished with that Doctor's daughter, you know. He's with a girl he met at a Young Conservatives do now. Oh it's all going well. In fact we've been invited to Barton Hall for dinner with his girl, she's called Felicity, and her parents, Sir Montague Storm and Lady Storm."

"Really?" Doris almost threw up on the spot.

"We don't know whether anything will come of it, or not, but we are hoping." Margaret shrugged, somewhat self-consciously.

Doris pondered for a minute.

"Aye, it must be grand to have your own. You know what you're getting that way."

Doris picked up a few bits of shopping in the Co-op once she'd left Margaret. It was only a short walk to the bus stop from the entrance to the Co-op store, but Doris felt like she hiked the Himalayas by the time she got there. The seat on the bus was very welcome indeed.

As she opened the Galaxy Bar in the comfort of her favourite armchair later that afternoon, Doris contemplated her misfortune and it all came down to Wayne.

Wayne, the second choice, who could never have been as perfect as Trevor.

Wayne, who had grown much too big for his boots ever since he had gone to that Grammar School.

Wayne, who had deserted Doris in her time of need by going off to college, less than two years after Frank had died.

Wayne, who didn't want to spend any time doing jobs for her.

Wayne, who didn't even know what job he was going to do after college.

Wayne, who would probably never come back to Shepton, full time.

Wayne, who would obviously abandon her to a life of solitary, lonely, old age.

It was quite obvious to Doris that Wayne had never thought that the Higginbothams were good enough. Oh no, not good enough for the likes of him.

Doris suspected Wayne's frequent visits to Ireland were not study trips at all, but that he was searching for his real parents. She hoped he never found them, or he would abandon her altogether and what sort of gratitude was that for all she had done for him?

Trevor wouldn't have abandoned her, or betrayed her. Trevor would have got a good job in Shepton, as a plumber, or a joiner, or in one of the mills. He would have married a local girl and lived nearby and then when Doris got too old to manage, he would have taken her in to look after the grandkiddies.

That's what good kids did.

That's why you have kids.

As she snapped off a square of chocolate Doris Higginbotham wished she had never clapped eyes on that ugly little baby with the ludicrous ears.

Thirty-Nine

Terri was not surprised when Dean asked for "five minutes" of her precious time when she called in to pick the kids up, one weekend in early September.

Conchita took the children off to play, while Dean fixed up a couple of Margaritas and suggested to Terri that they go sit by the pool.

Terri looked out over the edge of the back yard, at the view of Beverley Hills. Palm trees, endless blue skies and mountains in the distance.

"I miss Coldwater Canyon." Terri said distractedly.

Dean laughed.

"You're still my wife, sugar. You can come back any time."

"Not for much longer." Terri hissed caustically.

Dean smiled a reptilian smile.

"So, how's it going?" He asked as pleasantly as he could manage.

Terri scrunched up her nose.

"Great! Apart from the fact that just recently three more major mail order companies have removed me from their roster without any explanation. I wonder why?"

Terri glared at her husband, who waved a hand dismissively.

"Nothing to do with me honey, honest!"

Terri took a sip of Margarita.

"Yeah, right Dean. You wouldn't know honesty if it jumped up and bit you on the nose. One word from you and things close up like shutters in a riot. Oh well, you did warn me I wouldn't work in this town again. It's just a good job that there are other towns."

Dean grinned sheepishly.

"So you think I'm leaning on people? Is this why you've still got this "friend of Michael's" popping round to your place and asking questions here, there and everywhere?"

Terri shrugged.

"He's got nothing to do with me."

Dean put his glass down and took an envelope out of the inside pocket of his linen jacket.

He tossed it to Terri. She opened it and saw several grainy black and white photos of James Malone, entering and leaving Annie's front door.

Terri glared at Dean.

"It is none of your business, Dean Vitalia, whosoever comes to my door. I will tell you this though. James Malone is a reporter and he has been to see me twice, asking questions about you. I have not been able to tell him anything, because, like with your string of mistresses, I didn't know anything. If I had known anything, believe me I would have told him everything. I would have sung like a canary."

Dean smiled his reptilian smile again.

"So do you think Michael has put him up to it?"

Terri had never thought of that possibility.

"Why would he want to do that?" She asked, genuinely puzzled.

Dean stood and walked around animatedly:

"You're his Mom. I bet he hasn't been hearing the best reports about me recently. You know, my philanthropy, my charitable contributions, my helping little old ladies to cross the road."

Terri shrugged.

"Michael's a good boy. He'd defend his Mom, but I really don't think he'd send his friend out snooping around just to get at you."

Dean nodded, slowly.

"Terri, you tell your boy to be careful, huh? So, this Malone guy is working on his own, you think?"

Terri nodded.

"Yes, I'm sure of it."

Dean grimaced.

"If he thinks he's gonna make a schmuck outta Dean Vitalia, he's in for a shock."

Dean walked away from Terri and began to carefully examine a cactus plant growing in a pot near the pool.

Terri strolled to the edge. The smooth water looked so inviting.

She coughed to gain Dean's attention. He continued to ignore her and stared at the cactus. He put one of his fingers to a spine and gently prodded it. He pulled his hand away sharply and put a bleeding finger into his mouth.

"So is Conchita bringing the kids down?" Terri asked, her voice laced with impatience.

Dean glanced at her, as though he had totally forgotten she was there.

"Sorry." He muttered, "I was just thinking." Dean ambled around the edge of the pool until he was stood right beside his wife.

"So, you're still going ahead with the divorce?" He asked, softly.

Terri nodded.

"You're going to get served with the papers very soon."

Dean looked pained.

"We were good together, me and you, you know."

Terri grinned:

"'"Were" being the operative word. If we were so good together, why did you have to go chasing anything in a skirt?"

Dean sighed and clapped his hands.

"Ah, it's a man thing Terri. None of them meant nothing! Not like you." He laughed.

"It's my Italian blood."

Dean's face clouded over as soon as he had said the word Italian.

"So while we're on the subject of Italian traditions, I will tell you what I've been thinking about. Terri, right now we have a problem."

Terri twisted her face.

"We got a lotta problems, Dean." Her reply was now sarcastic in the extreme.

Dean snorted.

"I've still got our children, Terri honey. Don't be a wise guy. No, the problem is this:

You wanna divorce, you wanna big settlement, so you set up this reporter, private dick, whatever he is, to sniff around and catch me out being a bad boy. What then? The both of you gonna blackmail me? It ain't gonna work Terri. I want you to tell this guy to leave me alone, as he is putting the both of you in danger. If it really ain't you, I think you should ask your limey son if he is involved and if he is, to call off his bloodhound, or else."

For the first time in as long as she could remember, Terri Thorne reacted to Dean's insinuated threat with anger rather than tears.

"Are you seriously threatening me Dean? Don't you forget Dean Vitalia that I could ensure that you are denied all access rights to Marco and Marina. All I'd have to do is show up in court with a black eye or something and you are finished."

Dean walked slowly over to the fence at the end of the yard and stared out over Beverley Hills.

"Conchita is waiting with the children in the hall, Terri." His hands gripped the fence tightly, so tightly that his knuckles went white. As Terri walked towards the house, he turned back towards her:

"Don't forget what I said Terri." He shouted. Terri didn't turn her head, but marched on into the dark shade of the house.

Dean smirked and turned his gaze back towards Beverley Hills.

"That Irish stubbornness could be seriously bad for your health, baby. Infact, it ain't a good day to be Irish."

He whispered under his breath.

Forty

Sabine didn't really know why she was crying. Jim had been more tender and sensitive to her needs when they had been making love, than he had ever been before. They had made love for hours and hours. She turned and looked at him, lying on his back, snoring gently. It was weird, but in the tiny glimmer of red light, cast by her alarm clock he actually looked like Wayne Higginbotham.

That was the problem, wasn't it? Here she was, just having made love to the man who was almost her fiancée and all she could think about was stupid Wayne Higginbotham. Even his name was stupid. Despite her tears she smiled at the thought of Wayne being held up against a wall by a fascist bully of a policeman, his feet dangling uselessly, putting on a regal voice and pretending to be British royalty. She snorted slightly as she laughed and Jim turned towards her.

"You Ok?" he asked in a voice that sounded an awfully lot like Wayne Higginbotham's flat vowelled Yorkshire burr.

"Jim?" Sabine asked, pushing herself up on one elbow.

"Mmm" An indistinct voice replied, sleepily.

Sabine really couldn't see in the darkness, but she instinctively felt that something was wrong.

"Jim, is that you?" Her voice now sounded panicked, she turned quickly to put on the light.

When she turned back she saw Jim hiding his face from the blazing glare of the bedside lamp.

"Oh Jim!" She gasped.

"What's up, honey?" He groaned, "You having a nightmare?"

Sabine rubbed her eyes and looked at Jim again. He had dropped his hand and was looking at her, his eyes bleary, his long hair messed up. Funny she had never noticed that he had pointed ears before.

"Are you OK?" Jim groaned, his drawl sleepy and slow.

Sabine was taking in great gulps of air. She really felt like she was having a panic attack, even so, she managed to gasp.

"I'm sorry, I was having a real bad dream. Go back to sleep, sweetie." She whispered as she kissed Jim's forehead, then she turned and switched off the light.

"Can I help at all?" Jim asked, slipping his arm under her back as she reclined back on to her pillow. He nuzzled in close. She could feel the warmth of his breath on her cheek and the heat of his skin on her body, the touch of his flesh excited her. The way they had made love earlier was like she had read it described in magazines and love stories. It had been so sublime and yet...

She turned away slightly.

"Jim?"

"Mmmmm" He murmured.

"Remember when we drove up through Manchester, Vermont, you know, back home?" Sabine asked, her voice a tiny whisper in the darkness.

Jim grunted.

"We laughed so much that day. You told me I'd hate the English Manchester because it wouldn't look anything like New England. It would be all mills and flat caps and English guys talking in accents that I'd never understand."

Jim grunted again.

Sabine paused for a moment as though choosing her words carefully.

"I quoted Shakespeare. How pretentious: "parting is such sweet sorrow."" She let a short ironic laugh slip out.

"I said that the three years would seem like an eternity, but that we'd see each other on vacations and that we would come out so much stronger at the end."

Jim's grunt was almost a snore. She continued anyway:

"Honey, I've sure done a lot of thinking since I got here. I'm nineteen years old. I'm too young to live in a nice little house with a picket fence, waiting for my darling husband to get home so I can serve him a pot roast and apple pie every night. I want to get drunk, fool around, party, you know? I want to act like a teenager, Jim?"

Jim's grunted again.

Sabine sighed. She had known in her heart that it was going to end like this as soon as she'd said no to Jim's proposal. She had even had her doubts that glorious summer day when Jim had driven her up to Grafton, Vermont in his Daddy's open top Mercedes.

He had thought it funny that she was going to study in a place where it never stopped raining and that couldn't have more of a contrast to her native New England.

"You sure you don't want to go to school here?" He had laughed.

"I'm sure there must be a good enough college here."

Sabine had laughed too. She laughed at all his jokes, even though she had realised pretty soon in their relationship that Jim wasn't particularly funny. He was so mature, her prize Yale-grad. So driven by the Protestant work ethic, in fact Jim Hampshire was destined to be the ultimate White Anglo-Saxon Protestant, that so defined the East Coast's "Mayflower" aristocracy.

Tears began to roll down the sides of her cheeks as she realised what she was going to have to do as soon as the morning light broke through the drapes.

Sabine Andrews was going to have to break poor Jim's heart.

He had told her the previous evening that he had flown over on a courier flight. He'd only paid a few bucks and the chance had been too good to miss. He had flown direct from Logan to Manchester and that he had twenty four hours to rest up before he was due to fly back

"I can't live without you." He had said.

Sabine sighed. A deep, mournful sigh, that caused Jim to stir again. This time he turned over and removed most of the duvet from Sabine. She pulled it back gently. There was no point waking him again.

Sabine could feel the rise and fall of Jim's chest as he slept. Poor sweet Jim.

Surely it was better this way. It was good that he had come all the way to Manchester to get dumped. It was certainly better that she would be able to tell him to his face rather than sending him a "Dear John" letter. He would get over it. He was a tall, incredibly good-looking Yale-grad trainee stockbroker, with a Harley Davidson and an enormous trust fund. The way they had made love earlier would be her farewell present to him and that was the way she would remember him. Kind, sensitive, tender, generous and handsome. Good, old Jim.

So what about Wayne Higginbotham? Sabine smiled. Even the thought of his name made her smile. She was so obsessed with him that she was even imagining him when she was with Jim. Yes, she would go out with him for a while, but this time she would not make the same mistakes she had made with Jim. She might love Wayne, but not in a "lets spend the rest of our lives together" way, not yet anyway. She could act like a nineteen year old with him. They could get drunk, fall over, be cool, or uncool, whatever. She was going to have some fun now. She would not get serious with Wayne, not like she had with Jim. Sure she liked him, but Mrs Higginbotham? She smothered a snorted laugh as she felt Jim stir slightly again.

She couldn't help but grin though at the thought of all those English people with their Northern accents addressing her as Mrs Higginbotham. No, that was not going to happen. Wayne would always be a friend, she guessed, but this girl just wanted to have fun.

The first chink of light broke through her drapes and the sound of birdsong began to flood into her room.

A young American girl had a tough job to do and she wasn't looking forward to it one little bit.

Forty-One

Lucy Hetherington had made two major decisions over the summer. Her disastrous exam performance, which had seen her drop to a lower second status in some of her papers, was not going to be repeated. Daddy had already arranged counselling for her, as it had become quite apparent that all this birth family and adoption business had become very distracting. There was a danger she might even end up with a second-class degree. Her therapist had advised her to close her mind to the whole issue, until she had graduated, at least. Lucy had readily agreed; she was not going to ruin her chances of a spectacular career and a golden future, just because she was over eager to find out about her past. After all she might find out an awful lot of stuff that would totally destabilise her. All of that could wait. After all, she had managed without her twin brother and the rest of her blood family for nineteen years, so a few more would not be of consequence.

The second decision had been to change her degree course. Lucy had enjoyed classics, but she had decided that law was her true vocation. She had managed, via daddy, to persuade Sir Harry Delfont, an old family friend who had enormous influence at Oxford, to speak to the Head of the Faculty of Law. Her tutor at Queen's had also exerted his authority, so Lucy had been less than surprised to receive her acceptance during the summer vacation.

A long, balmy August, spent in Tuscany had seen Lucy strolling through the ancient streets and squares of Siena and Florence and climbing the towers of San Gimignano.

A large floppy hat protected her porcelain skin and pale complexion. A series of floaty, Dior, silk dresses drove Italian boys wild, much to her delight, as she affected a serene, English nonchalance.

Long, lazy lunches by the pool of her Uncle Toby's villa, had merged into delicious Chianti fuelled dinners, under tall, fragrant cypress trees, serenaded by a vast orchestra of crickets and floodlit by a billion stars.

By the time she got back to Jersey, the memory of the "dark satanic mills" of Shepton and the name of Higginbotham had almost been totally expunged from her mind.

September had been spent riding Flick along the beach and walking Spick and Span around the island. Mummy and daddy had made such a fuss of her that Lucy had been too busy to even think about her obscure background.

By the time the calendar had laconically rolled around to October, Lucy had almost been sorry to leave the island to return to Oxford.

She was soon glad that she had, however. It had been on her very first day back in town that she had literally bumped into someone who would change her life.

Lucy had been emerging from the front door of Blackwell's book shop on Broad Street, bearing a huge pile of legal textbooks, wedged precariously under her chin, when a tall, good looking, albeit confused individual, wearing the most ridiculously checked trousers she had ever seen, blundered right into her, knocking all of her books out of her hands and onto the pavement.

"What the hell…?" Lucy had shouted, but the tall guy immediately dropped to his knees and started gathering up her books:

"Gosh, Ma'am, I really am just so sorry." An American voice drawled as he struggled to stand up bearing the pile of texts.

"Erm, I was just staring up at your marvellous Sheldonian theatre building, over there, and I guess I was being careless. By way of an apology, can I carry these books for you to wherever you need to go?"

Lucy glowered at the ludicrously trousered, clumsy American.

"Erm, I'm Jonathan T. Sherman." He announced, sticking what looked like a dismembered hand out from under the pile of books.

"Erm, I guess you're a student here, given this amount of literature. Are there no decent libraries in Oxford?"

Lucy flinched:

"The best libraries in the world are in Oxford, actually. I just prefer to buy my textbooks, so that I always have them to hand and yes, thank you, you may carry my books. I was beginning to wonder how on earth I was going to manage, when you so kindly relieved me of that responsibility, Jonathan T Sherman."

She took the proffered hand and shook it by the tips of the fingers

"I suppose you'd better follow me." She declared haughtily, as she turned on her heels and marched off down towards the Radcliffe Camera.

Jonathan T Sherman started off after her, the pile of books wobbling in his hands as he tried desperately not to drop them.

"Are you visiting Oxford as part of a tour?" Lucy asked as she paused after a long embarrassing silence in which she had marched ten paces ahead of the awkward looking American, all the way to the Radcliffe Camera building.

"I suppose you've already done the rest of Europe over the last five days and this is your last stop before you go back to the States?" She continued, her voice laced with sarcasm.

"England, a country consisting of London, Oxford, Stratford upon Avon and Heathrow Airport."

"Erm, no." Jonathan T Sherman replied, trying to steady the top four or five books in the pile with his chin.

"I'm here for a couple of years, you know, post grad research stuff. I just got here yesterday and this has been my first chance to take in some of the sights."

Lucy raised her eyebrows, totally amazed that someone with such bad taste in their wardrobe should be a student at Oxford.

"Those trousers will have to go then, Mr Sherman, if you have any intention of staying here. I have never seen anything quite so repulsive in my life." Lucy declared imperiously.

"Erm, my pants?" Jonathan could not believe his ears.

"Erm, these were real expensive, I bought them at…"

"Unless you wish to be the laughing stock of the entire student community here at Oxford, then those ridiculous trousers have to go. My God, you wouldn't even be allowed on a golf course in those."

Lucy shook her head as she interrupted him and marched off again, only pausing once she had reached the porter's lodge at Queen's.

"Thank you, that was most helpful. You may continue with your sightseeing now."

Lucy stated arrogantly, as Jonathan carefully placed the books on the desk in her room.

"Why, erm, thank you Ma'am."

He replied without the slightest hint of irony.

Now that he had emerged from the behind the pile of books, Lucy was delighted to see that her first impression of him had been correct. He was good looking. Behind his black rimmed spectacles, he was very good looking indeed.

He turned and was about to go through the door and leave when Lucy's heart softened.

"Wait, Jonathan T Sherman, would you like a cup of tea? I'm Lucy Hetherington, by the way, from Jersey."

She held out a slender, long fingered hand.

Jonathan T Sherman turned back, grinned sheepishly and took her proffered hand. This time Lucy shook it properly.

"New Jersey?" Jonathan queried with a confused frown.

"No, old Jersey, the largest of the Channel Islands, you moron. I mean, do I sound American? There is a big world outside the good old U.S. of A. you know."

Lucy laughed as she pulled a box of teabags out of a cupboard.

"Erm no, well sure, you don't sound like any American I ever met."

Jonathan answered her question, whilst appraising the somewhat snooty English girl who had made him carry her books so far.

"What are you here to study, apart from how to be an accident waiting to happen?" Lucy asked, aware of his appreciative gaze as she poured boiling water into the teapot.

Jonathan scratched his head.

"Erm, er European Law." He groaned. "It sure sounds heavy. In fact having carried those law books of yours, it is real heavy."

"Oh yes, I'm reading law now too." Lucy declared with a giggle as she handed Jonathan a steaming mug of tea.

"I'd quite forgotten for a few minutes there."

"Erm, do you have any sugar?" Jonathan asked politely, after a quick visual search of the small dark rooms that Lucy occupied within Queen's had failed to come up with anything that looked like sugar.

"Oh, of course, how terribly rude of me."

Lucy jumped up to find sugar in the kitchen of her rooms. Jonathan was aware of cupboard doors opening and banging shut.

"I never take sugar, so I always forget to ask. I know mummy packed me some, ah, here we are." She stated as she returned with a plastic container.

Jonathan took a couple of spoons full and stirred them into his tea.

"It's a real nice room you got here. Mine's disappointingly modern, I'm afraid."

He took a sip of the tea and immediately spat it out, all over his checked, cream, black and red trousers:

"Jeez, eugh, that's awful." He coughed and spluttered. Lucy looked on, aghast, she had never seen such behaviour. Surely he could have taken a sip and said that's too strong, or too weak, or whatever.

"I think that container, holds salt." Jonathan T Sherman stated, as he slowly regained his composure and placed the cup carefully on a table.

It seemed to both Jonathan T Sherman and to Lucy Hetherington that they started to laugh at exactly the same time. He noticed how stunningly beautiful she was, underneath the snooty English veneer and she noticed how handsome he was, despite the glasses and those appalling American trousers.

When they discussed it later on in life; that was the moment when they began to fall in love.

For Lucy Hetherington, all thoughts of her real family, of her brother, Wayne Higginbotham and of her real mother, whoever she was, were displaced by love and by a gruelling law degree.

For Jonathan T Sherman, he had just lost his appalling bad taste in apparel and had just met his future wife.

Forty-Two

James Malone stood and stared at the small, nondescript bungalow. A lawnmower stood abandoned on the recently trimmed, neat front lawn. The fresh, sweet smell of cut grass still hung in the sultry, warm air. The afternoon sun's rays cut through the shifting leaves of two tall Cypress trees on the opposite side of the street, causing shadows to shift and dance on the plain white walls and shuttered windows of the house. It was a scene of good order, of the perfect American suburban afternoon. Children could be seen and heard playing on their bikes, down towards the bottom of the street. A woman was washing the Jeep on her drive a few doors away and a pristine "Old Glory" fluttered gently in the light breeze, as it hung from the neighbouring porch. A passenger plane flew noisily overhead and the muted roar of the Freeway could be heard in the distance.

It was another normal afternoon.

James had found Rory Benson's house quite easily, the address had been in an old phone book and it was in a part of Los Angeles that James knew well. The house stood on the corner of a typical suburban street in the North West of the San Fernando Valley, in the district of Granada. It was only a few minutes drive away from James' own home in Box Canyon, which made James feel slightly nervous.

Rory Benson had been an experienced reporter, just like Manny Schoenberg. In his time he had broken many sensational stories about the Hollywood elite that had been syndicated to news agencies all over the world. James recalled Manny's words:

"Rory Benson didn't come back to work the next day. In fact he ain't ever come back to work. Nobody's seen sight, nor sound of him since. Word on the street is that he's helping support a Freeway, somewhere up in the Valley."

It was hard to imagine that someone could be at work one minute and then quite simply never be heard of again.

James was used to death. As a young Priest he had administered the last rites many times and had seen a lot of old people drift off into the afterlife, peacefully and serenely.

He had also seen more tragic cases, where he had done what he could to calm the young victim of a traffic accident, or on one occasion a farmer who's Land Rover had rolled over him, where death had not come quietly. He had seen the terror on Father Dermot Callaghan's purple face when he had found him hanging from the rafters of the tiny

244

Church in Finool. He had watched in horror as Fr Francisco Pizarro had fatally wounded the man he had known as Mickey Finn and had then perished himself in the burning cottage. He had been frozen in terror in St Patrick's Cathedral, when Pierre de Feren had been about to stab him, just before Wayne Higginbotham's timely intervention with a carafe of cognac and a convenient, falling candelabra. James had watched his erstwhile assassin burn before his very eyes, until De Feren had run out of the Cathedral in agony and had hurled himself under a bus to end his torment.

So, James Malone had faced death and seen death. It was no stranger to him, but the thought of disappearing terrified him. Not only would there be no chance of absolution, but his darling Carrie and dear little Aoibheall would be left with no grave to visit. There would be nowhere they could go to mourn and comfort themselves. There would be no closure. They would be left forever, wondering, hoping forlornly, that one day he might just knock on the door and come back to them. It would be a sort of eternal damnation for them. At least he'd be dead. They'd be the ones suffering.

James Malone shivered and gazed out on the scene of mundane suburban normality that faced him. How could he be thinking such dark thoughts on such a perfect afternoon.

As he knocked on the frame of the mosquito screen that stood before the Benson's front door, James realised, however, that that must be exactly how Rory's widow must feel, left with a perpetual gaping hole in her life.

A female voice called from somewhere inside.

"Just a minute."

A couple of seconds later a smart looking lady of late middle age walked towards the door, unlatched a couple of bolts and a chain and greeted James with a friendly:

"Hi, how can I help you?"

James held out his hand:

"Hi, I'm James Malone, I'm working for the "Hollywood Sentinel." Would you be Mrs Benson, by any chance?"

The lady looked very surprised.

"My goodness young man, you are out of date. I used to be a Mrs Benson, but I've been a Mrs Danzigger for some time now. You're with the "Sentinel?" Well, golly gee, you better come in."

The woman gestured for James to pass on into the house. The gentle hum of an air conditioning unit seemed to be the only sound in the spacious, tidy living room. Lots of frilly cotton hung over the furniture and framed black and white photographs of all shapes and sizes stood on every available surface. A man, who was obviously Rory Benson, smiled out of most of them, accompanied by grinning movie stars like John Wayne, Steve McQueen, Barbara Stanwyck and Rock Hudson. James couldn't help but stare at one with a serious looking Rory Benson next to a taciturn Frank Sinatra.

"Please sit down, young man." The lady insisted as James stood awkwardly looking around the room. He sat down in a large armchair.

"Did I discern an Irish accent, there?"

James nodded:

"Yes ma'am."

The lady smiled. Her teeth were still bright and white, but naturally so.

"My mother was from Ireland. The Emerald Isle she used to call it. She always swore she'd go back one day, but she never did and I am ashamed to say that I have never been either. Maybe if my husbands had lived, I might have visited the "old country" one day, but I don't suppose it will happen now. Would you like a coffee, or a tea maybe?"

"Coffee would be lovely. You have a nice home." He gushed.

The lady beamed.

"Lovely, that is just so Irish. No one here says lovely. That's cute. How do you take it?"

James told her how he liked his coffee and the woman bustled off into the kitchen.

It sounded like she'd lost another husband since Rory. Maybe she didn't have such a gaping hole in her life.

"So you married again after Mr Benson?" James asked when Mrs Danzigger returned with the coffee.

"Why yes." She exclaimed. "Poor old Rory was legally pronounced dead two years ago. It seems that some hoodlum from the Watts district confessed to his murder when he was being tried for some other crimes. I was just pleased to know that I could get on with my life. Jeffrey, that's Mr Danzigger, had a heart attack at the end of last year. I suppose losing one husband counted as an accident, two they tell me is pure carelessness."

Mrs Danzigger laughed and James couldn't help but smile. After all his earlier morbid thoughts, it was so reassuring to meet a woman with the sort of indomitable spirit that didn't allow life's tragedies to crush her.

"So you're a young hot shot reporter on the "Jollywood Mental" as my dear, late, first husband used to call it?" Mrs Danzigger asked pleasantly.

James nodded eagerly.

"I'm such a hot shot, I'm on the verge of getting booted out before I've even really started." James laughed.

It was Mrs Danzigger's turn to smile.

"I presume you want to talk about Rory?" She asked, suddenly much more serious and business-like in tone.

James took a miniature cassette recorder out of his bag:

"Yes, I think I'm investigating the same thing that Rory was researching when……."

"When he was murdered!" Mrs Danzigger interrupted vehemently.

James nodded.

"Yes." He replied stiffly.

Mrs Danzigger took a deep breath and shifted her gaze on to one of the black and white photographs. James noticed it was Rory with Lucille Ball.

"Rory was a fool." Mrs Danzigger stated adamantly after a moments silence.

"Is that awful Jewish bully still working there?" She added, curling her lip in disgust.

"Manny Schoenberg?" James suggested.

Rory Benson's widow nodded:

"He tried to warn him, but he had stolen so many of Rory's stories over the years that Rory thought he was just going to expose that agency himself."

James nodded encouragingly.

"Rory had found out that that awful Italian, Vita, whatever his name was, was a hood."

"Dean Vitalia?" James almost spat the words himself. The more he was hearing about Dean Vitalia, the more determined he was becoming to exposing him for what he really was.

"Yes, him." Mrs Danzigger matched his contempt.

"Rory had found out that some poor girl had tried to blackmail the Italian and had ended up face down in the Pacific. Then of course, poor Al was found …………."

Mrs Danzigger's voice broke and her eyes misted over. She took a deep breath.

"Al Montelli was a good friend of Rory's. Al used Rory to get exposure for his people in the "Sentinel." Rory used Al for all the latest Celebratory gossip. It was an amicable arrangement. When Al was found, you know, Rory had his suspicions about who had done it. He swore at Al's funeral that he would expose that, that………."

Mrs Danzigger was lost for words.

"Manny Schoenberg said he was a good friend of Al Montelli's too." James interjected.

Mrs Danzigger snorted:

"Manny and Al had a huge fight not long before Al passed away. Manny Schoenberg is a good friend of Dean Vitalia. That's why he still gets insider information about what's going on in Hollywood, without ever getting his fat butt out of the office."

Mrs Danzigger's scorn was palpable.

James frowned.

"So Manny and Dean are buddies?"

He thought back to Manny's tip:

"You gonna have to be careful. Vitalia's a nice guy. He's gotta lotta friends. Funny how he don't have many enemies, ain't it?"

James was confused. If Manny was Dean's friend how come he'd given him all the information about Al's murder and the lead into Rory Benson's investigation. Unless the purpose had been to scare him off. Maybe there had not been a phone call telling Manny to warn James off. Maybe Manny was warning James off.

"Are you alright, honey, you've gone kinda pale?" Mrs Danzigger's concerned voice jolted James back into reality.

"Manny tipped me off about the Al Montelli "suicide" and gave me the lead towards the Sally Sedona case. He said he'd been told to warn me off."

Mrs Danzigger closed her eyes and shook her head slowly from side to side.

"Mr Malone, Manny Schoenberg has more faces than an Indian idol. He is as trustworthy as a wounded rattlesnake. If you are going to continue trying to expose that viper, Vitalia, be very careful around Manny."

James pondered Mrs Danzigger's statement for a few moments.

"Did the police not come up with anything about Rory's disappearance?"

Mrs Danzigger snorted her derision again.

"They said he'd probably run off with some budding actress. After all he was well known as a bit of "leg-up" in the career ladder. If a girl could get some press coverage from Rory Benson then that next big part was a whole lot more likely. It was all rubbish, of course. Rory was as faithful as the day is long. It was only when that kid confessed to his murder that the police accepted that Rory was dead."

James thought carefully about his next question. He wanted to get off the whole subject of her husband's murder, but Rory Benson's widow was the best source he had come across so far in trying to find incriminating evidence against Dean Vitalia.

"Did the guy who confessed to his murder, say why he'd done it?" James asked, grimacing at the directness of his own question.

Mrs Danzigger surprised the young Irishman by smiling:

"He claimed it was an entry test for a gang he was in. Rory was just in the wrong place at the wrong time. Funny how he'd had thousands of dollars in the bank."

James bit his lip and nodded.

"Thank you very much for your time, Mrs Danzigger. It's been a pleasure."

Rory Benson's widow caught his arm as he was exiting the front door.

"Nail him, Mr Malone. Get that slimy toad, get him for Rory, but please, be careful."

James Malone left Rory Benson's old house in a strange mood. As he climbed into the baking, oven like interior of his black Buick, he thought about his predecessor on the "Sentinel."

Had he had any idea how much danger he had been in?

Would he have carried on if he had known?

James thought about Aoibheall. Did she deserve to grow up without his support? Who would give her away on her wedding day?

Maybe he just wasn't cut out to be a journalist.

Forty-Three

Wayne Higginbotham was having the most delightful dream. He was lying next to Sabine on a pristine white sand beach. The sea was as calm as a millpond, a small band of white surf rolling on to the sand and then bubbling back with a faint swish.

Palm trees swayed overhead and in the distance a reggae band was playing a Bob Marley tune. A lone seagull drifted overhead, under a cloudless azure sky. Wayne could feel the heat of the sun kissing his face.

He heard Sabine flinch and groan.

"You Ok?" He asked, half asleep.

A beautiful red-haired girl in a white bikini was slinking by holding an ice cream.

On the horizon a tall sailing ship was just visible in the haze.

"Jim?" Sabine asked, sounding somewhat alarmed.

"Mmm?" He responded lazily. Man, this was paradise, maybe he'd go and get a beer.

"Jim, is that you?" Sabine now sounded upset. He felt her moving quite quickly.

The Caribbean idyll instantly dissolved and the memory of the previous night flashed into his head and as he felt the light blaze on his face, he rapidly reassumed the form of Jim Hampshire.

"You Ok, honey?" He asked doing his best to imitate Jim's voice again, while shielding his eyes from the glare of Sabine's bedside light and from her curious gaze as he fully adapted his features to look like Jim.

"Jim?" Sabine sounded utterly disorientated and confused.

"What's up, honey?" He groaned, "You having a nightmare?"

Sabine rubbed her eyes and looked at him again. Wayne had dropped his hand and was looking back at her. He knew his eyes were bleary and that his hair was messed up. He just hoped his pointed ears weren't visible.

Sabine looked like she was having a panic attack, she was almost gasping for breath. So was Wayne. He was aware how such carelessness could have cost him everything. He was like a swan, gliding serenely through current events while paddling crazily underneath his shape-shifted disguise.

"I'm sorry, I was having a real bad dream. Go back to sleep, sweetie." Sabine whispered as she kissed Wayne's forehead, then she turned and switched off the light.

"Can I help at all?" Wayne asked, slipping his arm under her back as she reclined back on to her pillow. He nuzzled in close. He could feel the warmth and softness of her beautiful, incredible body. The way they had made love earlier was without doubt the highpoint of his life. The only word he could think of to describe it was sublime.

Wayne felt her push him away.

"Jim?" Her voice sounded so soft and sweet in the darkness.

"Mmmmm" Wayne murmured.

"Remember when we drove up through Manchester, Vermont, you know, back home?" Sabine asked, her voice a tiny whisper in the darkness.

Wayne murmured again, hoping that she wouldn't ask him any questions that would catch him out. He still couldn't believe how he had got away with so much the previous evening.

Wayne had read in the newspaper just that morning, about people crossing the Atlantic cheaply by working as couriers. That had provided a great excuse for his "Jim" to come over and see Sabine for just one night. Their conversation had started with her apologising to him for not accepting his proposal back home. Wayne had wanted to run around the room punching the air in a wild victory celebration at hearing that news, but his eyes hadn't so much as flickered to betray the joy he felt. Of course, he had used all the usual platitudes and had expressed his love for her: "I can't live without you" he had said mustering as much sincerity as he could. He had declared that whatever decision she eventually made he would abide by. In reality he had wanted to scream at her and be totally abusive so that she would dump him there and then but that would have been out of character for Mr "smarty-pants" Hampshire, at least as far as Sabine had described her perfect Jim.

Sabine had appeared genuinely confused about her feelings, but had still seemed to be in love with Jim at heart, which did make Wayne feel a little bit guilty, but as they say: "all's fair in love and war." After all, he could have been cruel and selfish and finish her relationship with Jim there and then. It would have been all too easy.

Sabine had talked a lot and Wayne, as Jim, had smiled and nodded a lot. Eventually they had kissed and passion had just taken over.

As he listened, in the darkness of her bedroom, to Sabine talking about her trip to Vermont with Jim, he couldn't help but feel that although making love with her had been the best moment of his life, it was also sad, because it would mean that she would probably agree to Jim's proposal the next morning.

Oh well, Wayne knew that in his own guise, he was destined to be no more than a friend, a platonic companion for the American girl and that in doing what he had done, he was the luckiest guy in the world. He could get whatever he wanted and not hurt anybody's feelings in the process. He was, in fact, doing Jim Hampshire an absolutely enormous favour.

Eventually Sabine seemed to have been convinced that her Jim had fallen asleep, so Wayne turned, feigned a snore and pulled some of the duvet off her. He felt her pull it back.

Whatever happened, Wayne knew that he couldn't risk falling asleep again. He had almost blown his chances with Stephanie Fleming, three years earlier, when he had failed to maintain a consistent shape as the good lucking American, Mickey Finn, due to a surfeit of alcohol. He really couldn't make the same mistake again by falling asleep again and losing Jim Hampton's form.

He could hear Sabine's soft breathing and could feel the gentle rise and fall of her breast.

Had this been how it had been for Uther Pendragon?

Wayne wondered idly, as the long minutes ticked by. He had named his plan "Uther" after the legend of Uther Pendragon's seduction of Queen Ygraine.

King Uther had first set eyes on the Cornish beauty when her husband, the King of Cornwall had brought her to a feast at Uther's court. Uther had been so smitten by her that he knew that he had to have her, whatever the cost. He therefore persuaded his wise wizard, Merlin to help him to spend just one night with the object of his lust.

Merlin, having been aware of the consequences, had been a reluctant accomplice, but had eventually agreed. Uther's army had attacked Cornwall's castle as a diversion and while the King was out, defending his domain, Merlin changed Uther's form so that he resembled Ygraine's husband in every single way. Merlin had then managed to get Uther into the King of Cornwall's castle, "across the dragon's breath" and Uther, in the form of her husband, had had his wicked way with the beautiful Ygraine.

The plan was only discovered when the King of Cornwalll was found dead amongst his fallen warriors the next morning. So were seeded the fruits of hatred that eventually led to the downfall of the progeny of that night's encounter, King Arthur.

Wayne shifted awkwardly in the bed. Progeny? He wondered if Sabine was on the pill. Jim would have known. She certainly hadn't asked him if he had "protection."

Wayne suddenly felt quite nervous. What would happen when she rang Jim and thanked him for his flying visit and that night of transcendent passion?

What would happen if she was now pregnant?

What............

"Jim." Sabine's voice disturbed Wayne's bout of steadily, mounting anxiety. He opened his eyes and noticed that chinks of early light were breaking through the curtains.

"Mmm." He murmured as he levered himself up on one arm and turned to face the beautiful Ygraine-like figure next to him.

Sabine switched on the light again. She pulled the duvet over herself and pulled her knees up to her chin.

"Last night was the most beautiful moment in my life." Sabine declared, stifling a sob.

"Well that's great, honey!" Wayne gushed, in a big Bostonian drawl.

"Here she goes." He thought despondently. "Yes, I'll marry you, you big hunk of love, you."

Sabine continued:

"It means so much to me that you have come over like this and that you have been so nice to me, even after I turned down your proposal."

Wayne shrugged.

"Shucks!" He gasped, maybe just a little too disingenuously.

"But I've been thinking all night." Sabine whispered, desperately trying not to sob.

Wayne waited for the inevitable proposal acceptance with baited breath. He didn't even have a ring.

"And I really, really feel, that the beautiful thing we did last night and the way we were, should be how we both remember one another."

Wayne was now confused.

"What?" was all that he could utter.

"I am so sorry Jim, but we're through. I'm too young to settle down and dedicate myself to just one man. You are the kindest, sweetest, gentlest man I have ever known and may ever know. Last night was so beautiful, but that is why we have to split. I could marry you and live contentedly, but I would never have had fun. I would never have been a teenager, a student, a wild child."

Wayne scratched his head. He hadn't been prepared for anything like this.

"Erm…fun?" He managed to gasp.

"I can be fun."

Sabine had laughed. Not a nasty, sarcastic, acerbic laugh, but a sweet, sympathetic laugh.

"Jim, my dearest darling, you are almost everything a girl could wish for, but you are soooo not fun."

"Is all of this because of this Wayne guy?" Wayne felt he ought to act a little bit angry and disappointed. Jim had supposedly crossed the entire Atlantic Ocean in pursuit of the girl of his dreams and had just been dumped for his pains. He really, really wanted to laugh.

"No, it's not Wayne. Like I said, he's just a friend. It's me, just me."

Wayne's balloon had deflated a little bit, but even so he was finding it very difficult to stay in character, as the poor dejected, dumped Yale-grad.

"I'll errr get my stuff." He said sadly, climbing out of bed and grabbing his jeans from the nearest chair.

"Will you promise me, we'll stay friends?" Sabine pleaded.

"That's what they always say isn't it?" Wayne sniffed. He fastened his shirt and walked round to Sabine's side of the bed, doing his absolute best to look as if the bottom had just fallen out of his world.

"I will always love you, honey. Always and forever." He said and softly kissed the top of her head, breathing in the intoxicating aroma of her hair.

"Always and forever. Until the end of time."

Why had he said that? He wondered as he turned, picked up his bag and walked quietly out of her door, closing it quietly behind him. Oh well, it was probably the sort of thing that old superman Jim Hampshire would have said, before riding off into the sunset on his Harley Davidson. Over dramatic, over poetic, over American!

Wayne Higginbotham left the house and jumped into his Ford Escort Mexico "the Finn Flyer" which he had parked out of sight around the corner. He looked around to see that no one was looking, despite it being highly unlikely at that time of the morning, then resumed his normal, shorter form.

The Escort sped away and a voice might have been heard shouting:

"Yeeeeeeeeeeessssssssssssssss!"

Forty-Four

Doris Higginbotham could not get out of bed. She had never experienced anything like it before. It was as though the messages from her brain were not reaching her limbs. If the messages were getting there the limbs were not responding. She could feel pins and needles all over her left side.

It was still dark outside, Doris always rose incredibly early. It was a legacy of the time she had spent as a young woman, working in the cotton mill as a weaver.

"Poverty knocking" they had called it. It had been poorly paid, incredibly hard work. The mill had closed down in the Nineteen Fifties under the pressure of cheap imports. That was when Doris had been forced to re-invent herself as a cleaner and part time barmaid.

She tried to swing her legs out of the bed, but to no avail. The only phone in the house was downstairs and as Wayne had abandoned her, she was totally alone in the house.

Doris was frightened. She had not experienced anything like this before. She led motionless in bed, waiting for the feeling to come back into her limbs or for death to slowly take her. The first rays of morning light began to filter through the curtains, lighting Doris' polyester sheets in shafts of grey.

Doris couldn't even knock on the wall to alert her neighbours. Her arm felt dead and the wall in her bedroom was on the detached side of the house. At least on Cavendish Street, because the house had been a mid-terrace, two bedroom walls had been shared with her neighbours.

Once again, despite her fear and the amount of pain she was feeling, Doris Higginbotham began to curse her good for nothing, adopted son.

"If he'd had owt about him, he'd never have left me on me own like this." She moaned as she tried to shift her body up the bed.

"It's alright for him. He's young, but wait 'till he gets to my age. It'll come to him one day. He'll suffer like I have to. Nobody knows what it's like, being on your own."

Eventually, by mid morning, she began to regain some feeling in her left side, which enabled her to sit up in bed. By lunchtime she had sufficient feeling in her legs to clamber slowly and painfully out of bed. She staggered out of the bedroom and bumped one stair at a time down the staircase on her backside. Once in the living room, she edged around the armchair in front of her dresser and with a huge sigh of relief rang: the Doctor and then her sister, Margaret.

The Doctor tutted and shook his head when he finally examined Doris Higginbotham late that afternoon. She had ordered a taxi to get her to the surgery and had ordered him to wait outside.

"Quite simply put, madam, what you experienced was a major angina attack. It is similar to a heart attack, but certainly a lot less serious and very rarely fatal. However, it is a warning shot across the bows, as it were. You are carrying far too much weight and not getting enough exercise. Do you smoke?"

Doris shrugged: "Not many!" She muttered, somewhat indignantly.

"Drink at all?" The Doctor demanded.

Doris shrugged again: "Not much."

"Well certainly cutting down in those areas would help you enormously and you must get a lot more exercise. Oh and do cut down on the cream buns." His jovial smirk was immediately wiped off his face by Doris' apoplectic glare.

"Take these tablets, every morning and evening." The Doctor muttered as he scrawled out a prescription.

"Take my advice and you'll be bothering me for at least another twenty five years, Mrs Higginbotham."

Doris snorted.

"I don't want to live on me own that long. I've only once to die. It'll be reight!"

That was pretty much the tirade that Margaret received when she visited Doris later that evening.

"Oh aye, it was a heart attack. That's what the Doctor said. There's nowt they can do though. They've given me some pills, which should help relieve the pain, but he said it's only a matter of time. Wayne will have to come home from that college, of course. I won't be able to get by on me own, like I have been doing. He's going to have to look after me now, like we looked after him all those years."

As Stanley Houghton Hughes' Rover rolled serenely down Greenwood Avenue, Margaret accurately summarised the situation to her husband, who had waited in the car whilst his wife had visited her sister, so sick was he of Doris' moaning.

"I think our Doris is in for a bit of a disappointment, if she thinks Wayne is going to come home to do nothing but nurse her twenty four hours a day."

He murmured.

"And God help him if he does!"

Forty-Five

It was the muffled sound of breaking glass that first roused James Malone from a deep, dark, dreamless sleep. He looked at his alarm clock. 3:30 a.m. He pushed himself up on one elbow and listened carefully for what seemed like ages. Carrie was snoring very lightly and gently, next to him. The more James concentrated, the more he began to feel that he could actually hear the darkness, it was like a gentle whistling sound.

He could hear a dog barking somewhere nearby, but nothing else.

A police car siren suddenly whooped into action, but far, far, away.

A distant, mournful train whistle echoed in the valley.

James' eyes were heavy, they began to flicker closed. Sleep washed over him like a gentle warm wave. His rapid breathing began to relax and he started to snuggle back down into his pillow.

Thud!

The sound was louder and unmistakable. It had come from the living room.

James snapped into a sudden, adrenalin-fuelled alertness.

Carrie stirred.

"What? What's up?" She moaned sleepily.

James switched on his bedside light jumped out of bed and pulled on a white towelling dressing gown that he kept on a chair by the bed.

"What is it, honey?" Carrie whispered, much more urgently attentive now.

James held his finger to his lips as he picked up a large, heavy torch.

"I don't know. I'm going to take a look." He whispered, as he slowly edged open the bedroom door.

Carrie turned and picked up the telephone on her bedside table. She caught her breath for a second until she heard the familiar buzz that informed her that it was still connected. Her finger pushed the buttons urgently, dialling 911 as fast as she could.

James walked into the oppressive darkness of the living room.

The small neon standby lights from the TV and the Hi-Fi glowed ominously, like single eyes in the shadows. James flicked the torch around the room swiftly, its beam like a searchlight, picking out items of furniture, ornaments, books and pictures on the walls within its wide white circle. His first priority was to check on Aoibheall's room. The door was closed, as it had been when he had gone to bed. He grasped the knob and slightly opened the door. He could hear his daughter's sonorous breathing. He smiled

"She's going to snore like a pig when she gets older." He thought to himself before snapping back into a fully alert mode.

He could hear Carrie shouting instructions down the telephone. He could hear the panic in her voice as she urged the police to hurry.

They were both going to feel so stupid when the police arrived and there was absolutely nothing amiss.

He walked forward tentatively. Normal familiar everyday items took on a new, threatening, alien hue within the unfamiliar light of the torch.

James could feel his heart pounding in his chest, could hear his pulse throbbing.

His eyes were no more than narrow slits as he advanced slowly towards the kitchen. He could hear the huge double fronted refrigerator humming.

Then, in the beam of his torch he saw his briefcase lying on the floor by the dining table. He heaved a sigh of relief. He remembered half thinking that it had looked precarious as he had left it, before retiring to bed, but he had been distracted, so had forgotten to move it. The bag falling had been the bumping noise.

A number of things then seemed to happen simultaneously.

James reached down to pick up his bag just as the main living room lights were flicked on. From a rapid glance he was aware of Carrie emerging from the bedroom, her hand on the light switch and her voice shouting:

"The cops are on their way."

He momentarily wondered why he hadn't thought of switching the lights on.

He was also aware of seeing several shards of broken glass by the front door, where a glass panel had been smashed and of a sudden rapid movement in the corner of his eye, from the darkness of the kitchen.

He heard Carrie scream as he was bowled over by something, or someone large, heavy and fast. He felt a hard punch to his back as he tried to swing the torch around, using it like a primitive club to defend himself. James fell forwards as he felt another punch hit his back just under his ribcage. He twisted around, his torch flailing ineffectually as he tried desperately to hit out at hiss assailant. He was aware of seeing the face of a man, dressed in dark clothes wearing a balaclava helmet, his brown eyes stood out of the black cloth mask, they were wide, staring wildly at James, panic written into their expression.

He heard Carrie scream again, then the sound of the front door being wrenched open and someone else shouting urgently in Spanish. So, there was two of them. James' assailant cursed, punched him again and then jumped over him as he hurled himself towards the door.

James could hear boots scrunching in the gravel of his yard, He tried to stand and give chase, but felt strangely faint, his body wouldn't respond. He was aware of Carrie running towards him, still screaming. He managed to get as far as the door, but was then suddenly aware of feeling wet all over his back. Had a drink been spilled over him?

His front was wet too. Warm and wet.

James Malone looked down at his chest, dark liquid oozed rapidly through his white dressing gown, which was turning red all too quickly.

It was OK. The paramedics would know what to do. James Malone was a survivor.

James Malone survived everything.

He felt Carrie grab him as he stumbled. He saw his best kitchen knife lying on the tiled kitchen floor by the door, blood soaked to the hilt. It looked blurred. Everything looked blurred. He could hear a tremendous roaring noise, like a train, or a jet plane rushing towards him, drowning out the sound of Carrie's screaming.

"It's OK, I'm OK." He said trying to reassure her. He was conscious of smiling at her. She mustn't worry. He'd be OK. The police and paramedics would be here soon.

James could hear sirens in the distance.

Carrie's beautiful face was blurring rapidly. How had he ever managed to marry a girl so beautiful? She was calling his name, but he couldn't hear her, he could just see her mouth moving.

"Don't worry, honey, I'm indestructible, like Capatain Scarlet. I love you." He mouthed, had he actually said it? He couldn't hear himself.

It didn't hurt.

Why didn't it hurt?

James Malone could taste the blood in his mouth, but it was OK. It would all be OK.

"It's OK, honey, it'll all be OK." He murmured.

And then it all went dark.

Forty-Six

Wayne Higginbotham was not a fan of autumn. For him it signalled the end of what, in England, constituted an all too short summer season. Summer was a time of long balmy days and comfortably warm evenings. Autumn was a time of death. A long, slow, painful descent into the seemingly interminable grey chill of a northern winter. It was a time of mushy, rotting leaves littering the ground, of fierce chilling northerly winds and horizontal, stinging rain. Wayne had often wished that he could hibernate, that he could disappear at the beginning of October and not emerge from his winter hideout, stretching and yawning, until the calendar turned to May.

Yet, this particular Monday afternoon in early October, found Wayne as happy as he had ever been. Even the emotional reunion with his birth mother on an Irish hillside, over eight years earlier, had not felt much better than this.

As Wayne stepped out of the Faculty of History, he took a deep breath of the cool, moist air and heaved a huge happy and contented sigh. The courtyard area, in front of the John Rylands Library, was full of so much life and vital energy. Every subspecies of the student animal could be seen. Young boys and girls, probably mainly undergraduates saturated the ground, buzzing hither and thither like bees around an enormous hive.

There was a smattering of more mature looking men and women within the throng, both post and under-graduate. Then there was a contingent of be-suited teaching staff and freakily gowned professors. There were spiky haired punks, ginger Mohicans, long haired rockers, gaudy New Romantics and the odd pair of swotty geeks, with their perfect neat haircuts, beige ties and tweedy jackets. Afghans and duffle coats proliferated and black leather biker jackets could be seen almost everywhere. Dazzlingly, pretty girls seemed to be just about everywhere too. Blondes, brunettes, redheads, long haired, short haired, curly haired and afroed, spiky haired and dungareed. Wayne Higginbotham was in love with them all. Some were rushing to tutorials, or to lectures with concerned looks on their faces. Others glanced nervously at their watches. Wayne had hoped he might catch a glance of Sabine, he noticed her friend Kim in the distance, but there was no sign of the girl with whom he had just spent the best night of his life.

Couples walked hand in hand, enjoying the thin watercolour sunshine, after a typical Manchester morning of fine drizzly rain. Some ambled along in groups, laughing and joking, others strutted and preened as they checked out members of the opposite sex, pretty much like Wayne was doing as he walked up past the refectory and out onto the Oxford Road.

The spring in his step almost caused Wayne to skip as he passed the student Union building and it wasn't just the incredible success of the "Uther Plan" that had put him in such an ebullient mood. His first tutorial that Monday morning had seen his first major assignment of the year returned by the intellectual enigma that was Professor Bouma.

The work, a political paper on the Marxist influence within post war western European politics, had been marked with an A and Professor Bouma, by far the most critical of Wayne's tutors had told him that he had been very impressed by Wayne's work.

To cap it all he had then received an A+ for an essay on "Individualism and the Protestant Work Ethic" being central to British Imperialistic success," from Professor Balderstone in his economic history tutorial. Professor Balderstone had said that such work was the hallmark of a first class degree. Flushed with success, Wayne had daydreamed his way through a Politics lecture and had written a love ode to Sabine instead of making notes.

Ian McNight, a Police Inspector who had had such a meteoric rise through the ranks of the Merseyside Police force, that his superiors had sent him to University to broaden his ultimate career potential and who was a good friend of Wayne's, had mischievously stolen the paper bearing the soppy ode. McNight had added a disgusting last two lines that had almost seen the pair thrown out of the lecture for laughing.

The walk down past the Whitworth Park was almost poetry in itself. The trees were a cacophony of colour. Some still bore the last, lush, broad, green leaves of summer, while others exploded in shades of russet, ochre, orange, yellow and red. The soft breeze plucked the leaves from the branches above Wayne's head, scattering them over him in a haze of multi coloured confetti.

The Oxford Road was as busy as usual, bright orange-liveried, Manchester double-decker buses, ploughed up and down the road, usually in groups of three, all packed with vibrant young people, not only from the University, but also the Institute of Technology and the Polytechnic that all shared the Oxford Road as a location.

Rusholme's "curry mile" seemed to impart all the spirit and spice of the subcontinent to the English Autumnal afternoon. Wayne walked past Indian restaurants, sweet centres, sari stores, specialist food markets and butchers. His mouth watered as pungent, appetising aromas permeated the air. Ginger, cinnamon, curry, saffron and the heavy odour of garlic assaulted his nostrils and stirred his taste buds. He gazed in amazement at the vivid, flamboyant colours that illuminated the shop windows. Saris were available in every colour imaginable and in some that were totally inconceivable. Gregarious, gesticulating personalities spilled out of doorways onto the pavement, bartering and arguing animatedly; laughing and joking in languages alien to Wayne's ear, causing him to smile, as he swaggered past.

Wayne Higginbotham had never felt so vivacious, had never been so aware of the exhilaration of life, whether it had been in the previous night's act of love, the beauty of collective youth by the library, the intense splendour of the autumnal, park landscape, or the exotic and exciting peculiarity of the curry mile. It was all so vital, so effervescent, so alive. By the time he reached Platt Fields Park he was singing out loud:

"Love, love will tear us apart, again."

His deep sonorous tones boomed out unashamedly, as he walked towards the little redbrick terraced house, an idiotic grin wiped all over his face. Once inside, Wayne switched on the electric kettle, none of the other students were back yet, so Wayne had the house to himself. He put the 12" black vinyl single on his record deck and jacked the volume on his amplifier up to its maximum limit.

"Love, love will tear us apart, again," exploded from the large wooden speakers as Wayne danced, jerkily around the living room in imitation of the late Ian Curtis of Joy Division.

The music ended at about the same time as the kettle boiled. Wayne lifted the needle off the disc and proceeded to make a cup of instant coffee. He hugged the mug as he slumped, contentedly into an armchair.

"How much better can life get?" Wayne wondered, as he drifted off into a deep mid afternoon nap.

He was still extremely drowsy when he was suddenly aware of a hammering at the door. Wayne looked at his watch, 4:30pm. Ben and Neil had said they were both due to be back late, while John wasn't due back from a weekend jaunt to London until Tuesday morning. The knock on the door came again, this time it seemed even more urgent. Wayne, finally roused from his somnambulant bemusement, jumped up out of his chair and opened the door. Mrs Roper, the owner of the house and the student's landlady, stood by the doorstep, wringing her hands and looking extremely agitated.

Wayne wondered what the occupants of the house could have done that would have caused Mrs Roper to be so upset. The vision of all four of the students trooping out of the house, suitcases in hand, flooded into his mind. If he was going to get evicted, someone better have a good explanation.

Much to his embarrassment, Wayne realised that he had missed the first few words of what Mrs Roper was saying, but he was brought rapidly down to earth by the statement:

"Your mother is very ill, love, it looks like she has had a heart attack. She needs you at home as soon as you can get there."

Mrs Roper had a telephone and had insisted that the parents of the students in her house had her number and vice-versa. Wayne realised that she had been saying that his Aunt Margaret had called and asked her to get hold of Wayne.

"Oh right, thanks, Mrs Roper. I'll do that," was all that Wayne could mutter, by way of a response.

He turned back into the house and closed the door as Mrs Roper scurried back to her own house around the corner.

"Damn!" Wayne exclaimed angrily. "That's all I bloody need."

The euphoria of the morning and early afternoon now seemed like a distant memory.

The prospect of having to return to Shepton so early in the term was a nightmarish prospect, worse than that was the prospect of having to nursemaid Doris for goodness knows how long.

He trudged disconsolately upstairs to pack a few things, but before he had even reached his room there was another hammering at the door.

"What now?" The student muttered as he turned and stomped back down to the front door. This time it was Sabine's friend, Kim, who was standing on the pavement looking agitated:

"Hi Kim, what's up?" Wayne asked: "You look as though you've seen a ghost."

Wayne beckoned the girl in with a wave of his hand.

"Come in. Can I get you a coffee?"

Kim shook her head as she entered the spartan living room with its ancient three-piece suite and huge paper lamp shade.

"No, no thanks." She stammered.

"Wayne something really weird has happened. It's Sabine." Kim looked as though she was about to burst into tears.

Wayne frowned:

"Sabine? Sit down, Kim." He urged sympathetically: "What's happened?" He asked, concern suddenly beginning to grow: "Is Sabine alright?"

Kim stared at the threadbare carpet, shaking her head.

"It's funny what you said about looking like I'd seen a ghost."

Wayne sat down on the couch next to the girl.

"Do you believe in ghosts, Wayne?" She asked, suddenly looking up, her face betraying a welter of confusion, pain and fear.

"No, not as such." Wayne shook his head slowly.

"Why do you ask?"

Kim bent forward, rested her elbows on her knees and buried her face in her hands.

Wayne was, by now really concerned. Kim was an extremely level-headed girl.

Had something awful happened to Sabine since he had left her early that morning?

What was all this about ghosts?

Finally Kim seemed to regain her composure. She sniffed, dropped her hands from her face, took a deep breath, sat up straight and looked Wayne straight in the eye.

"Sabine asked me to come and tell you this, because she's not going to be around for a little while."

"What?" Wayne gasped: "But I only saw her..." He checked himself awkwardly.

Fortunately, Kim had interrupted him anyway:

"Sabine says that Jim spent last night with her. She said he'd flown over on a courier flight, just so that they could spend a few hours together."

Wayne nodded, encouragingly as Kim took a deep breath and contimued.

"We, well, that's me and the other girls in the house, all thought it sounded a bit weird, but Sabine swore that it was true and to be honest one of the girls did hear, you know, sex stuff."

Wayne nodded again.

"I'm sure she wouldn't have made it up." He said with a shrug.

Kim looked almost as if she was in pain.

"Sabine said that it was the most beautiful night she had ever spent with Jim, but that, at some point in the night, she had realised that she was actually in love with someone else."

Wayne took a sharp intake of breath, was Kim referring to him?

The girl continued her story, not noticing that Wayne was now wearing a very soppy grin:

"Sabine said that she finished with Jim, this morning, just before he set off back to the airport. She said he had looked so broken hearted that she had almost changed her mind."

Wayne couldn't help but swell with pride at his "oscar" worthy performance earlier that day.

Kim smiled sadly and shook her head.

"Even I thought I heard Jim's voice in Sabine's room at one point, during the night, but I must have imagined it. None of us saw him. No one but Sabine."

Wayne shrugged, his face was a portrait of amused confusion:

"Well, you probably did hear him. If Sabine says he came over......"

Kim interrupted him again.

"No Wayne, you don't understand. Sabine's father has just come up from the Midlands to take her home. He had a phone call from the States late last night. Jim Hampshire was killed on Saturday evening. It seems he crashed his Harley into a truck. He died at the scene of the accident. Jim Hampshire had been dead for over twenty-four hours by the time Sabine says he came to her."

Wayne's face went white and his stomach did a double somersault.

"She collapsed when her father told her the news. I mean can you imagine how she must feel?"

Wayne emitted nothing more than a small, pathetic gasp. Kim took a deep breath.

"So you see, this means either there are such things as ghosts, or poor Sabine has gone totally and utterly insane."

Wayne Higginbotham felt sick to the stomach.

"Oh...My...God!" He gasped, as he slowly collapsed to his knees.

Forty-Seven

His Eminence, Cardinal Warzowski, held his hand to his forehead in a moment of silent prayer. Father Abraham Reichmann gathered his papers together, picked them up and placed them in his battered, old, leather briefcase.

The heat of the Roman autumnal afternoon permeated the white walled room, leaving both men in their dark robes perspiring.

So, you are absolutely certain, Father Reichmann, that the "Sacred Order of Saint Gregory" is no longer functioning in any shape or form?" The Cardinal demanded impatiently.

Father Reichmann grimaced:

"As I said, your Eminence, there are now no survivors. The "Order" died along with Fr Bianca."

The Cardinal grimaced and nodded.

"And the rumours of the Holy child?"

Fr Reichmann held his hands up as if in surrender.

"There is no evidence that a Holy child ever existed, your Eminence. If the "Order" did indeed bring about the second coming of Our Lord, then they covered it up brilliantly.

If, however, they brought something else into the World, well, we shall find out soon enough, I suppose."

The Cardinal pursed his lips.

"And what is your opinion, Father?"

Father Reichmann scratched his head, through his thinning, frizzy, grey hair.

"My opinion, for what it is worth is that the "Order" survived for fifteen hundred years, undetected by either the mainstream religious, or the secular authorities, Your Eminence. They did not survive by taking fools into their midst. Madmen on occasion, yes, maybe, but not fools. However, sometimes even the cleverest individual can misjudge a situation. Whatever, or whoever it is, that has wiped out the "Sacred Order of St. Gregory" is, I believe, of their own creation. It is like when the Pharaohs murdered everyone who worked on their tombs, from the architects to the very last slave, so that no one would disturb their rest in the afterlife, or rob them of their treasure. I believe that the "Order" has brought a demon to Earth. A demon of such power, that even before he has reached the age of ten years old, has systematically exterminated every single last one of the very architects of his existence."

The Cardinal frowned.

"What can we do about this?"

Father Reichmann shrugged:

"We must be vigilant, Your Eminence. We must be alert, but most of all we must be patient. This creature will make itself and its purpose known in due course. Until it does, there is nothing more we can do, except to pray."

The Cardinal stood and rubbed his chin furiously.

"Abraham, I have known you since I was a little boy and you took me under your wing when you found me destitute and starving in the ruins of my native Poland. You are the finest Priest I have ever known; the most pious and dedicated individual that I have come across."

The Cardinal put his hand on the old Priest's shoulder.

"I also know that you can be a devious and manipulative old devil on occasion."

Father Reichmann roared with laughter.

The Cardinal shook his head in bemusement.

"You subtly inform me that there is a distinct possibility, that we have a demon of unimaginable power living amongst us. The assumed suggestion is that it is a demon that can only get stronger with the passage of time. Yet, you appear remarkably calm, relaxed even. You are quite prepared to wait until this creature makes its first move, rather than trying to anticipate its intentions. You would let it grow, rather than advise me to notify the wider Church and the relevant secular powers, so that all possibilities can be examined, every single stone turned over."

Father Reichmann shrugged.

"If I told you the truth of what I now believe, you would lose all faith in my judgment. The secular authorities would have me locked up in a padded cell."

The Cardinal's eyes betrayed his admiration for the old Priest.

"I believe that you know something that you are not prepared to share with me, you old scoundrel, Father Abraham Reichmann."

Cardinal Warzowski stepped back and sat on the corner of the desk, his eyes scoured Fr Reichmann's face, beseeching him to tell his superior all he knew.

The older man remained impassive, but his eyes shone with a quiet confidence.

The Cardinal smiled.

"I believe you are not telling me all that you know, for the same reason that your Pharaohs killed their architects and your supposed creature has exterminated the "Order." You are not ready to trust anyone else with the knowledge that you have, in case you too are betrayed. You have more than just faith, Abraham. You know something. You must tell me what you know, please."

Father Reichmann smiled and patted the hand of the Cardinal.

"You know me far too well, Pietr. It is all down to Faith, however. You too must have faith, Your Eminence. The Lord moves in mysterious ways."

Cardinal Warzowski smiled sadly.

"Abraham, do not try to carry the whole weight of the world on your shoulders. You are not getting any younger."

Father Reichmann stood up slowly and painfully:

"Pietr, Your Eminence, you must trust in me now, just as you trusted in me when I was but a skinny young German Priest and you were no more than a skeletal child. You hated all Germans, you said; they had killed all the members of your family and left you an orphan. Even so, somehow you managed to have faith in me then. You must have the same faith in me now."

Cardinal Warzowski bit his lip and shook his head sadly:

"I have faith in you, Abraham. May the Lord God bless and protect you. But you have found no trace of a second coming, or of the actual existence of a demon. The "Sacred Order of Saint Gregory" is now history. Whatever it is you know, Abraham, you must tell me. I need tangible evidence if your investigations are to continue. Otherwise I must reassign you to more mundane and tangible duties."

Fr Abraham Reichmann shook his head sadly.

"Then Pietr, Your Eminence, for now we must close this particular book. Like you say, I must protect what I know with my life."

It was as he was leaving the Cardinal's office that an exhausted Fr Doyle caught up with Fr Reichmann. The young Irish Priest was sweating profusely and breathing heavily. He had obviously been running.

"What is it my son?" Fr Reichmann asked concernedly.

Fr Doyle shook his head:

"I've just received a telephone call from California, Father. I have some bad news, I'm afraid. Very bad news indeed."

"And I have some bad news for you, too." Father Reichmann whispered sadly.

268

Forty-Eight

In the darkest corner of the underground car park, in a derelict industrial area of the San Fernando Valley, an old, dirty, grey Chevrolet Impala rolled slowly to a halt. A shiny black Lincoln town car parked nearby flashed its headlights twice. Two Hispanic youths, wearing baggy jeans, even baggier Tee shirts and red bandanas, climbed out of the Chevvy and swaggered towards the Lincoln, rolling their hips in a manner that oozed arrogance. A dark window on the Lincoln was lowered electronically.

"So, you did well, amigos." A deep voice rumbled from inside the car.

The two youths grinned, flashing pearly white teeth.

The taller of the two leaned towards the car:

"It was like taking candy from a baby, just like you said." He exclaimed:

"It was just another failed robbery, by some masked Mexican punks, probably illegals."

The youths laughed at the irony. The smaller of the two gave his companion a high five.

"Yeah, we just sent the Republican vote up ten points in the Chatsworth area."

The voice from the car interrupted the youths' display of bravado.

"We have an arrangement about payment."

The taller youth nodded eagerly.

"$5000 worth of merchandise. Fair payment for a job well done."

The voice in the darkness of the car laughed.

"The boss is very pleased. He don't like nosey people."

A rear door of the Lincoln opened and an unfeasably tall African American man, his head shaved to a perfect polished finish, climbed out. He pulled up his tie and adjusted his dark sunglasses, which seemed more than a little incongruous in the darkness of the car park. He slowly and deliberately walked around to the trunk, opened it and took out a black briefcase. The youths followed him eagerly, playfully punching one another's arms in celebration. The black man opened the case and took out a bag of white powder. He ripped it open with a grunt, then proffered it towards the youths. The taller one stuck a finger into the powder, sniffed it and tasted it. His eyes grew to huge round circles.

"Oh man, that's the real good stuff."

His colleague followed his example and nodded sagely.

"The best, man."

The black man nodded and closed the case carefully.

Both of the doors on the other side of the Lincoln Towncar opened and two dark haired white men, also very sharply dressed in suits and ties and also wearing black wrap-round sunglasses climbed out.

For an all too brief second, the youths continued to grin in euphoric anticipation of just how rich they were going to be when they had sold all of the merchandise down in the hood. Their smiles froze on their faces, however, when the tall black man and the two whites all rapidly shifted their right arms into their jackets in a perfectly choreographed movement and drew out three pistols.

The taller youth just had the time to say:

"What the…………"

Six swift sharp reports interrupted his question.

Both of the youths had tried to respond, both had had firearms tucked into the backs of their jeans, just in case, but neither of them had managed to even touch their own weapons.

The tall black man gently poked the tall youth's body with the toe of his immaculate shiny-black shoe.

One of the white men wandered around the car and did the same to the smaller of the two, the bag of precious white powder still tightly clutched in one of his hands.

"Hey Preacher, didn't you used to be in one of these gangs?" The white man asked the tall black man, while their accomplice climbed back into the car.

"A long time ago." The black man muttered, his face twisted, disparagingly.

"I was a crip, these two were bloods. They was just amateurs."

He spat on the ground near the tall youth's body.

The white man tutted.

"Ain't nowhere safe nowadays? A decent man ain't safe in his own home and two well armed hoods can't even go out a do a deal without ending up full of holes. It's all these illegal aliens and punks going and joining street gangs."

He laughed as he sauntered back around to the rear of the car. The huge black man shook his head.

"Killin' people ain't no laughin' matter. One day we all gonna be judged." He rumbled as he turned to climb back into the car.

"Even the boss man gonna get judged. Yes sir. One day he gonna have to justify each and every one of his actions."

As the Lincoln rolled almost silently out of the car park, the white man who had joked about safety snorted:

"I wouldn't worry about the boss, Preacher. I'm told Mr. Vitalia has friends in very high places."

The four occupants of the car including the driver, who had remained diligently at the wheel during the shooting, just in case a sharp exit had been needed, laughed raucously.

Forty-Nine

The green telephone that sat on the windowsill of 49 Greenwood Avenue rang three times, its annoyingly loud bell permeating every single room in the small semi-detached house.

Wayne put his mug of tea down in the kitchen and wandered unenthusiastically over to the phone and answered it.

"Hello." He said, the tone of his voice flat and miserable.

"Oh hello, Mr Higginbotham." A woman's cheery Yorkshire accent chirped out of the receiver:

"Doctor Windass has confirmed that your mother had an angina attack, not a heart attack. She'll be fine within a few days, so you will be able to resume your studies as early as next week."

"Thank you, thank you very much." Wayne replied with a celebratory punch of the air.

That news cheered him up immensely. The prospect of having to stay with Doris for an extended period had filled him with horror, which on top of the enormous amount of guilt that he was feeling about Sabine, had left him very depressed indeed.

The Doctor's report had provided a small chink of light in what had been a very dark and potentially, very long tunnel. Margaret had already told him that Doris had suffered an angina attack and was exaggerating her illness to force Wayne home, but now he had official confirmation. He would go back to Manchester on the Sunday, only having missed four days work.

Wayne had rushed back to Shepton in the "Finn Flyer" on the Monday evening, after Kim had delivered the devastating news about Sabine and the supposed "ghost" of Jim Hampshire.

Wayne had never felt as miserable in his life.

What had he done to that poor girl?

The death of the King of Cornwall, during Uther's perfidious impersonation of him, had exposed his own magical deceit and made Cornwall's daughter, Morgan Le Fay hate Arthur, the product of that union, for all of his life. Indeed that enmity eventually caused Arthur's downfall. Could Wayne have sealed his own doom in his irresponsibility?

No one in the rational modern world, no one in their right mind anyway, would ever believe that it had been a shape shifted Wayne who had spent the night with Sabine, just as few would believe that it had been the unfortunate Jim Hampshire's ghost. Poor Sabine was destined to have her sanity questioned in perpetuity.

The guilt weighed so heavily on Wayne's shoulders that he would have even offered to stay in Shepton with Doris forever, if he could just have turned back time. Yet, even he couldn't do that.

Wayne had also been worried that Aillen would also be furious with him. He had been almost apoplectic with rage when Wayne had attempted to use his shape shifting powers to woo Stephanie Fleming over three years earlier. Wayne knew that he could always retort that such magic had been the only way that Aillen had managed to seduce the young Theresa O'Brien and thus bring him into existence, but for whatever reason, Aillen remained conspicuous by his absence.

Wayne immediately telephoned his Aunt Margaret to inform her that Doris would be OK as long as she had the occasional visit from her sister, just to check up on her, and he would pop back a couple of times during the rest of the term. Margaret had been delighted at the news that Wayne would be able to resume his studies.

All Wayne now had to face was telling Doris the good news. Somehow he didn't expect her to react as positively as Margaret had.

He had only just replaced the receiver when the phone rang again.

Wayne scowled.

Who could be ringing in the middle of the afternoon? Doris only ever got phone calls from Margaret and him, and he had just spoken to his Aunt so it was unlikely to be her.

He shrugged and picked up the receiver again.

"Wayne, is that you?" A strangely familiar voice asked.

"Yes, yes it is." Wayne answered tentatively, desperately trying to fit a face to the accent and tone.

"Look Wayne, it's Dan, Dan Malone here." Wayne nodded as the memory of James Malone's older brother came back to him. Dan the man. Dan who had helped James to locate Wayne in Shepton and who had dealt with the sale of one of Wayne's pieces of "Tuatha" jewellery, the benefits of which Wayne had not yet seen, as most of the money raised had been placed in trust.

"Hi Dan, how the hell are you?" Wayne blustered, wondering why Dan was ringing him at home. He hoped there hadn't been a problem with his investment.

Dan had sighed heavily down the phone.

"Thank goodness you are there. I thought you'd be at University." The lawyer mumbled his soft Irish lilt now almost totally replaced by a posh London accent.

"I didn't know where else to ring." Dan apologised needlessly.

Wayne was now beginning to recognise in the flat monotone of Dan's voice that something was wrong.

"My mum's sick, so I'm home for a few days." Wayne stated, his mind whirling, wondering what else could possibly have gone wrong. Had Dan somehow lost all of Wayne's money?

Dan sighed again.

"There's no easy way to say this Wayne, but it's James. Carrie rang me yesterday.

He's been murdered, Wayne. James is dead."

The icy sensation seemed to start at the top of Wayne's head and slowly crept down his entire body.

He heard someone ask Dan when the funeral was going to happen and where, he knew the voice was his own, but somehow he felt totally detached from reality.

A strange buzzing appeared in his ears as Dan said he would let Wayne have all of the details as soon as he had them.

Wayne heard himself thank Dan and the Irishman promised to ring him back.

Then he replaced the receiver and slowly slid down the wall, ending up sat on Doris' appalling, patterned carpet.

James Malone had been the closest thing to a best friend Wayne had ever had, despite the age gap and the fact that they lived on different continents.

James Malone had been the only person alive who knew about Wayne's powers and had actually seen him use them in action. James had told his wife Carrie all about Wayne, but she had only heard the stories, she hadn't actually been there.

James Malone had been the only other person alive who knew and had met Aillen Mac Fionnbharr, both in the guise of Mickey Finn and as the last King of the immortals.

James Malone had been there, the night that Pizarro had assassinated Wayne's real father Aillen and his adoptive dad, Frank had punched him and disoriented the Priest enough for Wayne to finish him off, by blasting him back into the burning cottage.

James Malone had saved him from the basement fire in Cavendish Street when De Feren had tried to kill him and had succeeded in murdering Aoibheall the Banshee, masquerading as Stephanie Fleming.

James Malone had been there when Wayne had blasted his way into the inner sanctum of the "Sacred Order of St Gregory" in Ireland and had defeated the insane Pierre De Feren with the help of James and the repentant Bishop Donleavy.

Since Wayne Higginbotham had been a snotty nosed eleven year old, James Malone had been there in the key moments of his life and now he was gone forever.

For the first time since Frank Higginbotham had died, Wayne felt the tears flooding his eyes and then he did something that he hadn't even done when Frank had died. Wayne felt his shoulders heave violently and he began to weep uncontrollably in great racking sobs. Wayne wept like a baby.

The lads used to joke during heavy drinking sessions at "The Junction Inn" that if the bottom was falling out of your world, then the best thing to do was to drink copious amounts of Tetson's ale and watch the world fall out of your bottom.

Wayne certainly needed lots of Tetson's now.

Fifty

Dean Vitalia was a very happy man. In fact he was on top of the world.

He sipped his Margarita and watched appreciatively the motion of the lithe, lissom, bronzed body of his latest blonde girlfriend, as she emerged from the water and climbed up the steel ladder out of his pool. She turned and flashed him a dazzling, white, perfect smile. Dean grinned back. The girl certainly had an amazing body and the tiny white bikini didn't cover much of it. He watched droplets of water trickle down her bronzed flesh, as she settled down on a lounge chair next to his. She turned on to her front and undid her bikini top to avoid strap marks ruining her tan.

Dean shook his head:

"Did anybody ever tell you babe, you oughtta be in the movies."

Both Dean and the girl laughed at his little joke, with Dean laughing the loudest.

The searing heat of the Southern California summer sun had calmed down as Fall took hold, although temperatures didn't vary that much over the year, it was definitely more pleasant to be outside in October than in July.

The best news Dean had received all week was the final studio approval from the Fox network for the screening of a TV pilot that he was going to personally executive produce. He shuffled the script papers of the pilot in his hands, then carefully placed them on the table beside his chair.

The idea for the show had come from a good friend of Dean's called Max Stevens. Max had co-written several hit comedy shows for the major networks and had gained quite a reputation within writing circles as a future star. He also had a huge weakness for beautiful young starlets, which is how he'd got to know Dean. Dean's agency was awash with beautiful young starlets, just like the young blonde who had just emerged from Dean's pool.

Max's latest idea was for a new sitcom about a simple Amish family from Pennsylvania, whose daughter leaves the farm in order to become a successful Hollywood actress. In order to preserve her modesty and sense of morality, the entire family: Mom, Dad, Granny, Grandpa and the girl's five siblings decamp to Los Angeles, complete with horse drawn buggy and seventeenth century apparel.

"The comedy comes from the clash of cultures, when the puritan, primitive, naïve and techno-phobic Amish, meet their brash new L.A. neighbours."

Max had explained:

"It's going to be called "The Amishers." I tell you Dean, it'll be every bit as big as the "Beverley Hillbillies." The big thing is, every single episode will not only have a lot of laughs, but also a real cute, homespun moral message, you know, saying maybe we can learn something from these simple folk."

Dean had already cast his new girlfriend as the beautiful daughter who runs away to find fame and fortune in Hollywood. He had also managed to persuade Terri to allow him to use Marina as the baby of the family. She had agreed, on the condition that he used his influence to get some of her bigger and better old contracts back. Dean had readily agreed, after all, he wasn't bitter anymore, especially now that he had a stunning twenty three year old on his arm.

The other parts had slowly been falling into place, but the real coup had come about just a couple of weeks earlier, when his cousin Aurelio had called over during a business trip to Las Vegas.

Dean's nephew, Lucien, had screen tested for the part of a cheeky eight year old boy in "The Amishers" and had wowed everyone with his angelic, cute, good looks, his impeccable comic timing and his incredibly sharp wit. It had been as though the part of Hans Kirsche had been written specifically for him. Aurelio had been delighted that his son was going to be television star, so delighted that he had offered to do a little business for Dean at absolutely no cost.

Dean had mentioned the small problem of an over inquisitive journalist, who was beginning to get on his nerves, as well as too close to the truth in one or two murky corners of Dean's past. Dean had arranged for a private detective to follow the journalist, so that he could establish just how far his "dirt-digging" was getting him. The journalist had been sniffing around Dean's estranged wife, using the fact that he was friend of the Limey son she'd had adopted. When the journalist had visited the widow of another journalist who had gotten just a bit too nosey, Dean had decided to act. Unfortunately, he had lost all his old "underworld" contacts.

"Can you believe this schmuck used to be a Priest, in Ireland?" Dean had informed Aurelio.

"He shouldda stuck to dispensing salvation instead of sticking his nose into other people' business." Aurelio had stated as he slapped his cousin's back.

"Sticking their noses in other people business is what Priests do. Only they usually call it "confession" and demand a few "Hail Marys" Dean laughed.

Aurelio had immediately offered his help. Aurelio still had a lot of "friends" who dealt with such situations, for a modest fee.

"I've got a friend who does real nice job." He had boasted.

"You'll not believe this, but he's a preacher man too."

The cousin's had laughed at the irony of the situation

When Dean had first come out West, it had been his own friends who had proven invaluable in helping him to get set up in business and to keep his nose clean.

A few well-placed payments had ensured that no one had gotten too concerned with investigating felonies where he might have been expected to be a suspect.

Now he had gone totally legitimate, it was useful to have a cousin like Aurelio.

Dean lit a large cigar and took a contented puff.

"The Amishers" was going to make him a very rich man and young Luke, as Lucien now liked to style himself, was going to be a huge star.

And that schmuck James Malone was off his back, forever.

Dean Vitalia was on a roll and it wouldn't stop until he was as rich as God.

Fifty-One

Terri was totally taken aback by Michael's call. She hadn't caught the TV news in days and she had never been a purchaser of newspapers. The last thing she had ever wanted was to face an unfavourable review of one of her movie parts. Not that any of her parts had ever been big enough to warrant a mention in a review, but it had become habitual for her to avoid the papers.

So, when Michael had telephoned to ask if he could stay for a couple of nights, to attend a funeral, she had presumed that it must have been one of his college buddies who had maybe originated in L.A.

"Sure honey, I'll check it with Annie, but I think it'll be OK. Who did you say died again?"

Michael's voice had been barely more than a whisper, but the name stunned Terri Thorne.

"James Malone?" She repeated, incredulously,

"Your friend, James? Irish James? How? What happened?"

Wayne told her exactly what James' brother Dan had told him. James had disturbed two burglars in his house in the middle of the night and had been stabbed to death in front of his wife. Terri was stunned to silence. She felt the chill in her stomach and thought about her last words of advice to James when he had seen her in San Clemente:

"I mean what I say when I say be careful, James Malone. Dean could be up to his neck in this mafia stuff and I would never have known. I would hate someone so close to Michael to get hurt."

She said her goodbyes to Michael and poured herself a stiff drink. She thought about the biker who had followed James and wondered if he had been involved in the murder.

Did this mean that Dean really was involved in the mafia?

How could she have been married to him for so long and not known?

Did this put Michael in danger?

What about Marco and Marina?

What about Terri Thorne?

She walked out on to the condo's balcony and stared out over the ocean towards the vague outline of Santa Catalina Island, shimmering hazily on the horizon. The sun sparkled on the water as what looked like hundreds of little boats chugged doggedly through the waves. The white washed walls of San Clemente gleamed and the highway was full of cars and trucks, as usual.

Terri could see people on the beach, families, lovers, people walking dogs.

Ordinary people doing ordinary things, as they got on with their ordinary lives.

She wondered if any of them had problems that amounted to anything like hers.

A jumbo-jet turned noisily a few hundred feet above her head as it made its way to somewhere far, far away. Terri Thorne wished that she had been on that plane when it had taken off from Los Angeles International Airport, no matter where it was going. The very thought that someone she had loved could be involved in the murder of one of her son's best friends filled her with nausea. She felt sick to the stomach, right to the very core of her being.

She had even spoken to Dean just the previous day. He had been in an unusually wonderful mood and had agreed to lay off the fashion houses that Terri had modelled for as long as she allowed their daughter Marina to appear in a new sitcom that he was involved in. Terri had been delighted to agree. She had wondered if his good humour had been purely down to the new young, blonde, bimbo who appeared to have inherited her place in Coldwater Canyon.

Now she could see things from an entirely different perspective. Maybe he was in a good mood because James no longer presented a threat.

Terri did not know Carrie, James widow, but she did know of her and about their baby, Aoibheall. Michael had waxed lyrical about them on his last visit.

If Dean was involved, what sort of man was he, who could take a father away from a young family?

Terri poured another large drink and slumped into a wicker chair that looked out over the coastline.

Fifty-Two

"A funeral? In America?" Doris had shouted when Wayne had informed her that he would be flying off to Los Angeles on the Sunday, less than a week after he had arrived back in Greenwood Avenue.

"It's James Malone." Wayne had informed his adoptive mother.

"Remember, he was the guy who saved me from the fire on Cavendish Street?"

Doris' face had set in that intransigent scowl that had been a familiar feature of Wayne's childhood.

"I don't care who it is, or what he did. You can't just go jiggering off to America, leaving me here, all on me own, in this state."

Wayne had shaken his head and had held his hands up in a gesture that suggested that his mind had been made up.

"You are fine, mum. I spoke to the Doctor. You just need to take it easy and keep taking the tablets. I will get you enough groceries to keep you going and I was going to go back to Manchester on Sunday anyway. Auntie Margaret is going to pop in on you every few days just to make sure you're alright and you've got the phone there in case you have a relapse."

Doris' face had gone a peculiar shade of purple as she almost screamed at the son who she had come to regard as an enormous disappointment:

"Aye, it's alright for you, swanning off here there and bloody everywhere. You don't know what it's like to be left on your own, especially when you're not right well. Nobody knows what it's like on your own. It'll come to you though, young man, you mark my words. You'll not always be young. Anyway, t'phones no good down here if I can't get out of bed like last time."

Wayne sighed.

"I've already arranged for you to have an extension put by your bed. It's going to be fitted on Monday."

Doris had curled her lip petulantly, although she had calmed down a little. Her face was now back to a vivid pink.

"So that's it then. I suppose you'll be going straight back to college when you get back from America?"

Wayne had nodded.

"I'll not be there long. It's not exactly a holiday."

Doris had emitted a hissing whistle from between clenched teeth.

"I expected you to have the decency to stay here now, with me in this state, after all we've done for you. You could have been left to grow up in a children's home and then how clever would you have been? I've just had a serious heart attack and I'm going to be stuck up here all on me own. Our Trevor wouldn't have left me in this state."

Wayne had heard more than enough.

The Trevor card had been played almost every time Wayne had been in an argument with Doris, ever since he had discovered that he had been adopted.

He had never felt more alone in his life and here he had Doris bleating on about her own loneliness and expecting him to forfeit any chance of a decent career, just so that he could look after her. Well she could forget that.

"I'm sick of hearing about Trevor!" He had shouted at the top of his voice.

"Sick, sick, sick! If you adopted a kid, just so that you would have someone to look after you when you got old, then you'd have been a lot better advised to take out an insurance policy. And I'll tell you this much, if your precious Trevor had grown up with you and had half a brain, he'd have been out of here as soon as he could as well."

Wayne couldn't help but feel a little guilty as he stood next to Dan Malone at the cemetery in Chatsworth. He had followed his aggressive outburst with a short mind-wipe on Doris, that had removed his anger from her memory, but he was still embarrassed by the sheer vindictiveness of what he had said and by the bleak, look of utter despondency on her face, when he had driven away on the Sunday morning.

His relationship with Doris was now another source of guilt and remorse. She and Frank had scrimped and saved to raise him. They had been good to him despite the constant references to his perfect predecessor. He had never gone hungry. He had always been warm, had lots of toys and books and in his early years had been extremely encouraging, which had been the launchpad of his academic success. Doris was a bitter, jealous old bat, but who wouldn't be, faced with a lifetime of loneliness?

Shepton, Yorkshire, seemed an awful long way from the open graveside in the San Fernando Valley. It was a suitably cool day for a funeral. Wayne always felt that funerals should be held in the rain, just like Frank's had been. Generally, that was not really an option in L.A. Even so, an unseasonably cool wind had turned in off the ocean, causing the native Angelenos to take to coats and warm winter woollies.

Wayne was comfortable enough in his dark suit jacket. The suit was the one he had worn at his adoptive father's funeral, three years earlier. He had certainly not expected to be wearing it again so soon.

Terri had insisted on accompanying Wayne to the funeral. He had been glad about that.

Terri had known exactly what to say to Carrie, while Wayne had merely hugged her and mumbled some pathetic platitudes.

Ever since his reunion with his real mother; Wayne's initial hope, that it would be just like they had never been parted, had been dashed. Sure they were close, Wayne loved his Mom and he knew she loved him, but they were more like incredibly close cousins, than they were like a mother and her son.

There had always been a barrier of some sort, be it physical, or emotional that had stopped them normalising the relationship. Whether it had been the secrecy that Frank and Wayne had been forced to engage in, to stop Doris finding out about the reunion, or simply the width of the Atlantic Ocean and the American continent, somehow they had just not totally normalised the relationship. The demands of Terri's career and her marrying a husband like Dean Vitalia had only exacerbated the problem. The nadir had come when she had written to Wayne to say that they should terminate the relationship, at least for a while, because the press would use it to terminate her career as an actress. That had been around four years ago, when she had been pregnant with Marco. Wayne had been completely devastated.

Terri had blamed Dean and apologised profusely, just a few weeks later, but Wayne felt that things hadn't been quite the same since.

Wayne's two previous visits to Los Angeles, a clandestine rendezvous in Ireland, plus an average of half a dozen letters a year, had not closed the gap that eleven years apart had opened.

Wayne remembered the uneasy feeling he had had, the last time he had come over to L.A.

Had that been the threat of having to stay at Dean's house?

Had it been an inner knowledge that he was going to meet the kid with the spooky eyes, who Wayne believed to be the demon?

Or had it been that he knew that Michael Sean O'Brien was no more real to him than Mickey Finn had been?

Wayne's mind drifted back to that last visit to L.A. and James Malone's last words to him as he had said goodbye to Wayne at Terri's Coldwater Canyon house:

"Either I'll be over in the ol' country soon and I'll visit you in England, or you get yourself back here as soon as you can."

Wayne sighed, well here he was, but unfortunately James wasn't around any more.

He heard Dan blowing his nose loudly, James' father weeping quietly as he stood next to his other son. Just off to the right, Wayne saw the coffin being carried towards the grave, a Leeds United scarf and an Ireland International rugby shirt displayed proudly on the lid.

There were flowers everywhere: wreaths made to look like shamrocks, Irish tricolours, floral tributes made into leprechauns and harps.

Terri grabbed Wayne's hand. He looked into her eyes and smiled reassuringly. They might never be totally natural, but he knew that he loved her very much.

James' young widow, Carrie was stood on the other side of the grave, weeping into a white handkerchief. Wayne recognised James' mother comforting her.

There was no sign of Aoibheall, James' daughter. Carrie must have left her with a minder. Suddenly Wayne was aware of another figure off to his left. A figure in dark robes caught his eye and nodded courteously, Father Reichmann. The Priest Wayne had last seen in Rome.

James nodded back and attempted a smile that looked more like a grimace.

There were many people by the graveside that Wayne didn't recognise. James' colleagues and friends he had made; both in the United States and back home in Ireland.

There seemed to be scores of people, many were weeping openly.

For many of the people present, James Malone had died tragically once before, which made the circumstances of his demise all the more horribly ironic.

At least James Malone was getting a good send off. Wayne wondered how many people would attend his funeral. It wouldn't be a turnout like this that was for sure.

A drop of rain hit Wayne's cheek, or was it a tear.

The ritual of burial passed in a blur for Wayne Higginbotham. Incense burners were swung and handfuls of earth cast onto the wooden casket once it had been lowered into the ground and many meaningful words were spoken. Dan's eulogy for his lost brother was particularly moving, especially his reference to the five years lost when James had been presumed dead after the Finaan incident:

"To lose him once had been hard. To lose him twice was unbearable."

Terri held Wayne close, especially when she heard the choking sob well up in his throat.

Then it was all over and James Malone, Priest, Counsellor and Investigative journalist and friend, had been committed to the earth.

People began to move away from the graveside. Brief greetings were passed, grim nods and handshakes. Wayne noticed Carrie walking towards him, through eyes blurred with tears. Wayne hugged her again, noting what a beautiful wife James Malone had been lucky enough to have. She passed an envelope to Wayne.

"James' boss found some letters in his desk." She stated, sadly.

"He thought he was in danger because of the story he was investigating, so he…"

Carrie's voice broke and she sobbed heavily, almost immediately she lifted her head, took a deep breath and recomposed herself.

"I need to speak to you alone for a second." She announced, grabbing Wayne's arm and steering him away from Terri and a small knot of mourners.

"Wayne, I know what you will want to do. James thought that Dean Vitalia was a mobster and that if anything happened to him, then Dean would be behind it. The police have said that James' death was simply a burglary that went wrong. I don't believe them, but there is no proof that it was Dean."

Wayne was about to speak but Carrie put her finger to her lips:

"Wayne, listen to me. Go and fulfil your true destiny. You have far more important things to do than to go looking for vengeance. Do not go after Vitalia. Even with all your powers, you could end up getting hurt, or worse. An eye for an eye achieves nothing!"

She glanced back at James' flower strewn grave, then back at Wayne.

"Promise me. No revenge, Wayne. James wouldn't have wanted it. Don't forget he was a Priest."

Wayne nodded forlornly.

Carrie smiled and kissed him on the cheek.

"Come and see me whenever you're over to see your Mom, OK?"

Wayne nodded again and wished her well. He glanced at the envelope again. James' handwriting was on the envelope. He put it carefully in his inside pocket.

When he looked up, Father Reichmann was standing in front of him.

"It is a very sad day." The old Priest stated simply, sympathetically.

"Do you think this is anything to do with some element of the "Order" that we were unaware of?"

Wayne shook his head.

"No. I don't think so. I think poor James got too involved in a story he was researching. I think he was "hit by the mob," as they say."

Fr Reichmann nodded and glanced around. Terri was slowly leaving James' graveside and was starting to approach them across the cemetery.

He sucked his teeth and sighed:

"Like you, I believe the "Order" is now forever consigned to history. Mother Church in the Holy See believes it too. There is no trace of a child, be it Holy, or otherwise. The last Priest who had been involved in the "Order," Fr Bianca died a few days ago. Therefore, in its infinite wisdom, the Vatican in the shape of His Eminence, Cardinal Warzowski, has officially declared the matter closed. Father Doyle and I are being moved on to other matters. You are on your own, Wayne Higginbotham. Whatever it is that is out there, you must face it alone."

Wayne sighed and nodded.

"I always knew I was on my own really. I knew it as soon as I heard those Doctors whispering about me being adopted when I was a kid."

Father Reichmann smiled and touched Wayne's shoulder.

"You are never alone in the presence of the Lord, Wayne Higginbotham."

The old Priest pulled a velvet pouch out of his pocket.

"You may need these, young man. Although I haven't a clue what they are. Fr Bianca believed them to be extremely important. By giving you this gift, I am placing my faith in you. I hope I am not making the greatest mistake in my life."

Wayne took the pouch, a puzzled frown on his brow.

"Oh yes, this is yours too."

The German Priest slipped a ring off his little finger and slipped it into Wayne's hand.

"I wish you well. God bless you, my son."

The Priest smiled at Terri as she finally reached the two men.

"Father." She acknowledged Reichmann with a curt nod.

Father Reichmann returned her smile.

"God bless you, my child." He whispered, before scurrying off as quickly as his old legs could carry him.

"What was all that about?" Terri asked.

Wayne shrugged.

"Carrie thinks that Dean was responsible for James' murder. She asked me not to get involved. She doesn't think I should seek retribution."

Terri grabbed his hands.

"I agree with her. If you don't do it for Carrie, Michael, then please do it for me. Do not get on the wrong side of Dean. You are still a kid and I couldn't bear it if anything happened to you."

Wayne scowled at his mother:

"Is he a gangster?" He asked somewhat brusquely:

"He tried to break us up, mom, and now it's possible, no it's likely that he's killed my best friend."

Terri grimaced as Wayne's voice rose.

"I really don't think Dean is a gangster." She whispered.

"He's a philanderer, a liar and I hate him, but I wouldn't have had two babies by him if I'd have ever thought he was involved in the mob. Even so, please, Michael, don't go and do anything silly."

Wayne nodded once.

"OK." He muttered.

"I promise I won't seek vengeance."

Terri sighed and smiled:

"Good." She whispered. But as she turned back towards the crowd of mourners, she missed Wayne's almost silent, venomous hiss:

"Yet!"

And she certainly didn't see his crossed fingers on the hand he held behind his back.

Fifty-Three

Lucy Hetherington took to reading law like a duck to water. Her relationship with Jonathan T. Sherman developed wonderfully quickly and by Christmas she was already planning on moving out of her college, into the little student house by the Isis that Jonathan was renting. Daddy had eventually and with much difficulty, managed to persuade her to delay such a decision until the end of the academic year, when she returned to Jersey for the Christmas vacation.

"After all," He had opined: "there's really no rush, I hope. If this really is the real thing you have the prospect of the rest of your lives together."

Rupert William George Digby Hetherington had not been entirely thrilled by the news that Lucy had fallen head over heels in love. He had watched her admiringly in Italy as she had strolled sassily, as the Americans seemed to call it, around the ancient cobbled streets in her hat and loose, almost transparent dresses. He had watched young Italian men stare incredulously as she passed by. He had even seen one teenage scooter rider run straight into the back of a tiny Fiat, as his attention had left the road and followed Lucy's provocative progress along the street. Fortunately, only his pride had suffered serious damage.

Lucy had turned into a stunning and intellectually brilliant young woman and the Hetheringtons couldn't have been more proud. While they were in Italy, Rupert had remarked to Melinda how it proved that nurture could overcome nature, given the right circumstances.

"I mean," He had stated, with the confident candour of the totally self assured, "there must have been a certain amount of good stock there, you know, a fair degree of intelligence in the gene, but one does wonder what would have happened had she not had such a first class home and family backing her and of course, such a super standard of education."

Melinda lowered her menu and peered over the rims of her half-moon spectacles at her husband.

"What do you mean?" She had asked, raising a sceptically quizzical eyebrow.

The couple had been sat in a restaurant in a hill top fattoria near San Gimignano.

288

"Well," he had announced with a pained grimace as he swallowed a large mouthful of Chianti and struggled to find the right words to express his opinion.

"It's like horses. One can't make a racehorse out of cart-horse stock. It's nearly all in the breeding, but if one takes a pair of similarly bred Arabs, takes one and has it pull a cart every day, while the other is trained to run and race, then it is obvious that the one trained to race would win if the two ever came into competition."

Melinda frowned as she sipped her glass of iced water.

"I'm not sure I necessarily agree, Rupert." She shielded her eyes as the early evening sun appeared as an orange ball of fire from behind a screen of hilltop cypress trees.

"One has to consider the amount of love, affection and money that we have lavished on Luce. She was tutored superbly by Frau Strichler, before she went off to Prep school and Roedean was absolutely super. I think any child would have done well, given the circumstances." She sniffed as she contemplated her next sentence.

"One finds it intolerable to even consider what might have happened to her had she been raised in less fortunate circumstances. She can be frightfully impetuous on occasion and she does have an unfortunate stubborn streak that neither of us possesses. Plus, I do think she has been rather saucy in her dress sense this summer. I would have had a word, of course, but one doesn't wish to appear fuddy-duddy."

Rupert nodded.

"One can only imagine what ever became of the boy. One knows one shouldn't speculate, but siblings can display remarkable differences in degrees of intelligence. Take poor Toby; he struggled to get a third at Cambridge. It is possible that it was down to too much rugger, rowing and beer, of course, but I was always the more academic of the two of us. As for Lucy, if there ever was a possibility of finding out what happened to the boy, that really would be the best comparison. One can't help but wonder, can one?"

Melinda had shrugged and picked up her menu again as the waiter approached.

"Best not to, darling. Best not to wonder at all."

It was on the Christmas Eve, that Rupert brought up the subject of Lucy's birth family to Melinda.

"I see what you meant now, darling, about Lucy's impetuosity."

Melinda, busily checking her lists of instructions for the cook had once again peered over her spectacles, perplexed by her husband's statement which had come quite out of the blue.

"In what way, dear?"

Rupert had heaved a huge sigh:

"The poor girl has fallen head over heels for this American fellow. She's moping around here like a lovesick puppy because he's gone off home for Christmas. I'm afraid that even Flick and the dogs don't seem to be taking her mind off it. As for this moving in together business, well, it's an absolute nonsense! If she carries on like this she'll be lucky to get a third class degree. I mean it's all so distracting for her."

Melinda had sighed too.

"Yes, maybe there is a lack of sound judgment in her blood. I mean do we know much about this chap?"

Rupert sipped a small sherry.

"Good family, the Shermans'. Not quite Mayflower stock, but good people. Extremely rich, I believe and quite decent, as Americans go."

Melinda looked out of her window at the low, wintry grey blanket of cloud that was hanging over Jersey.

"Well darling, at least we've done our absolute best for her. She's a young woman now.

One can only hope that Lucy takes advantage of the opportunities that we have provided."

Fifty-Four

Wayne's lingering feeling of guilt over his treatment of Doris led to him deciding to go home to Shepton for the weekend. He had been in Los Angeles for just forty-eight hours and despite suffering from monumental jet lag he had managed to attend two full days of lectures and tutorials. Even so, he still had more than a week's work to catch up on, which losing another weekend would not help, but Wayne hoped that he could diffuse at least some of Doris' bad feelings towards him, if he popped back to Shepton, even temporarily.

He had read the letter from James that Carrie had given to him at the funeral on the plane on the way back to England. Its contents had not surprised him:

Dear Wayne,

I really hope you don't get to read this letter, because if you do, it means I'm dead and I really have no intention of meeting my Lord and Maker for quite a while yet.

I've been "dead" once already and I think that was quite enough for my poor old Ma and Da to go through.

Wayne had been forced to wipe away a tear at that point as he remembered the desperately desolate faces of James' parents at the funeral. He had been quite fond of James' mother in particular when he had stayed with the family in Dublin three years earlier. He had glanced round to make sure none of the other passengers could see him crying before he continued:

Anyway, I've got Carrie now, lucky beggar that I am, and I want to see Aoibheall grow up.

So if you are reading it, then things have gone horribly wrong.

I am currently researching your Mom's husband, Dean Vitalia. There have been many rumours about supposed mafia involvement in Hollywood over the years, going right back to the days of Frank Sinatra and I think it's about time Vitalia was exposed, especially after what he's done to your Mom.

We Irish have got to stick together, even the plastic paddy, English contingent (that's you, you eejit.)

I know it's potentially dangerous but I think I've proved I'm a bit of a survivor.

Anyway, this note is just to say that if anything does happen to me, then the likelihood is that Dean was responsible, SO WATCH YOUR BACK.

I don't want revenge. I know you could use those powers of yours to turn him into toast, but that is not the right thing to do. I still believe in heaven and hell, even if the collar was thrown away a long time ago.

Your powers have been given to you to be used for a much greater purpose than pointless revenge and I wish you well in that. I know you will fulfil your destiny, Michael Sean O'Brien, Wayne Higginbotham, or Mac Aillen. You will save the world, but <u>not if you try to take on the mafia.</u> Find Father Reichmann in Rome. I am sure he will help you, in the way a young, naïve, Irish Priest once tried to.

Yours
Your Friend,
James Malone.

Wayne had been forced to flee to the plane lavatory to wipe his eyes and compose himself. It was all beginning to fall into place. Perhaps there really was no such thing as coincidence, just a great big horrible grand design. Of all the people in the world, it just had to be his mother's husband's cousin who happened to be looking after the demon that had haunted Wayne's dreams. Now that same husband, Dean Vitalia, had murdered, or more likely, had someone murder, Wayne's best friend. It was all just too convenient to be coincidental.

So be it thought Wayne as he re took his seat.

"The phoney war is over. Let battle commence."

If Doris had been delighted to see Wayne when he arrived at Greenwood Avenue, then she did a marvellous job of disguising her pleasure.

"Oh, you're back then." She had muttered when he had walked through the front door.

"I thought I'd come and see how you are doing." Wayne had replied, trying not to sound disappointed by her reaction.

"Guilty conscience got to you, has it?" Doris had sniffed, huffily.

"How are you feeling?" Wayne had asked, pleasantly.

"Could have been dead, for all you care." Doris had grumbled, before bumbling off to the kitchen to put the kettle on.

Wayne had spent the rest of the afternoon trying desperately to rise above Doris' constant baiting. He had gone to the store and bought re-supplies of fresh groceries, taken Doris' dirty washing to the laundrette and had dusted and vacuumed the house. He had even sat and watched Doris' appalling Saturday night TV variety shows with her.

By the late evening, Wayne had been more than relieved to retreat to his bedroom sanctuary.

Once ensconced in his room, he had heaved a huge sigh as he thought about the prospect of fulfilling Doris' dreams of staying in Shepton and looking after her.

It really could never happen. He would have much rather faced Dean Vitalia and the entire combined forces of the "Cosa Nostra" without any of his powers, than face that.

Wayne wondered sadly if it would have been the same if he had been Doris' natural son?

He decided it was futile to engage in such idle speculation.

He took his vanity bag from the back pack that he used and was about to go off to the bathroom, when he noticed the small, velvet, drawstring pouch that Father Reichmann had given him. Wayne hadn't even opened it. He put his vanity bag back in the backpack and pulled open the pouch. Several shards of stone fell on to his bed, just like his own pieces of the Stone of Falias. So, Fr Reichmann had got Fr Bianca's stones and had trusted Wayne enough to let him have them.

With a mounting sense of excitement Wayne opened his underwear drawer.

He took his own stones from the hidden cashbox and carefully laid all the shards that he now possessed out on the bed.

Nothing happened.

Wayne could hear rain hammering against his bedroom window and Doris shuffling about downstairs as she prepared to get ready for bed.

Wayne looked up at his rain-streaked window. It was pitch black outside, he had yet to draw the curtains. Yorkshire in the rain, it made Wayne long to jump back on that plane, despite what had happened to James in L.A.

Suddenly, Wayne was aware that he could see bright colours caught in the reflections in the raindrops. Strange colours, vibrant shades of red and green, oranges and yellows, exploding, glowing then rapidly fading. It was like hundreds of little kaleidoscopes had been opened on the glass and were trickling down the window-panes.

His attention on the window was disturbed by a sudden change in the light of the room; it was as though his light bulb had suddenly dimmed. Wayne's first thought was that there had been a power cut. He looked back towards his bed.

What had been a plain and simple row of grey stone shards and pebbles on his clean, white duvet were glowing with the same coloured shades of light that he had seen reflected in his window. Even weirder, the stones were floating in a circle above his bed, like a ring of asteroids around a tiny invisible planet. The colours were mesmerising, getting brighter and brighter, until he had to avert his eyes. At about that same moment his third finger on his right hand began to burn.

"Ouch!" He squealed, as the ring he wore on that finger seemed to get hotter and hotter. He wrenched it off and tossed it on to the bed with a muttered curse.

The ring was all that had been found of Aoibhell the Banshee, after the conflagration in the Cavendish Street basement.

At least it had been her and not the beautiful Stephanie.

Aoibhell had adopted the form of Stephanie Fleming in her attempt to wrest the stones from Wayne and for a while he had been convinced that it had been poor Steph who had died in that basement.

Wayne plunged his little finger into his mouth and sucked it before shaking it violently to try and cool it.

The light faded and Wayne turned back to look at the stones.

Where there had been a number of pieces of stone floating in the air, now there was just one perfect, gently glowing sphere lying on his duvet, next to a blackened ring that had lost its stone.

Wayne heard Doris clumping heavily up the staircase.

"Wayne?" He heard her shout. "Are you alright?"

"Yes, why?" He responded as though nothing out of the ordinary had happened.

"I thought heard you shout." Doris replied, sounding a bit puzzled.

"Is sommat burning?" She asked as she loudly sniffed the air.

"Wayne, it smells like sommat's burning."

Wayne turned back to the sphere on his bed. It was still glowing, but very faintly now.

"Oh bum!" He exclaimed under his breath as he rolled the stone off the piece of scorched and blackened duvet.

He blew on the scorch mark urgently as he heard Doris walk along the landing towards his door.

With a swift flick of the wrist he turned the duvet over and nonchalantly sat down on the unblemished white cotton as Doris opened his door.

"Have you been smoking?" She asked suspiciously. Wayne thought quickly.

"Only a cigarette!" He lied.

"That's why, I shouted out. It was horrible. I won't be doing that again."

Doris, who smoked twenty cigarettes a day, much to Wayne's disgust, nodded.

"Doesn't smell like a cigarette. Your not doing that wacky baccy or whatever they call it, are you?"

"No, don't be silly." Wayne lied again, shaking his head just a bit too vigorously.

"You don't want to be starting that habit." Doris muttered. "It's bad for you. You'll be on that LCD before you know it."

Wayne smiled weakly.

"I'm not that daft."

Doris had not been long gone, when the green mist began to form by Wayne's bed.

"Hello father." Wayne whispered as loud as he dared to avoid Doris hearing.

"Long time, no see, as they say."

Aillen Mac Fionnbharr emerged from the mist in his Tuatha robes and bearing the gold circlet on his head and the heavy Torc around his neck:

"My visits are sparing, my son, unless something changes. I do not visit you just to see how tall you are growing, or how handsome you have become. I no longer even bother to come to tell you when you have been foolish with the use of magic."

Aillen glowered knowingly at Wayne and Wayne knew that he was talking about the "Uther plan" incident.

"You are no longer a child, my son. Many mighty warriors have died at an age much younger than the years you have reached. My visit this night is to urge you to action now. You have now taken possession of the reformed stone of Falias. Yes, we felt the power of its reformation, even in Tir Na Nog. You now have two of our great treasures. Fortune favours you, for the reformation of the stone was beyond our wildest hopes. You have faced much in your life so far, my son, but there is still the greatest of your challenges to complete. It is by far the most important of the three tasks that were preordained for you. Your destiny awaits."

Wayne bit his lip.

"They've killed James Malone."

Aillen put a hand on Wayne's shoulders, sympathetically.

"He was a worthy Holy man and a good friend to you."

Wayne nodded sadly:

"He saved my life."

Aillen took his hand off Wayne's shoulders and balled both hands into fists.

"Then strike now! You have delayed long enough, my son. You must find the demon spawn and destroy him. I have no doubt that he is somewhere behind the death of your friend."

Wayne nodded again:

"I'll do it during the Christmas holidays. I'll find the kid and bring it all to an end then."

Aillen smiled proudly.

"I used to like the dog in the "Tom and Jerry" cartoons on the telly, when I was in the form of Mickey Finn. As he used to say: "That's my boy!""

Aillen grinned at his son, then turned, stepped back into the mist and was gone in an instant.

Wayne shook his head.

"Most guys have fathers who work in an office, or put thingummys on to widgets in a factory. I have a father who turns up as a spectre in a green mist, wears bronze-age gear and chooses to spend most of his time in another dimension. Yet the most inspiring, motivational quote he can come up with is from "Tom and Jerry." Now that is weird."

Wayne pulled the duvet off the perfectly spherical stone. Although it had stopped glowing, Wayne felt immense power surge through him making every part of his body tingle, it felt like he was experiencing a mild electric shock. Wayne could feel his hair standing on end as he carefully placed the stone in his underwear drawer.

The Stone of Falias was his. The spear of Lugh was his. Wayne Higginbotham knew exactly where the Getty Villa in Malibu was; the sword of Nuada was as good as his. Aillen Mac Fionnbharr was right, his power was now almost immeasurable. His destiny to fulfil the role of "Slanaitheoir mor" was imminent. Wayne Higginbotham was on the verge of achieving legendary glory.

So why did he feel like running away and hiding?

Thousands of miles away, a young boy with cherubic features and a cascade of blonde curls falling on to his shoulders, suddenly felt a sharp pain in his head. His private tutor noticed him grimace unexpectedly. The boy sharply grabbed his forehead as though he had just received a hammer blow from inside his skull. Surely his Latin lesson wasn't that boring.

The boy had recovered quickly but had asked if lessons could end for that day so that he could retire to bed, due to a massive headache. The tutor had agreed, of course.

After all, the boy's father was going to be a Senator and the boy himself was destined to be incredibly famous, according to all the entertainment critics in the newspapers.

"The Amishers" was definitely going to be as big as "I Love Lucy", or the "Beverley Hillbillies" and Lucien Vitalia, or Luke Lively, to give him his stage name, was going to be the star of the show.

Fifty-Five

Terri had decided that she was not going to be subtle with Dean when she arrived at the house to drop off the children for his weekend's access. It was all just too much of a coincidence for her liking. James Malone had been investigating Dean's supposed mafia involvement, then, out of the blue, strange men on motorbikes had been watching her house and had covertly followed him. Then, James' had suddenly and extremely suspiciously died, purportedly the result of a bungled burglary. Yeah, right!

She pulled up the drive to the Mexican styled, white walled house on Coldwater Canyon and stopped the car outside the front door. Despite the fact that she had been mentally rehearsing her speech for days, she still wasn't exactly sure of what she was going to say, but she knew that she wasn't going to let herself be intimidated by her soon to be ex-husband. Terri Thorne was determined to get to the bottom of the matter and find out the truth. She owed it to James Malone and to Michael. Just in case his involvement with James had put him in danger in any way.

She heard the front door of her old house open behind her as she struggled to extract Marina from her baby seat. Her heart pounded as she lifted her daughter out of the car and turned to face the man that she had once loved:

"Ah, Mrs Vitalia, it is so good to see you." Conchita greeted her with a huge smile.

Terri heaved a quick sigh of relief as she kissed her old Mexican housekeeper on both cheeks.

"Conchita, how are you?" She exclaimed before gripping the smaller woman's shoulders and examining her face.

"Is that good for nothing ex-husband of mine treating you well?"

Conchita shrugged as she lifted Marina out of Terri's arms. She glanced around furtively to see if they could be overheard.

"Mr Vitalia is fine, but his new girlfriend, she's a beetch."

Both women laughed as Terri walked into her old home beside Conchita, Marco tightly gripping her hand.

"Talking of my soon to be former husband. Is he here?" Terri asked as they entered the kitchen. Conchita nodded and with a brief movement of her head indicated the pool area.

Terri pursed her lips, left the children with Conchita and strode confidently out into the afternoon brightness of the back yard and on to the poolside patio.

Dean was carefully applying sun tan lotion to a young blonde's naked back.

Terri coughed politely.

The blonde swiftly reached behind her back to fasten her bikini top, as Dean stood up abruptly, a supercilious grin creasing his mouth.

"Hey, hi, honey, is it that time already?" He pretended to gasp as he glanced surreptitiously at his watch.

Terri smiled back with a smile as disdainful as she could manage:

"Yes, honey. As they say time flies when you are enjoying yourself and you certainly look..." She glanced at the girl with her eyebrows raised contemptuously,

"....as though you are enjoying yourself."

Dean laughed:

"Oh I am baby, trust me. I am. Are the kids here?"

Terri smiled sweetly:

"Of course they are, sweetie, they're with Conchita. I wouldn't dare to let you down, darling."

Terri was aware of the blonde staring at her, incredulously. Appraising her every feature, every single imperfection that age and childbearing had wrought on her. Terri grew more furious with every passing millisecond.

Dean leaned over the blonde girl and whispered in her ear. She smiled and turned her gaze away from Terri.

Dean picked up a Hawaiian shirt and slipped it over his arms. He approached his estranged wife with a concerned crease etched on his brow.

"What do you mean by that?" He whispered quietly as he cupped Terri's elbow in the palm of one of his hands and started to guide her off the patio back towards the kitchen.

"By what?" Terri asked innocently as she allowed herself to be led towards the door.

"That you wouldn't dare to let me down." Dean hissed, particularly emphasising Terri's use of the word dare.

There was no sign of Conchita, or of Marco and Marina, Terri assumed that they had moved upstairs.

"I really can't think what you are getting at, Dean, dear." Terri responded; her voice edged with sarcasm. She turned to move into the hall.

Dean physically turned her body towards him.

"You can stop with the sweetie, darling, dear stuff, enough already. If you are referring to your little friend's recent mishap, then please don't go making accusations against me. I had nothing to do with it."

His voice was little more than a whisper, but was oozing menace.

Terri smiled sweetly.

"James Malone was a good man, Dean. For goodness sake, he was a Priest for many years. It just seems a bit uncanny, just a bit too much of a convenient coincidence, that as soon as he starts to investigate the Vitalia clan, he suddenly comes to an unfortunate and sticky end."

Dean pursed his lips and glanced around uncomfortably.

"We live in a sick society, honey. A man can't sleep safely in his own bed these days without some knife-wielding hoodlum coming to rob him. Like you say it must have been an unfortunate, uncanny coincidence. Stuff happens, welcome to L.A."

Terri smiled a humourless smile. Her eyes narrowed to little more than slits.

"Swear to me, on the lives of our children, Dean; that you had absolutely nothing to do with the murder of James Malone."

Dean Vitalia snorted.

"Do you think I am stupid? He's a journalist trying to set me up. Trying to pin some gangster rap on me. Who's going to be the first suspect?"

Terri glared straight into Dean's eyes.

"Swear to me." She insisted.

Dean swallowed nervously.

"I did not kill anyone. I swear." He growled.

"Swear you didn't arrange the murder." Terri whispered urgently as the sound of children's laughter echoed through the hallway.

"What is this? Are you working for the cops? Are you trying to frame me now?"

Dean whispered angrily.

"James Malone wasn't the first journalist to "disappear" while investigating you, Dean, was he? Swear you did not arrange for James Malone to be murdered." Terri continued to stare directly at Dean, her blue eyes probing his shifting brown.

Marco rushed into the room and grabbed Terri's legs.

"I don't wanna stay with poppa. I wanna go home." He wailed.

Dean glowered at Terri.

"Nobody can pin nothin' on me. Nobody!" He hissed, averting his gaze from his ex-wife and waving his hand dismissively.

"It ain't my fault that a couple of schmucks have had unfortunate accidents when they've gone out to dirty my name. Maybe somebody up there is lookin' out for me."

Terri grimaced, pursing her lips angrily and pointed to the floor.

"Somebody down there, more likely."

Before Terri could persist, however, Dean turned and retreated into the kitchen.

Terri picked up Marco.

"You've got to stay with Poppa, Marco." Terri soothed her son. "Just for the weekend."

Conchita appeared with Marina and took Marco's hand.

"Look after them, Conchita." Terri almost sobbed as she gave a little wave to her children.

"Love you!" She waved again then ran out, through the front door to the Chevvy.

Dean had not sworn on his children's lives. Did that make him a murderer?

Was his "Nobody can pin nothin' on me" statement a confession?

Terri was not sure, even so, leaving her children with a man who might just be involved in murder, had just got a whole lot harder.

Fifty-Six

Doris had been pleasantly surprised when Wayne had walked in on the Saturday morning and announced that he would stay until the Sunday afternoon. Not that she would ever have let Wayne know that. He was still a disappointment as far as she was concerned.

Even though she couldn't remember exactly what he'd said to her that had upset her so much, she did know that he'd insulted her and that by refusing to come home to look after her, he had betrayed everything that she and Frank had ever done for him.

What had really pleased Doris, however, was how miserable and unhappy Wayne had seemed. Even the smoking in his bedroom incident hadn't upset her too much. If he wanted to waste his money on cigarettes, that was up to him. After all, Doris smoked, so it would have been hard for her to preach to him. It wasn't that she was happy just because Wayne was generally unhappy. After all he had just been to the funeral of a chap who was supposedly a good friend and was bound to be in mourning. It was the fact that he didn't seem quite as delirious about Manchester any more.

Over the summer holidays, he'd inadvertently mentioned the same girl's name a number of times and had seemed really excited about going back to Manchester. Now he just seemed to be incredibly miserable all the time and when Doris had subtly probed him about the girl, he had snapped back that he didn't have a girlfriend and was too busy to get involved with anybody. When Wayne had promised to drive home again the following weekend to check up on her, Doris had been even more suspicious that maybe things weren't going all that well for her adopted son at college. She had told Margaret about her speculation when she had telephoned later that week.

"Aye, I think there's a chance he's had his heart broken." She reported with no mean amount of glee.

"If it's upset him so much, you never know, he might pack it in and come home for good."

Margaret Houghton-Hughes tried to temper her sister's enthusiasm at the prospect of Wayne quitting his tertiary education.

"I very much doubt that he'll pack it in, Doris. He's bound to meet someone else. I wouldn't build your hopes up." She had stated with a sigh.

"And don't forget his mate has just died. He saved his life didn't he?"

Doris had snorted:

"Our Wayne's not bothered about anybody else but our Wayne. Mark my words, sommats happened at that college and he's not happy there any more. It wouldn't surprise me if he packs it all in and doesn't go back after Christmas."

Doris was even more delighted when there hadn't been any change in Wayne's downbeat demeanour when he had visited the following weekend.

Finally she had come straight out and asked him:

"Are you happy at that college, Wayne? If you're not, you could always come home."

She had simpered as sweetly as possible.

Wayne had simply looked surprised.

"No, I'm fine mum, honest." He had replied, unconvincingly.

Doris Higginbotham knew her son better than that whether he was her own flesh and blood, or not.

Wayne Higginbotham was not happy at the University of Manchester and that made Doris Higginbotham very happy indeed.

Fifty-Seven

It was true, Wayne Higginbotham was not happy at Manchester University. He had struggled to make up for his lost week and a half in the early part of the term and by the time the Michaelmas term was beginning to draw to a close for the Christmas holidays, he still had a pile of essays to do and several books to read.

It hadn't helped his time management that he had forced himself to make the journey back to Shepton at least once a week, since the quick visit when had got back from Los Angeles. Wayne couldn't help but feel guilty about Doris, if only for Frank's sake. Wayne had loved his adoptive Dad, even if he had been embarrassed by his job in the thingummy factory and his lack of aspiration. Frank had saved Wayne's life when all had seemed lost and the least Wayne could do in return was to help Doris as much as he could. Doris' demands on him, however, were getting increasingly unreasonable. The prospect of a whole month's vacation spent in Shepton with a ton of work to do and Doris to look after; left Wayne with the distinct feeling that life really could not get any worse.

Then the letter arrived on the last Friday of term. It was from Sabine and was postmarked "Cambridge Mass." Wayne ripped it open excitedly:

Dearest Wayne,

I'm sorry to have to write to you like this. I know I led you along last year and that you care for me a great deal. I am so sorry that I was so cruel. I guess I used you for company because Jim was so far away and you are such a fun guy to be with.

You made me laugh so very much.

The thing is, over the summer vacation, I realised that I care a great deal for you too.

Far more than I had realised. I thought about you all the time, even when I was with Jim. Fun was the last thing that Jim was. He was just so heavy. I could never have accepted his proposal of marriage.

Dear Wayne, you ought to know that I was going to finish with him, so that we could be together. I had decided that such a long distance relationship could not work any longer and that I wanted to be with you. I wanted to behave like a nineteen year old and to have a laugh.

I guess Jim's death has changed everything. My whole life is in meltdown.

They all think I'm mad, even my Dad.

They say Jim cannot possibly have come to England, as he was already lying dead in a fridge in the hospital mortuary. Dad checked with the airlines and there was absolutely no record of Jim ever having made a courier trip to Manchester. His passport never left his Mom's house.

It's just all so weird. They say that I must have dreamt it all, that I've had a nervous breakdown and that I must be mentally ill. They use nice words, of course.

The strange thing is, I know I was with him, that I made love with him that very Sunday night. What's even funnier though, is that I remember waking and imagining that it was YOU in the middle of the night, I really fantasised that it was your voice that I heard, not poor Jim's.

The biggest joke of all is that I've just had to have a termination. I was eight weeks gone. The psychiatrists and the therapists and the doctors and the specialists can't explain that one.

How did a ghost get me pregnant, hah!

Dad's got a job in California. He thinks it best if we start again, somewhere else. Somewhere where I can get the best treatment money can buy.

So I guess this is goodbye, dear Wayne.

Maybe we'll meet again, one day, if they ever let me out of the funny farm.

With all my love,
Sabine.

Wayne found that he couldn't breathe. His chest was heaving but so rapidly that he didn't seem to be able to take in any oxygen. His eyes had misted over, he wasn't crying but he couldn't see. His legs had turned to jelly. He felt nauseous, sick, he wanted to shout and scream. He needed to explode. He managed to run upstairs and to throw himself on to his bed. He buried his face in his pillow. How could things get any worse? Why was he being punished in this way? Not only had he lost his best friend, but also the girl he was crazy about and now he had lost his unborn child. Had he known that Sabine was going to dump Jim for him then he would never have had to resort to the "Uther plan."

He had really believed that Sabine had accepted Jim's proposal and that a worm like him had absolutely no chance of wooing a girl like Sabine.

This was an even bigger disaster than Uther's. At least Ygraine had given birth to Uther's baby and that child had led Britain through a brief but legendary golden age.

Wayne's child had been put in the trash.

There really was absolutely no one else to blame. It was all Wayne's fault.

Magic was not a toy to be used frivolously. He should have learned his lessons after the near disaster with Stephanie Fleming, but oh no, he was too smart for that. Doris had been right in saying that he'd got too big for his boots.

Slanaitheoir Mor? Saviour of the world?

He was a moron, an idiot and he'd ruined an innocent girl's life and killed his own child.

What he had done was tantamount to rape.

Wayne let all his emotions flood out. Fortunately, all his housemates had already left for early lectures so no one heard the sound of deep heaving sobs and wails that came from his room.

By the time that John Lancaster returned to the house, Wayne had recovered some semblance of normality, although John did query the peculiar redness of his eyes.

"It's nothing." Wayne had lied, "I just had some more bad news from the States."

He informed John about Sabine's illness but refrained from mentioning his part in the tragedy, not that John would have believed it anyway, and he didn't mention the termination.

"Come on." He announced, "It's the last night of term, tomorrow it's back to grim reality, let's get hammered."

"Yeah." Wayne mumbled, "At least things can't get any bloody worse."

By half past eleven Wayne Higginbotham was well and truly hammered. He could hardly stand up. The noise of the disco music, the flashing lights and the loud cacophony of laughter and chatter was beginning to get on his nerves:

"Just one more!" He announced to an almost comatose John Lancaster, who eyes were closing even as he sat on the long red leather banquette seat that surrounded the student Union dance floor.

Wayne was staggering back to the table he was sharing with John, with two brimming pint glasses in his hands, when a large, thuggish-looking, skinhead turned suddenly and barged Wayne's arm. Half a pint of cheap lager splashed out of the glass and soaked Wayne's tight, white, drainpipe jeans. The thug turned away without so much as a word and re-engaged in conversation with a slutty looking girl.

Wayne put the beers down on a table and prodded the skinhead's back with a finger. He turned, his eyebrows almost covering his eyes in a Neanderthal scowl.

Wayne smiled and announced pompously and extremely loudly:

"Had I spilt your beer, my friend, I would have at least had the good manners and the decency to apologise."

Wayne shook his head and muttered "moron" before staggering off back to his table with the beers. He had just put the two plastic glasses on the table and had not even had the chance to sit down, when he felt the tap on his shoulder. Wayne turned slowly, vaguely aware of some sense of an impending threat. His eyes narrowed to slits.

"Are you alright Wayne?" A girl he knew from his course asked.

"Of coursh." Wayne slurred.

"Ohhh what's with the angry eyes?" The girl asked, "They're very red. Are you wearing contacts?"

Wayne shook his head:

"No, I'm just a bit drunk, I think."

The girl, who Wayne had quite fancied before Sabine had come onto the scene laughed:

"More than a bit, I think. You can hardly stand up."

Wayne made a dramatic gesture that was meant to indicate: "Oh well" and which amounted to emitting a huge sigh and raising his head towards the heavens.

He was not even fully aware of the girl being brusquely pushed aside, or of the thug pulling his arm back and punching Wayne squarely and firmly on the chin.

Wayne, for the second time in his life, flew through the air with a shower of sparks and stars exploding in his brain. He landed flat on his back on the edge of the dance floor amid much screaming and panic. He was aware of the acrid, metallic taste of blood in his mouth and the skinhead leaning over him and shouting:

"You embarrassed me in front of my bird."

Cold fury erupted in Wayne's mind. Suddenly he was very, very sober, but as he climbed slowly and deliberately to his feet, blood pouring from his mouth, down his chin and on to his shirt, he felt his arms being grabbed from behind and in the periphery of his vision he saw John Lancaster being grabbed by "Muppet" the six foot four inch tall, black security man. He worked out that the man who had him in an arm lock must be "Murphy" the Irish ex-boxing champion who headed up the Student Union's security.

"Now come on lads, we don't want any trouble." He heard Murphy say as he felt himself being manhandled out of the disco doors.

Ten seconds later and John and Wayne found themselves stood on the pavement of the Oxford Road, outside the Union building. Wayne's shirt was covered in blood and his jeans were still wet from spilt beer.

"Suppose that's that then." John muttered as he staggered off down the road, too drunk to even contemplate waiting for Wayne.

Wayne's face cracked into a wicked grin.

"Oh no, it isn't." He hissed as he looked around. He took a few steps into the darkness at the side of the Union building. He had not been this angry since Baz Thompson had flattened him when he was eleven.

The figure that emerged from the darkness resembled Mickey Finn, the American that Wayne had invented to charm Stephanie Fleming back in Shepton, three years earlier. This Mickey Finn, however, was taller and much better built than the youth who had almost succeeded in wooing Steph. Wayne strode back into the Union and flashed his student Union card. Muppet was on the verge of challenging him, but a quick glower from Wayne and a suggestion aimed directly into his mind, persuaded the giant bouncer to attend to other matters. Wayne strolled into the Union disco bar and glared into the darkness. It took him a few seconds to refocus in the gloom, but he soon recognised the thug, now standing with two of his mates and two or three sycophantic giggling females. Wayne noticed the thug passing over a small white packet and one of the girls handing him some cash.

Coloured disco lights flashed blue, red and green. A glitter ball sent rays of white light spinning around the dance floor.

Wayne marched purposefully across the dance floor, his now very red eyes gleaming. He was conscious of people gasping and moving out of his way. Some complained as he barged them unceremoniously aside. The noise, the disco beat, the laughter, all annoyed him immensely. The skinhead was laughing along with his mates and the girls. Wayne could still feel blood seeping into his mouth despite his shape shift.

"You effing ugly effing skinhead. You hit my mate." He bellowed over the noise of the disco.

A strobe light clicked in sending everyone's movements into a black and white parody of an ancient movie.

Flash, flash, flash.

The thug turned, his face set in an aggressive sneer as he prepared to give a hiding to another student weakling. Wayne grinned evilly.

Flash, flash, flash.

The strobe made Wayne look even more demonic than the blood on his mouth.

The thug blanched as he saw the huge figure before him, shirt covered in blood, red eyes blazing, visible even in the surreal stacatto light.

Flash, flash, flash.

"I think we take this outside." The demonic figure that Wayne presented drawled in an American accent. Wayne wasn't sure whether to go for Clint Eastwood, or Darth Vader, it came out somewhere in between.

Flash, flash, flash.

The thug looked at each of his mates in turn. Panic etched all over his face.

He nodded at another skinhead on his right and then immediately charged towards Wayne.

Wayne merely lifted the palm of his hand towards him and concentrated. The object of his ire flew ten feet backwards through the air and landed in a heap against the back wall.

Flash, flash, flash.

There was a loud thud as the thug's head knocked a huge dent in the plaster.

Flash, flash, flash.

The thug's mates stood staring open mouthed. It had looked like a slow motion replay in flashing black and white. Almost like a kid's flicker book.

The strobe light stopped and the revolving disco lights started again.

Wayne was still stood at least ten feet from where his earlier assailant had been lifted off his feet. He smiled at the thug's bewildered mates and their cheap girlfriends, then turned and walked straight back out of the Union Bar, satisfied that justice had been done and honour had been restored.

He passed the doormen, Muppet and Murphy who were both rushing back into the disco. Now maybe they'd get around to throwing out the bad guys instead of the victims, he thought as he opened the Union buildings main doors and stepped back out into the fresh air and down the steps back on to the Oxford Road.

A single piercing scream split the air. It seemed to emanate from somewhere behind Wayne and it was followed by a lot more screaming. He snorted. It was probably the three girls who had been with the thug and his mates.

"Sorry to ruin your night, girls." Wayne muttered sarcastically as he stepped into the shadows and swiftly re-emerged as Wayne Higginbotham once again.

The next morning Wayne emerged from his room with a pounding hangover and a massively swollen mouth.

John Lancaster was sat at the dining table clutching a cup of coffee, his face as white as a ghost's.

"I want to die." He muttered.

"Me too." Wayne mumbled through his incredibly sore mouth.

"My head is going to explode." He slumped into a chair and put his head in his hands.

"Oh God, what happened last night?"

John shrugged:

"We got drunk. You got into a fight. You lost by the way. After that I don't remember anything."

Wayne laughed, even though it hurt.

"Yeah, I sort of remember that bit. I also looked in the mirror. At least my teeth are still all there."

A key was turned in the lock of the front door and Ben Johnson, strolled into the house.

"So, looks like somebody got lucky last night?" Wayne taunted his housemate.

Ben grinned sheepishly.

"Of course, I did. Mind you, looks like somebody didn't though."

He pointed at Wayne's swollen mouth and bruised chin.

"You should see the other guy." Wayne quipped.

"Talking of fights, did you hear what happened at the Union last night?" Ben chirped as he put the kettle on.

"Well no, not if it happened after we got thrown out, due to Mohammed Ali here, getting knocked out in round one, punch one." John stated sarcastically, nodding in the direction of Wayne.

Ben laughed.

"Well you were lucky by the sound of it. Somebody went and got themselves killed in the Union disco." Ben stated in a matter of fact manner.

Wayne felt a strange buzzing noise in his ears, as all his senses seemed to go numb.

"What?" He asked, a sickening, nagging sensation inside told him what he already knew.

Ben turned towards his housemates, his face animated with excitement.

310

"No one knows exactly what really happened, but it seems this skinhead bloke had been drinking, smoking dope and openly selling bags of charlie all night. Then he started throwing his weight around, him and his mates. They beat some law student up in the toilets, made a right mess of him and then he smacked somebody else in the main bar. The security guys were terrified of him and his mates. Nobody knows how he even got into the Union. Some girl must have signed him in. He was probably the one who did for you, Wayne."

Wayne nodded:

"Probably." He muttered.

Ben continued to relate the tale of the previous night's excitement:

"Anyway, it seems this big fellow came in, just looking for this skinhead drug dealer bloke. Somebody said he was covered in blood. Anyway, he walked straight up towards this drug dealer and they exchanged a few words. The next thing, the skinhead was thrown up in the air like a rag doll, even though the fellow that had come in looking for him was still stood yards away from him. He must have had a gun hidden in his pocket or something. What was really freaky was that it all happened under a strobe light. Anyway, so even though the big fellow never touched the skinhead, he flew through the air and hit the wall so hard that he split his skull open. It was like, a real gore-fest. Probably all drug related, you know what it's like in Moss Side and Hulme. The dealer's dead anyway.

The funny thing is they reckon there was no bullet wound on him, no sign of him being hit or anything. The police are out in force this morning, I can tell you. The Union's a total no go area. Crime scene tapes everywhere."

John Lancaster whistled:

"Must have been a hell of a blast to lift him off his feet like that. I'm glad we got thrown out when we did Wayne, Wayne?"

Wayne Higginbotham was already on his way to the bathroom, to be violently sick.

Fifty-Eight

Terri Thorne knew that Dean wouldn't like her decision, but since their divorce had been finalised, she didn't care much what Dean thought anyway. What was he going to do, have her shot?

Dean had even been pulling back on his access rights in recent months, so Terri was sure he'd be reasonably happy at the prospect of her taking the kids away for Christmas. He had never really liked the schmaltzy, traditional festivities anyway.

It was as she was collecting the children from a weekend with their father at Coldwater Canyon, therefore, that she announced to Dean that she would be taking Marco and Marina out of the country for the first time. Dean had frowned disapprovingly:

"So where are you planning on taking them?" He asked.

"Ireland! To see their grandfather." Terri replied coldly.

Much to her surprise, Dean nodded.

"Good! Family is real important. Just make sure you bring them back."

Terri couldn't stop herself baiting her ex-husband.

"Why, would you send someone to shoot me?"

Dean grinned sarcastically.

"I might. Talking of shooting, don't forget Marina starts shooting the next episodes of "The Amishers" on January 4th."

Terri nodded.

"We'll be back by then."

Dean watched her put Marco and Marina in their seats in the back of her old Chevvy.

"Will you be seeing your boy, while you're in Europe?" Dean asked.

Terri turned and stared at him.

"Probably, why?" She demanded; her suspicions aroused.

Dean carelessly kicked a pebble into a flower-bed.

"Oh, I just wondered." He stated with a shrug. He sniffed, then screwed up his face.

"Does he think I'm in the mafia too?"

Terri ignored the question for a second while she completed strapping Marina into her safety seat. Then she turned and shaded her eyes. Dean was standing with the sun behind his head.

"I've no idea." She lied. "You'd better ask him yourself the next time you see him."

Dean bit his lip.

"You know, I still think your son was the one who sent that Irish Journalist friend of his after me. I think he did it as revenge, you know? Because of what he thinks I did to you."

Terri laughed.

"Michael did not set James up to do anything. James was his own man and as far as I am aware, Michael doesn't give a fig as to whether you are a Saint, or the Godfather himself."

She climbed into the Chevvy and wound the window down.

"Just one warning Dean, whether you have mob connections, or not. If you, or any of your buddies, ever harm so much as one hair on Michael's head. I will kill you myself."

Dean held up his hands defensively and laughed.

"Hey, easy tiger. I told you already, I never had nothing to do with that schmuck's murder and if your boy did set him up to get dirt on me, then hey, he's a good boy who loves his momma. It's about family honour, you know? I'd do the same sort of thing in his place."

Terri glowered at the man she had been married to, but now found almost unrecognisable.

"Yeah right." She hissed as she started the car and slammed the automatic gearshift forward. She didn't look back towards Dean but sped away in a cloud of dust.

Dean smiled.

"I hope he didn't send the schmuck, Terri, because if he did and if he carries on trying to play the wise guy, he might just meet with an unfortunate accident too. And I would hate to have to do that to you Terri honey. I really would."

Fifty-Nine

Wayne was carefully replacing the top stone on the cairn when the mist first appeared. It was a beautiful, crisp morning. The blue sky, streaked by several thinning vapour trails, was reflected perfectly in the Lough and the small islands that peppered its surface seemed to shimmer in mid air. The sun was bright, but impotent, as the chill winds of an Arctic winter blew in off the Atlantic Ocean. The mist had a green tinge, so Wayne knew that it wasn't a rogue cloud that was about to spoil his day, but something far more serious.

The mist gathered near the stone cairn that was now about four feet tall. Aillen Mac Fionnbharr walked out of the mist on to the mountain-top, his face grave.

"What are you doing, my son?" He asked, his brow furrowed in confusion.

Wayne continued straightening the stone, after a few seconds of silence he suddenly exclaimed:

"There! Good as new."

"If I am not mistaken, you have buried two of the sacred treasures of the Tuatha de Danaan in there?" Aillen asked, obviously bewildered.

Wayne ignored the question.

"Wow, this is quite a family gathering. Mom is down there in the cottage with my little brother and sister."

Aillen glanced down towards the cottage.

"Theresa is down there?"

Wayne nodded.

"Her decree nisi, or whatever it is, has come through. She's single again, but I don't suppose you'd have much chance with her. Having left her pregnant and alone once already and I suppose being dead does count against you, a little bit, of course."

Aillen sighed:

"I have matters to deal with that are even more important than my beloved Theresa. I repeat: have you buried the sacred treasures of the Tuatha de Danaan in there?"

"Yep!" Wayne quipped, flippantly.

"The reformed Stone of Falias and the mighty Spear of Finias, that the legendary Lugh bore in his prime, are now safely hidden deep within the cairn."

Aillen shook his head.

"But why, my son?" He asked, anguish and bewilderment evident in his tone.

"You promised me, swore to me, that you would go and fulfil your destiny. How will you do that without the treasures?"

Wayne shrugged. He had carefully avoided his father's gaze since his appearance and he now stared out over the fabulous panoramic view from the top of the western ridge of Buckaun. He could see a pillar of smoke rising from his grandfather's cottage, far below.

"I'm sorry, father. I'm through, I quit, I resign." He announced.

Aillen's mouth dropped open.

"Quit?" He repeated stupidly.

"Yes, I officially hand in my notice forthwith from the position of "Slanaitheor mor," great saviour of mankind and great white hope of the inhabitants of Tir Na Nog and the planet Earth and I willingly forego any associated pension, holiday entitlement and other benefits that I may have accrued in service."

Wayne turned and looked at the shocked and appalled phantom visage before him.

"Seriously, father, I really can't do this. I am embarrassed to say that I am not capable, or indeed worthy of fulfilling my destiny."

He said the words slowly and deliberately, with tears welling in his eyes as he spoke.

Aillen closed his eyes.

"I have been aware of magic being used in recent days, your magic. What is it that has persuaded you to act with such folly?"

He asked, his expression pained, his voice laced with disappointment.

Wayne's head dropped. His chin almost touched his chest.

"I killed a man, father. It was an accident, I think. I was too drunk to know."

Aillen Mac Fionnbharr sighed heavily and shook his head as Wayne continued:

"So in the nine years that I have had these powers, I have managed to give a bully, but a kid all the same, permanent brain damage. I have seen two fathers killed. I have effectively raped a beautiful girl and sent her completely insane and lost my first child in the process. My best friend has been murdered and now I have killed a man. And all because he happened to spill my drink and hit me. That's not to mention the tiny misdemeanours, like a bit of drink driving and almost getting arrested for being drunk and disorderly. The demon in my dreams cursed me. He told me that my magic would bring only heartbreak and that it would hurt everyone it touched."

Aillen nodded sadly.

"I have tried to counsel you many times, my son. Magic is only to be used for great purposes, not for the satisfaction of carnal lust, or for satisfying petty arguments. The demon's curse is a red herring, as they say. It is your own arrogance that has cursed you, not the demon."

"Oh yeah, like getting my Mom pregnant was a great purpose was it? Don't tell me you never used your magic to satisfy your own needs Aillen Mac Fionnbharr. How many men have you killed in your time?"

Wayne shouted at his father with such vitriol that Aillen was totally taken aback.

"I...I..." He stammered.

"You gave me the keys to the sweetie shop, father and expected me to never even try one tiny, little jelly bean. Well, I'm sorry, my supernatural daddy, dear. It must be my human half that doesn't quite match up to the high standards of the almighty "Tuatha de bloody Danaan." I'm supposed to be a saviour? Do you think Jesus Christ got pissed, screwed around, got into fights and killed people? I don't think there'd be many Christians if he had. It's over, Father! Maybe the "Order" was right all along. Maybe I'm the bad guy after all. Maybe the demon is my own ego, my id, like in that "Forgotten Planet" movie. Maybe the kid that the "Order" brought to Earth is the Messiah. Well he can have the Earth. He can do what he wants with it. I really don't care any more. I will never use magic again as long as I live."

Wayne slumped to the ground, sat on a lump of turf and buried his head in his hands, whispering over and over.

"I'm so sorry, I'm so sorry."

Aillen Mac Fionnbharr nodded sagely.

"It is as well that you have come to this choice. It is better that a weak animal hides in the safety of the herd and is never found, than that he steps out to challenge the hunter, only to be slaughtered like a tethered lamb."

Wayne looked up:

"You can't bait me, Father. Your mind tricks won't work on me." He snorted derisively.

"I am not weak, I suppose. I'm just stupid and I don't want to hurt any more innocent people. I have no guilt about Pizarro, or De Feren, or even the Banshee; but I do care about Sabine and our baby and I do feel bad about Stephanie Fleming and even Baz Thompson and the skinhead. I know Baz was a bully and the thug was dealing drugs, but they didn't deserve what happened to them. I could end up with a list a mile long, if I carry on like this. Every driver that cuts me up, "blam, kapow", he's toast. Every hooligan and thug who I think is threatening me: "zap, kaboom," he'd be history. My life would be like one long, bloody comic book! What was the Spiderman thing? With great power comes great responsibility. Well, I think I've well and truly proven that I am not responsible, not in the slightest."

There was along silence.

Even the immortal Aillen Mac Fionnbharr was lost for words.

"The police came to question me you know. They thought I might have sent this big fellow in to the Union to get revenge for this guy hitting me. Yet, as the cop who came to see me admitted, the big guy never even touched him. Obviously nobody had any idea that I was actually the big guy. Witnesses said it was as though Barton had deliberately thrown himself ten feet backwards, and smashed his skull on the wall. Suicide by Olympic standard, gymnastic backflip!"

Wayne looked out over the blue expanse of the lough.

Finally, Aillen approached his son.

"You cannot give up, my son. Whether you wish it, or not, you are the "Slanaitheoir mor". Yes, I have killed men in the past when my temper has boiled over. Some deserved their doom, others did not. It is a part of who we are. And yes you are right. I did use my powers to seduce your mother, just like you did with this girl who stole your heart."

He put his hands on Wayne's shoulders.

"You will never fully absolve yourself of the guilt of your mistakes, but life goes on, or at least it will until the power of darkness decides to cleanse the earth of mortal life. There will be no hiding place amongst the herd for you then, my son."

Wayne wiped his arm across his eyes. He stood up and sighed:

"Que sera, sera, whatever will be, will be, as they say."

Aillen stepped back.

"There is no curse on you Michaeleen. You will realise that one day. You just need to be more judicious in your use of magic. You will be back one day, my son. You will emerge from the herd and you will stand tall to fulfil your destiny. The tragedy is, that by then it will probably be too late, for in truth you do not seem to possess the power that I thought you might have by now and the demon's strength grows every day."

Wayne laughed, a sarcastic bitter laugh.

"What, should I be able to nuke entire cities?"

Aillen shook his head sadly:

"I will not see you again, not until the day comes to pass, when you decide to seize your destiny. Only when you come back to this sacred place to gather the great treasures of your ancestors. Only when you have decided that you do have the strength and the courage to complete the prophesied third task. Only then shall we talk again. Goodbye my son!"

Aillen Mac Fionnbharr turned and disappeared into the mist without looking back.

Wayne took a deep breath.

"Well that's that! I suppose."

He took a yellowing piece of folded paper from his pocket and read Father Reichmann's spidery black handwriting for probably the thousandth time:

"A child no mortal man shall sire
By mother's blood Royal line acquire,
Shall suckle he no milk white breast,
Shall rise in exile, unwelcome guest,
Shall learn to change his form at will
His shape, his face, his ways to kill
Unseen, unheard, his telling blow,
His doom to lay The Messiah low,"

Wayne knew the prophecy by heart. He screwed up the piece of paper and tossed it onto the cairn, then he descended the mountain down one of the easier paths.

Terri greeted him by the cottage. He had been with her for two days, but it was the first time that she'd actually caught him alone. Daideo, or Katie, or the children had always been around. Wayne knew that she needed to discuss something serious with him by the sombre expression on her face.

"Michael, we need to talk." She whispered as she took him by the arm:

"Let's walk down the lane a while."

Wayne felt the hairs on the back of his neck creep up. Had his run of bad luck not bottomed out yet?

Terri remained silent until they had almost reached the five bar gate that marked the edge of Wayne's grandfather's farm. Sheep wandered across the field, running swiftly away as Terri and Wayne passed.

"It's about James Malone." Terri finally whispered as she clung tightly to Wayne's arm.

"I do now believe that Dean may have had something to do with it. You told me at the funeral that Carrie certainly believed that."

Wayne nodded thoughtfully as he avoided a large cow-pat. He took a deep breath, as though what he was about to say caused him a certain amount of pain.

"James wrote me a letter, only to be opened in the event of his death. He said that if anything happened to him then Dean was probably behind it."

Terri grimaced.

"I asked him outright, you know? I asked him to swear on the lives of his, of our children that he wasn't involved. He couldn't do it. He could not swear that he had not been involved."

Wayne smiled sadly:

"The trouble is, he's so powerful now. He can buy the police and the judges and so on. They'll never get him."

Terri smiled at her son, the sadness obvious in her eyes.

"That's why I'm going to ask you to do something for me."

Wayne steeled himself.

Terri blew her nose into a tissue:

"I'm going to ask you to stay away from L.A. for a few years. Dean seems to think you might have asked James to bring him down, you know, in revenge for what he's done to me."

"What?" Wayne exclaimed incredulously.

As going to Los Angeles was something that Wayne had enjoyed immensely, Terri's request came as yet another hammer blow to him.

"Great! So how am I going to get to see you?" He asked his mother.

She shrugged:

"I guess we could meet here as often as we can, every two years or so."

Wayne blew out an exasperated sigh.

"I had absolutely nothing to do with James getting on Dean's case."

Terri smiled sadly.

"I know honey, but I don't want you putting yourself in danger. It's not worth the risk."

Wayne heaved a huge sigh.

"Look I'm not frightened of Dean Vitalia. Trust me, I can take him."

Terri flashed him one of those looks that said:

"Men are so stupid."

"Do it for me Wayne." She pleaded, as she looked deep into his eyes.

"I lost you once, I don't ever want to lose you again."

Wayne sadly nodded his agreement.

As he drove the souped up Escort back towards the ferry port in Dublin, Wayne pondered his second year at the University of Manchester so far.

He had seduced his intended girlfriend by magical deception, had got her pregnant and had inadvertently driven her insane, when all along, she had intended to become his girlfriend anyway.

He had lost his best friend.

His adoptive mother had suffered an angina attack and had become even more dependent on him.

His baby had been aborted.

He had accidentally killed a man.

His birth mother had effectively banned him from visiting her.

He had let down his father and his people and possibly all of mankind.

Like he had said to Aillen, not to mention the drink driving and the drunk and disorderly.

Wayne Higginbotham looked at the reflection of his eyes in the rear view mirror of the car. The green-blue eyes that stared back were not those of a demon. Just a careless, self-centred youth who needed to do an awful lot of growing up.

Wayne smiled sadly:

"Report conclusion: "Could do much better!"

The thought briefly crossed his mind that people who could use magic should be licensed, like spies that get a license to kill, then he realised how incredibly stupid the thought had been. If he was the last person on earth who could wield magic and he had retired, then there was no need for a licensing system. Could that really be true?

Was Wayne Higginbotham, born Michael Sean O'Brien, truly the last person on the planet capable of performing real magic?

Suddenly he felt very lonely, very lonely indeed.

Wayne Higginbotham, an average, unremarkable skinny student from Yorkshire, had unilaterally declared the end of the age of magic on Earth.

And no one, not one living soul, would ever know.

Sixty

The music was annoyingly catchy, the sort of thing that one finds oneself inadvertently whistling whilst showering, or in unguarded moments. Postmen and milkmen could often be heard whistling the refrain as people woke from their night-time slumbers. It was a jolly, infectious tune that made people happy.

Doris Higginbotham settled back into her chair and heaved a contented sigh.

Wayne would be home tomorrow. He was in the third year at college now and had a beautiful new girlfriend. He had promised to bring her home. The only problem for Doris was that she had a Russian name that Doris couldn't quite get her tongue round and she sounded a bit posh for Doris' tastes, but that would certainly impress Margaret.

Whatshername was definitely a lot more stunning than her nephew Cedric's fiancée, Felicity Storm. Although it had irked Doris enormously that Margaret had been able to announce a wedding date the following August and could now claim that she would soon be related to the local aristocracy.

Doris hadn't forgiven Wayne for sticking it out on his course at Manchester. She had really thought he was going to quit at the end of his second year, he had seemed so unhappy. When she had asked him outright, however, he had said that he had quit a lot of things, but he was not going to give up on his education. Doris had presumed he had meant he had quit smoking. Not that she had ever seen him smoke, but she had smelt smoke in his room on that one occasion and he had looked extremely guilty and had even confessed.

It was also true that his home visits had become less frequent since her health had improved, but at least now, she had the prospect of him gaining his honours degree and letters after his name, which Cedric Houghton-Hughes couldn't claim. Mind you she never let him forget that she was disappointed in him. Wayne Higginbotham had always been a poor substitute for Trevor.

Her mind moved back to the TV in front of her as the catchy theme tune came to a close and the show started. She didn't really understand why the main family in "The Amishers" show seemed to be from hundreds of years ago, while everyone else was typically modern American, but their antics were hilarious, especially the cute, blonde curly-haired lad, who was always involved in the most uproarious escapades, but was incredibly lovable.

The boy turned to the screen, winked and Doris almost split her sides. Now if only Wayne had been more like him.

Margaret Houghton Hughes started to laugh. She always laughed before the show had even started. It was peculiar because Margaret didn't particularly like comedy shows, especially imported American ones with canned laughter, but "The Amishers" was hilarious. Even Stanley had been known to splutter a laugh from over the top of the Telegraph on the rare occasions when he had been home early enough to catch an episode.

Cedric and Felicity often came over to watch the show when he had finished work at the bank and Felicity had dealt with all the horses at the Storm's stables. After the show the conversation would roll invariably round to the wedding and all the arrangements that the Storm's were making. It was beginning to sound to Margaret like it was going to be the Prince of Wales and Lady Di all over again.

It was a huge relief, therefore, that for half an hour, Margaret Houghton-Hughes could forget all about the pressures of the upcoming nuptials and having to live up to the standards of Sir Montague and Lady Storm and just enjoy a really good laugh.

On this particular evening she was watching the show alone. The prospect of not having to face more demands from Felicity had made her incredibly happy anyway. How she laughed as cute little Hans snuck off to the drive in movie in his parents' horse drawn buggy, having convinced his fifth grade friends that he could drive and that he had "cool" transport. The looks on their faces when he pulled up outside their houses on his ancient buggy was worth the licence fee on its own. That boy was just too funny.

Lucy Hetherington hated TV. She hadn't been encouraged to watch it at home and she certainly didn't have time to watch it at University, especially now that she was in the middle of a particularly trying term. Yet, for some reason, probably at Jonathan's suggestion she had tuned in her small black and white portable set to watch a new American sitcom called "The Amishers." Jonathan had assured her she would laugh until she cried. For several minutes Lucy had been aghast. How could the boy she loved, like anything so pointedly moronic? Jonathan T. Sherman had the sharpest intellect she had ever experienced. How could he enjoy something that was about as amusing as cholera?

Then the cute ten year old, or whatever he was meant to be, snuck a bottle of Cola into his family's Seventeenth Century kitchen under his ludicrous tall hat. His parents both left the room for a second, giving the boy time to try and sneak a surreptitious mouthful of the deliciously wicked, forbidden soda. In trying to remove his hat and pick the plastic bottle off his head, however, he dropped it, making a huge fuss about spinning it round and juggling it, as he made a protracted, albeit futile attempt to catch it. Just as he had managed to retrieve the violently shaken bottle from under the huge wooden table and had started to open it, a look of fevered anticipation covering his perfect features, his father walked in and challenged him. Naturally the boy turned towards his parent as the cap came off and of course, in the spirit of classic slapstick, he totally and utterly soaked his abject senior in an unfeasibly, powerful stream of sticky black liquid.

Lucy couldn't help laughing. She wasn't even sure why. The timing was just so good and the expression on the cute kids face was priceless. Lucy Hetherington was hooked. Her thesis on the diverse principles of law in the United States compared to the Napoleonic Code and the English model could wait. Jonathan had been right after all, as usual.

"The Amishers" was absolutely hilarious.

In his small sparsely decorated room, Fr Reichmann poured himself a glass of water and switched on the ancient TV set. He was not a fan of the television, occasionally tuning in to catch up on world events, or to watch classical music concerts. Yet for some reason he stayed in his chair after watching the news and allowed himself to watch an appallingly dubbed American sitcom. The plot was as ridiculous as the quality of the dubbing was bad. A traditional Amish family and their misadventures in modern Los Angeles, yet he could not bring himself to turn the TV off. The young boy who played a naughty, but golden hearted prankster was positively angelic in appearance and the show ended with a sound moral message about honesty prevailing and family ties being the most sacred of bonds.

Fr Reichmann even had to stifle a couple of guffawed laughs. He would definitely tell Father Doyle about "The Amishers." There was nothing sinful about innocent laughter.

In the small cottage under mighty Binnaw, in the West of Ireland, Tom O'Brien poured himself a large cup of tea and settled onto a chair by the kitchen table. The little TV in the corner flickered into life as he pressed the remote. The catchy music was just finishing and the mischievous son of the Amish family in L.A. that were the main subjects of the show, was seen plotting with two of his modern Angeleno friends how he was going to obtain a copy of Playboy. It was obvious that his scheme was doomed to end in failure or embarrassment, but it was funny anyway. It was when the Amish mother appeared with her infant daughter, however, that Tom's chest swelled with pride. The little girl was his granddaughter, Marina Vitalia and she was cute as a button. Tom had very few good words to say for his ex-son in law, but credit where it was due, he had made Marina a star and Tom was the proudest man in all of Ireland.

Terri Thorne had just made a cup of coffee and was about to go out to the local mall for some groceries when she heard the familiar music echoing from the small TV she had forgotten to turn off in her bedroom. They were showing an afternoon repeat of an "Amishers" episode from the recently completed first season and her daughter was in it.

Terri swelled with pride when she saw her little girl being carried onto the Amish set by her "Mom" in the show. Her pride soon soured, however, when, a few minutes into the show, the actress playing the errant eldest daughter of the Amish family appeared on the back of her boyfriend's motorbike. The beautiful blonde actress was Dean's current girlfriend, in fact she was now his new fiancée and she was certainly young enough to be his daughter.

The girl on the TV climbed off the bike and provocatively stretched her lithe, lissom figure, clad only in a pair of ridiculously tight shorts and tee shirt. Terri scowled. The girl took off her helmet and shook out her long, luscious, shining blonde hair which tumbled sexily around her shoulders, much to the horror of her strictly puritanical watching Amish family.

Terri clicked the remote and the TV was silenced. She shrugged, oh well, some you win, some you lose. At least the "Amishers" had been commissioned for a second season and Dean had promised her that Marco would have a part in a few episodes. He had been as good as his word about Marina so she had no doubt that he would not let his own son down. The "Amishers" was the biggest thing on TV and seemed to be doing well around the world. For a brief second Terri felt a pang of jealousy, if she had stayed with Dean, maybe she would have been in the show. She swiftly shook the thought out of her head and headed off to the Ralph's store at the mall.

Natalia Robson shouted for Wayne:
"Are you coming to watch it tonight?"
Wayne put the novel he was reading down and sighed. He had deliberately not watched "The Amishers," which everyone seemed to be talking about, despite the fact that his own little sister had a leading

324

part. He just hated that sort of sitcom and all the "canned" laughter and he was having an extended fit of pique anyway. His Mom had written to him saying how good the show was and how great Marina was in it and Doris had gone on ad nauseum about the cute ten-year-old boy and how funny he was. Wayne had decided to avoid it like the plague. Even Natalia was now raving about it.

Wayne had met Natalia very early in his third year. After a long period of introspection following the series of disasters that had happened to him in his second year, Wayne had decided to stick with his course. Giving up and retreating to the boredom of Shepton had never really been an option. The thought of looking after Doris on a permanent basis had scared the hell out of him.

A summer spent idling in the Greek islands after a few weeks working in a Shepton factory, had fully rejuvenated the twenty-year old student. His guilt about Sabine had been helped by an encouraging letter, in which she had described how well she was doing and how she was going to go back to University in San Francisco, once her recovery was complete. As for the late Carl Barton, the skinhead drug dealer, after one brief police interview in the immediate aftermath of the event, Wayne had been absolved of any guilt. In his own mind, Wayne knew that he would always carry the burden of Carl Barton's demise, but he hadn't exactly been a nice guy, so it was case of "getting on with it."

Wayne and John Lancaster had opted to go back into University halls of Residence in the third year, this time of the mixed sex, self-catering variety. Beech Court was in the Fallowfield student village area and was a hive of frenetic student social activity.

Wayne had noticed Natalia who lived in a flat above him in the very first week of term and had been stunned by the young brunette's beauty, but had been equally bemused by her habit of wearing her hood up even in the mildest October weather.

He had watched the young fresher from his window as she had come and gone over that first month, hood up, come rain come shine. Eventually he had approached her in a disco and asked why she wasn't wearing her hood on the dance floor. Her first reaction had been to wonder why a third year student was asking her such a stupid question, but they had eventually engaged in conversation and she had decided that he wasn't the idiot that she had first presumed him to be and he had decided that she was totally and utterly gorgeous. By December, they had become inseparable.

Natalia Robson was from the North East, although her accent was devoid of any regional inflections. Her mother had been a fan of Russian literature, hence her name and her father a celebrated tenor.

Wayne Higginbotham was head over heels in love with her by the time she had asked him to come and watch the episode of "The Amishers."

Wayne stood and entered the girl's flat's common room. Each student flat in Beech Court consisted of six boys, or six girls, the boys occupying the downstairs flats, the girls upstairs. The familiar strains of the "Amishers" music was still playing as Wayne slumped into the sofa next to Natalia. All five of the other girls in the flat were sat around along with one boyfriend.

"Wayne's little sister is in this." Natalia announced proudly as Wayne rolled his eyes.

"Fortunately, as she's not yet three, she doesn't have too many lines." He responded with just a hint of self-deprecatory sarcasm.

The beautiful blonde girl skipped along the beach in a skimpy bikini. Natalia playfully covered Wayne's eyes. The blonde laughed as a surfer dude tripped over his board as he stared at her.

The camera panned back to a boy in a traditional Amish outfit standing on a cliff top nearby peering through a pair of binoculars. Blonde curls tumbled out of his tall black hat.

"I tell you, our Eliza is going straight to hell. She's driving the English wild."

The boy exclaimed in a slightly Germanic accent. A typical American ten-year-old kid in shorts, tee shirt and sporting a Dodgers baseball cap was standing next to the Amish boy:

"Give me back my binoculars Hans. I want her to have a chance of driving me just a bit more wild, before she disappears off to hell in an explosion of sulphur and brimstone."

The Amish boy on the TV screen passed the binoculars to his buddy and the camera zoomed into his grinning, mischievously perfect features.

Wayne Higginbotham felt a chill in the pit of his stomach and every nerve ending on his body tingled and every single hair on the back of his neck rose.

He knew that face so, so well.

He knew those eyes better still.

www.ingramcontent.com/pod-product-compliance
Lightning Source LLC
Chambersburg PA
CBHW060523030726
47498CB00004B/1055